# THE COURIER'S COLLECTION

## THE BOLAJI KINGDOMS BOOKS ONE-THREE

### T. S. VALMOND

THE COURIER'S COLLECTION

The Bolaji Kingdoms Series One-Three

T.S. Valmond

PRINT ISBN: 9 7 8 1 7 7 5 3 6 1 0 8 4

# THE COURIER'S CODE

BOOK ONE

The irony of waiting for a princess to rescue him wasn't lost on Lu. One rarely complains when waiting for rescue even when the timing could mean the difference between his life and death. Lu hung from a hook in the ceiling, his hands tied together and his boots dangling four feet from the floor. In the room the scent of burnt wood and iron permeated everything.

A fire at one end of the room was still ready and prepped for steel work, a set of pokers waiting nearby. A large wooden table dominated the center and sat empty except for a small tin cup. There was a wooden stool on each side of the table. The large red man stood between Lu and the table pacing back and forth. Then he stopped long enough to cross his arms and glare at Lu.

"What's a greenie like you doing sniffing around here?" The man's skin a crimson red accentuating the black of his eyes.

"I told you, I'm a courier. I'm in the middle of a delivery. Really, you're going to laugh when you realize your mistake. I'm no threat to you at all."

"You haven't yet told me who sent you."

"I haven't told you because it's classified. They don't even tell me. Those are the rules. What kind of service do you think we're running? Let me go, you don't want any trouble over this. If they ask me what happened I'll just tell them it was a misunderstanding."

The man shook his head and prepared a poker in the fireplace, getting it red hot.

"Let's say I'm just a concerned citizen of Bolaji. I don't suppose a people like the Tero-Joro, trained to spy, would be hanging around my place without looking for trouble. Let's see if we can't get to the real reason you're here." The man's black eyes didn't waver.

"That was a long time ago, we don't do that kind of thing anymore. It doesn't matter anyway since I've renounced any allegiance to Tero-Joro to become a courier for all ten kingdoms."

The man pulled the metal poker from the fire and waved it under Lu's nose. His eyes never left Lu's face, even when someone knocked on the door.

"Ah that should be for me," Lu said, twisting in his restraints.

"No, you and I aren't done," he said.

The man opened the door and another red brute carrying an unconscious young girl entered. He arranged her on a second hook. Lu saw she had a bloody cut on the side of her head.

"Rash, are you okay?" Lu turned to the man. "What did you do to her?" he exclaimed.

"What's this? Is she with you?"

"If you hurt her, you'll be sorry." Lu hissed through his teeth as he shook against the restraints.

"This whole time you've been holding back. Now we see a little fire from our small green friend." He turned to the other man and asked, "Did you get it?"

"Yes." The red Karmirian held the item up between two fingers. It was a round disk no bigger than the fingers holding it. Neither of them noticed that the girl had woken up. She mouthed something to Lu. He shook his head, not understanding her. She rolled her eyes before closing them again.

She groaned in pain. Both men turned their heads in her direction and stared at her. She groaned again.

"Looks like someone has something to say."

"I'll talk, just leave her alone," Lu called out.

"No, you had your turn. Why don't we give this little Chilalian a chance? I've always wondered what the purple girls were like." The man snickered and gave his companion a poke in the ribs with his elbow.

He moved closer, and the girl groaned again. He leaned his face in next to hers. She swung her head back and rammed it into his, making a loud crack. She swung her legs up and snaked them around his neck. Using him for leverage she removed her bound hands from the hook.

The man flailed and beat on her legs but she held fast until he passed out and dropped to the floor. She jumped off of him, landing in a crouch.

The other man wasn't coming empty-handed. He'd grabbed another hot poker from the fire and swung it at her. She smiled, encouraging him to step forward. He twirled the poker then tried to jab her with it. She dodged it and moved to his right. When he turned toward her, she leapt for the stool and then the table. She kicked the stool at his head and he swung at it, leaving him open. She spun and kicked him in the side of the head. His eyes rolled as he fell to the ground, and the poker fell, clattering away from him.

"What took you so long? I thought he was going to skewer me with that thing. Where are your swords?"

"Cutter and Blade are well hidden. I had to make sure he had the disk." Rasha jumped from the table and using her toes, retrieved a knife from the first man and cut her hands free of the rope. She pocketed the disk and turned to Lu. She lifted him off of the hook before cutting his hands free.

A small squeak came from the can on the table.

"Don't," Rasha warned Lu as he walked over to investigate.

Inside was a small beastie, with gold and cream-colored fur covering a wide face with oversized paws. Its large ears lay against its head and came to a point at the ends. It shivered and whimpered when Lu reached to pull it out of the can.

"Well, look what we've got here. I've never seen one of you before," he said.

"Come, remember what happened the last time you picked up a stray?"

"Must you always bring that up?" He stroked the little beastie in the palm of his hand until it stopped shivering.

"Only because it's relevant."

"My mom always said I had a way with animals." Lu took in the little animal's large ears and big brown eyes.

"I think I'll call you Temi." He lifted him up and tucked him in the pocket of his vest.

"Why do you bother naming them?" Rasha asked, shaking her head.

"This coming from someone who named her short swords," Lu said, following her to the door.

"That's because they've never failed me and they'll never die."

## 2

"I've never seen anyone so thrilled to see a disk. I wonder what's on it," Lu said as they walked away from the client's home in Tero-Joro.

"That's not for us to know. Let's keep it that way." Rasha pulled out a palm-sized square disk and pressed her thumb to it.

"Rasha Jenchat, fetch and delivery complete, record one hundred percent, rating ten, payment complete."

"What's it like to be seventeen and have a two-rotation perfect run?" Lu asked as he pulled out his own square communicator.

"I enjoy my work."

"I suppose so." Lu looked down at his own communicator and frowned.

"What's wrong? Was there a problem with your payment?"

"No, nothing, I just have to go take care of something. I'll meet up with you later."

"You know where to find me."

"Yes, of course." Lu stopped short and turned to her. "Why do you go to places like that? They won't give you drink."

"I'm not there for the drink," Rasha said and turned to go.

---

RASHA SAT in a dark corner of the tavern with one foot on a chair in front of her. She caught bits of conversation as the other couriers from on and off world sat and discussed their latest fetches and deliveries. Mixed in were a few travelers and locals who sat at the bar in their usual seats. The lighting was at twenty percent and they were nowhere near capacity. Many of the tables sat empty since it was midweek. There were a few seats open at the bar, but she ignored them. Rasha had made the mistake once of sitting at the bar. Those seats were for people taking drink only, not for someone her age. She'd been tossed out on her backside and told to mind her manners in all things concerning the bar.

The barmaid, wearing less than the imagination required, came over and put a glass mug in front of Rasha.

"Rash."

"Silae."

9

Silae sat across from Rash in the empty chair and stared at Rasha's boot on the other. Rasha glanced over at her boot with a grin in challenge. Silae had reddish-brown skin and long, dark, wavy hair. Her eyes were as black as night. She was part Karmirian and part human, a unique mix. Her almond eyes and full mouth always seemed to smile. Rasha enjoyed their banter even more than the non-fermented juice she drank.

"What's a nice young girl like you doing in a ruffian's drinking hole like this one?" Silae asked.

"Minding my own business, which is what you should be doing," Rasha said.

"I'll take note of that, just before I ignore it. Sorry I can't offer you ferm or something stronger."

Rasha smiled at her brazen attitude and ignored the comment about the drink.

"Where's that adorable green partner of yours, with the big ears?"

"He has somewhere else to be."

"What a shame. He's got such a nice way with people, unlike his traveling companion. Before I go, I thought you should know The Choosing has begun."

Rasha kept her face and features still as her stomach flipped. It took too long for her next words to come out.

"Why should that concern me?"

"I didn't say it did. I thought you'd want to be informed." Silae, always the sly one, slipped out of the seat with a toss of her hair and returned to the bar to get more drinks served.

Rasha's heart raced as she pulled out her communicator and watched the feed. It was true. The eligible princesses in the realm were making their way to Adalu, the first kingdom. The current prince would choose one of the pure-born princesses to be his bride. Her hand shook when she reached for her juice and she pulled it back again. She raised her eyes to the bar and saw Silae watching her with a knowing smile. She wanted to pull out Cutter and Blade to slice that smile right off of her face. Silae turned to another customer before Rasha let her imagination go wild.

"Ruins is what it is. I can't get to my trade routes for the all the parading around these princesses do," she overheard a tradesman the next table over complain.

"Like a bunch of pikos, strutting around for the crowned prince. The whole thing is ridiculous," his companion replied. "It'll be tough getting anything on or off this planet for a while. I'm thinking of taking work in the far reaches."

"I'm not that desperate. Besides, the princesses aren't half bad to look at, not like this lot," the tradesman said, waving a hand at the room.

Rasha only felt a tinge of shame being lumped in with the rest. She'd been considered a beauty once. Her grey eyes in contrast to her purple skin often caught people's attention. That was another time, another life, where she dressed and performed for the approval of others. Few noticed her in the clothing she wore now. She kept her hands and arms covered and a hood concealed most of her head and hair. No one here would even recognize her. Besides, why would anyone look at her? A princess wouldn't be seen in a tradesmen's bar drinking unfermented juice. She stroked the amulet around her neck and whispered a prayer under her breath.

## 3

*L*u found the jail just as he'd left it the last time. A grungy, dark building with the dank and pungent stink of sweaty humanoids. He didn't bother to pinch his nose. His ears caught a laugh he recognized, and he clenched his teeth and balled his fists at his side. She'd done it again, and this time getting her out wouldn't be easy.

"Poobari!" Lu exclaimed as he approached the overweight jailer.

"I wish I could say it was a pleasure to see you. She's in for good this time." Poobari's creamy skin folds made grimy rings on his shirt and pants.

"There must be something I can do. A large basket of Majiwan delicacies?"

"I can get that on my own."

"You haven't seen the latest tech in the Twinlands. I might be able to get you the newest listening device."

Poobari opened a drawer and pulled out three such listening devices.

Temi let out a half yawn and growl catching Poobari's attention.

"What have you got there? Hey little fellow, want to come to Uncle Poobari?"

Temi growled and retreated deeper into Lu's pocket.

"Sorry, he's a good judge of character."

Poobari frowned. "She's not getting out, so go on about your business."

"What? You're joking. I'm one half of the best team of couriers Bolaji has ever seen. I can get you whatever you like."

Poobari stopped and looked up at him with beady eyes half buried in folds of skin. He gave Lu toothy grin.

"Perhaps there is something."

"Anything, I'll do it."

"I have a special fetch and delivery request. It's half on-and half off-the-books. You need to go through official channels to accept but I can make sure you're the only one who gets the offer. Agree to it up front here with me and I'll send it to you."

"Sure, what is it?"

"Since when does a courier need to know what the package is? Aren't you supposed to be discreet?"

"I am, I am. Poobari, you're amazing. I'll take the fetch. Thanks again. Can I go back and see her? I want her to sweat a little."

"You horrible little yahtz. Sure, just make sure you're

both out of here within the half hour. I have another prisoner in transfer, the cell will be filled again before night's
end."

"You have my word." Lu didn't bother to shake
Poobari's hand. His nod was enough. Poobari released the
locks on the cell door. Lu entered the cell and Poobari
locked it behind him with a loud clang.

The reek only grew worse within the walls but he
followed the corridor down to the fifth cell on the left.
Several of the inmates whistled and called out as Lu
passed. He got too close to one side and had to remove his
tunic from someone's gnarled grip. When he reached her
cell, she was hanging by her fingers from the ceiling and
pulling herself up. Her green skin and large eyes and ears
were a perfect blend of her Tero-Joro parents, one from
each of the Twinlands.

"Told you boys I wouldn't be here long," she said and
dropped to the floor. They groaned and yelled obscenities
at her. She brushed her hands off on her fitted pants.
"Well, hello big brother."

---

LADI, two rotations younger and half a head shorter than
him, swaggered up to the bars of the cell and rested her
arms on them. She didn't seem at all bothered by the smell
of the place. She pulled out a piece of dried meat and
gnawed on it. Lu shook his head and leaned against
the bars.

"What's it going to take with you?"

"What do you mean? Hey, who's the new little beast-ie?" She reached out a hand and Temi purred at her touch.

"His name is Temi." Lu pulled away from the bars, stepping just out of reach. "When is it going to be enough?"

"I'm enjoying myself and making lots of money. So what if I get caught sometimes, I have plenty to bring home when it's all done."

"Mother and Father are well taken care of," Lu said between clenched teeth. He dropped his shoulders and relaxed his jaw. "You have the skills to work legitimate jobs, I don't know why you won't take them."

"They don't pay as well."

"I wish you wouldn't worry our parents so much. I won't always be able get you out."

"But you got me out this time, so why are we still talking through the bars?" she asked, tapping them with one finger.

"Because I want you to understand something." Lu waited for her to meet his eyes. "This is the last time." She didn't flinch as he stared her down. "I don't have a problem seeing you punished for criminal activity. Next time they'll take more than just your money."

"What? Poobari, you scheming, two-faced ranglefort!" Her voice carried down the corridor and their ears picked up his belly laugh.

"You let him take my money?" she said, turning back to Lu.

"Let him? I'm not sure what kind of position you imagine you're in but you put yourself here."

"No, I didn't. Who do you think hires me to do all these off-the-books fetches and deliveries?"

"Well, not anymore. If you get into trouble again, you're on your own." The cell door's mechanical locks clicked and the door slid open. Lu noted it was just before the half hour mark.

Ladi strolled out of the cell and down the corridor, not waiting for her brother to catch up. "So, he took the money, which means you're doing something for him. What is it?"

"That's none of your business."

"You're doing a run for him. I can help you. We can have it knocked out in a day. Debt paid and I never have to worry about it again."

"No, you're going home, right now. I've been missing Mom's baked beti and you need an escort."

"I need no such thing."

"Well, no, but I'm desperate to see your face after Mother and Father finish with you."

He chuckled when she glared at him.

## 4

*L*u was already waiting downstairs at the bar when Rasha made her way down the steps of the inn.

She held up a hand at Lu while she paid the barkeep. The man lifted out a black box he kept behind the bar and she swiped her disk across the top. The confirmation beep ended the transaction. Silae slithered out of the back before she got away and called out to Lu. "Well, if it isn't my favorite greenie."

How could she be less dressed than before? The small shirt managed to cover her chest leaving her shoulders and midriff bare. The skirt, a thin material, hung around her ankles but didn't hide her legs, which could be seen when the light shone behind it.

"Hey, Red, you're looking charming this morning. Shouldn't you be sleeping after an overnight shift?"

"Not when there's a chance I might see someone like

you. I was telling your partner last night it wasn't the same without you."

"Next time. I promise. Any news?" he asked.

"Not really. They announced The Choosing has begun, so be careful on the trade route. You know how competitive these purists get," Silae said.

"Have you seen who's in the running this rotation?" he asked without looking up from his communicator as he checked the facts.

"The Sidoans are offering a princess of age for the first time. She's striking, they say. With the mines in Sidoa now offering the rarest gems ever found in the ten kingdoms, she'll have an even better chance of being chosen."

"My money is on the Karmirians, they're the closest other than the Chilalians, who don't even have a pure daughter to offer. Crazy, right, Rash?" He still didn't look up.

"Yeah, isn't it?" Silae said with a significant glance at Rasha.

Rasha's hands clenched at her sides. Silae was pushing their fragile acquaintance with her insinuations.

Lu didn't seem to notice. He leaned over the bar and whispered something to Silae that made her laugh. Rasha grit her teeth and turned to go.

"Rash, wait, where are you going?" Lu called after her. He gave Silae a kiss on the cheek and bolted after his partner.

Rasha reached the cool fresh air and took a deep

breath. What did Silae know, anyway? Why was she giving her those looks?

"I'm not spending another night here. The place is far too loud and, if you ask me, overpriced. How was your business last night?"

"Fine," Lu said looking at his feet. Rasha was ahead of him and didn't see his hesitation.

"Where'd you sleep last night?" she asked.

"I—,"

Before he could answer, her communicator signaled. She looked down at the screen. "What the yahtz?"

"What?"

"Central is sending us a mandatory."

"Oh, well, glad I didn't skip town right away, now we can take care of this and then I can go visit my family."

"This is madness. I should contact Central and find out what the mix up is. We just finished a one-month fetch and delivery due to theft. Why do we always have to be the ones?"

"We're the best, that's why they call us."

"Yeah, but why is this one mandatory?"

"You think they'll tell us?"

"No, of course not. It's all the way in Sidoa."

"The tenth kingdom!" Lu slapped his leg. "Well, then let's go, it'll take us longer if we stand around complaining. We'll worry about the rest later." He adjusted his pack on the back of his tuskin and led him toward the woods.

Rasha thought for a moment. True, she couldn't ask

them why they wanted to send her. Besides, it was a mandatory. She didn't have a choice.

"Wait a minute."

Lu stopped short and looked back at her.

"How's your family? Did you get to talk to them at all?"

"Yeah, they're fine."

"They'll be sad you missed them."

"I'll send them a message when we're well on our way."

"Fine, but after this assignment I'm turning off my communicator and throwing it into the nearest river."

Rasha grabbed her large riding beast, a tuskin, and the animal's short tail wagged in greeting. She didn't notice. Her mind was on the journey south. Lu pulled out a piece of gale fruit and gave it to his tuskin, who gobbled it up in a saliva filled slurp. He rubbed his curved horns against Lu in thanks. Lu rubbed his knuckles up and down between the beast's eyes.

Temi made a faint cry of complaint from Lu's pocket.

"We should pick up supplies. Our animals are hungry and it will be much warmer in the south. We might pick up a few things while we're there," Rasha said.

"Like some jewels," Lu smiled.

"Something like that."

## 5

The journey South to Sidoa was pleasant and uneventful. The climate warmed day to day as the sun's rays grew stronger and longer in duration. This time of year, storm activity increased. Rasha and Lu found comfortable lodging at a few nice inns they'd frequented before. Most of the time an inn would balk at their ages. Young and in trade they weren't always offered a room on the premises. There were a few places they'd stayed that knew their reputations and allowed them access to some of the nicer establishments.

"We should be there by nightfall," Rasha said, looking up at the orange sky. The two moons were visible to the north.

"What do you think it will be?" Lu asked.

He was referring to the fetch. "Only the gods know."

"Jewels. I bet its jewels." Lu pulled Temi from his

pocket and set him down on the beast. He'd grown a little and could keep himself on the moving beast's saddle.

When they reached Sidoa, they followed a small road off the main thoroughfare to the location of the fetch. The locator led them to the middle of nowhere and nothing. Lu checked the position twice.

"How can this be the place? There's nothing here." Rasha asked.

Lu climbed down from his tuskin and tied the reins to the nearest tree. He cocked his head and listened.

"Someone's coming this way. It's a wagon."

"That's promising," Rasha said. "What do you see?"

"Nothing from here. I'll climb up and see if I can get a better look. The sun is already down, so no promises." He held Temi out to her.

"What?" Rasha asked, looking down at his hand as if he held a poisonous slithering stolken.

"He doesn't like heights." He grabbed her hand and put Temi down.

Temi had grown since Lu found his tin cup. His limbs now dangled over the edges of her hand while she gripped his midsection. Temi never took his little eyes off of Lu and he whined when he lost sight of him in the tree.

"There, there, little fellow, he's just getting a better view. He'll be right back." She ran her thumb across his head as she'd seen Lu do and the beastie stopped crying.

A moment later, Lu was climbing back down and Temi's whole body wiggled with joy.

Rasha pushed the little beastie back into Lu's hands as he spoke.

"There are three men, two of them Sidoans, and they're hauling a large crate. Looks to be heavy, we'll need to team up our beasts to pull it."

Rasha bit her lower lip.

"Okay, since we're not welcomed in the kingdom we won't be sleeping here tonight. I say we make our way back toward the inn we stayed at last night," she said.

Lu nodded. "They have seafood, I could live there."

"We aren't staying long. She climbed down from her beast.

They didn't have to wait much longer for the three men to reach them. The men were a mix of dark and light-skinned. Their trader outfits and size suggested the shady end of dealings. Temi growled as the men approached them, but soon climbed into Lu's pack to avoid being seen.

"My hero," Rasha said, looking at Temi. She addressed the men. "Out for an evening stroll, gentlemen?"

"Are you the Jenchat?"

"I am."

"You're Chilalian."

"Yes."

"We have a fetch."

"Well, now, that's convenient."

They looked at one another with confused expressions, then at Lu and Rasha.

"How old are you children?"

Rasha didn't like proceedings starting with this question. It meant not only did they not trust her abilities but they wouldn't process her digital paperwork. She wasn't in the mood to lose money. They'd travelled five days and wouldn't even be able to trade for the famous gemstones they'd heard about.

Rasha pulled out her disk. She held it up and let the Central data do the talking for her.

The robotic female voice spoke loud enough for all of them to hear, "Rasha Jenchat, certified courier, record: one hundred percent over two rotations. Satisfaction level: ten." Rasha pocketed the disk.

"I showed you mine, now you show me yours."

The large brown man in front held up his square and keyed in his purchase code. His device beeped as he tapped the edge of her disk, which beeped in return.

"Fetch complete, thank you for your business," it said.

"Are we done here?" Rasha asked.

"I hope I don't have to tell you that this package is precious."

"You just did," Rasha said. She and Lu transferred the harness to their tuskins.

"Please, protect it with your life."

"Fetch, delivery, and satisfaction guaranteed," Lu said.

The men still seemed worried. In fact, they waited for them to ride out. The only thing that would change their minds was a successful delivery and Rasha planned to give them one. This assignment was as important as all the other ones had been for their clients.

"It's gems, isn't it?" Lu asked when he was sure they were out of hearing distance.

"Without a doubt," she said. Rasha shivered. She turned in her seat to glance behind them.

"What is it?" Lu asked.

"I have the feeling we're being watched."

Lu looked around, then tilted his head into the wind and away.

"Anything?" she asked.

"No," he said. "Want me to send out a pulsar?"

"No, it's probably a wild animal looking for a morsel," Rasha said, but she shivered again.

At the word 'morsel' Temi poked his little head out of the pouch and sniffed the air, letting out a low growl. Lu gave the beastie a pat on the head.

"See, Temi doesn't believe you, either."

## 6

*B*y morning, Rasha was sure they were being followed. The fellow wasn't even trying to hide it. He left broken branches and prints all over the place.

"What do you make of it?" Rasha asked as they rode along.

"They're skilled enough to stay hidden," Lu said.

"But not to cover their tracks?"

Temi seemed annoyed by their scent and he'd growl at the wind. Now he sat on the saddle in front of Lu, content to rest his large head on his paws.

"They don't seem in any hurry to overtake us," Lu said.

Rasha didn't respond as she kept her eyes on the surrounding trees. This fetch was all wrong. First, it was mandatory, after a rotation of optional fetches. A march into the woods of Sidoa, meeting with people that didn't trust them to deliver feed, let alone whatever was in the package. Not even a day later they're being followed by a fangledort who didn't cover his tracks.

"You've got that crease in your brow. I think we should've traded for a vehicle," Lu said.

"No, a vehicle would just make it easier for whoever it is to track us." Rasha tried to relax her face but soon felt the tug between her eyes. "It's this assignment. It's all wrong."

Lu shrugged. "They're all the same to me. I just want to get it done. A vehicle will cut our travel time by more than half. We can make delivery and take a well-deserved holiday. Besides, the money will help my family."

"Your sister is still not willing to legalize?" Rasha asked.

It was Lu's turn to frown. His large eyes cast down as he spoke.

"She's so different from me. I wish I could reach her."

"You sound like an old man."

"Sometimes I feel like it. I know the burdens of this life weigh on you, too. I can't wait until we retire from it. We'll be like a couple of royals with servants caring for our every need."

Rasha shook her head. "That's not my kind of thing."

"Since when is pampering not our thing?"

Before Rasha could answer, Lu held up a finger and turned his head to the right. He glanced back at her and nodded once. There was someone out there. Perhaps the person that was following them. Rasha pulled out her short swords and slid off of her beast. She passed Lu the reins and, with a nod for him to continue, she slipped into the trees. She waited for a moment behind one of the older trees and then doubled back. Rasha found male boot prints along with the prints of a large beast. The tracker still made no secret of following them, but remained hidden.

Rasha listened and watched for several moments but there was nothing other than the rustle of leaves and a soft cool wind from the north. Rasha raced back through the trees and caught up to Lu. He slowed down and stopped so she could remount.

"Want to use the pulsar now?"

"No, they're not close enough. We'll wait until they relax a little more."

They reached the small inn they stayed at the night before and settled in with their cargo for an early evening. The inn wasn't very busy this time of year and the barkeep didn't mind their age at all.

"Help me with the cargo, then find cover for our beasts. There's a storm coming." Rasha said looking at the sky.

Lu looked up. "Yes, but not for hours."

"I'd rather make sure they're out of the elements anyway."

They hefted the large crate into the inn but made it no further than the bar.

"This thing is heavier than it looks," Lu said as he strained to shift it behind the bar and into a nook. He paid the barkeep to cover it with supplies so that no one would notice it. They'd have to retrieve it in the morning.

They sat at a table watching people come and go for several minutes before the barman came over to take their order.

"No ferm for you two. What else can I get for you?"

"I'll have a floral juice."

"I'll take a fauna."

"Any food for you? Kitchen closes in half an hour."

At the mention of food Temi poked his head out and sniffed the air.

"No beasts allowed inside. Take him outside if you want to feed him," the barman said, turning away without their food order.

"Great, now we'll starve thanks to your little friend," Rasha said. "I don't think I have to remind you what happens when I don't get fed."

"He's harmless. I'll put him in the room upstairs. Order me a seafood plate." Lu got up and headed for the stairs. The entire second floor offered rooms for rent and they'd bought one with two beds. Another benefit of the season: there were lots of options.

Rasha turned up her nose. She wasn't a fan of seafood but she ordered his plate and a meat plate for herself. When the barman returned with their drinks, she placed the order and used her own disk to pay.

The sound of an all-terrain vehicle approaching the inn made Rasha turn and look. Two large men climbed out and strolled into the bar. One slapped the other on the back, and they laughed as they took their seats. That gave Rasha an idea. Before Lu returned, she put the plan into action.

Rasha sauntered over to them and looked them over from head to toe as if trying to determine their clothing size.

"Can I help you little miss?" the bearded one asked. His dark hair stood in spikes on top of his head.

"I was just wondering how the two of you managed to get that all-terrain vehicle. It seems a little expensive for a couple of fellows from the ninth kingdom."

"How do you know we're from Buku?"

"Your clothes and that smell. I'm not sure what it's called." Rasha grimaced and waved a hand front of her face.

It had the desired effect.

"Go play with your dollies, little one. We haven't got time for your games."

"Not even a game of Hands?" She gave the men a smile as she pulled out her disk and set it on the bar. "Four hundred credits says you're no good at it."

"You can't be serious. Gorg never loses." The beardless one was mouthy. His buddy, Gorg, tapped him on the chest to keep him quiet. Rasha was already calculating her winnings.

"Sure, little purple one. I'd love to take your money and teach you a lesson in how a lady should behave."

Rasha laughed. "A lady? I had no idea you had so much experience." The man rose from his seat as if to hit

31

her, but Rasha didn't flinch. He was flexing his muscles. He wouldn't hit her, a girl-child in his eyes. Taking his money would be fun.

Rasha invited them to her table and Lu joined them a moment later. His confused expression became a smile after she explained what game they would play. The men didn't suspect a thing even after she'd thrown the game and raised the stakes. A crowd gathered around them. A few onlookers cheered them on. The others were for the big guys. Rasha looked at her partner and gave him a subtle but rapid double blink. Lu knew his part, and Rasha counted on him to make it good. He didn't fail her.

"Oh no, I've got nothing Rash," he groaned and then covered his mouth as if remembering he wasn't supposed to say anything. The crowd that had been supporting them groaned.

She kicked the table in front of his knees and he flinched as if she'd kicked him. She rolled her eyes to the crowd as if he'd just ruined the entire game for them. The two men smiled at each other over the cards they held.

"What's it going to be little one? Your partner has nothing. Shall we end this game?"

Rasha bit down on her lip as if she were working out a complex problem. The crowd around them doubled in size. Money passed from hand to hand as the people placed bets on the game.

"I've got the rest of my earnings for the month. What have you guys got?" She knew they'd already finished the credits they'd planned to use. She pushed for more.

The two men nodded to each other and shrugged.

"We've got our vehicle, the one you admired, if you're interested?"

Rasha looked to Lu who shrugged as if he didn't know what to say.

"I guess so. But this has to be the final round, I can't afford to lose anymore," she said loud enough for the crowd to hear.

"Oh, us too. We don't dare bet anything more." Gorg gave his partner a knowing a smile.

"Place your hands, gentlemen," Rasha said, calling all of their cards to the table.

They put their cards on the table and Rasha put hers down trying not to giggle. "I think I won." The crowd erupted, and some slapped Lu and Rasha on the shoulders in congratulations. The crowd collected their own bets on the game. Rasha returned to the bar to get the credits she'd given the barkeep to hold for them. The men were angry but with the large crowd there they didn't dare fight the outcome. They'd lost and now they'd pay up. Gorg shoved his friend, who was still running his mouth about how unfair the game had been. He pushed back. Gorg gave him a swift jab with his elbow before he got the key to the vehicle and held it out in front of her.

"Are you sure it's not too much vehicle for you?" he asked her.

"I'm sure," Rasha said and she slipped the card in her pocket and turned to leave.

## 7

*R*asha's insides threatened to bubble over and explode out of her mouth. They'd covered a lot of ground with the all-terrain vehicle, but at a price. Its wheels sped over the uneven roads. Lu sat behind the wheel like a happy little twyllo. He rushed headlong on the road, heedless of the bumps and bruises Rasha was accumulating while holding on to her insides.

"I had no idea you had such a weak stomach," Lu said as he skidded along one edge of the road and then the other.

"Do we have to go so fast? I'm going to spill my guts."

"Don't be so dramatic."

Rasha swallowed down bile and shook her head.

"Nope, not drama. Stop," she called out grabbing his arm.

Lu came to a neck breaking halt and Rasha fell out

headfirst and vomited in the trees. When she finished, she turned slowly back to the vehicle. She glared at Lu, who was looking at one of his devices.

"Next time, I drive," she said as she leaned her head against the side of the door.

"You don't know how."

"Neither do you."

"Get in," Lu said, putting his device down and revving the engine.

"I'm not ready yet." She shook her head and backed away.

"Rash, get in the transport, now." The urgency on Lu's face was unmistakable.

"What's wrong?"

"We've got company. I'm going to try to outrun them."

"It might be better to let them catch up to us," Rasha said, half in and half out of her seat.

"Nope, there's too many of them, they're closing in fast on our position."

Lu took off before she settled. Rasha looked down at the device Lu placed between them. A red dot in the center of the screen pulsed. Around it were numerous green dots coming from all directions.

"What is this?"

"It's an ambush."

Rasha held onto the side of the vehicle and clutched her amulet.

"May the Universal help us," she whispered as she secured the straps around her middle.

"Hold on," Lu said. It wasn't necessary since Rasha hadn't let go of the side since their journey started.

Maybe it was the speed of the vehicle or the terrain, either way they'd never know. When the all-terrain got to the felled tree in the middle of the road, there wasn't enough time to do anything but try to go over it. The vehicle's wheels lost traction and vaulted into the sky several feet before it rolled onto an embankment, then hit a row of trees and shut down.

RASHA CAME to after a few moments and realized she was hanging upside down by the security straps. Her neck already ached from the awkward angle she'd been hanging from. As she pulled her leg from the crumpled frame, she realized she was alone.

"Lu," she groaned. Her voice didn't carry beyond the inside of the vehicle. Rasha tugged herself free from the vehicle's straps and searched for her partner. She stumbled twice before her balance returned.

She found the device first. It must have been thrown from the vehicle into the brush. The screen was blank. She shook it once before tossing it aside. At the moment, Lu's whereabouts were more important to her than that of those who had ambushed them. Her head ached and she was still nauseous, but she walked on until she found the fallen tree. No wonder they'd gone flying. The tree was old and thick around the base, but it had been felled deliberately onto the road. The crash hadn't been an accident.

Voices in the distance got her attention. Rasha crouched down behind the branches of the tree, reached for her swords and found only one, Cutter. She'd lost Blade in the crash. That would be inconvenient. Rasha watched with one short sword at the ready.

She didn't have to wonder what they were after when she saw the damaged cargo being hauled into another vehicle. She recognized the two men doing the hauling as Gorg and his partner from the game of Hands the other night. The third man gathered his gear and started at the sound of a pebble hitting a tree on their left. Rasha threw another to their rear that forced them all to turn toward it. She watched them agree to separate, just as she hoped.

When the unknown man reached her, she swept a foot out and watched as he fell over it. Before he recovered, she leapt up and hit him in the back of the head with the butt of her sword, knocking him unconscious. The talkative man from the game heard her before she jumped on him and pulled out his own sword, blocking her. Their swords clashed several times, making her arms ache. The man's upper body strength was solid. Every blow against Cutter reverberated through her already weakened muscles. She fell to her knees and had to get creative to avoid his sword. She rolled forward, cutting each of his thighs, slowing him down enough to slice his back. He fell forward onto his face before blacking out.

"Well, little one, aren't you two hands full of trouble?"

"That's what they tell me." Rasha tried to keep from throwing up again as he circled her. He carried a long sword, which meant she'd have to avoid his lunges if she wanted to survive this fight.

He focused on her with such intensity he didn't see Lu stumbling forward, looking greener than usual and holding something out in his hands.

"You're going to be fun. Is that all you've got, purple one?"

"I don't think so."

Rasha stopped circling and forced him backwards right into Lu. His device zapped the man's back and his eyes rolled up in his head before he fell forward. She heard the crunch of the small bones of his nose breaking on impact.

"You okay?" Lu asked.

"Nope," Rasha said as she turned and vomited again.

Lu HELD up his tracking device.

"What's wrong? Is it working?" she asked. The thing made a few beeping noises before turning off.

"It's working fine, but there were at least eight dots on the screen before and there are only three men here."

"You think the rest took off when these claimed the crate for themselves?"

"I'm not sure. It might have been a planned attack, but they weren't here, all in on it together," Lu said.

"These two were greedy and took care of the rest," Rasha said, finishing his thought.

"Looks like they damaged the cargo crate. We should secure it."

Lu followed her to the back of the new vehicle. It was almost identical to the last, which had a horrible effect on Rasha's stomach. As she'd seen while the men were moving it, the lid had broken open and some kind of smoke was leaking out of it.

"I bet it's new technology." Lu's excitement was palpable.

"No way, it's jewels. Only jewels bring men to a fight like this one."

Lu reached in and lifted the lid of the crate.

"Holy yahtz," they said in unison.

Inside the crate, next to a leaking oxygen tank, was a girl, dressed in array of fine and flowing materials and her jewelry glimmering against her dark skin. She lay curled up in a ball on her side.

"It's the princess of Sidoa," Rasha said.

"How do you know?"

"I just do."

The last thing she wanted was to discuss how she recognized the princess. Rasha had met the girl before in another life. She'd been much younger back then.

Lu reached in to touch her but Rasha slapped his hand away.

"What if she's…?" Rasha asked, fearing the worst.

"That's what I was trying to find out." Lu reached in and felt for life signs while Rasha held her amulet.

"She's alive," he said.

"We've got to get her out of here." Rasha said, looking into the trees. The feeling they were being watched hadn't gone away after the fight. "She won't make it the whole way in this broken crate, and we can't have her waking up to another fight."

"Why do you think she's being transported in a crate instead of traveling to Adalu like the other princesses?" Lu asked.

"Based on what we've seen this afternoon, I'd say because they feared she wouldn't make it there alive." Rasha turned and gathered up the rest of their supplies and put them into the new vehicle.

"I need to find Temi. He jumped out of the pouch during the crash and I haven't seen him since." Lu walked into the woods.

It took some time to gather all of their scattered things, including her missing sword, Blade. Rasha had packed the second vehicle with their belongings and was waiting when Lu returned. He still hadn't found Temi.

"We don't have time for this, we've got a princess to protect. There will be more of them coming," Rasha said when Lu hesitated.

Lu swore under his breath and called out for Temi one last time.

"He may have gotten scared and run off. I'm sorry." Rasha hated to see him like this again, but she had no other words to offer. She put a hand on his shoulder and hoped it was enough. "He belongs in the wild."

"Okay," Lu said, his head and shoulders drooped with resignation. He took one last look around before he climbed into the driver's seat.

"Let's take it slow, I want my insides to stay on the inside this time."

## 8

*R*asha and Lu placed the sleeping Sidoan princess on the bed that dominated the small room at the inn. There was also a chair and a lamp, but the room had no decorative ornaments. Not the first place royalty would take refuge, Rasha noted. But if she had wanted to travel in style, she wouldn't have picked a crate. She was beautiful. Rasha looked her over as they laid her on her back with her arms at her sides. Her skin was so black it was almost blue. She wore a blue gown. Her tumble of hair framed her face. She wore a crown of colored gems and jewelry everywhere from her from neck to her ankles.

Lu must have been admiring her too, because he said in a half whisper, "She's beautiful isn't she?"

"She's trouble. If we don't figure out what happened and fast, we'll be up to our eyeballs in trackers and assassins." Rasha paced back and forth. "I need to contact Central."

"I'm not sure that's a good idea." Lu fidgeted from one foot to the other.

"Someone needs to know what's going on."

"When has Central ever cared about what happens out here in the field?"

"This is different. Someone in the Courier's Keep might be able to help us. My record is perfect and clean, they might listen to what I have to say."

Lu watched her apprehensively, with a fingernail between his teeth.

"Courier Jenchat-42769 speaking," Rasha said into the thin communicator square.

"Voice identification confirmed. How may I help you?" The automated voice spoke in a clipped and impatient manner.

"I need to speak with someone about a fetch discrepancy."

"We deliver: we don't ask, we don't tell, the—"

"Courier always delivers." Rasha tapped on the square, impatient to get a real live person. "I'm aware of the code, you robotic pumseed. No, this is above and beyond the code."

"Please enter your job number." Rasha sighed.

"Fetch & Drop Assignment 2-4879, confirmed, in progress, requested and accepted." The computerized voice droned.

"Incorrect, not requested. I demand an audience with anyone in the Courier's Keep. I don't want to talk to an artificial—"

"Fetch & Drop Assignment 2-4879 requested by Luduru Moren, accepted by Rasha Jenchat."

"Requested? No, there must be a mistake."

"Voice confirmation of Luduru Moren-62513 received."

"We didn't ask for humanoid cargo."

"Transport of humanoid cargo is cause for immediate dismissal and license revocation for all couriers involved. Moren-62513 and Jenchat-42769 licenses are now void. Thank you and have a nice—"

Rasha switched off the device with the tap of her thumb. She slipped the clear square back into her pocket before turning to Lu. He backed up but not fast enough. Rasha hauled him up hard by his vest and slammed him against the nearest wall.

"What in the yahtz did you do?"

"Wait, I can explain."

Lu's boots dangled a few inches off of the floor and Rasha dropped him, only to pull him a breath away from her face. She had to look down to look him in the eye.

"How do you explain transporting humanoid cargo and losing our licenses?"

Lu gave up resisting her and hung his head.

"Ladi."

"Your sister? What does she have to do with this?" Rasha asked, letting go of his vest.

"Remember the night I had to take care of something?" At her nod he continued, "Ladi was in jail, again."

"Poobari's."

"Yeah, and he was like a stone wall this time. I had to give him something to get her out."

"I'm sure the ungrateful wretch didn't even thank you."

"No, I gave him the money she'd earned, and I promised him I'd take this job. She was less than pleased."

"I'm glad. She should pay for her own mistakes. Why didn't you tell me all of this in the first place?"

"I knew what you'd say."

"That she should rot in jail like the little fangledort she is?"

"The plan was to be back in Adalu before it even came up. I'm sorry. I'm already working on a way to get our licenses reinstated."

"You don't get it, do you? Without our licenses, we don't have access to any of the privileges that come with being couriers. We're on our own. Not to mention all our courier payments are subject to investigation." Rasha wanted to punch something but Lu's face was the only thing close, and that wouldn't do. He was still her friend, and they'd need each other now more than ever.

"Get rid of that all-terrain vehicle and use the money to get two beasts and bring the rest back. We need supplies."

A startled scream got their attention, and they whirled around and saw the princess staring at Temi. He crouched

on her chest, ears back and growling six inches from
her nose.

## 9

"*C*ome here Temi, where have you been? I've been looking all over for you." Lu reached over and grabbed his little beast before they hurt each other. Lu stroked the animal, and he stopped his growling and licked Lu's green finger.

The princess sat up and looked around the room and its furnishings. Her eyes fell on Lu and he couldn't help smiling at her. She looked up at him through her lashes. She noticed they weren't alone in the room when her eyes found Rasha and her mouth fell open.

"You're purple."

Rasha rolled her eyes. "We're not finished," she said to Lu before storming out of the room.

"I'm sorry, that was indelicate of me. I will choose my words better." The princess shook her head.

"No, don't worry about it. Rash is," Lu struggled for a

word that was honest and yet not too honest, "well, she's Rash."

"Rash," The princess said.

"Rasha," Lu corrected her, pulling the small stool over and sitting down on it so the princess wouldn't strain her neck looking up at him. She slid down on the pillows. No doubt she was still a bit confused about what happened.

"I'm Lu, and you are?" He held up his hand in greeting.

"I'm Chiza," she said pointing to herself and speaking slowly. Many of the newer kingdoms had not mastered the common language as his people had. They also hadn't learned the cultural norms—she stared at his raised hand for a moment before remembering she should raise her palm to his.

"It is a pleasure to meet you, princess." Lu lowered his head to her and watched Temi stare at him in wonder.

"What happened? How is it that I'm here in this place with you and not at the palace with prince Bashir?"

"What's the last thing you remember?"

"My mother and father putting me to sleep. They said I'd be carried to the first kingdom and wake there. Are you my abductors?" Chiza, all at once, seemed to understand the dangerousness of the situation.

"No, we were commissioned to carry you to Adalu, but we were attacked on the road. That's how your crate was damaged."

"I understand. Things are not going according to the

original plan," Chiza said and bit her bottom lip, a habit Lu found alluring.

"I suppose you weren't planning on being tossed about by bandits. Do you know why these men are after you?"

"I'm from Sidoa," she said as if that were enough.

"I don't understand. None of the other princesses had such trouble."

"Their lands are also not small. We are farmers by trade. When they discovered gems in the caves, it changed everything. Now the surrounding kingdoms all want to take our lands by force. The only way to do that is to make sure I don't become the next queen."

"Your father tried to sneak you out using less than reputable channels thinking it would keep you hidden?" Lu asked.

"I believe so. He told me he'd paid enough in gems to ensure I'd arrive and be opened by the prince like a gift.

"I can imagine his expression when he opened the crate." Lu gave her a halfhearted laugh.

"We hoped he'd be pleased," Chiza said, casting her eyes down to her lap.

"He will be," Lu said, wanting to talk about anything else. "Now, let me introduce you to Temi. It seems you got off to a rough start."

"Temi, this is Chiza, the princess. Princess, this little guy is Temi."

"I've never seen another like him." She reached out a hand to touch the top of his head and he bowed to her as Lu had done.

"Well, aren't you a smart little beastie?" Lu said, laughing.

"Where ever did you find him?"

"In a tin cup."

"He wouldn't fit in a cup," Chiza laughed as Temi rolled over onto his back and exposed his belly.

"Not anymore, he's grown since we found him." He reached out and rubbed Temi's stomach until he purred.

"Your friend, she's upset with me?"

"No, it's not you. She doesn't much like humanoid cargo since it's bad for business. You see, we've lost our couriers' licenses because of this misunderstanding."

"Oh no, please accept my apology on behalf of my family. We didn't think things would go this far astray."

"So, you knew you were being put in a crate like cargo? I hope I'm interrupting." Rasha entered the room carrying a bag, and closed the door behind her.

Lu popped up off his stool. Rasha gave him a glare like he'd just done something stupid. "No, I was just getting the story." The words tumbled out as if he'd rehearsed them. Why did he feel like he hadn't any right to be there?

"She says her father was trying to keep her hidden, out of fear for her life." Lu forced his voice to sound controlled.

"He was right, it seems," Rasha replied, dropping the bag to the floor and sitting on edge of the bed as if the two girls were longtime friends.

"Not at all," Chiza said. She was far too innocent. Lu

recognized the look on Rasha's face. She was preparing to eat her alive. Lu tried to diffuse the situation.

"Chiza was telling me that their kingdom is at risk."

"Chiza?" Rasha's smile was a warning.

"Princess?" Lu asked. "The seventh, eighth, and ninth kingdoms are all a threat. They'd double their own lands and gain the gems along with it."

"Well, this is more than a small problem here. I'm sure my partner failed to mention we lost our licenses due to this little venture."

"Yes, he mentioned that." Chiza said. She seemed almost pleased.

Rasha turned to Lu, and if her eyes could cut, she'd have sliced his head off.

"Did he also mention that as couriers we've renounced all loyalty to any one kingdom? This isn't our problem."

Lu had already prepared an answer. She wouldn't like it but he was ready for her.

"We're no longer couriers and if we should deliver the princess to prince Bashir, I'm sure he'll want to make sure we get our licenses reinstated." He said.

"We're not qualified for this," she snapped.

"We're the best team of couriers this kingdom has ever seen. Our perfect record proves it. Who better than us?"

He was right, Rasha didn't like his answer, and if her hand twitched toward her belt again, he'd make a run for it to avoid her short swords.

It was Chiza that saved him.

"Do you think the prince will be disappointed not to get his present?"

That turned Rasha's attention back toward her.

"Don't you feel, I don't know, at all embarrassed to be passed off to the prince like nothing more than common goods?"

"It's a privilege and an honor to be chosen by the prince. I've been preparing for it my entire life. I can't imagine a better way to serve the ten kingdoms than to be its queen." Chiza's eyes glazed over as if she was seeing her life unfold in front of her.

"Your privilege and honor remind me of a decorated collar on a short leash," Rasha told her.

The princess remained silent. Rasha gestured at the bag she'd brought in with her. "Princess, you'll want to change into something warmer. We'll be traveling at night and heading north. We'll keep you as comfortable as we can but it won't be an easy trip. The crate would have been more comfortable, but that's no longer an option."

Chiza nodded and pulled out a cloak from the bag. It was black with blue lining. She would look amazing in it.

"Lu?" Rasha asked.

He tore his eyes away from Chiza and raised his eyebrows at Rasha.

"Isn't there a vehicle you need to take care of?"

"Oh, yes." He remembered now. "I'll return as soon as I can." He bowed to Chiza. "Princess."

"Don't hurry back," Rasha said, giving him her most bored and annoyed stare.

## 10

$R$asha snuck them out the back of the inn. They had no money for the room they'd occupied most of the day, another mark on her once spotless record. The southern air created droplets of sweat on her temples. The princess, covered in her new cloak, rode behind Rasha on her new tuskin. She kept a warmer cloak of her own packed away among her things for when they reached the north. She couldn't trust Lu with her anymore. He kept giving Chiza odd looks while the princess laughed and giggled as if he were the prince she needed to impress.

"We're still being followed," Rasha said after they'd been riding for some time.

"You think it's the same guys from the card game the other night?" Lu asked.

"No, it's someone else. Just one, a tracker."

Chiza yawned wide before asking, "We're being followed?"

"Since we left Sidoa," Lu added. "I'll go this time and see if I find anyone.

Chiza sat up straight. "Be careful."

"I will." Lu turned his beast around to hunt for the unwanted follower.

"What was that?" Rasha asked.

"I'm sorry?"

"Nothing." The last thing she wanted was another debate with the princess. She seemed bent on being one of the prince's ladies on display.

Rasha enjoyed the silence as they rode along. She listened for any movement in the trees. She heard Lu as he returned. The princess had fallen asleep against her back, so Rasha used signals to communicate with him instead.

Lu gave her a shrug of his shoulders. If the guy from Tero-Joro, a people with advanced vision and hearing, couldn't find the tracker they must be amazing. Rasha admired him a little. Her own skills in tracking had become something of note among her fellow couriers, but this was beyond special. Lu stayed behind them as the road narrowed and they had to travel in a single file.

They rode through the night. As dawn approached, she felt Chiza wake up with a start behind her. Rasha and Lu continued on in silence for a moment before Lu gave his morning greeting.

"May the sun greet you with kindness, brother. I'm happy to see you are safe," Chiza said to him.

Rasha tried not to laugh at Lu's reaction. Being a non-religious person, he didn't seem to know what to say.

"Are you a worshipper of the sun god, like the Karmirians?" Rasha asked.

"No, not at all. We worship the Universal as your people do. Are you much for worship, Rash?" Chiza asked, forgetting she shouldn't use the familiar name as Lu did.

Lu smiled this time.

"Yes, when I can, I visit the temple of my people."

Chiza yawned.

"I'm sorry," she said.

"You've been riding all night, your highness. You're entitled to be tired. I apologize, however, since we've still got a long way before we stop again."

## 11

When Rasha rode off to check behind them for the tracker a weight lifted off of him. She had a way of making him shy around Chiza. He figured the princess felt the same since her grip tightened around him as soon as Rasha disappeared into the woods. He slowed his tuskin to make the ride a little smoother. She didn't complain about it but he knew how she must be suffering. His own body, accustomed to the riding, didn't notice it yet, but by evening he'd have his own pains to suppress.

A sound in the trees to their right caught his attention. He turned and scanned the area until he saw what had made it. A beady-eyed creature with a tail it used for throwing itself from branch to branch among the trees.

Chiza was busy humming under her breath. It was a pleasant tune, and he asked her about it.

"Something I picked up as a girl. I had a mermaid for

a friend once. She sang all the time."

"I sort of imagined you growing up in a castle or something. I didn't think princesses could have friends," Lu said with a laugh.

Chiza didn't giggle as she did when she found something funny.

"I'm sorry, did I say something wrong?"

"No, it's only that you're right. Growing up, I had few friends. Most don't understand the training involved in this life. The mental preparation, knowing you will give your entire purpose over to one person who may or may not even choose you."

"Well, like it or not, you made another friend. This Tero-Joro can keep in contact with all of his friends, near and far."

Chiza put her head against his back.

"Thank you, you're too kind."

"No, you're the kind one. I'm a courier and you will one day be my queen. I'm sure that once the prince sees your beauty, generosity, and gentle spirit he'll be just as enamored with you as—" Lu stopped himself before he finished that dangerous thought. Instead he cleared his throat, and said, "As any man would be after meeting you."

When he heard Rasha's whistle he returned it with one of his own. She used the signal to check on them and their distance. His confirmation would let her know they were both all right and she could continue her hunt for their tracker.

Chiza didn't seem to notice that he whistled back to Rasha. Instead she hummed again to herself and he listened before trying to repeat the song, making Chiza laugh aloud.

"Wasn't that right?"

"Only if you're trying to imitate the mating call of a dying piko." She laughed again.

"Okay, well, are there any words?"

Chiza hummed for a moment then shook her head. "I can't seem to remember them well enough."

Lu tried again to copy the tune, which sent Chiza into giggling hysterics.

"Well, I'm glad that the tracker now no longer needs to follow the tracks of our beasts I did so much work to cover. Now he can just follow your laughter straight to our graves," Rasha snapped.

"I'm sorry, Rash, his tones are so wayward that I don't know how his people ever learned to communicate with the mermen."

"Well, hold your tongue, we're not out of danger yet."

Chiza leaned close to his back and said, "Isn't she a horrible taskmaster?" which made Lu's shoulders shake with laughter though he kept his mouth closed. She was full of surprises. He'd never known a princess to be so open and honest. Although, if he were being honest, he wasn't on a first name basis with any royalty.

"Are all the Chilalians like her?"

"No, they're a kind and quiet people. Of all the kingdoms, the Chilalians travel least. They don't like living in the other kingdoms and prefer to be called on when needed instead. They are similar to the mermen, in that way."

"So, a peaceful people."

"In general," Lu said and glanced in Rasha's direction. She wore a fierce expression. No doubt the hunger and fatigue were getting to her. He wondered what it would take to get them through another night. They wouldn't be able to stay at another inn. They'd be sleeping in the elements and there would be little food if they didn't catch something soon. He'd have to get a fire going, cook them something. He hoped Chiza's delicate palate tolerated the food he prepared.

"I need to get something for us to eat tonight."

Rasha slowed her animal, and he slowed to match until they came to a halt. Rasha waited for the princess to join her. Chiza still clung to his waist, not understanding what was happening. Lu climbed down and held out a hand to her.

"I'll be back soon with something to eat," he said to her.

"Oh, I see," Chiza slid down off of the back of his tuskin. He used one arm to ease her down to the ground. She looked up at him and flashed him a smile such as he'd never seen. Her joy lit him up from within. With her smile on his mind and the setting sun in front of them, he rode off to go hunting.

"Your highness," Rasha said, holding out her arm. Chiza used it to climb up behind her.

*R*asha enjoyed the quiet, watching the setting sun to the north. It didn't last long.

"I know who you are, Lady Indari," Chiza said, shattering Rasha's internal and external peace.

Her back straightened and she didn't speak for several moments.

"Don't call me that, ever. Where did you hear that name?"

"I was educated about all of my competition from an early age," Chiza said, as if she were speaking of mathematics or some other school subject.

"I'm not your competition."

Chiza didn't speak for a moment, then said, "I suspect Lu isn't aware of it. If he was, I think he would treat you with the respect he gives me."

"That's not respect he's giving you."

Chiza didn't respond to that as Rasha hoped she

would. She'd rather talk about anything than her own past.

"Why won't you do your duty? Doesn't it shame your people to leave them with no eligible princess for the prince to choose from?" Chiza asked.

"Doesn't it bother you to be handed over to man you've never met to serve as the commodity of your nation's greed for power?"

"I choose to serve my people, I'm not forced or coerced."

"But they persuaded you to believe it's what should be done. The idea has been forced on you since birth." Rasha heard Lu returning and pulled up. "I won't be lined up like a beast of burden to be chosen by any man. It is not for him alone to do the choosing. Shouldn't I also be able to choose for myself?"

"No," Chiza said. Her answer was confident and sure. She added, "For the sake of your people you forsake that choice to better your kingdom. If the royal house was passing to a princess, it would be her duty to choose from the princes. It makes no difference the gender of the royal doing the choosing. We should be proud to be among those given the opportunity. There are so many, due to an accident of birth, who will never get the chance."

"I'm a courier, with no allegiance to any one kingdom or nation. I deliver, and I do it well. It's better than being a pawn of the palace," Rasha replied.

She itched to have the princess as far away from her as possible. The question was coming. One she dared not answer. The one that made the acid in her stomach churn until she thought she might be sick.

"The day may come when you must choose a side. I hope you and I will stand on the same side on that day," Chiza said.

Rasha's breathing returned to normal as the silence ate up her last words. It wasn't the question she'd been expecting—the one that always seemed to tear her from the inside out.

Lu returned, food in hand, and found the two in the middle of the heated debate, neither able to occupy the same space on the back of Rasha's beast.

"She's right, we may have to choose a nation someday. I've thought about it myself, and I'm with Chiza."

"Of course you are," Rasha said, sliding off the beast and leaving Chiza to find her own way down.

"What does that mean?"

"It means only this: be careful which side you stand on. You've known her for but for a few days, and you've known me for two whole rotations. Which of us is more likely to betray you and slit your throat?" Rasha stormed off into the woods. Lu and Chiza were becoming unbearable.

Rasha wondered why Chiza failed to use her endless supply of self-righteousness to learn a proper skill like combat or defense training. The girl got on her nerves. The princess lacked the most basic of survival skills. Rasha used her short swords to cut through the brush as she marched through branches and weeds.

She couldn't leave the two of them for long, so she returned to where she left them and found that Lu and Chiza had already made camp. Lu had the meat over the fire and rotated it every few minutes, cooking it evenly.

Lu frowned at Rasha. Maybe he noticed the set of her jaw. She shook her head. Lu couldn't know. Chiza shouldn't know. There was nothing to do about it now. She'd deliver her cargo to the palace of Adalu and be on her way as fast as her tuskin beast's pace allowed.

Lu and Chiza twittered back and forth until Chiza fell asleep on his shoulder. Neither of them spoke to Rasha as they ate and prepared for bed. Rasha rolled her eyes. What did she care if they wanted to be more than friends? Lu was getting into serious trouble. He had the same look on his face as when he found a new beastie. The heartbreak would come, it always did. This girl, promised to the prince, would never choose him over her duty. Rasha wouldn't get involved. She'd made that mistake before.

Instead, she rested with her hands behind her head on her patch of covered dirt and looked up at the sky. One large and one small moon lit up the night sky making it difficult to see any other constellations. Rasha reached for her amulet and said a brief prayer to the Universal for their safety on their continued journey. They needed all the help they could get.

## 13

---

The next day, Rasha was grateful Lu and Chiza had kept their chattering and giggling to a minimum. Thinking of what might lie ahead was difficult enough, trying to navigate through areas where it might not be acceptable to bring the princess or places where they would be recognized. They hadn't had an incident in almost a day. The competing kingdoms would strike soon. That's how she'd do it. Maybe that's why she heard them coming before they attacked.

Lu was talking to Chiza about his family at the time. Startled, he looked over at Rasha, who nodded as she climbed off of her tuskin and brought it to him. Chiza slipped from Lu's to Rasha's. He pulled Temi's pouch from his shoulder and placed it over Chiza's. Something in her eyes caught Rasha's attention, but she didn't have time to decipher it. They were closing in.

Lu handed the reins of his beast to Chiza, who shook

her head and whimpered. Lu slid down to the ground so he could cover the row of trees opposite.

Rasha grabbed a long dry branch from the ground and struck the backs of both beasts and yelled, "Now."

Rasha listened to their approaching voices and confirmed it wasn't who'd been following them before. The roar that burst through the trees was not the stealthy tracker.

Rasha nodded at Lu to cover her six, and when the men came through the trees, she saw from their clothing they'd come from the eighth and the ninth kingdoms. The men they'd fought earlier were with them, and, although still damaged from the last time, led the charge against them now. Gorg's partner, the one with the broken nose, came for her, but she was ready for him. She pulled out her swords and held him off, giving Lu more time.

Lu was behind her prepping his equipment.

"How long?" she yelled. She fought him off more easily this time with two swords.

"I'll need at least two minutes," he yelled back as he backed closer to her.

"Two minutes? Are you sure it will work?"

"Yes, but it needs two minutes!"

"Great, then, a minute after we're dead they'll be down."

Rasha kicked the man nearest her in the sensitive area between his legs, then slammed an elbow into his back. She pushed off of him and landed a kick to the side of the man opposite her. Lu bobbed backwards trying to avoid getting a blade to the face from an attacker with a long sword. Rasha stepped between them and took the brunt of the clash against her own sword, the hit almost knocking it from her hands. She fell backwards, taking her swords with her and luring the man away from Lu.

Lu used his speed to get around two large guys that tried to pummel him with tall staffs. Lu grabbed the end of a staff and used it propel him around the men. From behind Rasha, a man grunted as he raised his sword to cut her down. Rasha pivoted to the right and the man in front of her dropped the sword against her blade. Their swords clashed with a loud crash.

"Lu, now!"

"It's not ready!"

"I don't care!"

Lu sat the device on the ground and jumped behind the nearest tree.

"Now!" he yelled, and the device sent a pulse that moved so fast it was invisible and every man within ten feet of it dropped, unconscious.

"Where's the princess?" Rasha asked. Before Lu could shrug a scream pierced the quiet of the woods. They ran toward it. Chiza hadn't gotten very far, and the frightened beasts had run off. She was struggling with a man that stood head and shoulders above the others they'd been fighting. Rasha moved in front of him with her swords drawn.

He pulled out a sword of his own and held it to princess' neck.

"Lu?" Rasha asked between clenched teeth. Things were getting more out of hand than she liked.

"No, it will take too long to prepare."

"Suggestions?"

"Nothing I want to give away."

"Well, if you're going to do something, do it," Rasha told him as she circled the man holding Chiza by the neck.

Her screams echoed for miles. Lu moved to the left, and the man grunted and pulled the sword closer to Chiza's neck. This only scared her more, and she screamed even louder. Something whizzed past her ear and landed on the large man's cheek and stuck. He swatted at it but it was too late. The small projectile, no larger than a pin, stopped him. The sword in his hand tumbled to the ground, and he fell to his knees and flat on his face. Rasha was looking at the dart, so she didn't see the other man come out of the trees in time.

He was on her in seconds. He landed a punch that made her see stars. She groaned and spun away from the punch to get out of the way before he could hit her again. She didn't make it. He dropped the butt of his sword on her back and it brought her to her knees. She fell beside the larger man she'd just taken down. His pungent sweat assaulted her nose and she wondered if this would be the last thing she'd ever smell.

A grunt came from somewhere above. A man had propelled himself from the woods and stood between Rasha and her opponent. He raised his long sword in challenge, giving Rasha time to crawl out of harm's way and see who had come to her aid.

The young man's moves seemed almost to be in slow motion to her as her brain tried to capture and retain what she saw. His long hair swirled around him as he spun his long sword, landing a fierce blow that sent the other man backwards. He tried to raise his sword, but his awkward thrust missed the young man by a mile. Instead his young opponent ran him through, and the shock on his face mirrored the shock Rasha felt.

The young man's sun-kissed skin identified him as another humanoid. When he turned toward her, he still had his teeth bared from the fight. But in an instant his features relaxed, and he smiled at her. His bright blue eyes and dimpled cheeks made him look even younger than she imagined him. He couldn't be much older than her.

Rasha crumpled to the ground before the young man could reach her.

THE POUNDING in Rasha's head woke her. That or the screeching from the back of her skull. No, not inside her head, she realized. Outside. Chiza was still screaming. Strong hands lifted her from the ground and helped her stand. She was about to thank Lu when she realized the face she saw was the stranger's. She stared at the young man who'd fought off the last of their attackers.

"You've got a nasty bump there. I'm sorry I took so

long." He reached out as if to touch her face and she backed away.

"Shut her up, Lu, or I will," she warned, startling the princess into silence.

"I'm Jak Ostari." He held up a hand, palm out, waiting for her to greet him, but she didn't move her hand from the tender spot on her head. He realized she wasn't going to return the greeting and dropped his hand. "I hope I didn't startle you. I heard the commotion and came to help. The screaming reached all the way to the main road. There were a couple beasts wandering around that way. I assume they're yours." His smile reached his eyes.

Rasha knew of Jak. A former courier with a reputation as good as, if not better than, her own. Before she'd come along, he'd been the best, with a perfect record. Until about a rotation ago when he didn't retrieve a fetch. No one knew what the fetch had been or where it went, only that he'd refused to do it. Afterwards, he quit being a courier and became a tracker.

Lu raised his hand to welcome him.

"I'm Lu, thanks for your help," he said, still standing with Chiza. She clasped his arm with both hands as if he kept her safe. Rasha wondered if Lu noticed.

"Nice to meet you Lu, I'm Jak. Who is this lovely vision?" Jak said turning his attention to Chiza.

"Chiza," she replied. She didn't elaborate or seemed charmed by him. That made Rasha smile. Chiza was smarter than she'd given her credit for.

"Jak? The Jak?" Lu stammered.

"I don't know if I've earned the article, but my name is Jak."

"You're the most famous courier I know, other than Rash. Well, I feel like I know you. I mean, we've never met but I've seen your work. I mean your former work. I know you don't deliver anymore. It's a shame, because everyone says you're the best."

His babbling embarrassed Rasha. She'd recognized him too, but she wasn't swooning.

"I mean, four rotations. No one has even come close. You're a living legend. I can't believe you're here."

"Not four rotations. Three rotations and seven months." He seemed embarrassed by the praise. He pulled at the collar of his coat. The tattoos on his neck didn't hide his blush.

Rasha had enough of Lu's gushing and cleared her throat.

"Lu, let's get the animals. We need to be on our way." Rasha found her footing and started toward the beasts.

"No, don't trouble yourselves, I'll get the animals. Just rest. You need it," Jak interjected, and started off into the woods.

"It's a good thing we ran into Jak." Lu beamed with happiness.

"He did seem to be here at just the right time," Chiza said.

Rasha thought so too.

"A little too convenient to be coincidence," Rasha said.

"What do you mean?" Lu asked, but Rasha began

swaying on her feet, and he leapt to catch her. "You need
to sit."

Rasha didn't have much of a choice in the matter. Her
ears rang and her back ached.

She slid into a sitting position. She tried to lean back
against the tree but the pain in her back made it impossible, so she turned her shoulder to it instead.

"See to the beasts."

"I'm not leaving you alone."

"I won't be alone," she sighed. Lu seemed to realize
that Chiza was still clinging to his arm with both hands.
He gently detached himself before going off to follow Jak.

"Do you think it's safe to leave them alone?" Chiza
asked, sitting down on the ground beside her.

She'd come a long way, Rasha noted. Before this little
journey she'd never sat down in the dirt on purpose.

"It's fine. If he'd wanted to hurt us he would have let
the others take us and then picked off the survivors." She
didn't need to name herself as the one being picked off
while she sat with a tree holding her up.

"Are you going to be all right? I've never seen you
like this."

"I'll be fine." Rasha said and hoped it was true. She'd
never sustained such a blow before. The man, though
smaller than the others she'd fought, got close enough to
lay his hands on her. "Is Temi with you?" she asked,
distracting her reluctant caretaker.

"Um, I'm not sure." Chiza looked into the pouch and
lifted the lid. Temi wasn't inside. "Oh no, he's not there."

"No doubt he got scared when the screaming started," Rasha told Chiza with what she hoped was a playful smile.

Chiza smiled back and said, "I was scared too. That man was so big. Where did that dart come from?"

Rasha frowned. She'd forgotten about the dart in all the confusion.

"Was it Lu?"

"No, I was looking right at him." Chiza's voice trailed off at and she looked down at her fingernails. She'd admitted to something she hadn't wanted to.

## 14

*J*ak and Lu returned leading three tuskins with them. Temi bounded alongside them. Jak's beast looked identical to theirs. She considered that and came to a conclusion. No doubt he had followed in their tracks making it impossible for them to discover him.

Jak and Lu leaned over and reached for her at the same time, helping her from the ground. She twisted out of Lu's grasp, and he retreated to help the princess get to her feet. Jak, however wouldn't let go, ignoring her attempts to shake him loose.

"How long have you been following us?" Rasha asked. She knew the answer, but she wanted hear it from him.

Jak laughed. Lu and Chiza were standing there looking shocked at her brazenness. The idea either hadn't occurred to them, or it had, but they'd been afraid to make the accusation. Temi growled as if just noticing that he didn't belong. Jak looked at them and then back to Rasha. He would answer her. She figured he was debating about whether he should tell them the truth. Not that it mattered now, here he was. He came to the same conclusion.

"I've been following you since you left Sidoa."

Lu gasped, but Chiza seemed unsurprised.

Rasha didn't let their reactions affect her. She waited for him to elaborate.

"I'm not at liberty to share with you my mission in any detail. But I can tell you I'm not here to hurt you in any way." He offered them a warm smile.

The three exchanged glances, then Lu and Chiza waited for Rasha to speak. Temi sniffed at his ankles, exhaling in short huffs.

She shrugged. "Let's not debate it out here. It'll be dark in a few hours. We need to get Chiza someplace safe." She tried to pull herself up onto the tuskin, but Jak's hands gripped her waist and lifted her onto the beast. Then he climbed up behind her.

"What are you doing?" she snarled at him.

"You're not well enough to ride alone. I'll be here in case you tip off," Jak said. slipping his hand around her waist. Lu helped Chiza up onto Rasha's beast. Lu mounted his own, bringing up the rear.

He had quite the nerve. Rasha was seething. She was more than capable of riding by herself. It hadn't been her first fight. Rasha spurred her beast and the tuskins following her increased their speed to match. They hadn't gone more than a half a mile before she was dizzy with nausea. She had to breathe deeply to keep her head from spinning.

"Ho," Jak said holding up a fist to stop the others.

Rasha's dizziness subsided, but only a little. Jak took the reins and clicked through his teeth to urge the animal forward at a slower pace. Her stomach settled enough for her to speak again. She was grateful, but she wasn't ready to admit it. His arm around her middle made her squirm, and she pushed it away.

Jak laughed.

"I haven't forgotten that you haven't told us. Why are you following us?"

"I can't tell you that, I'm still bound by the code. But I'll tell you this. The road we're on is no longer safe. It will not get you to the first kingdom unharmed."

"How do you know where we're headed?" Rasha turned to look at him, and got another dizzying headache for her trouble.

"You're going to Adalu. Why else would you be taking the north road this time of year? I'm no stranger to this road. No one else takes it to visit the Twinlands. You're headed to the first and you've brought enough warm clothing to survive a few days on the road until you get there."

"Have you ever noticed that you talk a lot and say nothing of importance?"

"I've been known to rattle on."

"What happened to you? Why aren't you a courier anymore?"

Jak didn't laugh off the question this time.

"You fight well, for a Chilalian," he said.

"You fight well, for a human," she retorted.

"The rumors about you aren't true."

"I'm not concerned with tattle."

"I don't find the purple strange at all. It's extremely attractive."

Rasha stiffened and kept her eyes forward. Jak laughed.

"Don't be so nervous, I'm only giving you a compliment."

"I'm hardly nervous," Rasha gritted her teeth. His comment shouldn't bother her. So why was she annoyed?

"No?" Jak leaned out to look at her face. Why did he have to be so intrusive?

Rasha jabbed his chest with her elbow. It wasn't enough to hurt, but enough to warn him she wasn't interested in being scrutinized. He took the hint but every time the beast came to a stop or made a quick movement his arm caught her waist again. She reasoned to herself that she was tired of pushing him away. It didn't do any harm. Rasha had always imagined having someone looking after you once in a while would give you the sense of security. She didn't feel secure. She felt vulnerable.

THE SKY WAS gold with the setting sun and one moon

could be seen high in the sky when Jak stopped them at an inn.

"We can't stay here," Rasha said, and started to turn her tuskin.

"We can and we will," Jak said. "I've got the credits, it's not a problem." He spoke as if he was aware of their troubles.

Rasha was debating whether to allow him to pay when the princess rode up next to them.

"A proper bath will be so nice. I can't see prince Bashir in this state."

"We're staying here?" Lu asked as he joined them. "I might be able to get a proper link to the communicator and contact a few friends. They might tell us what's up ahead."

"Good thinking. Let's go get settled," Jak said.

Rasha didn't know what to say. Her back was killing her, and she wasn't sure she didn't have a concussion because her head was still spinning. She didn't know how to view his offer. Jak's surprise arrival, tracking them, and apparently being on a mission running parallel to theirs, but they didn't have any details. What if he planned to kidnap the princess? She couldn't be sure until she had the truth.

What was that saying? 'Keep the eye of your enemy in sight and your friends at your back.' She'd do that and make sure that this Jak fellow didn't hinder her delivery. It didn't matter if he was a legendary courier and wielded his sword like an extension of his arm. Rasha refused to give any more thought to his skills or the lock of dark hair that fell in front of his gorgeous blue eyes when he spoke to her.

Jak climbed down from the beast first and pushed the lock of hair away from his eyes before reaching up to help her down.

"I'm not an invalid," she said more forcefully than necessary.

"Of course," Jak said, "but you need rest."

He ordered them two rooms. Rasha and Chiza shared one, Jak and Lu took the other.

Rasha tried to thank Jak but the words stuck in her throat. It was Lu who expressed their gratitude. Chiza headed straight for the bath. Rasha wanted to lie down but knew she'd fall asleep. Instead she left the room to tend to their beasts. They'd need food.

Lu was already there.

"What are you doing here? Shouldn't you be resting?" Lu said when he saw her.

"I'm not sure I should lie down just yet."

"I see. Well, while you're here, pass me the bristle brush there on the stool."

"Grooming?" she asked as she passed him the tool.

"Yes, they need to brushed and their hooves checked. Small pebbles get in there and make it difficult for them to travel long distances. We've got a journey ahead of us yet."

"Any word?" Rasha asked.

"No. I'll keep checking, though. It was nice of Jak to

pay for us to stay here. I don't think Chiza could have slept on the ground one more night."

"We can't let Jak stay with us."

"No." Lu said without looking up from the hoof he was examining.

"It's kind of him to help us, but this delivery is far more important than any one man."

"Maybe he wants to make some new friends," Lu suggested.

"If he wants to make friends with us, he can try when we're not in the middle of this mess with the princess. Too many people have a stake in her arrival to the first kingdom."

Lu nodded but didn't answer.

"Does it matter I sort of like having him around?"

"No," she said firmly, looking at him. When he met her eye, she gave him a sharp nod and turned to go.

WHEN RASHA WOKE UP, the room was empty and dark. Chiza must have gone out with Lu. They were never too far away from each other.

Rasha did herself and everyone else a favor and took a bath. The cleanliness rejuvenated her. She no longer had the nausea in her stomach. In fact, she was hungry. Rasha wondered how far Jak's generosity stretched. Would he also pay for their meals? He hadn't shared his plans so she'd set up a tab in his name with the barkeep. She smiled at the thought. Served him right for trying to take care of her.

She wondered why she wanted to punish him for it. Then the answer came. She didn't trust him. She'd learned early on not to trust every person coming with an open hand and a smile. They always wanted something in return. Jak Ostari wouldn't be any different. He wanted something. She couldn't fathom what it was yet, but she'd find out.

*L*u worked on his communicator, trying to reach anyone who had information on what was ahead of them. It didn't look good. He'd already received two reports. There were a couple of illegal requests for hired men from the Wilds. Hunters and trackers for the tenth princess, as she'd been seen in the area.

He didn't like the sound of that. Men from the Wilds were lawless, if you trusted the reports. Assuming the pay was high enough, they'd be ambushed again by morning. He got up and grabbed his communicator. Rasha would be down at the bar by now, sipping her juice. Jak might be down there too since he didn't seem like the tuck-in-with-a-good-book kind of guy. He'd have the room to himself tonight, if Jak's reputation proved true.

A soft knock at the door changed his plans. He opened it and the beauty before him made him forget everything else. Lu's heart leaped into his throat every time he saw her, making it hard to speak. His face broke out in a smile. When the silence between them became uncomfortable, an idea formed in his mind. He imagined she'd be sleeping the night away, and he said so.

"I thought you'd be asleep by now."

"I tried but I can't seem to settle. May I come in?" she asked.

He held the door wide enough to allow her to pass.

"Sorry it's so messy, I wasn't expecting company." Lu pushed his things off of the chair where he wanted her to sit, and sat on the bed across from her.

Chiza had changed into another one of her dresses. This one a simple pink, no doubt for sleeping. But the lace on the edges drew his eye, and he had to work not to wonder what was underneath all the sheer layers. What was wrong with him? Lu shook his head to clear it.

"I'm so sorry to intrude," Chiza said as she surveyed the room.

"No, I like company. I miss having people around. My family is close and we talk about everything," Lu replied as he picked at his boot buckle.

"Mine too." Chiza cast her eyes to down to the floor. She seemed sad.

"Are you worried about them?" he asked.

"Yes, their worry is contagious. It doesn't make any sense, I'm sure they're fine." Chiza said.

"But they're anxious and it concerns you. I have the same problem at home."

"Really? But what you do isn't always this dangerous," she said.

Lu remembered his last job and hanging from the ceiling on a hook waiting for Rash. What if things hadn't gone according to plan?

"Well, it's not as safe as they would like. My parents would prefer that I stay in the Twinlands and settle down and have a family."

"Don't you want that?" Chiza asked.

"Yes, I do. In the future, I mean, I'm still young. There are some things left to do while I can. I want adventure before I go back to ordinary life. The problem is my little sister. Like me, she wants adventure, something extraordinary. Unlike me, she often puts herself in danger. Which is another reason I have to do what I do. I enjoy being available to help out when I can."

"I've always wished for a sister. With no siblings, all of my parent's hopes for our kingdom rested on me." Chiza dropped her gaze.

"Are you sure you want to go through with it?" Lu asked. The question tumbled out before his brain registered what he was asking. He made a quick recovery. "I mean, are you having doubts?" He realized too late that the second question wasn't any better than the first, but Chiza answered it.

"To be honest, no. I know my duty and I'm thrilled with it. I've been studying the other princesses and the prince for rotations. I'm the ideal wife and partner for him. But will he see it too?"

"If he doesn't, he's a fool," he blurted.

"Be careful of how you speak of our prince," Chiza said with a flash of anger.

Lu held up his hand then chose his words with care. "I only meant if he can't see what a treasure you are, then he might not be using all of his mental capacity."

"That's not any better," Chiza retorted.

They both laughed.

"I know, and I am sorry for it." Lu's laughter died down and he asked her a serious question. "What do you want?"

Chiza pondered that for a moment. She understood there were many things wrapped up in that one question. "I guess I want the dream, the fairytale. No matter what happens, I want a family. I'd like to live a peaceful life and should prince Bashir choose me I'd like to improve on the kingdom as its queen and not make it worse."

"How? I mean in what ways?" Lu leaned forward. She had his full attention now. What did she want to improve?

"Well, for one, it's a shame that more people don't learn the native languages of the nations within our realm. The Twinlands where you are from are proficient, it's your culture, but the rest of us need to do more work. We have our common language but we lose a deeper understanding."

"I'm intrigued. What else would you do?"

"I'd want to regulate our intergalactic trade. We need more tradesmen off world and more off world relations.

We should explore alien cultures in more depth. There's more we can do to help each other thrive.

"You speak like someone born to the Twinlands. My people also speak of the future this way. We want those things and more."

"What's one thing you would change, if you had the power to do so?"

"I wish for the prince or princess the freedom to marry whomever he or she chose. A union not based on bloodlines, but common interest and affection." Lu swallowed hard. His mouth had gone dry and he wasn't sure he hadn't overstepped his bounds. She'd already said she desired to fulfill her promise and marry the prince if he chose her. So why did he have to keep sowing seeds of doubt?

At that moment, Temi decided he wasn't getting enough attention, and he plopped over and put his large front paws on Chiza's lap. *When had he gotten big enough to do that?* Lu wondered. Chiza giggled and stroked his belly the way he liked and Temi purred with happiness. She spoke to him in her language the way you would to a baby. Temi loved it. Lu admitted to himself he enjoyed it too. He watched them with a twinge of longing. He wanted to be the object of her affection. Something she was incapable of giving him without breaking her vow to the prince.

## 16

*R*asha sat nursing a juice in the corner of the bar downstairs from their rooms. When Jak stumbled in with a girl on each arm, she felt something in her gut tighten. She wasn't surprised to see him with multiple women. He'd made her think she was special. Here was the proof he'd misled her.

Jak sat at the bar drinking and singing, of all things. He was so embarrassing. Rasha hadn't worn her cloak and now she wished she had. She could hide in it and go unnoticed. Not tonight, though. She'd come down here to think about what to do, not to hide from Jak. She couldn't avoid him all night. She glanced up to see if he'd noticed her, only to meet his eye.

His smile widened, and he winked at her. Winked! She wanted to pull out her short swords and stab him. Instead, she looked away with a calm she didn't feel and yawned. It was something she'd learned rotations ago. It had been an older man that time. A much older man, and he didn't want to take no for an answer. So she yawned in his boring face and that had done it.

Rasha didn't have to look at Jak this time to know his reaction. She hoped she'd injured him. Maybe then he'd leave her the yahtz alone. She sipped from her drink and stood up to go. But it seemed Jak hadn't gotten her message.

"Rash, come on join us."

"No, I've had enough." She started for the door.

"I doubt you've had any," he said with a knowing look at the ladies around him. They all cackled along with him. "Come on, at least have a dance with me."

"No, thank you." She bowed her head and turned to leave. But then he started singing again, to her.

"There was an old bard from hither and to, who traveled the lands meeting people like you." He tapped a finger on the nose of the girl on his right.

"He sang and danced and pranced around gaily." Jak separated himself from both girls and danced over to her.

"But deep in his heart he longed for a lady. A beautiful lady with long white hair." He wrapped a finger in her hair and lowered his voice.

"To tell her his feelings he wouldn't dare." Jak dropped her hair and turned to the other ladies who spread their arms wide to welcome him back.

"She'd sneer, and she'd snap cause that's what they do,

Purple girls who love an old bard, Deep down yes
they do."

Cheers erupted all around—the entire bar was egging
him on. Jak sang with a beautiful voice and no doubt sang
well the language of the mermen. That explained the
mermaid on his left arm. Jak held out his arms to Rasha,
and she smiled back at him and took a step forward. He'd
embarrassed her as he'd intended but she wasn't interested
in being another one of his decorative arm pieces. He'd
have to learn his lesson and fast. She raised a finger and
pointed in his direction.

*Me?* he mouthed as if surprised she'd been persuaded.
She shook her head in the negative. Then pointed again.
Over his right shoulder was a young man whose eyes had
been stuck on her since she'd strolled into the bar. He was
young and inexperienced with farmer's clothing and
unkempt hair. His first time in a bar, if she had to guess.
His eyes lit up at everything he saw and he'd also been
drinking a juice. All of this made him perfect.

When he noticed she was looking at him, he pointed
to himself with a large grin. Rasha nodded and crooked
her finger in a 'come here' gesture. He didn't hesitate. He
edged through the crowd until he was in front of her. She
grasped his hand and wiggled five fingers back at Jak,
whose jaw was on the floor. Rasha led the young man into
the corridor leading to the inn. Once there in the half
light, she pulled him in by the collar and kissed him hard.

Rasha didn't think he'd ever kissed a girl before in his

life. He didn't understand his lips should be firm and his tongue inside of his mouth. She ran her hands roughly through his hair and pulled his shirt out of his pants as if she wanted more. The kiss left him dizzy. It put Rasha in a bad mood.

"Good night," she said, turning him toward the door to the bar and walking up the inn stairs.

"Good night to you, miss." He smiled and sauntered back to the bar like someone who'd been kissed senseless.

"Good night Jak," she whispered to herself.

Rasha reached the second floor, still hearing the revelry of the bar downstairs. She hoped Lu and Chiza hadn't been listening to any of the nonsense in the bar. When she reached the door to her room she overheard Chiza's unmistakable giggle. Not from inside, but from Lu and Jak's room behind her. Rasha stood at the doorway—it was slightly ajar—and listened to Lu talk about princesses making their own choices. She clenched her fists. He was trying to make the princess doubt her duty. It wasn't fair. She had too much to lose.

She knocked once on the door before pushing it open. They both jumped as if caught doing something they shouldn't. Another bad sign.

"Can I talk to you for a moment?" she asked Lu.

Lu stood up and followed Rasha across the hall and into her room. She shut the door behind her and then spoke to him in a growl.

"What in the yahtz are you doing you pumseed?"

Lu's hands came up in front of him. "What, what did I do?"

"I heard you," she said with her jaws clenched.

"Chiza and I were just—"

"Oh, I know what you were just doing. You should stop before you both get hurt."

Lu tried to speak, but she raised a hand.

"She's not yours for the asking or the taking. She belongs to the prince and your interference might cost us this delivery, or worse, your life. Have you forgotten the last time someone came between a princess and the prince?"

Lu squared his shoulders.

"I didn't realize you were taking on the role of my mother on this journey."

Rasha opened her mouth to speak but this time he held up a hand.

"I know what I'm doing. Keep to your own business and don't worry about my life, I can take care of myself."

Rasha held up two hands in surrender. He was right. She'd done her duty and warned him, but it was up to him to decide what he'd do. Since when did he ever listen to her?

"Please tell me you haven't been up here this whole time flirting with the princess?"

Lu sighed before he answered, "No, of course not. I've been on the communicator with some of the local greenies. It's not good."

"Not good? How not good?"

"You're underwater with the mermen without a breather, not good."

"So are we talking bounty hunters?" Rasha asked.

"More like assassins, trackers, and bounty hunters."

"I see. Things are going to get thicker than I'd like."

Rasha took a deep breath. They wouldn't last the night in this place if there were that many people after them. Assassins meant they would shoot to kill anyone who stood between them and their goal. Rasha needed to prepare. If they'd sent an assassin, they weren't at the inn yet.

"I need you to throw off the communications."

"You know that's not really how it's done."

"This time it will be. I want the assassins, trackers, everyone else looking for us in the wrong place. We're getting off this road north and leading them in the opposite direction. Send them west."

"There aren't many roads leading north on the west end." Lu said with a hint of complaint in his voice.

"I don't care, create one, and make sure everyone thinks we're on it."

Lu nodded.

"Oh and send the princess over," Rasha said, and he glared at her.

Lu returned to his room and Chiza came out a moment later.

"Oh, sure, thanks for listening. I'll see you in the morning," Chiza said to Lu.

Chiza looked up and met Rasha's eye. Bold, she didn't

flinch under Rasha's glare. She didn't have time for this. Rasha turned toward her room, intending to speak to the princess. Jak stormed up the stairs and straight into her room. She hadn't expected the furious expression on his face. It threw her off guard. Her surprise was complete when he slammed the door in Chiza's face.

## 17

"*H*ave I done something to hurt you?" he asked. When she didn't answer he continued, "Since meeting you have I treated you in a way that's causing you to distrust me and think ill of me?" Jak stood there with his arms crossed.

Rasha saw where he wanted to go with this. He'd rescued them in the woods and after some playful banter perhaps he thought they should be ready to begin some kind of relationship. She had other plans. A little huffing and puffing from him wouldn't intimidate her. Rasha rolled her shoulders back and placed her hands on the swords at her hips.

"I don't have any reason to trust you, and a million reasons not to. I don't care if the Universal himself says you've been sent from the stars, I'm not going to let you pull me into whatever this is." Rasha waved a hand between them.

"This," he repeated her hand movement, "is called friendship. I'm surprised you don't recognize it. If you need help in the future, I'd be glad to point it out, except I doubt anyone would bother if you treat them all this way."

He was right. She kept people at a distance and she didn't show herself to anyone. But she had reason not to let anyone in. That discussion could wait for another time. For now, she only had to remind him of one thing.

"You've been tracking us since we left Sidoa and you still haven't told us why. I'm supposed to take it on faith that a trained tracker and courier is helping us?" Her voice had risen an octave.

Jak grabbed her left arm, and she drew Cutter and held it steady at his neck.

"Whoa!" He dropped her arm. "I wanted to put something in your hand."

Rasha sheathed Cutter and nodded for him to reach for his pocket. He took a deep breath, reached into his pocket, and pulled out his communicator. He scrolled through until he found the document he wanted, then he scrolled to the bottom and showed it to Rasha.

THUNDER ROLLED IN THE DISTANCE. The weather outside grew ominous, the sky filled with dark rain clouds.

"What is this?" Rasha asked as she stared at the order. It had an official Adalu royal seal.

"The king of Adalu hired me to track you all the way to the first kingdom," he explained.

"Why didn't you say that before?"

"It's confidential. I'm not even supposed to know. The reason I do is because I did some back-channel checking. I learned that the king of Sidoa had hired not only a group of illegals to transport his daughter, but also bounty hunters and trackers to make sure she never made it," Jak said.

"I see." Rasha understood this was more about the wealth of Sidoa and less about his daughter's potential marriage to prince Bashir. "The tenth king wants to honor his promise to the royals and hold onto his wealth."

Jak nodded.

"You're here as backup in case something should happen to the original couriers." Rasha said.

"You weren't supposed to track me while I tracked you, it's jeopardized the entire mission. Besides that, I thought your pride wouldn't like it very much."

"Don't concern yourself with my pride." Rasha clenched her fists. "What do you plan to do now?"

Jak was expecting something, but not that. He blinked twice as if he needed a moment to register what she'd asked. Rasha didn't understand at all why he hesitated. It wasn't a crazy question. He'd admitted what his mission had been and to breaking the rules of engagement. She only wanted to see how far he'd go now.

Instead of answering he grabbed the back of the neck and kissed her hard on the mouth. She felt her lip hit her teeth. Rasha struggled against him but his mouth melted against hers, demanding and needy at the same time. She couldn't catch her breath. She had to push against him with both hands as she gasped for air.

"I—" Jak stammered. Something in his eyes went dark, and he turned and stormed out the door, leaving it open behind him.

What in the world was that? They'd been fighting, arguing about the princess and then he'd kissed her. Rasha shook her head as Chiza came in.

"What was that all about?" she asked.

"I don't know," Rasha replied.

He was a fantastic kisser, that she would concede. Her wobbly legs forced her to sit down on the edge of nearest bed. She hadn't been kissed in a while, she thought. That must be it. Then she remembered the boy from the bar. She decided that didn't count since she only did it for spite.

LU LEFT her a written message on her communicator. He'd discovered a route they might take if things got more complicated. Though she did wonder how much more complicated things would get. They'd already lost their licenses. Lu was pining for the princess who was promised to the prince. Bands of assassins, trackers, and bounty hunters were chasing them. Jak had kissed the brains out of her. Things were beyond complicated.

Chiza turned in while Rasha sat in the chair looking out at the night. She wondered what it would be like to kiss Jak again. He wasn't bad looking. He had a dark look about him that brightened when he smiled. His laugh, she had to admit, was contagious too. He was a skilled fighter, and he had a beautiful voice. She preferred songs that didn't revolve around her. Rasha held two fingers to her lips, remembering how his lips felt.

It was from that moment and vantage point she saw the men coming for them. They filtered out from the trees like hungry insects on a neglected plate of food. Dressed in black, they were almost invisible against the dark sky. The cloud cover diminished the light of the two moons.

Rasha watched them for a moment, counting. When she got to twenty, she leapt from the chair to wake the princess. The door flew open before she reached the bed.

"We've got to go, now," Lu called, moving toward the princess. Chiza heard him and scrambled out of bed.

"I've got her," Rasha said. "Go to the stables and get our beasts to the spot you showed me on the map. We're on our way."

"Where's Jak?" He asked.

"He's not with you?"

"No, he never came back. I assumed you were still together."

Rasha didn't want to let the comment bother her. What did it matter anyway? Lu didn't care one way or the other, so why was she so annoyed by it?

"No, I've been here with Chiza the whole time."

Lu gave her a strange sidelong look before he turned to leave. Temi, now too big to fit inside of the carrying pouch, scampered behind him.

97

Chiza stood at the ready, her own bag in hand. Rasha grabbed her cloak and ran down after Lu. But instead of going out the back, she took Chiza through the bar and out the front door. Both of them were cloaked. Rasha put a chummy arm around Chiza and stumbled out singing and swaying. Chiza got the idea. She couldn't imitate the singing but she pretended to be half carrying Rasha. The two walked out past the first row of men. They weren't assassins. Rasha stole a few glances and noticed one man who had pink hair from the ninth kingdom of Vol. There were several others in varying colors, but the Buku from the eighth kingdom and the Winakans from the seventh she recognized.

They made it as far as the edge of the woods before they were spotted.

## 18

*R*asha pushed Chiza ahead of her through the woods. She ran with her hands in front of her to protect her face from the small branches whipping at her head and face. Under the cover of the trees they were less visible and Rasha dared a glance back. She didn't see Jak, but he could take care of himself. If Lu made it to the stables, he'd have two beasts with him and would wait up ahead.

"How much further?"

Rasha looked back at the men running toward them. The sky decided at that moment to open, and torrential rain drenched them. The pounding water drowned out Chiza's startled shriek.

"There, up the tree."

"What?" Chiza looked from Rasha to the tree and then back again. "You want me to climb up there?"

Rasha wanted to scream herself. Why hadn't she

shown her some basic fighting skills or something? This girl would be useless in a fight and this was worse than a fight. For her own sake, Chiza's people should have taught her more defense and less dancing.

An arrow whizzed past her head as she covered Chiza.

"Up the tree now. Use those knots." She boosted the princess up the tree. "Up you go."

When Chiza was out of reach and out of sight, she called up to her, "I'll be right back," the sound of the rain and thunder almost drowning out her voice.

"What?" Chiza called back down to her.

Rasha raised a finger to her lips instead of answering her. She ran from the base of the tree where the princess was hiding and then crouched down behind some brush to wait for her pursuers.

She'd teach them not to come after her in the night with only twenty men. Rasha pulled out Blade and Cutter, testing the grips in each hand. They didn't slip and slide in the water. Her gloved hands were tight on the hilts. A man on her right didn't see her until he was on top of her and she forced him down with a sweep of one leg. He fell backwards, and she got on top of his chest and held her sword to his throat.

"Why are you after us?"

He ground his teeth together, refusing to answer. She didn't see the other man until the first one smiled at her and his eyes flicked above her head and on the right. Balancing on the man under her she kicked out with her right foot and slashed his stomach open. The man under her grunted, and she returned Blade to his throat.

"You were saying?" The man looked less confident now, with water cascading down his face. He sputtered, but she didn't let up.

"We've been paid in full to kidnap the princess."

"By who, and don't make me ask you twice."

"The king of Sidoa."

Rasha's blade froze against him. That was the same thing Jak had said.

"Why would the king pay for us to deliver the princess, and for you to kidnap her back from us?"

"A fickle bunch, royals," the man replied.

She didn't trust this man any further than she'd trust a slithering stolken, so she hit him with Blade's hilt and he went to sleep.

Rasha ran back for the princess with a weight in her chest. How many people had the king hired for this job? What had she gotten herself into? The tree was where she'd left it but the princess wasn't anywhere. She looked down at the ground and found a green leaf lying at a peculiar angle, out of place. Something only a greenie would do. Lu had come for the princess and put her some place safer.

It was a good thing she remembered the map. She ran to catch up with Lu. When she heard the sound of men fighting nearby she ducked behind a tree. She saw Jak, holding off two men. His sword danced through the air slicing and jabbing. She debated about going to help him but she needed to get to Chiza. Jak would be fine. At least, she hoped so.

She raced for their alternate route. Rasha managed to avoid a group heading in the opposite direction when she saw Lu. He and Chiza were each on a beast, waiting for her. Chiza made room for her to get in front and take the reins. As soon as she mounted the animal she urged the animals into a run.

"Now, Lu," she yelled back at him.

"What about Jak?"

"Now!"

Lu triggered their trap, and a pulse went off behind them, knocking every man off of his feet. Some flew up in the air and landed on their backs. Others were pushed forward and landed on their noses. There was no one left standing, or cable to follow them.

They rode hard for quite some time before they pulled up. Lu stopped next to her and they panted as if they'd been running the miles themselves.

"Have we lost them?"

"No one's following us." Lu smiled as he checked the biometric locator. "We're good."

"We need to keep going. You lead since you know the way. Thanks to the rain our tracks will be impossible to follow."

"Chiza?" Lu asked.

She was clinging to Rasha's back.

"Won't they ever stop?" Chiza asked, tears streaming down her face.

"Don't worry, we'll keep you safe," Lu reassured her.

"What good is that, if you all die in the process? I don't think I could live with myself."

"About that, we have a problem," Rasha interrupted.

"What?"

"I pulled an attacker aside. He wasn't an assassin. He said he'd been hired by your father to track you and then deliver you back to him."

"What? How can that be?"

"It seems your father is not inclined for you to marry the prince and take your newfound gems with you."

"That can't be. My father would never dishonor his family in such a way."

"I want to believe you, but Jak told me the same thing only a few hours before. He'd been hired by the king of Adalu to see you safe if something should happen on the way. Either way, it changes nothing. We're going to make it to the first kingdom."

"Agreed," Lu said as he looked at the princess. "Stop worrying about us. We can handle this." Lu moved on ahead and Rasha followed without another word.

They continued east on the alternate road and by noon the rain was drying up. They reached the edge of Winaka and Wilds lands by late afternoon. With no food yet and damp from the rain, they all needed to get dry and eat something. Rasha noted that Chiza was quieter than usual. Lu tried several times to engage her in conversation, but she didn't respond. The shock of everything was getting to her and they'd need to consider making camp soon.

Rasha scanned the base of the southern ridges and didn't see any caves or places where they could hide for the night. Their best move was to double back. She'd seen a cave several miles behind them that might do, but she'd hoped to find something closer. Before she could decide, she heard the rumbling of more thunder. They would get even more rain tonight. Rasha tried to remember what it felt like to be dry.

## 19

"*Y*ou're hungry," Lu said. He wasn't asking, he knew that look.

"How do you know?" She gave him what she hoped was a skeptical look.

"You start looking around as if a plate of food will materialize out of nowhere." Lu couldn't hold back his laugh. "I'll go get us something."

"I don't think so, there's no shelter. We've got rain on our backs in two hours."

Lu looked up at the sky. He debated about which direction to go.

"We'll go back to that cave we passed. Maybe we can scare whoever's in there out and camp for the night."

Lu nodded and they turned to go back.

They reached the small cave as the clouds rolled in and lightning lit up the sky in every direction. The cave, half hidden by brush and trees, faced away from their route.

"Set up camp, I'll be back," he said.

Lu dismounted and hefted Temi from his new, larger bag and placed him at Chiza's. She still seemed sad. He'd have to do his best to cheer her up later. Lu wanted to touch her, to give her some kind of reassurance. The thunder reminded him he had little time to get food and prepare it before the rain was on top of them.

He reached down and pat Temi on the head.

"You take care of the girls." Temi growled in response and nuzzled his head against Lu's hand.

Lu TOOK a small pack that he strapped across his chest and disappeared into the woods. It didn't take him long to track a medium-sized beast drinking at a nearby stream. The animal sniffed the air. It trembled with nervous energy, ready to run on its spindly legs at the first hint of danger. Lu raised his arm and aimed, but a noise from behind him startled the beast and it bolted.

"What the yahtz?" He turned back to retrace his steps and see if he could find another beast. He found something even better.

"Jak!"

"Hey Lu," Jak swaggered over to him. "Looking for food, I see."

"Yeah, girls have to eat or they become little beasties, you know."

"I do. I picked something up to help with that." Jak

pointed to the animal he carried over his shoulders. "Shall we? My tuskin isn't far."

"Sure." As they walked, Lu said what he knew Rasha wouldn't. "I thought you'd be angry at us for leaving you behind. Then triggering the pulse without warning you. It wasn't meant for you, I hope you know that."

"I know, you have a delivery and that takes priority—and it should. The princess' life is all that matters. The pulse was a surprise, but I recovered from it."

"Rasha told us about your mission. Why did you agree to it?" Lu asked.

Jak considered for a moment before answering.

"I gave up being a courier because I didn't like taking jobs without knowing all the details. This one was upfront from the start and it seemed like something I wouldn't lose sleep over."

"Yes, this job makes me think we should have asked a few more questions before accepting it."

Jak turned toward a stand of trees. His tuskin was feeding behind it, still wet from their travel through the rain. Jak didn't bother mounting; he strapped his kill to its back. The tuskin stamped his legs but then settled. Jak led it by the reins and followed Lu back toward the cave.

"The king of Adalu hired me to follow you in case you ran into trouble. At first I didn't know who you were. When they ambushed you on the road with the princess I couldn't stand by and do nothing."

"The men from last night. One of them said Chiza's father hired him."

"That doesn't surprise me."

"Rasha says you knew about Chiza's father."

"I suspected the father might not honor his promise to the first kingdom. Her transport arrangements and the recent discovery of the gems in the caverns of his lands meant something had to be done."

JAK DIDN'T SAY any more. He seemed to be deep in thought. It was a while before he spoke again.

"How is the princess?" Jak asked.

"She's unwell. This journey and its dangers were an unbearable weight on her mind."

"Well, it's good then, she has your companionship."

Lu said nothing more. It was true they were friends, if only that were enough.

"Does she know about her father?" Jak asked.

"We've told her what we've learned, but she's finding it hard to believe."

"No one wants to believe that their own family member would put them in harm's way just to hold on to a few gems."

"No," Lu agreed, but he was thinking about his own family and how often his sister had put them in danger with her own selfish pursuits.

"Has she guessed yet how you feel about her?"

"What?"

"I can imagine it must be hard to keep your distance.

She's gorgeous and exotic. Her belonging to another man can't be the best of circumstances."

"No, it's not like that," Lu lied. He didn't know what he felt, but he was certain he didn't want to share it with Jak.

"If you say so," Jak smiled. He hummed under his breath as they walked on. When they reached the camp, the fire was going just inside the mouth of the cave. The weather wouldn't hold forever, and they needed to move fast if they wanted to have enough food prepared before the rains came.

Rasha had placed the tools for Lu to prepare their meal at the side of the cave. When she saw Jak, something passed between them. A look… was she blushing? It was hard to tell under all the purple. Lu reminded himself that it was none of his business and went about preparing supper with Chiza.

"What's going on there?" Chiza asked, tilting her head at Jak and Rasha.

"I would ask about all her intimate relationships, but I know Rash, she'd rather cut me with one of her swords than share her feelings."

"I see," Chiza said. Their eyes met, but she quickly looked back down at her hands. He sighed and wondered how long it would take before he saw her smile again.

"Jak brought us some meat, let's see how much of it we can get ready tonight. Are you hungry?"

Chiza shook her head.

"I could use some help."

Chiza's mouth turned up at the ends "I wish I could help, but I'm not much for cooking either. It's not a part of my training."

"Well, then together we might make something just above edible." Lu smiled and bumped her with his shoulder. She smiled back. There it was. He'd been waiting for it all day. The smile that could light up the night.

Temi scooted closer to them as they worked, making smacking sounds in anticipation.

"Not yet, we've got a lot of work to do before we eat, little one."

"Do you feed him raw meat?"

"No, I figure he'll learn that little trick on his own, and since I don't know how big he'll get I better wait. For now, it's a good thing he's dependent on us for his meals."

Temi's incessant whine made Chiza smile again.

"Well, at least we'll have one who'll enjoy what we make no matter how horrible it turns out."

"He'd eat a ranglefort if you put it in front of him."

Chiza's face scrunched up at the distasteful idea.

Lu looked up when Rasha and Jak moved off.

"The storm is almost here," Chiza observed, looking up at the dark clouds.

"You have no idea," Lu replied, watching Rasha.

## 20

*J*ak stood in front of Rasha with hurt etched across his face. She looked down at the ground as she tried to think of something to say. Something that made how she'd left him behind okay, or at least forgivable. She couldn't think of anything.

"You left," he whispered.

"A courier delivers," she replied.

"Don't." Jak took a step forward and Rasha took a step back.

"You kissed me and then you left."

"I didn't kiss you. You kissed me," Rasha retorted. She looked over to see if Lu and Chiza had overheard them. They were deep in their own conversation. She took several steps away from the cave.

"You kissed me and then left without returning to your room. If you had, you'd have been there when we had to run."

"Look, I know everything is a little complicated, but I thought—" Jak ran a hand over his face. "I told you why I was following you. Why didn't you let me in on the plan?"

"I didn't sit down for tea and sandwiches and go over my ideas with you. I saw the place surrounded, and I had to make a run for it. You were nowhere in sight."

Jak raised a hand to stop her.

"I didn't come here to argue the point. I want you to understand that, despite my pumseed behavior, I'm here for you. You can trust me."

Rasha heard the words, but she watched his face. When he said the last line he looked up at the sky. He was still lying about something. She didn't know what it was, but she'd learned how to read deceptive body language and his was screaming at her. But when he looked at her with that hunger, he was being sincere. It was there again, in his stormy blue eyes.

Rasha's instincts were screaming. She should run, she shouldn't trust him. But the passion in his eyes, his feelings for her, were real. He was telling the truth about that. He stepped closer and his arms enveloped her before she could think. His mouth found hers, but this time their breathless kisses were warm and soft. Neither noticed the rain that fell around them. The droplets pattered their faces, but neither let go. Rasha didn't realize that her hands were gripping him until he pulled back.

He looked at her smugly. The look she hated.

"Wow, that wasn't just me kissing you that time."

Embarrassed, Rasha let go and started back toward the cave.

"Wait, I'm being a fool again. I'm sorry. Listen, I didn't come just because I had to, but because I *wanted* to. Do you at least believe that?" His eyes searched hers while hers searched his.

Not taking her eyes off of him she said, "Yes."

His shoulders dropped and his arms fell to his sides.

"Good, now let's get you something to eat. You look hungry." Jak had the audacity to reach out and grab her by the waist.

Rasha slapped his hand away and took a swing, but missed his head—he was ready for her.

Jak was laughing now, and he tried to put an arm around her shoulders but she shook him off before Lu and Chiza could see. She didn't know what they were yet, but she wasn't ready to declare it.

Rasha and Jak were both wet from the rain. Lu had set up a place for them to hang their cloaks to dry. He and Chiza had already gotten out of their wet clothes and were warming by the fire. She and Jak did the same. The smell of the cooking meat reached her and her stomach groaned in complaint. She'd gone without food the night before. That must have been the reason for her spinning head and racing heart.

Jak sat next to her by the fire. Chiza looked ready to curl up in Lu's lap. The two looked adorable together. What was she thinking? No, they couldn't be together and seeing them reminded her that it jeopardized their mission and the reinstatement of their licenses. She needed to say something. Jak grabbed her leg and shook his head before she could stand.

What did he mean, no? Didn't he understand what losing their licenses would mean? No, he'd already lost his own license. Rasha gave him a hard stare and sat back down. Chiza fell asleep with Lu as her pillow.

"I'll take the first watch," Jak offered.

Rasha gave him a nod and positioned herself two feet from the fire and watched him. He crossed his legs and closed his eyes as if he were in deep prayer. Perhaps he was meditating or just listening for any sounds. He must have felt her gaze, because his eyes opened and he smiled when he caught her staring at him. She didn't blink, but she yawned and looked at the fire. She woke up to a gentle hand on her shoulder.

"I'm tired. Can you take over?" Jak whispered. His eyes were drooping. He still looked wet.

She reached out and touched his shoulders.

"I went scouting our location to make sure I wasn't followed. I need to rest."

"Yes, it's fine, I'm awake." She sat up to prove it.

She relinquished her place to him and hung his cloak so it could dry. The fire was low and they would need more wood if they wanted to make it until morning without getting too cold. Her blood was thick enough, but the princess had snuggled close Lu to keep warm and Temi lay curled up in a ball beside them.

Rasha couldn't stop thinking about how much things

had changed since they'd picked up Chiza. They'd picked up a tracker and several groups that her father hired trying to bring her home again. Central claimed the delivery was void after losing their courier positions. But there was no record of a new fetch and delivery being created.

Rasha also wondered why the king of Sidoa would risk his daughter's life by sending so many illegals after his daughter? Didn't he know many of the couriers he'd contacted worked in less-than-reputable channels? Her own contact to this job had been Poobari, a jailer with a well-known criminal history.

What motive could her father have for making such careless choices for his only daughter? There was something about it all that bothered her. Her brain hurt trying to figure out the strange puzzle. She wasn't used to knowing this much about a fetch and delivery of a package. But this wasn't a normal package, this was a person. By law, upon discovery the sender should be fined, but instead they'd sanctioned the couriers. The system at Central might have been having an off day, but she doubted it. Rasha would ask Lu to tug on his connection to Poobari. Maybe they could find out more about who was behind this.

Rasha was cooking meat for breakfast by the time the others woke. Temi had been sitting at her side the moment she started. Jak was the last to wake up as he'd been up most of the night. Lu set up his equipment and contacted Poobari.

"Well, I didn't expect to hear from you so soon, Gree-nie. How'd that fetch and delivery go?"

"That's why I'm contacting you, and I think you know why."

"I don't have the slightest idea, but I'm sure you're about to tell me, so let me sit down and have a listen." Poobari rearranged his bulk and sat down in the chair just behind him. "What's the news?"

"I was hoping you could tell me. It appears we're not the only ones hired for this fetch and delivery."

Poobari put up his hands in a shrug.

"You went through the proper channels. I don't know how Central handles their business, but I'm sure they've got computers and machines making sure that kind of thing doesn't happen." He had the audacity to wiggle his eyebrows.

"We don't—" Lu began before Rasha snatched the communicator from his hands.

Rasha looked into the camera and waited for Poobari to acknowledge her.

"Rash, love, I haven't seen you in ages. How are you?"

"I'd be better if there weren't a bunch of mukes chasing after my fetch. Who hired them?"

"I don't know what you mean. I haven't got a thing to do with them." Poobari's chins quivered with denial. His eyes, however, shifted to the left.

"Do you remember the last time I caught you in a lie?"

"I wouldn't lie to you, love. I swear I don't know why there are so many chasing after one little princess."

Rasha waited for Poobari to catch his own mistake but the pumseed wasn't that bright.

"I never mentioned that the fetch was a princess." Poobari's pale skin turned a bright red. "Here's what's going to happen next. You'll tell me who hired those other men and everything thing you know about this thing or I will fetch you and with the help of my friends, Cutter and Blade, deliver you to the Universal's front door."

Poobari looked around the room.

"I ain't supposed to say a word about it. I can't, you see. If I do, there are worse things than dying by your swords, little girl." He looked from left to right as if he expected someone would interrupt him at any moment.

"The king hired those men."

"Which king?"

"The King of Sidoa." The communication cut off, and the screen went transparent.

"What happened?" Rasha said, holding out the communicator to Lu.

Chiza's eyes were wide with shock.

"One lying jailer isn't to be trusted," Rasha said, moving to sit next to her. "It explains nothing."

"Could it be true? Could my father be responsible for the men chasing us?"

"To be honest with you, I'm not sure." Rasha placed a hand on Chiza's back as the young woman wept. "Look, this is bigger than any of us suspected. We'll figure out the details of what happened, and we won't give up. You'll get your prince and I'll be a licensed courier again."

Chiza wiped her eyes and nodded. Rasha wasn't as sure as she sounded, but one way or the other, they would get answers.

"Let's go," Rasha announced.

"What about Jak?"

"Where is he?"

"I don't know, he was here a moment ago."

Rasha groaned as she stormed off into the woods to look for their tracker.

## 21

*R*asha followed Jak's tracks into the woods. It took several tries to pick up his marks when they veered off of the path she was on. What was he doing all the way out here? The sound of voices made her hesitate, and she ducked into the bushes. She peered around them to see Jak talking with two men who were waving their hands in agitation.

One tall, dark man appeared to be Sidoan. The other was from Winaka, the seventh kingdom. Rasha stared, wondering what they could be doing here meeting with Jak. They didn't talk long. Jak dashed away, leaving the two men alone. They didn't have any animals with them. But they hadn't walked this far out here. Instead of following Jak back to the cave, she followed the two men.

Ducking behind trees, she managed to follow them for half a mile to the north. They were in an encampment of more than a dozen men, dressed like the men that attacked them the night before last. The two seemed to be reporting something back to the others. Rasha couldn't make it out, but her stomach felt queasy. She recognized the feeling: betrayal.

Rasha didn't wait to be discovered. She raced back through the woods to the cave where the others were waiting. Lu gave her a look, but she shook her head. She wouldn't explain now.

"Rash, what's with your bathroom habits? Between you and Jak I don't know who's worse." He was covering for her.

She nodded and laughed it off.

"My stomach always gets a little nervous before we go into unknown territory." Rasha said as she eyed Jak. He was leaning against a tree as if he'd been waiting for hours.

Chiza was sitting on Lu's beast. Rasha didn't bother speaking to Jak for the moment—she'd let things play out. He was up to something, and she wouldn't trust him until she knew what it was. Jak rode ahead of them most of the way. She needed a different way to go about getting information this time.

When they stopped to water and feed the animals, she pulled Lu away from Chiza. It was difficult, as Chiza didn't want to leave his side. Their bond was closer than ever. She wondered how they would fare in the presence of the prince. She doubted he'd be okay with his intended choosing someone from the Twinlands after he'd gone through so much trouble to ensure she arrived at the first kingdom.

"I need something from you." Rasha spoke to him without looking, keeping her voice low.

"Anything."

"Tell me you brought some kind of listening device. Something you can pin onto someone without them being aware that it is recording."

Lu looked up and tracked Jak's movement from the animals back to Chiza. She was laughing at something he said.

"You know I do."

"I need you to slip it to me without anyone seeing you. I'll do the rest."

"You still don't trust Jak?"

"I don't trust anyone who has secret liaisons in the woods with the men trying to kidnap the princess."

"To what end?"

"I don't know, but I think we need to be cautious."

"We won't get much out here. We've got no working communicators."

"He may not use one."

"I'm not trying to sound condescending, but have you considered just asking him?" Lu asked.

Rasha *had* considered it. Considered it and dismissed it as another chance for Jak to use her emotions against her. "Just get it for me, and don't let Chiza see you," Rasha said with a knowing look.

Lu gave her an indignant look before he turned to go back. Temi came over and looked up, expecting something.

"What?" Rasha asked

Temi growled and moved closer then sat and stared up at her.

"You want something?"

Temi gave her another growl. At a loss for what else to do, she stroked Temi under the chin before heading back.

"Your beastie is getting almost too big to carry," she said to Lu. He was digging something out of his pack and, as she hoped, she got Chiza's attention with her remark.

"He's so big now, I can't believe it. I wonder when he'll stop growing," Chiza said.

"It won't be long now. We should see his true size. Did you take care of beasties at home Chiza?" Rasha asked, looking at Chiza to keep eye contact with her.

"Not really. We weren't allowed animals inside our home. My mother thought it uncivilized."

That was a word she hadn't heard in a long time. Rasha recalled her own mother using just such a term to describe her only daughter.

---

## 22

*T*he sun was just above the horizon to the south when they packed up and continued east. They reached the Ridge an hour later. The Ridge was a low mountain range and a natural separation between the Wilds and the ten kingdoms of Bolaji. Their peaks, though not high, were grueling to travel on foot. The animals they'd brought would have just as hard a time navigating the rocks with their wide legs.

"The ridge is treacherous," Lu pointed out.

"I know, that's why no one will follow us there," Rasha said.

"We could cross the ridge and make our way on the other side," Jak suggested. They both looked at him with disbelief.

No one said anything for almost a full minute as they all considered the possibility.

"I don't like it," Rasha said at last. Chiza nodded in agreement, though she didn't have a vote.

"I do. It's brilliant. We'd have the best of both worlds. No one wants to deal with the Wilds and they won't be able to track us through the desert. I think we should do it," Lu said.

"Are you getting any communications?" Rasha asked him.

"Nothing. I'm still blacked out. Nothing going in or out. It won't be better on the other side of the Ridge, but it also means we'll have less of a chance of being traced or tracked."

"There's nothing on mine either," Rasha said looking at the blank square.

"So, are we agreed?" Jak asked.

THEY TOOK a few hours to traverse the Ridge. The tuskins had been hard to convince to navigate the rocky land-scape. The Wilds close to the Ridge were desert lands made up of hard-packed and cracking dirt and a layer of shifting sands.

Their view was broken by a scattering of trees, bare branches reaching up to the sky as if to petition for more rain. The terrain wasn't as rough but, although dry, they were far from warm.

Jak led the way. He knew where to stop for water, where to rest, and where to set up camp for the night. This time of year, the night winds were cold, the four of them (along with Temi) huddled together for warmth.

"How do you know so much about this place?" Lu asked.

"This is the route my mother took when she fled Winaka, the seventh kingdom, to raise me in the Wilds."

If he'd said he'd been born with two heads and two horns they couldn't have looked more shocked. Rasha clicked her tongue for her beast match the pace of Jak's.

"You were raised in the Wilds?" she asked. She didn't hide her surprise any more than the others.

"Yes. It's not how people describe it. Just because we don't abide by the laws of the ten kingdoms doesn't mean we run around nude with spears in our hands."

Rasha stifled a laugh. Jak looked at her sideways.

"What? Were you imagining me in the nude?"

Rasha's mouth fell open in shock, but she recovered and rolled her eyes. "Not in the least."

Chiza giggled somewhere behind them, which only encouraged her.

"That said, I'm sure that your thin legs wouldn't look *too* bad."

"My thin legs?" Jak looked down at his legs with concern.

"I'm sure with a little spear hunting you could improve on them," Rasha told him as her tuskin overtook his.

## 23

*L*u and Jak wouldn't stop singing and it was making Rasha's teeth grind together. Their fluency in the language of the mermen was astounding; even she had to admit that it was skillful. They encouraged her to join but she refused. Singing was not a skill she'd learned. Chiza didn't sing along, either. She enjoyed it though, because she clapped with enthusiasm after every single song. By the time they reached the border between the Wilds and Chilali, Rasha knew she couldn't go any further. Things would change tomorrow, and she needed one night of peace to prepare herself.

The sun hadn't gone down yet, but Rasha could already feel the cold creeping into her bones. She pulled the cloak tighter around her ears and neck. Jak rubbed his hands together and blew into them. Lu busied himself with making the fire as Chiza danced in place hopping from one foot to the other and rubbing her arms. They were only one kingdom away from Adalu and then this whole delivery would be behind her.

"You know you're irresistible when you get that worry line down the middle of your forehead?" Jak asked.

Rasha looked up as he spoke. She'd been so far in the back of her mind she hadn't understood him at first.

"What?"

"Where were you just now?" He reached up and touched her face with the back of his hand. "You have nothing to worry about."

Rasha pulled away from him. "Not now."

Lu caught her eye as she gathered more wood for their fire. The trees in this part of the Wilds were thriving, and although most of them were bare, a few kept their bright foliage She brought the wood she'd collected to Lu, who added it as needed to his growing fire.

"What's wrong with my purple princess?" Jak asked.

Rasha's head snapped up, as did Chiza's.

"Don't call me that," she growled.

Jak held up his hands and shrugged.

"Have you ever known a girl so disagreeable?" he asked Lu.

One look from Rasha and Lu held his tongue. Lu, Chiza, and Jak ate while discussing the change of scenery. Rasha kept to herself. She even sat a little apart from the others. Rasha couldn't get out of her own head. The thought of her home in Chilali weighed on her. Would they still be angry with her for leaving? What would her parents say? Did they know of her reputation as a courier? Did they even care about her accomplishments?

Rasha stared at the fire but found no answers there. The smoke rose into the night and then dissipated into the black. Above them, the constellations brightened the heavens. The two moons were doing their best to brighten the night and doing a fine job. The blue moon hung in the east and seemed to be right above them, while the orange one to the south seemed to kiss of the horizon.

"Rasha, would you like more?" Chiza asked.

Rasha looked down at her plate. She hadn't touched it. She shook her head. Most of the night she'd kept to herself and gained inner calm, despite her lack of appetite. Instead of waiting for him to come to her again, she called Jak over, making it clear she had something important to tell him. He gave her a wary look, but shrugged and joined her. She couldn't blame him for being confused, she'd snapped at him most of the day.

## 24

*T*he warm fire couldn't compare with the warmth Lu felt inside. Chiza talked less and less of her preparation as one of the chosen and more and more of her own dreams and wishes. Lu didn't know what it would mean for him, but he braced himself to do something he'd never considered before.

He'd found a small white flower and tucked it away. Now he pulled it out of his pouch. Temi growled at him and shook his head around, pawing at the ground.

"Go on, there's no reason to be jealous, my friend, this is for the lady." He held the flower between his finger and thumb and tucked it behind Chiza's right ear. The contrast between the flower and her ebony skin and black hair was stunning. He started to tell her so, but his hand itched.

"Oh no, what's the matter with your hand?" Chiza asked. She grabbed it and looked it over.

"I don't know." Lu stood up, out of instinct wanting to

run from his limp and useless hand. It had doubled in size and he couldn't move his fingers.

"What in the yahtz?" Rasha asked as she saw Lu stumble backwards.

Jak came running. "What happened? What did you touch?"

"Nothing, I picked a flower earlier and when I pulled it out just now my hand itched and now I don't feel anything. The numbness is traveling up my arm," Lu said as his arm went limp. "I can't lift it." He felt his wide eyes get wider.

"When you picked it earlier, were you wearing gloves?"

"Yes, I was."

"That explains why you didn't experience any effects until now. What did you do with the flower?"

"I gave it to Chiza." As one they all turned toward where Chiza was sitting and saw her lying by the fire. Jak dashed around the fire and over to her. He snatched the flower off of her ear and threw it into the fire with one gloved hand.

"Rasha, I need you to come here and hold the princess up like this, keep your gloves on."

Rasha did as asked and though she looked uncomfortable, she squatted down and lifted Chiza's head and shoulders onto her lap.

"Her breathing is shallow," Rasha said.

Lu felt his insides drop. Then his leg weakened under him and he fell to his knees. What had he done? This was all his fault.

"I need to hurry or we'll lose them both," Jak said as he turned away.

"Where are you going?" Rasha asked her voice shrill. That meant she was more scared than angry. Lu had only heard it once before.

"I'll have to get the antidote. The plant is one I've seen before but in the dark it'll be harder to find. I need to hurry. Lu, prop yourself up against Rasha, she won't be able to lift you and soon you won't be able to crawl," Jak said as he turned back and half dragged Lu to Rasha's side. "I'll be back as soon as I find it."

"There's a light, in my pack. Take it." Lu's body was slowly numbing. He couldn't feel his legs at all.

"I'm sorry Chiza, darling, you don't deserve this. I already miss what we could have been."

"Shut up, you're not going anywhere, so stop saying goodbye," Rasha snapped.

Lu heard the fear and anger in her voice, shrill again. It was strange what you could hear when your body was so quiet. The numbness was reaching up to his waist. His stomach and chest would be next.

"Rash, I think I was in love with her," Lu confessed. Saying the words felt good, like he'd relieved something pressing on his chest. Another pressure replaced it but this one he couldn't lift. Temi had moved in and rested his head on him. He whined. Had the little beast tried to warn him about the flower? He wanted to put his hand out and reassure Temi, but the other hand was numb now

131

too. Temi had been loyal and helpful. If only he'd been paying attention.

"Of course you are, you pumseed." Rasha's reached out, and he didn't feel her fingers, but saw them as they dug into his numbing chest. His breathing was ragged now. He didn't know if he could stay conscious.

Something wet fell on his face. It was raining. Fitting. A quiet rain for the overwhelming sadness he felt. He'd killed himself and Chiza with a pretty flower. When the black came, he welcomed it.

"WHERE THE YAHTZ HAVE YOU BEEN?" Rasha screeched when Jak returned.

"Finding it took me more time than I'd hoped. I'm sorry." He had a hand full of green leaf clusters.

"What do I do?" Rasha asked, feeling helpless with the weight of her friends resting on her legs.

"Nothing, these are poisonous to anyone who isn't affected by the white flower. He pulled off several leaves and put them inside of Chiza's cheek and did the same with Lu on Rasha's other side.

"How long does it take for it to work?"

Chiza coughed on the leaves. She gasped and then chewed on the leaves in her mouth.

"Good, that's good, chew them up until they're pulp, but don't swallow.

Beside her Lu let out a similar gasp, and then he

chewed the leaves. Jak threw the rest of the leaves in the fire. They crackled before they went up in smoke.

Lu and Chiza each sat up and eased away from her, testing their limbs and smiling around the green in their mouths.

"You should both be fine now. Spit out the pulp and rinse out your mouths with water."

"How did you know what to do?" Lu asked.

"This is the Wilds, I grew up here. There are many natural dangers here. Most people only think of the lawless, but they don't think about the untamed nature that surrounds them. Jak raised his hands palms up and spread them, encompassing everything outside of their fire.

Lu turned to Chiza after they'd both spit out the remaining leaves and spoke in a voice Rasha had never heard Lu use before.

His voice husky and deep, he said, "I'm so sorry, please forgive me. I only wanted to make you smile."

"You made me smile and I don't blame you. How could you know they were poisonous?" Chiza smiled to prove it. "Next time don't kill me." That made them all laugh. Distracted most of the evening, Rasha had time to think now that morning was just a few short hours away. They'd have a long day tomorrow. She needed to sleep.

Jak was the first to lie down, exhausted from searching the woods. Temi hadn't left Lu's side, and neither had Chiza. Lu was taking the first watch, but it was like the three stayed up watching each other, afraid to close their eyes. Rasha watched them huddled together for a moment. Focused on each other, they'd never notice when she placed the listening device on Jak. She wanted to trust him. After what he did for them that night she almost did. Rasha moved closer to Jak. She kneeled close to him and when she was a breath away, she reached out to place the tracker on the collar of his cloak. Jak's eyes flew open and his hand snaked out and caught her arm.

## 25

*J*ak held her arm and Rasha's fingers closed around the device. He wasn't looking at her hand. He stared into her face. Rasha struggled for control over her own features. She only hoped he couldn't read her plan, written all over her guilty face.

"I knew you couldn't resist," Jak said as he pulled her in and kissed her hard.

Rasha's body went limp, and instead of pulling away she melted against his side. He turned toward her, cradling her head in the crook of his arm, and kissed her again. He bit her bottom lip, and she felt a sigh escape her lips. This only encouraged him and he tangled his fingers in her hair, keeping his mouth firmly on hers. When they came up for air, she looked in his eyes and wasn't sure what she saw there. They were half closed, and he smiled as he settled in and fell asleep with his arms wrapped protectively around her.

Rasha only had to shift to place the tracker inside the collar of his coat. Once it was connected, she closed her eyes and pushed the sick feeling of betrayal in her stomach down.

THEY'D BEEN RIDING against the northern winds for most of the day when they finally entered Chilali lands. Rasha had willed sleep to come, but, in the end, didn't sleep at all. The others were careful to avoid her, as she was still prickly. With the wind in their faces they were less inclined to make small talk. The small communities of people they passed weren't out in the elements. Many of them looked out from their windows and doors to see who would be foolish enough to be traveling north this time of year. Rasha was careful to keep her own face hidden.

"We'll need a place to rest for the night," Jak called out against the wind.

"This is Rash's territory," Lu said, and then turned to Rasha. "Is there someplace out of the way we can take shelter?"

Rasha started to say something but then bit her tongue. Chiza was giving her the wide eyes of a conspirator. It was obvious she wanted Rasha to tell the others about her status. Rasha shook her head and straightened her back.

"I know a place," she said and rode to the front. Her mind raced. How would she be received after a two-rotation absence?

Avoiding the populated areas became more and more difficult. Chilali had many developed areas, and, like in Adalu, the city center had grown and spread, while the outer edges were only a little less populated. Rasha steered her tuskin to a home that sat on the west edge of a small community. Rasha rode up to the door and gave a high three-note whistle.

It didn't take long for the door to open. A plump woman with purple skin and a long white braid came out with a long sword in one hand.

"What do you want?" The woman asked, squinting at her.

"It's me, aunt," Rasha said, raising her hands but not getting off her beast.

"I know who it is. What, you think I'm blind or something? I could see you coming when you climbed the ridge. I asked, what do you want?"

"My friends and I need shelter for the night. May we enter?" Rasha asked, keeping her voice level even though she felt her insides getting cold and threatening to chatter her teeth.

"So you think I'm just going to risk my life sheltering you?" She looked them over for an agonizing minute. "Put the beasts in the barn and come in before you freeze to death." She turned and went inside, leaving the door cracked for them to enter.

Rasha slid down from her tuskin and handed the reins to Jak. He gave her a questioning look, which she ignored. Then she reached for Chiza.

"Let's get you inside, princess."

Chiza didn't seem surprised they'd separated her from the others. Rasha would have to speak to her aunt and the only person who could be there was Chiza. She also needed to warm up. This weather was no doubt a shocking change from the warm winds of the south.

"They will learn the truth," Chiza whispered as they walked to the door. Rasha nodded, but she hoped it wouldn't be tonight.

RASHA FELT the heat of the fire the moment she stepped inside. The smell of spices and food with herbs mingled in the air all around them. Rasha's stomach growled.

Chiza and Rasha stood at the door. Chiza kept shifting her weight from one foot to the other.

Rasha moved to the table and pulled out a chair.

"Can I get your highness something to drink?"

Rasha's head snapped up.

"I meant the other one." Her aunt said without looking at Rasha. "I may be old but I know my princesses."

"Yes, thank you so much," Chiza said with a smile.

Rasha spoke up when she saw her aunt pull four cups down to the table and poured the warm liquid into each of them. She'd made bazil, a spicy drink she remembered from childhood that could warm her from toes to temples.

"I'm grateful, for everything. We'll be gone at sunup tomorrow."

"I know you will. Do the people traveling with you know who you are?"

"Chiza does, but the others do not."

Her aunt made a disapproving sound in the back of her throat. She went to the pot of stew she'd been cooking and put it on the table, along with four bowls. Rasha's mouth watered at the sight. She'd been so nervous before, she didn't have time to be hungry. Now the growling in her stomach grew insistent.

"You are very kind, mistress," Chiza thanked her.

"Happy to oblige one of the royal family. You may be queen someday, and I hope you'll remember my kindness."

"Queen or no, I will remember."

The door opened and Lu and Jak entered. Hesitant, they waited to be addressed. When her aunt turned around and saw them she whistled.

"Now I know why you never visit. I guess I wouldn't either with these two handsome fellows following me around. Come on in, sit down at the table. We're about to eat something."

"Whose name should I use when asking for a blessing on your behalf?" Jak asked her.

"Aren't you charming?" She reached out a hand and took his.

"This is my Aunt Sochi," Rasha introduced her, leaving off the formal last name to avoid any questions. Her aunt caught her eye as she did so and she gave her head ever so slight a shake. Not now.

"Well, my home is your home for the night."

"Thank you so much, Mistress Sochi," Lu added as he took his place next to the princess and across from Rasha. She wanted to kick him under the table. Why did he have to be so obvious in his affection for Chiza?

Aunt Sochi gave Rasha a meaningful glance she could only respond to with a roll of her eyes and a shrug. She hoped it was enough, but her aunt was perceptive and outspoken.

"You two are so handsome and well mannered," she said, addressing both young men, and added, "you shouldn't be wasting your time with girls who are already promised to someone else."

"Aunt Sochi!" Rasha's tone was a warning.

Her aunt shrugged and lifted her hands palms up in surrender. "Oops, maybe I shouldn't have said anything."

"You're promised?" Jak asked.

"I'm not," Rasha hissed.

"Really, well, someone ought to tell your parents. They're under the distinct impression you are. I'm sure that's why you've avoided them," Aunt Sochi observed as she continued to bustle around the kitchen.

Rasha saw Jak's back stiffen at the words, and Lu's mouth hung open, making him look like some kind of reptile.

"What are Rasha's parents like?" This time she did kick him under the table. "Ow!" Lu grabbed his leg and changed the subject.

"They're parents," she replied, putting an audible period at the end of the statement.

"I suppose they could be worse. No offense, princess, but had I a father like yours I'm not sure what I would do," Aunt Sochi asserted.

Chiza looked up confused, "Beg your pardon?"

"It's no secret what he's done. Sending you off by courier so they could be robbed of their package and the princess never delivered. All so he could keep his precious gems."

"Where did you hear that?" Lu asked as he reached for Chiza's hand.

"It's all over the broadcasts. How could you have missed it?"

"We came by way of the Wilds," Lu said, looking at Jak, who shrugged.

"The Wilds? Now that's taking your life in your own hands. Not that it matters much. They'll be waiting for you the minute you try to cross the border into Adalu. Her father paid a handsome sum to make sure there's enough bandits mixed in so that no one will suspect a thing. If she's killed or something goes amiss, he'll still get to keep his gems."

The four sat in silence, none of them knowing what to say. Chiza was stunned and silent, neither eating nor drinking. Lu patted her hand and whispered something to her that made her nod, but otherwise not a word.

That news changed the color of the landscape. She and Lu had their licenses revoked over this job. If news got out that the entire thing was a conspiracy to keep the princess from Adalu, would the prince be grateful or annoyed to meet her? Rasha looked over at Lu, but he wasn't thinking about their jobs. Jak hadn't looked at her since he heard she was promised. How could she tell him that that wasn't even the worst of it? If he knew the truth, he'd be shocked. Worse, she'd never know if he liked her, or if he had some kind of hidden agenda. She couldn't take the chance.

The rest of the night was uncomfortable, but nothing compared to the morning. Jak still wasn't speaking to her. She tried to engage him but with her aunt watching it was near to impossible to be herself.

Chiza was helping her aunt with breakfast.

"Eat up everyone, we've still got a journey yet to the palace." She scooped up porridge and passed them around. Lu and Chiza ate with vigor. Jak played with his food and Rasha left her own bowl untouched.

The banging on the door at sunrise didn't bode well, and they looked from one to the other and to Aunt Sochi. Sochi waved a hand for them to sit down but Rasha and Jak were already on their feet, swords in hand. Lu, thinking fast, put Chiza behind him.

The insistent banging on the door was accompanied this time by shouting. "Open, by order of the king."

Rasha felt her heart leap and then sink to her toes. This was the moment she'd been dreading since they discovered the princess was the package. The information she never wanted out. She sheathed her swords and Jak looked at her, the confusion clear on his face. He wanted to know why she wouldn't fight. He'd soon hear the truth for himself.

Aunt Sochi opened the door.

"To what to I owe the pleasure of such an unwarranted and early visit?"

They stormed in past her, pushing her aside. They didn't see the fire that flared in her eyes, but Rasha saw it. She recognized it. They'd dismissed her again. She was the king's sister, and they walked all over her.

"Princess Rasha Jenchat Indari, by order of the king, you and your companions are under arrest." She didn't fight when they bound her hands and took Cutter and Blade from her. Rasha didn't see the expressions Jak, Lu and Chiza wore, but she could imagine the betrayal, shock, and confusion she'd find there.

## 26

*R*asha sat alone in her cell. They'd hauled off Chiza in one direction and the boys in the other. She'd known she'd be arrested, but she hadn't thought them capable of putting her in the dungeons. It was cold, damp, and dark. Only two small, spire-shaped lanterns hung on either side of her door lighting the small space. Lu and Jak might be together. The prison covered the entirety of the lower level. She could be a corridor or two away and not even know. Chiza, a princess, would not be held here. Her parents wouldn't be so cruel and no doubt recognized her.

Rasha heard the sound of heavy boots on stone headed in her direction. They brought light with them and it preceded them down the corridor. Her suspicions were correct. Chiza stood on the other side of her cell along with two guards holding the light above them.

"Please open the cell," she asked.

"I cannot, the king's orders," the guard said, standing straighter.

"You expect me to stand *here* to talk to the prisoner? I don't think so. Open the cell and you can close the door behind me," Chiza insisted. They conceded, and she was allowed into the cell with Rasha.

"You must be desperate for company if you want to sit down here with me," Rasha said.

"Your parents have been very kind to me. They gave me a very nice room where I can rest. It's pink with a lot of lace. I think it was yours once."

Rasha didn't reply. She didn't want to talk about her old room. She'd hated the pink, but her mother had insisted on it.

"The castle is beautiful. The grounds were well kept and there are lots of beasts to ride. They offered to let me go riding. I declined. After all the riding we've done, I could use the break."

Rasha stood but still didn't speak. The guards stood outside, one on each side of the door, no doubt listening. They were always listening.

"Won't you speak to me?"

"Did you come here to discuss the castle highlights?"

"No, I'm just not sure what to say."

"Did my parents send you?"

"No, of course not." Chiza stood up to face her. "I wouldn't have come if they had. I would never come between you."

"There's nothing between us."

145

"You're wrong." Chiza reached out a hand and held Rasha's arm. "They love you, in their way. Keeping your room as it was, is just an example."

"No, you're wrong. If they loved me, they would have changed that room long ago. I never liked it. No, they're holding on to what they wish their daughter to be, not what she's chosen to become."

Chiza sighed. Rasha didn't like arguing with her. Their views were just too far apart.

"You might be right, but ignoring them won't get you understood, or even seen by them, either."

"Have you spoken with the prince?" Rasha asked. She'd rather talk about anything but herself right now.

Chiza sat back down on the slab of stone where Rasha was to sleep. She was careful not to lean back. "I have, he's in good health, and he's expecting my arrival. He says the other girls are already there, and they are excited."

"You mustn't let the other girls worry you," Rasha offered, wanting to get out the advice she'd been planning to give. "You have every right to be there, as much as anyone. Maybe more, since your little misadventure has taught you how to react under pressure and unpredictable circumstances."

Chiza laughed. "That's true enough." She had a far-off look in her eye, as if she were thinking back over the trip. A smile spread across her face and she looked down at her folded hands.

"What are you doing?" Rasha asked.

Chiza blinked and then sobered. "I beg your pardon?" The formality had returned.

Fine, that would work for her. "I recognize those feelings. You're going to hurt him."

"I'd never dream of hurting my prince and future king." Chiza smoothed out her dress over her knees.

"He's not the one to whom I was referring." Rasha gave her what she hoped was a meaningful look.

"Oh." Chiza's mouth formed the word, but it came out in a whisper.

"He's in love with you and you'll crush him. It's not fair to practice on him."

Chiza searched for the words to respond. "I never meant for—"

Rasha stopped her with a wave of her hand. "Of course you didn't. But look at what you've done and tell me you can just walk away from him as if he meant nothing."

Rasha paced the cell like a caged animal and kicked at the bars. It was a long moment before Chiza spoke again, her voice a whisper. "How do you know he's in love with me?"

Rasha turned and faced her. Chiza's eyes remained cast down and her shoulders slumped forward.

"Because when he thought you were dead, and he was dying, he told me so."

"Why didn't he say anything?"

Rasha's anger flared again.

"Are you that ignorant? You've studied the other

princesses in The Choosing but haven't studied royal history? What is he supposed to do, declare his love for you only to be killed? All of this while you secure the affection of the prince? Fickle girl."

Chiza didn't speak this time. She wept, her silent tears falling to the floor.

Rasha put an arm around her. It hadn't been her intention to hurt her feelings. Chiza had become a friend to both her and Lu. She noticed that Chiza had cleaned up. She was dressed in fine clothes that had come from the closet in her old room. The dress was a warm yellow and unlike Rasha, it suited Chiza.

"What am I going to do? I think I'm in love with him, too."

Rasha knew she'd be putting Lu in harm's way to encourage anything between them.

"There's nothing you can do. How does that pink cage in the upper tower feel now? Perhaps you understand a little now why I left it behind."

"You were in love with someone else?"

"No," Rasha shook her head and lifted Chiza's chin so she could see her face. "No, I wanted the choice."

Two royal guards entered the jail and stopped in front her cell. The two guards that arrived with Chiza straightened up.

"Their royal highnesses the king and queen request your presence in the royal chambers," the guard informed Rasha. He opened door of the cell and waited for her to exit.

They wouldn't leave her in peace for long. She'd been expecting to be summoned. She'd have to answer for her betrayal of her parents, the kingdom, and her royal position. This was a moment two rotations in the making. Somehow, it didn't feel the way she thought it would.

Chiza wiped her face and looked up at Rasha.

"What will they do to you?"

Rasha waved airily. "Don't worry about me. Promise me you'll be honest with yourself and with him." She didn't need to clarify to which 'him' she meant. "If you break his heart, you'll lose two good friends."

Rasha stepped out of the cell and held out her hands, but the guards did not bind them. They turned around, and she followed them out, leaving Chiza sitting alone in the open cell.

## 27

*J*ak was face down on the stone floor, pushing his body up and down, keeping his back to the bars. His breath came hard and fast. He alternated between that and pulling himself up using a U-shaped bar welded to the ceiling. Lu watched him as he continued to work himself into a heavy sweat. It was cold and dank as most cells were, but Jak wouldn't be able to feel it. In fact, he'd already removed his cloak and outer clothing.

"I know you're mad, but I'm sure she has a good reason for not mentioning it. I mean, she's not the kind to keep secrets. I mean, not these kinds of secrets."

Jak jumped up from the floor and looked down at Lu as if he were an insect he wanted to stomp out of existence. Lu cleared his throat.

"I mean, she's never done it before, and she was protecting us. Considering we're in a prison cell, I can see why we haven't visited her folks before. I guess they don't approve of her profession."

Jak lay on his back now, and putting his hands behind his neck, he used his abdomen to lift his torso from the floor. He hadn't spoken a word since they'd arrived, and Lu couldn't stop talking.

It wasn't like he didn't try. He'd even used the bar on the ceiling a few times before the muscles in his arms trembled from exhaustion. He climbed trees, he didn't lift dead weight from the floor.

"Her Aunt Sochi seemed like a decent woman. I see where Rash gets her edge. The woman seems quick, and her eagle eyes miss nothing. I mean, you heard the way she was talking to us. That's because she knew about Rash and Chiza being princesses."

Jak used the bottom of his shirt to wipe the sweat from his face. There was water in a basin with a cup for drinking. The water was fresh and Jak took several cups before he threw the cup back in the water.

"They all knew. Chiza, Sochi, and Rasha. They all knew the truth, and they kept us in the dark," Jak said.

"Chiza wouldn't—"

"When are you going to figure out you're only hurting yourself?" Jak asked angrily.

"What?"

"They're princesses, and this is the rotation of The Choosing. They are *both* promised to prince Bashir until he decides otherwise. We have no claims to them." Jak walked to the bars and gripped them until his knuckles turned white.

Lu sat down on the nearest ledge and tucked his legs up underneath him. He'd been struggling with that exact problem. Lu knew he'd lost his heart to Chiza. But he hadn't planned on sharing his feelings with anyone. Now, Jak needed to deal with it as he had. Maybe hearing about what he went through would help Jak.

"I joined Rash about a rotation ago. I couldn't believe I was teamed with one of the youngest and most reckless couriers," Lu said. "She takes time to get to know, but we found a rhythm that works. Honestly, I can say I was never more content away from my family than when I was with Rash. That's until Chiza came out of that box. I've never seen anyone so beautiful or kind. When she meets my parents, they'll like her too. My sister Ladi won't, but she doesn't like anyone. Chiza feels for me the way I feel for her. I have no doubts when I say the prince won't choose her. She and I will be together."

"You don't know that," Jak said, anguish all over his face.

"There's one thing I know about every man in the world. What you might call a universal truth." Lu looked up and saw Jak waiting for him to continue.

"No man wants a woman that belongs to another." To Lu it was just that simple. Once he realized it he never had another doubt. Chiza would present herself to the prince because it was her duty, but she wouldn't be chosen.

Lu watched Jak's expression soften. "Rash already

made her choice," Lu said. "She won't allow herself to be chosen. If you can't see that her heart belongs to someone else than you're a pumseed and a fool."

Jak nodded. Lu watched the realization pass over his features, relaxing them. Jak didn't say anything more. Instead he dropped to the floor and continued his circuit of training. Lu waited a moment longer than necessary, but when he realized the conversation was over, he launched into more free-form rambling.

"I hope Rasha's Aunt Sochi is looking after Temi. I'm sure he's a little upset about being separated from me. Does he look bigger to you?"

---

*T*he guards led Rasha to one of the guest suites. "What is this?" she asked.

"You'll prepare yourself to meet your king and queen. Make use of the room. There is suitable clothing available inside. Everything you need is there," the guard said.

The guard nudged Rasha into the room and locked the door behind her. Inside, the room smelled of flowers and something familiar, something spicy and sweet. Could that be bazil in the teapot by the bedside table? Impossible. She rushed to it and poured a cup and drank some of it down. She felt her core warm with the delicious liquid. A contented sigh escaped her lips. A sound from behind her caught her attention, and she dropped her cup and reached for Cutter and Blade, but her hands met empty sheaths. They'd taken her weapons.

"Yahtz." She turned and was almost knocked down by an excited Temi. "Get off me, beastie. Who let you in here? I'm supposed to be getting cleaned up, I don't think they meant you."

"No, they meant me," her Aunt Sochi said, stepping out of the bathroom.

Rasha rushed to her.

"They let you in? Didn't get enough chastising in last night, I see," Rasha said and embraced the older woman.

"No, I had to sneak in. I thought you could use some encouragement before you get dressed down by your father. Come." She gestured toward the bath.

How many times had her Aunt Sochi been there when she returned from riding lessons with her father and etiquette lessons with her mother? Rasha peeled off her clothes. Her aunt turned her away and picked up a long-handled brush and the soap and brought them over.

Rasha was neck deep in the milky water when Sochi turned back. Her aunt didn't speak at all. Rasha used a smaller brush that sat on the rim of the large oval tub to scrub at her hands and feet. It was large enough for three people but she kept to the edge where her aunt could reach her. Rasha sat back and let her aunt unravel the braids and the knots that entangled her hair. Her own white braid was pinned up to keep it from getting wet. When she'd finished Rasha's hair, Sochi helped her bathe, using the brush to get the skin at her back. Rasha felt wrinkled and cleaner than she had in forever. Sochi held out a towel for her hair and a plush pink robe.

"I know you hate this color, but that's all there is."

"It's fine," Rasha replied. She didn't mind the color so

much at the moment. She was enjoying the peace her aunt brought with her presence. It wouldn't last, but she was determined to take advantage of it.

The vanity mirror and table both had gold edges, and the chair had a plush seat and back. Rasha sat down and watched in the mirror as her aunt squeezed the water from the ends of her hair. Rasha loved the feel of the soft bristles against her scalp as her aunt brushed. Sochi looked at her niece in the mirror.

"So, the young man, Jak. He was wounded this morning. Do you think he'll be able to accept the truth?"

"Accept the truth, yes, but understanding requires a little more than he might be capable of giving."

"If he's smart enough for you, he'll figure it out. No one in his right mind would let you get away."

Rasha laughed. It sounded a lot like what she used to say when she was encouraging her to prepare for the prince's choosing. She laughed and said, "You used to say any prince in his right mind."

"That was before I knew you for who you are, not for who I wanted you to be," she replied.

Rasha nodded.

"They still don't know you for who you are. You won't find any understanding from them." Sochi was speaking about her parents.

"Yes, I know." Rasha rolled her shoulders back.

"You're older now. What they feared the most passes. It's time you show them who you've become. I taught you to fight, now I'll teach you to stand up for yourself."

"I already know how to do that. I'm a courier. I fetch, and I deliver without fail."

"Yes, and you've been too afraid to confront your parents for the last two rotations."

Rasha held her tongue. She hadn't had the time. That's what she'd told herself. Lu visited his family all the time, but she hadn't felt like dealing with the disappointment on her parents' faces. They'd threatened to keep her in the dungeons and they'd done it. Wasn't that enough of a reason to avoid dealing with them? Maybe she had been a little afraid to return. Now that she was here, she felt guilty about not at least visiting her aunt. Sochi had always stood by her.

"I'm sorry." Rasha couldn't meet her aunt's eyes.

"For what?"

"I should have come to see you."

"The circumstances weren't ideal for visits, I understand. I followed the reports from Courier Central. You've made quite a name for yourself among your peers. I don't know what you'll do now you've lost that, but I'm sure you've got a plan."

Rasha stood up and faced her aunt.

"It's temporary. I'll explain matters to his royal highness of Adalu. It was all a misunderstanding, we'll get our licenses back." Rasha would see it through, not just for herself, but for Lu.

"Good, that's the fire I want to see. Make sure your mother and father see it too. They'll be hard on you, but it's nothing you haven't heard before."

"Either they'll see me for who I am or I'll be confined to a cell." Rasha shrugged then looked down on saw a peach-colored gown that was laid out for her.

"What's that?"

"The dress they left for you." Sochi let out a laugh at the look on her face. Rasha must have looked disgusted. "Yeah, that's what I thought you'd say. I'll leave you alone to get ready. Your tuskins are in the stables. Leave this beastie here where he can't get into any trouble."

Rasha nodded as she looked down at Temi, who, for the moment, could have deceived anyone, because he looked as innocent as a lamb.

"Be careful on your journey, and don't forget to come and see me once again in your lifetime."

Rasha rushed over and threw her arms around her aunt's neck. "I will," she whispered.

Sochi rapped on the door. The guard opened for her, and she left the room. Rasha missed her strength already. She couldn't help but wish for the millionth time that Sochi had been her mother. The woman had taught her to be who she was in every way that mattered. Rasha looked down at the dress and wished she had her swords.

Rasha followed the guards to the royal chambers. The tower to their rooms was on the opposite side of the castle from her old room, where they'd taken Chiza. Guest rooms weren't even on the same level of the castle. The ornate door to their chambers had once intimidated her. Now the gleam of the handles and the lion's face carved on the door had no hold on her.

"Enter," her father's booming voice replied to the guard's knock.

The guard opened the doors wide, ushering her through before closing them behind her.

"What is this?" her father asked as he looked her over. His dark purple skin was wrinkled with age but his eyes were like stone, cold and black. Her mother, as usual, was perfectly turned out without a hair out of place. Neither wore their royal robes, choosing to meet with her in what they considered casual attire. Her mother's cream gown reached the floor and her ankle and neck jewelry were in gold and bronze.

Rasha knelt on one knee and put her fist to her heart as did all the guards and servants when greeting her parents.

"We left you a dress. Why aren't you wearing the dress?"

"I have no need of gowns, Mother. The clothes I wear are good enough for me, and for you," Rasha stated. Keeping her tone even took effort.

"What? You would refuse our hospitality?" her father blustered. He pounded a fist on the breakfast table and the dishes all jumped, some tinkling to the floor.

Her mother's handmaid hurried to gather them together and put them on the service stand for removal.

"I did not refuse your hospitality. Downstairs, the cell was comfortable and adequate. A bath in the guest suite was also a kind gesture. The dress is not mine. I have no use for that kind of finery in my line of work."

The look of disappointment on her mother's face made Rasha angry. She wasn't there to prove anything to them. Couldn't they see that? She wasn't one of them.

"Child, come here. Enough of that," her mother fussed. "Take a chair and sit so we may speak with you."

The handmaid was ready and put a bright yellow chair in the middle of the room for Rasha to sit on. She sat, even though the low chair made it easier for her parents to look down their noses at her.

"I will answer your questions if you will hear me."

"We will hear you," her mother said.

"Why do you shame us by not taking your rightful place among the chosen?" her father asked.

"Haven't you toiled enough as a domestic for the ten kingdoms?" her mother followed in quick succession.

Rasha waited for the questions to stop before she spoke.

"I am sorry to have shamed you, but you know I will not agree to be chosen by the prince or any man. I have the right to choose and I exercise my right."

Her father shook his head angrily, denying her words. She turned her attention to her mother. "I've been earning my own money as a courier and I like my job. I have no plans to quit in the immediate future."

"So why are you here?" her father yelled banging his fist on the table again, startling her mother and the handmaid.

"I'm here because you had me arrested. I had no plans

to return at the moment. I have a very important delivery to make to prince Bashir."

"Yes, Chiza of Sidoa. We've met her." Her mother rolled her eyes in annoyance. "She's not a princess, she's the daughter of a farmer."

"A man who'd as soon sell his daughter as give up his jewels. Selfish ranglefort," her father criticized.

"Mind your language," her mother rebuked him.

"How do you know about that?" Rasha asked. It took everything in her to stay seated and not pace the room.

Her father waved a hand. "Everyone knows that greedy man has hired half the kingdom to keep his gems from going to Adalu as his daughter's rightful dowry."

"Darling, we would never treat you in such a manner. You have a plentiful dowry. We only want to see you take your rightful place. You have a duty to your kingdom, and you've overlooked it for far too long. If a farmer's daughter can do it, how is it you find it so difficult a task?"

Aunt Sochi was right. They hadn't changed. She'd grown older, but they still spoke to her as if she were a child. They didn't understand her even after she'd refused to put on the dress they'd given her.

"I'm sorry, but that matter is closed."

"Closed?" Her father blustered again, but this time she regarded his dramatics with the boredom it deserved.

"I will not marry the prince, even if he were to choose me sight unseen. I don't love him and I don't want him or his life." Rasha watched her parents' mouths gape open as she continued. "I will carry on as a courier."

"But your license has been revoked. It is illegal for you to continue," her father said.

This time she did stand. How could he know such a thing? There were only two ways, and she doubted it was because he cared about how she was doing. Rasha took two measured steps closer to her seated father, who now had to look up.

"What do you know of my career as a courier?" She spoke in a low and even tone that barely contained the rage she felt.

Her mother started to speak but Rasha held up a hand that stopped whatever excuse her mother planned to offer. Rasha stepped back and shook her head as if to clear it.

"It was you." Rasha had to fight to keep the emotion from choking her.

"What are you accusing me of?" her father demanded and stood.

He paced the room as if he were trying to figure out what to say. He turned back to face her.

"Don't be a coward now, Father. You had a hand in getting my license revoked. Surely you don't fear the wrath of your daughter. Can't you admit it to my face?"

"Transportation of humanoids is illegal," he declared.

Rasha nodded. It was the closest thing to an admission she'd receive. Before she could stop herself her anger propelled her across the room in three rushed steps that put her within striking range of her father. Her hands dropped to her empty belt again, but before she registered that her hands were empty, a heavy slap struck her face. Rasha stumbled back.

"No," her mother exclaimed, rushing forward. But her father raised his arm and held her back. His face had gone an even darker shade of purple.

Rasha steadied herself, and calmly asserted, "You won't tie me down and force me to live in this castle as your trophy princess."

She dropped to one knee again and put a fist to her chest. "I appreciate all you've done for Princess Chiza. She's not just a mission anymore. Lu and Jak are my friends and have done nothing wrong. I beg you let them go. They are more than capable of escorting the princess on my behalf."

Rasha kept her head bowed, waiting for an answer, then remembered something.

"Oh, and I'd like your permission to go to the temple before my imprisonment."

## 29

"Come with me."

Four guards stood just outside of Lu and Jak's cell, waiting for them to come out. With two guards in front of them and two behind, they were led from the dungeon.

"I wonder if they're having some kind of feast for us. Big confusion, sorry we didn't realize you were that princess," Lu said under his breath.

Jak was in better spirits too. He had no problem poking fun at the guards as they walked.

"I think the furry caps on their heads might be squeezed too tight. See how their faces are all pinched? Not at all a good look for these purple guards."

Lu snickered, but caught himself when one of the guards half turned to glare at them.

"Fine accommodations you have below stairs, would you like us to inspect the rest of the castle? We'd be thrilled to serve the king and his princess," Jak said. This time Lu laughed.

When they reached a small temple beside the castle, the guards stopped some distance away. One of the guards pointed his long metal-tipped staff first at Lu, then at Jak. He said, "You will hold your tongue. This is our holy temple. Your presence is requested but not required. I hope you understand my meaning." The guard squared his shoulders, preparing for a fight. Lu wasn't interested in fighting with Rasha's people. He was too fascinated by them. Jak held his chin up but didn't respond.

Lu was about to ask what they were doing out there when Chiza arrived. He felt his insides light up as soon as he saw her. She was being escorted down the front steps by one guard.

"You look fresh. I guess the female cells are much nicer than the men's," Jak said with a wink.

"Cells? You've been imprisoned?"

They both held up their bound hands.

"You weren't?" Lu asked.

"By the Univers—" Chiza caught herself as she'd noticed the temple. "Of course not. I'm the princess of Sidoa. We don't want to go to war with these people any more than they want to. I can tell you all the nonsense we've been through would be nothing compared to a war. If my family were to discover I'd been placed in jail, it would be worse for them than anything we've experienced so far."

"Where have you been?" Lu half whispered as the guard escorted them to the temple doors.

"I've been in Rasha's old room," Chiza shrugged.

"I take it she didn't leave a journal of her escapades and lost loves?" Jak asked her.

"Nothing of Rasha lives in that room. Nor in this castle, I'd say."

Temi came around the back of the temple and took a defensive posture as the guards raised their weapons. Lu whistled, and the beast relaxed.

"Are we finished with these?" Jak asked raising his bound hands.

One of the other guards stepped forward and released them. Jak proceeded inside ahead. Chiza followed. Lu started in with Temi beside him.

The guard snapped, "The beast is not permitted inside." He spat on the ground. The idea of the animal occupying such a holy place was disgusting to him, it seemed.

"As you wish, sir, he'll stay out here with you." Lu flashed them what he hoped was a wicked smile like Jak's, then turned and followed the others inside.

Chiza had stepped inside the doors, but no further. Jak stood just ahead of her. It took a moment for Lu's eyes to adjust to the darkened room. All the windows were made of colored glass, and fifty rows of benches flanked an aisle leading to the altar. In front of the altar, Rasha was kneeling in front of a glowing ball of light. Her head was bowed and her hands were clasped. Her mouth moved,

but from where they were nothing of her voice could
be heard.

Chiza pulled Lu aside by the lapels as soon as the
doors closed behind them. Instead of entering the temple
area, they stood in the back of the building behind the
barrier between the servant's corridor and the altar room.
It was a space where the servants could pass unseen. This
part of the temple was less ornate, made with polished
wood floors and panels.

"I must speak with you. It's urgent," Chiza whispered.

Lu took one more look toward Rasha. Maybe he
should find out how things went after their arrest. Jak was
already moving toward her. Lu turned back to Chiza. The
corridor ended at a wall where a round window let in light
a few feet above their heads. Chiza was waving him over
from beneath the window.

"Are you well?" Lu asked.

"Yes, I'm well. Now that I see you again I feel much
better."

"Me too." Lu reached out and grabbed both of her
hands. "I've missed our talks."

"I have as well. This is what I came to say." Chiza took
a deep breath. "I think that I am no longer fit to marry the
prince."

Lu watched as Chiza's eyes filled. Something inside of
him clenched, and he realized she'd been in agony over
this. Lu couldn't bear to see her so distraught. He'd do
anything to make her happy. If she told him to go, he'd go.
If she said they could never speak again, he'd do it.

Anything, if it meant removing the hurt he saw swimming in her eyes.

"I can't marry him. I won't."

This wasn't what Lu expected or wanted. It was dangerous for her to speak this way. Rasha had been right. They'd gone down a very dangerous road. Rasha had made her choice, but few would contradict her blades. Chiza was no fighter. How would she stand before the prince and declare she wouldn't have him?

"You must go to the palace. You must meet with the prince. Let him choose someone else, but you must go. You can't risk bearing the shame of your family forever. They could arrest you, declare you a traitor to the first kingdom, or worse. All of these are good reasons to follow through with your vow. I want you to."

Chiza was shaking her head now, the look on her face determined. "How can I marry him when I know I'm in love with you?"

Lu stared at her a moment, not sure he'd heard her correctly. Chiza smiled and tilted her head.

"Is it so strange that I could fall in love with you?" she asked.

He smiled then. "I was thinking this whole time that I was the only one in love."

Chiza let out a little squeak of pleasure and threw her arms around his neck. "You do?"

"I think I've loved you since the moment we pulled you out of that box." Lu put a hand on her face and leaned in to her. He'd wanted to kiss her for almost as long. Now was his moment. He wrapped his hand around the back of her neck and her lips parted with a sigh as soon as his lips met hers. They were so soft and warm like the rest of her. She pressed up against him and his other arm reached into her coat and slid around her waist.

"I won't marry him," she whispered in his ear.

"I know. But you must go. I will stay as long as I am allowed. You'll meet the prince and the other princesses, you'll make friends. There's nothing wrong with more friends. I will return to the Twinlands and wait for the prince to choose another. Then you'll join me there and meet my family."

"You'd do that for me?"

"I would do anything for you. Waiting for your return is nothing. Have you ever been to the Twinlands?"

"I have, we went there when I was a girl. My family did all the trade negotiations with the other nine kingdoms in person."

"Then you know much about my nation already, but I hope to be your guide when next you come."

"I'd like that," she said as rested her head on his shoulder.

"There's plenty to occupy our time. I've got money saved up and we can go visit your father."

"Yes, my father will want to meet you."

"Yes, I know. I have a few things to ask him," Lu said, as he tried to rein in his anger.

Chiza pulled back from his embrace to look him in the eye.

"My father is not a perfect man. But I believe whatever he did, he thought it best for our kingdom."

"The kingdom, perhaps, but not for you, his daughter. You deserve so much better."

"Don't be angry, my love." Her words, so light, so casual and intimate made him burn with desire for her. "I've seen the reports and I admit his behavior has shamed us. But I won't add to our shame. I'll be able to fulfill my duty, but only because your promise will be close to my heart."

Chiza leaned in and brushed a finger down the front of his forehead. Lu pulled her close again and this time he let his need for her fill him. She sighed with her head against his chest. Lu smiled as he thought about how things had changed between them. From this moment on their lives would never be the same.

## 30

*R*asha kept her head bowed even after her friends were brought to the temple. She finished her prayer to the Universal and tucked her amulet back under her shirt. She'd been released. Her parents had sent word through the guard. She and her friends were free to leave if they chose. Rasha stood without turning, keeping her face to the eye of the Universal. She felt Jak behind her. She wasn't sure how she knew it was him. Maybe it was all the nights of him tracking them. She'd gotten used to his stealth.

"Where are the others?" she asked.

"They're talking somewhere." Jak let his voice fade. He looked around, taking in the temple.

Rasha turned and faced him. "I wanted to explain why I didn't say anything about all this before." She gestured at the castle. Her fingers trembled, so she locked them together.

"You're a spoiled little girl," Jak said.

"What?"

"You were bored, so you left. I get it. The castle life must have been tough, all these servants attending you." Jak waved a hand and turned in a slow circle, the disdain for the room and its furnishings on his face.

"Careful," she warned.

Rasha's hands remained clenched at her sides. She'd wait and let him get this out of his system. He needed to vent.

"No, I get it. Too much love and affection from this family of yours so you pack up and leave to become a courier. Something with a bit more freedom to be the spoiled brat that you are." Jak said. "I can see why you left. I mean look at this place, the gold, the gems."

"Are you mocking me?" she asked.

"Well, I don't much see any reason to avoid the place for two rotations, or to lie about it."

"You know why I can't tell people who I am."

Jak nodded. Then he ran his thumb across his neck like a knife.

"They wouldn't dare," Rasha said. He was teasing her.

"No, they won't come after you. They'll punish your family." Jak said.

Rasha nodded. That's what bothered her parents. They'd been shut out of royal events because their daughter refused to conform. They were proud and her actions were a constant blow to their status. Two rotations ago, she hadn't given it another thought. Now she wondered if there was a way to restore her family and still maintain her own freedom. Hadn't she done everything she could to distance herself from them?

"How do you come in here with the Eye of the Universal condemning you?" Jak asked.

"I'll have you know that Eye has been in my family for generations. Only the guilty are condemned." Rasha waited a beat and then asked him the question that had been worrying her since their arrival. "Are you still angry with me?"

"No," Jak replied. The ease with which he said it calmed her heart. Perhaps Lu had said something to help him understand. She'd have to ask him about it later.

Rasha, feeling bolder and more at peace, took a step toward Jak. "I'm glad. I wouldn't want this to come between us."

"Between us? Is there something between us?" he asked, his false innocence making her tighten her lips to keep from laughing.

She made a show of looking around and in between them.

"I don't see anything between us." She took another step closer. She tilted her head and her lips parted.

"Princess, are you going to kiss me?" Jak asked, tipping his head forward and staring at her mouth.

"Don't call me princess. Are you going to stop me?" she asked, a breath away from his lips.

Jak nodded but he let her kiss him. His hands gripped her waist before they slid up her back to her neck and into her hair. When they parted he ran a finger down her cheek and frowned when she winced.

"What happened here? Your skin—it's swollen, and your lip." He ran a finger along her busted bottom lip. When she tried to look away, he held on to her chin. "Who did this?"

Rasha gave him what felt like a half smile. "It's a parting gift to the spoiled princess for speaking her true feelings to her father."

Jak's jaw clenched as his eyes traced the outline of the handprint on her face.

"We should get going." Rasha wanted to be on her way before this conversation got any more uncomfortable.

"Yes." Jak let go and straightened his coat. Rasha glimpsed the small disk she'd placed just under the collar. He hadn't seen it. She reached up and grabbed for it. A guard chose that inconvenient moment to open the temple doors and announce himself. Rasha's hand dropped back to her side.

"Your highness." The guard inclined his head in her direction. Not a full bow. "The king sends his regards; your presence is no longer required. You are all free to go."

The guard turned back around and exited the temple, the doors closing soundlessly behind him.

"Your parents aren't ready to meet me, I suppose." Jak pretended to be offended.

"Come on." She pulled him along. Then she yelled for the others, "Lu, Chiza, it's time to go."

The two hadn't gone any further on the inside edge of

the temple. They were in the small entrance hall, with swollen lips and clothing askew. Jak laughed and gave Lu a pat on the back when they reached all reached the doors. Rasha shook her head. What could she say about it?

As if her parents couldn't wait for them to be gone, the beasts were waiting outside the temple. Temi finished up a bowl of food they'd brought to pacify him. He trotted to Lu like a domestic animal and licked his hand. Lu gave him a pat on the head before helping Chiza up on their tuskin. Temi, too big to sit up on his lap anymore, trailed along beside them. Jak followed them with a smile and a wave to the guards.

Rasha raised her eyes to the windows of her mother and father's rooms in the southern tower. There was no movement. She hoped someday, as her aunt had, they'd see her for who she was instead of what they wanted her to be. She had her aunt. Rasha would have to make more of an effort with her. Sochi had given Rasha shelter even after a two-rotation absence. She was like a mother to her. A shame she'd never married and had children of her own.

## 31

They rode hard and fast over the next two days. They'd been delayed enough, and with a winter storm on their heels they needed to hurry or risk being caught in the coming snow.

When Lu let out a warning whistle, they all came to an abrupt halt. Rasha rode up beside Lu as he cocked his head and stared into the woods ahead of them. "What's wrong?" she asked in a whisper.

"We've got company."

"What's wrong?" Jak asked.

"The royal guard doesn't come out this far to meet or greet princesses. Besides, no one is supposed to know we're coming today, which means they've been set up here for some time."

"How many?"

Lu jumped down from his tuskin, leaving Chiza to hold the reins. He pulled out his eye gear and disappeared into the woods. None of them spoke as they waited for Lu's return. A few minutes later, he was back.

"It's a blockade. Three large groups waiting on the border for anyone who should pass by."

"I could ride up ahead. Get a closer look. If they take me, it won't matter. You'll have the princess and you'll know to find another way around," Jak offered.

"Why would you do that when we could all just go around? There's no chance we can sneak Chiza through so let's not go the martyr route until we must," Rasha replied.

"There might be another way," Lu said. He had his screen out again, and he swiped through the images until the right one appeared. "There. I have a way through."

"Through?" Jak said.

"Not exactly through, but under. There are tunnels. They're escape tunnels for the palace but they've been all but abandoned for the last hundred rotations of peace."

"How do we know that no one else has already found the tunnels?" Jak asked.

"One, the men at the border are nowhere near the exit tunnel, and they only go one way. The doors to the tunnels are locked from the inside and the only way through is if someone on the inside opens the doors."

"If they're locked how will we get in?" Chiza asked.

"Working on it," Lu said as he bit his bottom lip and used his communicator, tapping out several sequences.

"Is it an electrical system, could we use one of your devices to disable the lock?"

"No, this is an original, antique locking system. There's no breaking a code to get through it."

"We need someone in the palace to open the doors." Jak paced.

"Yahtz, I can't get through to anyone." Lu said. "The palace is packed with princesses so there's no getting through to anyone inside." Rasha could think of nothing more unpleasant than a pack of princesses. She looked over at Chiza, an idea forming.

"We don't have time for this," Jak said. "Let's just go around while there's still light."

"Wait, Chiza, I need you to come with me," Rasha said and tipped her head to the right.

"Are you going to tell us what you're doing?"

"One step at a time. Just give us a minute." Rasha smiled over her shoulder and led Chiza into the woods.

Rasha and Chiza returned a few moments later wearing each other's clothes. Chiza stood transformed into a warrior princess. Rasha wore Chiza's pink gown. It came down just to her ankles. On the tuskin it wouldn't be noticeable if she could keep their eyes off of her feet. She couldn't manage to squeeze her large feet into Chiza's delicate sandals. The pink dress offered no support to her stomach and back, and the thin straps were snug over her arms, but otherwise it fit. She sat tall and kept her bare feet in the stirrups of her mount.

"What is this?" Jak asked. He reached out and fingered the bottom edge of the soft material just above her ankles.

"It's called a plan."

RASHA RODE ON HER BEAST, keeping her distance
behind Jak. He sat well in his seat on the mount, riding
with a straight back and fierce expression on his face.
She'd put on her best princess act and they'd stuffed
Chiza into a bag. This time, though, she was fully
conscious. Lu rode several paces behind Rasha, creating a
buffer around her. Chiza lay draped over the mount, her
arms and legs on opposite sides. When they reached the
border, several men jumped from the trees in an attempt
to stop them.

Jak pulled his sword, ready to fight, and Lu readied his
charge emitter. It wouldn't take down all of them but,
enough to get Rasha and Chiza through.

"What have you got there?" The man said, looking
over Rasha and Lu.

"We are on our way to The Choosing. The royal family
of Adalu is expecting us. I have the Princess Rasha Jenchat
Indari from Chilali and her manservant. Why do you
detain us?" Jak looked ready to take their heads. "Well,
what is your business here?" He demanded.

"We are looking for someone. A black princess traveling with a purple courier."

Jak laughed in their faces.

"Well, take a closer look, boys. Do you see a black
princess or a purple one?"

"She's purple, but—" the man closest to him stammered, but didn't drop his long sword.

"Is she a courier or a princess?" Jak asked leaning down over his mount.

"She's a princess, but—"

"Jak, what is the delay?" Rasha called out, using her mother's tone.

"Your highness, these men seem to have mistaken you for a courier."

"A what?" Rasha moved her mount forward, looking down her nose at the man who appeared to be the leader. "A courier?"

"Lucius!"

"Yes, your highness."

"This man on the road seems to think I'm a courier. I told you not to dress me in this manner. I look far too common. Now the prince will think I'm some kind of domestic."

"I'm sorry, mistress. I will correct it at your convenience." Lu gave her a gracious bow. He reached out a hand and pressed it lightly to Chiza's back.

"We must be on our way. If there's nothing else?" They waited a beat. The men continued to stare at each other in confusion. "Good day, gentlemen," Jak said, urging his mount into a hurried trot. Rasha followed, with Lu beside her. She knew it must kill Chiza to be on her stomach. They needed to hurry out of view.

"We're almost there, Chiza, hold on my sweet," Lu said when they were out of earshot.

As soon as they reached the hedges around the palace, Jak and Rasha stopped behind a stand of trees. Lu untied

Chiza from the bag and helped her to a seated position in front of him. Chiza gave them a nod when she was ready to proceed and she led them in a race toward the palace. Rasha looked over at her and realized that Chiza's strength and bravery weren't always on the surface, but today she was a force. Wearing courier clothes, she looked like an ancient warrior queen.

WHEN THEY ARRIVED at the gates of the palace they were admitted at once, based on Rasha's description. They all assumed she was there as a princess to meet the prince. The confusion only worsened when Prince Bashir himself came out to meet them. He was as white as snow and his hair and eyelashes were the same. He admired Rasha, looking over her figure twice before reaching for her hand.

"My dear, what an arduous journey you must have had. I expected you ages ago. What's kept you?" The prince bowed and placed a light kiss on her hand. Rasha pulled her hand from his and kept it at her side.

"I regret to inform you, your highness, that I am the courier and the princess and I had to engage in subterfuge to get past the border."

"I apologize for my attire, your highness. Allow me a moment to change before making my introductions," Chiza said.

Rasha regretted that they hadn't thought to change her mount. Sitting on the tuskin with Lu holding the reins from behind her made Rasha look at the prince to see if he noticed anything between them. But the prince went to Chiza and took her hand.

"It's of little matter, you are a vision in anything you wear." He lifted her hand to his lips and reached up to help her down. "My apologies for overlooking you." He raised a hand and two of the servants came forward.

"Please help these men with their animals, there should be a guest room available to them. Escort Princess Chiza and Princess Rasha to their rooms so they can... change." He gave them both a knowing smile before turning to go.

Rasha had the distinct feeling he knew she wasn't there for The Choosing and was forcing her to stay. Rasha kept her mouth closed and her eyes down as the guard escorted them, carrying both bags with ease. How stupid to think she could just show up here. She'd vowed not to be anywhere near the first kingdom during the time of The Choosing, now here she was right under his nose.

When she looked back Jak was staring at her. 'It'll be all right,' she wanted to say. Halfway up the steps to the palace she couldn't risk saying anything. Rasha pulled her shoulders back and lifted the dress and followed Chiza and the guard inside, where things only got worse.

## 32

*R*asha and Chiza were brought to the east wing of the palace where the princesses were staying. They entered a corridor lined with doors. They were all open, and the girls were milling about between rooms. When Chiza and Rasha arrived, a general silence fell on the group as they stopped to stare at the new arrivals.

They whispered behind their hands and looked at them as if they'd interrupted an exclusive party. As Rasha thought about it, perhaps they had. Chiza held her head high as she passed them and Rasha tried to do the same. The dress didn't make it easy. It swayed above her ankles, showing off her large and dirty feet.

"You will be in side-by-side suites here." The guard pointed to the doors and bowed. He refused to lift his head until they'd both entered. He shut both doors behind them. Rasha took in the luxurious room. The furnishings were not overstated, but every piece was made of precious metals or decorated with precious gems.

A knock at the small door to her right startled her.

"Open the door, it's me," Chiza called from the other side of the door.

Rasha opened the door and saw a similar door. Through that was a unique room on the other side. Rasha looked behind her to make sure there wasn't another door there and found the washroom instead.

"Have you seen the bath? It's divine. Thank the Universal this will be a comfortable place to pass the time." Chiza strolled past her and dropped Rasha's courier clothes down on the bed. "Oh, my goodness, have you seen this mirror? I've never seen anything like it." She ran a hand over the gems and then stopped and turned back to Rasha, who was redressing in her own clothes. She'd been missing the boots and sat down on the edge of the bed to tie them on.

"I wouldn't do that if I were you," Chiza said.

"What?"

"The prince, he expects you to stay. You mustn't disappoint him."

Rasha shook her head and stood up, resting her hands on the hilts of her swords. "I'm not staying here."

Chiza's head dropped with her voice. "You could do what I'm going to do."

"What's that?"

"Make sure that the prince doesn't choose me, so I can have Lu."

Rasha tried to imagine herself faking her way through The Choosing. No, she'd known that wouldn't work for a long time.

"No, I can't. I'm sorry. I know you don't want to be here on your own. The problem is, I can't be here at all."

Chiza seemed to try to work something out in her mind.

"Forget about it. There's nothing you can say to convince me to stay here during The Choosing." Rasha went to the door to the corridor.

"Yes, it's fine. I just wanted a friend while I'm here."

Rasha stopped. She respected Chiza, despite their different opinions about duty and honor.

"You have a friend here." Rasha wished things could be different, but the palace walls were already closing in on her and she didn't want to stay any longer than she had to.

"I need to meet with the prince to discuss my license. Now you've become a princess again instead of a courier, you need to see him again, too. He'll need to hear an account from you of all that's happened."

Chiza rolled her shoulders back as if preparing for battle.

"Yes, you're right. Let's go."

Rasha opened the door and stopped dead. The other princesses were waiting for them in the corridor.

## 33

They all came forward, offering Chiza greetings as they took her hands, hugged her, and kissed her on the cheek. Some of them gave her enthusiastic handshakes and fiddled with her dress and jewelry. The princesses from the Buku, Winaka, and Vol kingdoms seemed less than excited to see her. Chiza's arrival was most shocking to them, no doubt.

"Princess Rasha, what are you wearing? You can't be wearing that to see the prince." It was the princess of the Karmir, her dark red skin decorated with the traditional four white dots down the center of her forehead. She'd left her hair loose, unlike the others, who were in intricate braided styles.

"I-I'm not here for The Choosing," Rasha said, not sure how to respond. "How do you know me?"

"My name is Osika. I'd know you anywhere. I studied

you as a child. We were here together once, you and I. To be honest, I didn't expect you to come."

Another girl, the one from Vol, stood with her arms crossed. "What do you mean you're not here for The Choosing? What else would you be doing here?"

"Your highness," Rasha said with a quick bow. "I have urgent business. Perhaps we can talk more later."

"Of course." Osika stepped aside and the others allowed her to pass by. The whispers about their mysterious arrival died down as they reached the stairs.


"Rasha Jenchat Indari, I knew I'd seen you someplace before," Prince Bashir spoke as they descended the stairs. He'd been waiting for them, it seemed. "I'll meet with you in just a moment. Let me welcome you, Chiza. Your journey was arduous and grueling, I hear. That you made it at all is tribute to your excellent couriers."

"Your Grace, it was nothing, knowing I could fulfill my duty to my nation and my kingdom."

Prince Bashir looked her over and made a sound in the back of his throat. Rasha wasn't sure if it was disapproval or annoyance. "Well, that is interesting. My home is your home now, please explore and make yourself comfortable."

He bowed to Chiza once more before taking Rasha's hand and pulling her away. He walked right out the doors and down to the gardens. The manicured drive they'd glimpsed at the front was mirrored here behind the palace with an identical drive. The hedges were brown, as the cold temperature had killed most of the color here. Rasha imagined there would be flowers everywhere in the warmer months.

"Your attire, Princess, is," he seemed to search for the right word, "odd."

"I'm not here as a Princess, your Grace, I'm here as the courier bringing you the princess from the tenth kingdom. I hoped that you might restore the licenses of my partner and myself. They were revoked over a misunderstanding. Perhaps you've heard of it by now? We received live human cargo on a mandatory fetch and deliver."

"Yes, I see where that could be a problem for your employers."

Rasha waited for the prince to say more. Instead he stopped in between two hedges. Rasha didn't know where they were. She'd been looking at him instead of where they were going. His long white hair and snow-white skin glowed in the soft light passing through the clouds above them.

"So, you would like your licenses and the freedom to just leave?" he asked.

Rasha's heart sank. This is the conversation she'd wanted to avoid her whole life. This was the reason she didn't want to be here during The Choosing. The prince would never understand.

"May I ask why I'm so repulsive that you won't even give me the decency of a trial?"

Rasha didn't want to get into her ideals, but it didn't look like she had a choice.

"Forgive me, your grace, but I don't believe in a system where women are paraded around a palace for several weeks to be chosen, or not. It may sound like treason to you, forgive me, but I want the option to choose. If you are the only male here, what options are there for me?"

Prince Bashir laughed. It was a deep, from his belly laugh, and it lasted so long that Rasha looked around and wondered if they were being watched.

"Oh, Rasha." He wiped a few tears from his eyes and smiled at her. Then he took her hand in his and raised it to his lips. "My thoughts precisely." He kissed her hand but didn't let it go.

Rasha didn't know what to think of this prince. Was he crazy or insightful? Perhaps he thought her mad.

"Many rotations ago, when we were about half the age we are now, you came here to the palace. We played together. I'm not even sure you remember it."

Rasha remembered. They'd picked up sticks and had been dueling when her father discovered them. He'd grabbed her by the back of the neck. Then he marched her out of sight where he whipped her for being seen as less than a princess in front of the king.

"You were the only princess out of the ten I'd begged my father to let stay." Bashir stopped, and, stepping close to her, brushed a wisp of hair from her face. "I adored you. When you arrived today, I didn't notice Chiza because you looked so stunning I couldn't take my eyes off of you."

Rasha turned away from him but she didn't pull her hand away. His admission made her uncomfortable. She didn't feel that way, and it was embarrassing to listen to him.

"I'm making you uncomfortable," he observed. "I see it in your eyes. You don't have those feelings for me. You don't know me."

He let go of her hand at last and continued walking the gardens.

"I've always had a problem with the system myself. Half the girls are in love with some boy or other before they arrive, anyway." He stroked his hairless chin.

"I've given this some thought. What if we invited all the eligible princes and princesses to the palace as a kind of meeting place?"

"It would serve some but not others. What about the prince or princess of the first kingdom? If they don't find a mate, then it's all for nothing."

"Not if done in a more creative way," Prince Bashir's pace quickened. "What if after The Choosing we opened the palace to everyone interested? Anyone who did not find a mate among the princes and princesses could look elsewhere." His hands waved in excitement.

Rasha didn't hide her shock as she raised her eyebrows and looked at the prince. He had thought about this. It surprised her that he'd be so open to the idea.

"It's revolutionary. Not everyone, including the council, will like the change, but you've got my vote." Rasha put out her hand to shake his, and he did. He laughed again and turned back to the palace. The wind whipped at their faces, his alabaster cheeks and ears turning pink.

"I want you to consider staying. I know it's not what you'd planned. However, I'd like to have some lively conversation and someone on my side when I bring this up to the king and queen."

Rasha almost choked on the words, "The king and queen?"

"Yes, my parents aren't open to change. Perhaps the two of us can convince them."

Rasha's thoughts were racing along with his, leaving her feeling disoriented. "Stay here in the palace with the rest of you?"

"Not just us. I'll send out an invitation to the other eligible princes. We'll make The Choosing fun again. I know you've already decided against me but I hope after you get to know me you might reconsider. I'm not so bad." His grey eyes implored her to change her mind.

Rasha's thoughts were on Jak. What would he say if she stayed? They hadn't talked about what they'd do after their delivery was complete and they had their lives back.

"I'll think about it," she said. Then she remembered why she'd come. "Our licenses?"

"Yes, of course, your licenses are already restored." He waved his hand. "I need to see to the other girls now, they're still jealous of each other. Don't let it bother you. I'll reserve a seat for you on my left at dinner." He flashed her a winning smile before he made his way back inside.

Rasha looked down at herself and wondered what she'd wear to dinner.

JAK WAS PACING the floor of the foyer when she found him. Rasha wondered if she should wait to tell him the prince's idea. He seemed agitated. Before she could ask him what was wrong, he held up the small circular disk that she'd placed under the collar of his jacket.

"What's this?" Jak asked.

"Let me explain."

"No, I know what it is. It's you not trusting me. If you wanted to know something why didn't you ask me?"

"That was a long time ago, before we," Rasha didn't need to finish the sentence she lifted his left hand and held it between hers. "I didn't trust you when I put that on your collar. Now, I do. I trust you with my life."

"When?" The guards looked up when he raised his voice. Rasha grabbed him and pulled him into a quiet seating area just off the front entrance.

She lowered her own voice. "The day I found you meeting with some men in the woods. They looked like the ones that were tracking us."

Jak nodded.

"They were. I travelled with them for a time to throw them off your trail. Then I directed them through seven lands so they wouldn't follow me. I explained to them I was going home to the Wilds. They believed me."

"Why were you following us in the first place?"

"The king and queen hired me to ensure princess Chiza's safe arrival. I told you all of this before. With all the tricks that her father had pulled, they didn't believe she'd make it. They were right."

Jak threw the disk down on the marble floor and Rasha stepped on it, rendering it useless. He seemed satisfied. Now wasn't a good time at all to talk about staying at the palace. She'd wait until they were both calmer.

Jak pulled her close, but she wiggled out of his grip.

"What's wrong?"

Rasha shook her head. The last thing she wanted now was to have to explain why she was staying.

"Have you seen Lu?"

"He went to say goodbye to Chiza."

"Oh." Rasha wanted to tell him they might not be leaving, but instead settled on something she thought they'd all enjoy. "We've been invited to stay for dinner."

"That's good, we could all use another good meal before we head out. It looks like a storm is coming," Jak replied.

He had no idea.

## 34

*L*u peeked around the corner and into the room where Chiza sat with the other princesses. She looked miserable. His heart soared at the sight. He'd been willing to go along with this plan, but when he met the prince he wasn't so sure she wouldn't fall for him anyway. He was tall, handsome, and mysterious-looking. What chance did a greenie from Tero-Joro have with a princess when she was promised to a prince like Bashir?

Lu took several steps into the hallway and whistled like the birds in the woods. Chiza had liked that best. It didn't take her more than a few seconds to leap up from her chair, and, ignoring the concerned questions of the other girls, step into the hall. He waved to her from around the corner and she joined him. There was no one here, but it wasn't private. Someone could come their way at any moment. Lu reached out and grabbed Chiza's hands.

"Are you all right, darling?"

"I am, thank you. I will be so miserable without you."

"As will I." He pulled her close and kissed her hard and desperately. "I don't want to leave, but I must."

"I understand. You won't forget about me while you're off having courier adventures with Rash, will you?" Chiza threw her arms around his neck.

"I won't. Even when we're not in communication, I'll be thinking of you every minute." Lu put his arms around her waist and squeezed her tight. He heard someone enter the corridor, and he jumped back and away from her. He gave her one more longing look before he dashed down the hall.

Lu's heart was racing. He'd wanted more time, no, needed more time. Chiza would be all alone here. The other princesses were notorious for jealousy and unladylike behavior during The Choosing. He only wished he could spare her that.

When he reached the lower level, he found Jak and Rasha in the room where they'd cleaned up. Not a room, more like a suite with a separate bedroom and bathroom area. Jak and Rasha sat on high backed upholstered chairs in the seating area. Like most of the other rooms in the palace, it was decorated with luxurious fabrics in deep rich colors. This room's primary color was red, covering the carpeted floors, bed, and draperies. A rug in intricate designs of varying reds covered most of the floor in the entryway.

"Where have you been? You don't want to get Chiza in trouble!"

"I had to see her one more time," Lu said. He hoped his feelings weren't too obvious. Not that it mattered too much. They were his friends. His secret was safe.

"We've been invited to dine with the prince this evening, so make yourself comfortable," Rasha said. There was something playful in her eyes when she said it.

"I'm looking forward to a royal feast. I think we've earned it," Jak remarked. He lifted Rasha's hand to his lips and kissed it. *When had they become so intimate?* Lu wondered. Rasha wouldn't allow anyone to touch her, let alone kiss her in public. He felt jealous of them. Jealous that their love would be open and public in hours and his had to wait the months until The Choosing ended.

"Did you talk to the prince about our licenses?" Lu asked, leaning over her shoulder.

"Yes, he says it's already done," Rasha replied.

"Then I'd rather get going," Lu said.

"What?" Rasha jumped up and rushed over to him. "I thought you'd be thrilled to be seeing Chiza again, what's wrong?" She sat down on the bed while he packed.

"I've said my goodbyes. There's no way I can sit around watching the prince fawn all over her and the others."

"I see," Rasha said. "Well, I've already told the prince I'll be staying. I understand if you feel you have to leave."

Lu dropped his bag. She'd already given her word. He'd wanted them all to leave together, but maybe this was the way it would be now. She had Jak, one of the most well-known trackers and couriers in the ten kingdoms. Why would she need him?

"You all have a nice time. I'll be on my way."

Staying there waiting around made his stomach ache. He couldn't bear it. He finished packing, and the others got ready for dinner. They'd all be gathering in the great hall. Temi whined; he'd been confined to the room all day. Ready to leave, he paced back and forth between Lu and Rasha as if he understood they weren't all going together.

Lu opened the door with his bag in hand and bumped into the prince outside their door.

"Hello," Bashir said. "Are you going somewhere? You're all invited to stay for dinner. I hope the invitation wasn't lost."

"No, I was—" Lu looked around for an answer and found Temi. "I wanted to take Temi hunting."

"Oh, of course. We have food here for him too. I'll have someone bring him some treats after our meal. Your companion?"

"Yes, Jak's coming," Lu took a quick glance behind him at the closed door.

"I'm glad I have the chance to speak with you alone. Lu, is it?"

"Yes, what can I do for you, your majesty?"

"I was hoping you could tell me about your impressions of Chiza."

Temi growled at his feet. Lu silenced him with a hiss between his teeth. Temi sat down, his eyes never leaving the prince.

"Chiza?" Lu's mind raced. What could he say to the prince that wouldn't be an encouragement nor disgrace Chiza?

"Yes, you spent time with her on your journey. What were your impressions of the young lady?"

Lu tried to think of something but nothing came to mind that didn't sound like raving praise from someone in love with her.

"She's a nice person." Lu could kick himself for being so ridiculous.

"Nice?" The prince nodded. "Any indication she's got someone waiting for her at home?"

Lu's face was green. Had he been any other color he'd have gone three shades of red.

"What makes you ask that?"

"Our introduction earlier. It felt cold, as if she were holding back. I've seen it before. It's a sign that the young lady's heart is elsewhere."

Lu's own heart soared at his words. The prince had already noticed that Chiza was in love with someone else. She would not be chosen. She was safe.

"Um, well, I couldn't say for sure, your highness. A woman's heart, who can know its depths?" He remembered that quote from a famous Tero poet.

"True. I see the others are coming. Shall we go to dinner?"

"Well, um, sure," Lu replied as he was swept along.

"I'm afraid your beastie will have to stay, there will be far too much food to tempt him."

Temi half whined and half growled as Lu directed him back to the room.

"Just a little longer, fellow, then we'll be on our way."

"Change your mind?" Rasha asked, walking out of the room with Jak in tow.

"Yes, well, the prince is here."

"He's what?"

"I thought I would escort my guests to the dining hall. You're the only ones here who don't know the way," Bashir said, popping into view. "I thought you were upstairs," he gave her a once over, "getting changed."

"Jak and I had business to discuss. I'm sorry. I'll hurry upstairs and change."

"No time for that now. Dinner will be served in moments. My parents don't like to be kept waiting. Please, follow me." He put out his arm for Rasha.

Rasha seemed flustered, but she took it and let him escort her. As they followed, Lu looked over at Jak. His expression was unreadable.

## 35

The dining hall was filled. There had to be more people there than were staying at the palace. Young men and women were mingling all around the table until the prince arrived. The immaculate table was decorated with flowers, gold-rimmed plates, and above it all, a large chandelier that dominated the room. The girls were all atwitter about Rasha and how she'd chosen to wear her courier clothes. There were even whispers and disapproving looks from the servants. Lu couldn't imagine what her parents would think of this. "If you'll both excuse me," the prince said as he bowed to Lu and Jak. He took Rasha's hand, and he led her away to the end of the table where he sat her down next to him. Chiza was placed on the opposite side of the table from him.

"How are you feeling about dinner now?" Lu asked Jak.

Chiza gave Rasha a strange look as she sat down. Lu watched Chiza from across the room. She'd be sitting directly across from the prince. Something in his stomach churned at the sight. She looked up and met his eyes. There was a longing there. He didn't want to sit through dinner like this.

He didn't have to sit for long. A guard approached him.

"Sir, you need to come with me, there are some strange noises coming from your rooms. The beastie sounds upset."

"I'll see to him right away," Lu said.

"Traitor," Jak said under his breath.

Lu shrugged, but gave Jak a smile, bowed toward the prince, and met Chiza's eyes.

Then he walked as fast as his legs would carry him. When he reached their suite, he heard Temi inside growling and knocking things over.

"What the yahtz?" he wondered aloud as he reached for the door. Temi growled and bolted. He was down the hall and out of sight before Lu could get him back.

"What's gotten into you?" Lu picked up his tracking device. He pulled up the bio-signatures and found Temi's red dot running toward the back of the palace, into a line of other red dots.

"I hope it's not my fault you left so early?" Chiza said from behind him placing a hand on his shoulder.

"No, we have a problem," Lu said looking down at the device.

"Yes, we do," Bashir agreed as he stepped out of the shadows. "Is there something you two need to tell me?"

Chiza's face went slack, and she opened and closed her mouth, unable to find the words.

"Yes, Your Grace. But that can wait. For now, we've got something of a bigger problem. There are intruders entering the castle from the north gate." Lu tilted the device so that the prince could see the evidence for himself.

"Guard!" Bashir yelled directing the men to go to the north gate. The screams coming from the dining hall set the three of them in motion.

RASHA WATCHED Lu leave the table and then Chiza. The prince had seen them too, because soon after Chiza jumped up to follow Lu, Bashir excused himself.

"Bashir, wait," Rasha said.

"This won't take long, I promise." He lifted her hand to his lips and placed a kiss there. The kiss didn't go unnoticed by Jak, who glared at them from the other end of the table. Rasha shook her head, but he looked down and stabbed a piece of meat on his plate. The princess next to Jak took notice of his mood and looked like she was trying to cheer him up. Her red ponytail was high on her head but reached her shoulders, where it bounced in big curls.

Rasha knew she didn't have much time before she'd have to explain to Jak what had happened between her and Bashir in the gardens. The queen sat on the opposite side of the table and smiled at Rasha. She was about to say something to her when the rumbling started. The girls gasped and panicked as the ground shook beneath them.

Rasha couldn't place the sound.... It reminded her of a stampede of tuskins. When the door flew open and they saw what made the sound, it was much worse. A wolf filled the doorway, growling as it entered. The guards did their best to hold him off, but directly behind him was another large beast. This one, a dragon, stomped into the room and devoured the king in two pieces. His wife stood speechless with her husband's blood splattered on her face. She was mauled by a large white bear that stood even taller than the wolf when on two legs. The beasts went after everyone in the room. The bear slashed his claws across Osika's chest, killing her. She fell onto the heap of bodies forming around the table.

Rasha pulled out her swords and leapt across the table, killing the white bear, before she jumped down on the far end of the table with Jak. The beasts were busy devouring everyone in sight. Jak grabbed her hand and managed to slip out the door behind a beast that had a bull's head on a man's body fighting off two guards.

They stumbled out of the doors, covered in blood and panting.

The Prince arrived with Lu and Chiza right behind him. "Run!" Rasha yelled to them She slipped on the blood and was skidding helplessly until Jak grabbed her arm.

"Who is it?" Bashir demanded.

"Not who, what!" Jak shouted. "Beasts of every kind. They killed the princesses and your parents. We fought, but the princesses were defenseless against them."

All of them backed up into the foyer.

"Where are the guards?"

"Most of them are still out patrolling the border. I sent them out moments after I heard about your encounter. They haven't returned," Prince Bashir replied.

"How many beasts are there?" Lu asked.

"Maybe half a dozen. But they're huge and some of them can speak," Rasha said as three beasts entered into the foyer. A birdlike man flew in. Another stomped in, the one with the body of a man but the head of a bull. The third was the largest grey wolf he'd ever seen.

"Where are your friends?" Jak yelled, holding out his long sword, still bloodied from the battle in the dining hall.

"They weren't given the warm welcome they deserved." The bird-man spoke in a high-pitched voice. The feathers on his wings were tipped with talons. The face of the beast was like a man's, but instead of a nose he had a horned beak.

"Well, come and get a real Bolaji welcome," Jak challenged.

"Bolaji is more than your feeble kingdoms and it's time you learned that," the bird-man replied. His talons clicked on the marble floor as he hopped around. Then, with a nod, he signaled the other two beasts.

The wolf got down on all fours and lunged at Jak.

Chiza screamed as the impact hurled Jak backwards. The bull-man came toward Rasha and she had her swords ready. He was slow and a little clumsy, but powerful. One blow had Rasha seeing stars as she landed on her backside. She used her legs to kick his legs out from under him. He hit the floor so hard, it floor cracked under him. He scrambled up, but not before Rasha leapt up, and with one boot landing on his face, knocking him back, away from Chiza and the others.

She sliced the bull-man across the chest with both swords, finishing him. Rasha turned toward the bird-man, but it was too late. He was heading for Chiza and Prince Bashir. Chiza screamed and at the last moment, Lu jumped in front of her, the bird-man's talons ripping across his chest instead of hers. Still in the air with his wings flapping, he took aim again and went after Chiza. Prince Bashir pushed her behind him. But they were against the wall with nowhere to retreat.

"No!" Rasha screamed and she dived for the bird-man.

In the same instant Temi leapt from the ground, onto his back and sank his teeth into its neck. While he writhed, Rasha leaped and sliced his belly open with her swords. They fell to the ground together.

Jak delivered a last stab to the wolf and, still panting, ran to Lu. He was fading fast.

Chiza leaned over him, covered in his blood.

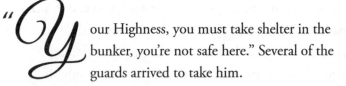"our Highness, you must take shelter in the bunker, you're not safe here." Several of the guards arrived to take him.

"No, wait, she's one of the last surviving princesses," Bashir said.

Lu reached up and gently ran a bloody finger along her cheek.

"I'm sorry, my love," he whispered.

"No, no, don't leave me." Chiza's tears were running down her face.

"I don't want to." Lu choked as blood filled his lungs. "You're the love of my life." He choked and looked at Rasha, an unspoken question in his eyes. His thoughts were with his family and she knew what she had to do.

"Of course I will, I'll look out for all of them," she promised.

Jak reached out and touched Lu's shoulder.

"Rest, my friend. All will be well."

Temi hadn't moved, his head resting on Lu's knees until his last breath. When Lu was gone, he howled with a cry of grief that was heart wrenching. Rasha wanted to scream with anger but she held on tight to it. She'd use it, as she always did.

"How many beasts are left?" she asked the guard.

"Maybe a dozen. They're concentrated on the east gate."

Rasha nodded to Jak, and he stood with her. They'd grieve for Lu later.

"Get her to safety," Jak said to Bashir as he pulled Chiza up from the floor.

Prince Bashir took Chiza's hand and led her away from Lu's body, dragging her along after the guard, through a passageway hidden in the walls. Rasha and Jak went to the east gate. The guards had made some headway and there were fewer than a dozen when they arrived.

There were even more types of beasts here. One that looked like a polar bear already cut in several places that was mauling one of the guards became Rasha's first target. She put her blades in the back of the beast and it let go of its victim. It tried to swing around to get her but couldn't lay paws on her. Finally, the animal collapsed.

Rasha and Jak fought for another two hours, taking down more bull-men, wolves, and bird-men. The last of them, one bird-man and a wolf, retreated before they could get to them. The remaining guards yelled in triumph. Rasha didn't feel triumphant. She dropped to her knees, even her anger spent.

Jak must have seen it because he sheathed his sword and went to her.

"Let's get you some rest."

It was only then that Rasha realized the hour. It had already been dark for some time. She followed Jak back to the castle, and when they entered the foyer Lu's body was still there. Temi was standing over him, growling at the servants who were trying to move him. Rasha moved to catch Temi. He fussed and whined, but the servants were at last able to wrap Lu's body and lift him up.

"Where will you take him?"

"The prince insists that he be given a proper sendoff. He'll be cleaned up and placed on the front lawn with the rest of the guard who perished and burned at dawn."


RASHA RAN the bath and made the water as hot as she could stand. The entire floor was empty now. It had felt like walking through a tomb. There was no laughter, no talking, nothing. She'd gone straight to her room, with Temi following, and locked the door behind her. Temi lay whimpering under the bed.

When the bath water was ready, she climbed in. The water turned dark as she washed the blood from her skin and hair. She let the tears fall as she sat there, wishing she had been a little faster. Maybe there was something more she should have done to save Lu. Her mind wouldn't rest until she'd gone over every possibility.

She emptied the bath and rinsed it. She couldn't stand to look at the blood. Rasha wrapped herself up in a towel instead of looking for something to wear. She climbed into the bed and curled up in a ball, waiting for the grief to stop. She didn't want to, but she'd have to go and tell Lu's family. Temi came to her and rested his head on the edge of the bed. When had he gotten big enough to do that?

Temi sniffed at her and gave her the saddest eyes she'd ever seen, the poor beastie. She'd never imagined he'd outlive Lu. She rubbed a hand over his face and neck. He didn't purr, but he did seem to settle. She closed her eyes and fell asleep with her hand on Temi's face.

Rasha woke to arms around her and warm breath on the back of her neck. Jak was on top of the covers and had wrapped himself around her. He smelled of soap. Rasha just lay for a moment, soaking up his warmth. Taking comfort in having someone's arms around her, protecting her.

She liked Jak, more than she wanted to admit. Maybe he'd consider being her new partner. He was no Lu, but he was good in a fight. She'd seen it firsthand. He'd slain as many beasts as she had and she'd seen how fast he moved with his sword. He'd been graceful and lethal at the same time.

She slipped out of the bed and wrapped herself in the towel again. She couldn't bear to put on her bloodied clothes again, so she went to the closet and found a gown in a beautiful blue she could wear. She changed in the bathroom. When she came out, Jak lay on his back, awake and watching her.

"You look stunning," he said.

She felt her face warm at the compliment. To avoid any more of that, she picked up a hairbrush and handed it to him. She settled herself on the edge of the bed and he sat up to brush her hair. After a while, she pulled it to one side and turned to face him.

"How did you get in here? I'm sure I locked the door."

Jak shrugged. "Locked doors are just an invitation to try harder to get in, because there's something of value inside." He ran a finger down the side of her cheek.

"What are we going to do now?" she asked.

"I've been wondering the same thing. We need to make sure that Bashir and Chiza are secured and then find the council. They must know something about these attacks. Maybe the king and queen knew this was coming."

Rasha nodded. That was sound. She should have thought of Chiza and Bashir. In the confusion, she didn't have time to process what had happened to them. Rasha couldn't imagine the grief Chiza must be feeling. Like it or not, everything they'd thought would happen had changed. Rasha had no idea how much things would change for her until she found the council.

*J*ak and Rasha didn't have to go far to find the council. The guard that showed them the way knocked on the door once and then the doors swung open. Though it was still very early, they were all summoned into the chamber of the council, accompanied by Prince Bashir and Chiza.

"Ah, there they are, Rasha, Jak, welcome. We've been expecting you."

Rasha raised her eyebrows in question.

"We'll explain everything, please join us at the table." The oval table made of marble and stone dominated the room. A member from almost every nation stood around the table.

The Chilalian raised a fist to his chest and bowed to Rasha as she approached. It made her insides squirm as it always did when someone recognized her. She gave the purple man a nod.

"We're honored that you are here with us, Princess Rasha, and that you and your friends were here to protect the kingdom from the beasts of the north."

"The honor is ours," she addressed the red Karmirian councilman as he spoke for the others.

"The group you see here represents what's left of the council and the royals."

"Let's dispense with the pleasantries for now. We have a request to make of you." This came from the man with pale skin and brown hair with grey at the temples. He was from the seventh kingdom, Winaka. "It won't be easy and we ask that you consider our proposal before you give us your answer."

Rasha nodded, though the knots in her stomach doubled.

"You may or may not have heard the king and queen of Adalu perished last night in the dining hall."

"Yes, I remember, I was there." Rasha was growing impatient.

"The servants are busy preparing the dead for a ceremonial cremation," the Karmirian councilman added. He looked to one of the female council, a mermaid. Her multicolored hair and turquoise skin was radiant even in the limited lighting of the chamber.

"Princess Rasha Jenchat Indari, we the council of Adalu, along with the remaining royals ask, no, beg you to consider being our princess incumbent," she said.

"What?" Rasha took a step back from the table and toward the door.

"You would be princess and council member only until the threat against the royal family is ended. No one outside this room knows Prince Bashir and Princess Chiza live."

Rasha's mind was racing. Why her? What about Chiza and Bashir? "I don't understand." She would have taken another step back if Jak hadn't used his body to block her.

"What purpose would that serve?" Jak asked.

"The ten kingdoms are about to go to war with the beasts of the north. We cannot remain united and defeat them without leadership," the councilman from Winaka replied.

"Constancy," the mermaid added. "If the people knew there were no royals, or worse, if the last of the royals were attacked and killed, the people could lose hope. You are both strong and able. We can keep the real prince and princess in hiding during their," she looked over at Chiza and the prince, "grief."

"Both?" Jak asked and stepped forward. "What have I to do with this business? I'm no prince."

"On the contrary. You are," the man from Winaka countered. "You know nothing of your biological father. He is a pure Winakan, once a prince himself. Your mother is also a pure Winakan. She would have been a princess at the time of The Choosing had they needed females. You are as much a prince as any of us."

The council murmured agreement and Rasha looked up at him, seeing him for the first time as royalty. She wanted to laugh when she thought of how her parents had treated him. If they had only known. She couldn't stifle her laughter. They all looked up at her, puzzled.

"I'm sorry, this is ludicrous," Rasha laughed.

"I beg your pardon, your highness," the Chilalian said to her. "On the contrary, this is what the council has debated most of the night. We feel this is the best way to keep the royals safe. You have already sworn a duty to all ten kingdoms as a courier. Is this so different?"

"Somewhat different, yes," Rasha said wiping the tears from her eyes as she got control of the hysterical laughter.

"Perhaps," the mermaid replied, "but will you at least take the time to grieve and return to us with an answer? Your kingdom still needs you. This role may not be what you're used to, but it is a noble one."

The Karmirian raised a hand. "That is all for now. The council is dismissed. I regret, Your Grace, that you and Princess Chiza cannot attend the ceremony for your parents, but our thoughts and prayers are with you and your future bride."

Rasha looked at Chiza, then put her own feelings aside and remembered what she'd been through. She'd lost the love of her life and now was promised to another all in one day. She'd be in hiding until the war with the beasts was over. Her suffering must weigh heavy on her shoulders.

Rasha walked over to Chiza before they disappeared behind the chamber wall.

"I'm so sorry." Rasha placed her hand on Chiza's back but to her surprise, Chiza embraced her. Rasha patted her back gently.

"You're a good friend. I know you'll help us." Chiza sniffled and then was ushered along by Prince Bashir, who nodded to Rasha before turning to go. He hadn't said more than a word to her or anyone else since his parents' death. He seemed resigned to stay with Chiza and hadn't made any more advances in her direction. Maybe it was because of Jak and the roles they were being asked to play.

The dark rings under Bashir's eyes said he wasn't done grieving for his lost family. He and Chiza would have a lot of time together. She hoped it served them well. The kingdom would need them again.

The only question left was what would she do? Would she stay and be a princess alongside Jak? Would Jak even accept it? He was speaking now with one of the council, the Winakan, and it didn't appear that he liked what he was hearing.

"May I speak with you?" The man from the seventh kingdom asked Jak.

"Of course."

"My name is Xeku Ameenu. I believe I have answers to the questions you haven't yet asked."

"My father. You know him?" Jak asked.

"I do."

"He lives?"

"He is alive, yes."

"Can you have him meet me?"

Xeku laughed a little to himself. "Come sit down." He gestured to one of the seating areas that hadn't been destroyed in the fighting. The servants were bustling about trying to set the palace back to right.

"I'm your father, Jak." His eyes rested on Jak's face, waiting for a response.

"I don't understand. How?"

"Your mother and I were young lovers in a time of The Choosing. It was treason to fall for anyone other than the princess. Your mother was captivating. She and I, well, we were inseparable, until my parents sent me north to make myself available for The Choosing."

"But you weren't chosen."

"Correct."

For every answer his father gave, he had a million more questions. He settled on the most important.

"Why didn't you leave, find my mother, and be a part of our lives?"

"I was asked to join the council. It wasn't the same as being chosen by the princess, but still a great and honored duty. I sent word to your mother, but she'd already fled to the Wilds, taking you with her. Your birth was a secret, and she wanted to keep it that way. Perhaps to avoid something like this."

Xeku lifted a hand and gestured to the palace.

"I see."

"I don't think you do, but let's assume so. Now you know the truth of your parentage, will that help you decide to stay and fight with us?"

Jak nodded.

Xeku put a hand on his shoulder.

"Think about it son. It's a huge responsibility. If I'm not mistaken, you already have feelings for Princess Rasha. If that's the case, then you're ready to stand at her side. That's all we can ask of you."

"I need time to think." Jak bolted out of the room.

Rasha gave him a questioning look as he dashed past her. Jak wasn't ready to talk to her about this just yet. His father was alive and a councilman. Xeku had been there the whole time. Jak was a prince of Winaka. A place he didn't know, with family he'd never met. All he could think was that if they knew the truth about him, they would never have asked him to stay.

---

## 39

*J*ak, along with Rasha and the others watched the bodies of almost fifty people burn on the front lawn of the palace. The king and queen, along with the princesses, were in the center, while the soldiers and servants killed were laid out around them. The smell of them burning wouldn't leave him. Jak couldn't eat that day, but he grabbed bread and meat to save for his journey. He slipped them into his pack and flung it over his shoulder.

He walked to Rasha's room and placed his hand on the door, listening. What would he do if she were awake? Would she be able to talk him out of leaving? Best not to find out. His heart already ached at the thought of not seeing her in the morning. The hour was late, and the patrol was out. As Prince Jak Ostari Ameenu, no one questioned his strange movements, but a few gave him sidelong glances.

It didn't matter. He couldn't stay. Not even if he wanted to.

He reached the west wall before he heard someone call out in the Winakan language. He stopped and turned.

It was Xeku.

"Wait," he said.

"For what?" Jak asked.

"You feel like this is the only option, but it isn't."

"What do you know of what I'm feeling?"

"I know what you're feeling. I abandoned my responsibilities once. Don't make the same mistake I did. You'll regret it for the rest of your life." Xeku held out his hands, pleading.

"I don't even know you, don't think you can show up now after eighteen rotations and play the role of my father. You don't know anything about me."

"You're wrong. I know why you're running. I also know you can't marry the princess. Not yet anyway. But that can be resolved." He waved a hand in dismissal.

"How do you know about that?" Jak asked, his eyes narrowing.

"You think I'd have a son and not at least learn something of him? You can fix your problem later. If you leave, you'll break Rasha's heart and her faith in you will be lost."

"You don't know her. She's strong, she'll move on." Jak readjusted his pack on his shoulder.

"Your mother was strong, too."

Jak hesitated. He thought about his mother. She had

been strong once, but she'd never moved on. That meant something. "I can't stay."

"If you leave, you're no better than I was, and you don't deserve her."

Jak walked to the wall and scaled it without looking back. He was on the other side in less than a minute. He hesitated, and then he started out into the woods on foot.

## 40

The next morning Rasha met with the council to give them her decision. She'd struggled all night. Her life as a courier was over, for now, but with the impending war with the beasts of the north it mattered little. She didn't like being the face of Adalu. That's what bothered her. The reluctant princess, they'd called her in the past. How true that turned out to be.

With Jak, she knew she'd be able to do anything. There wouldn't be any beast that could stand in their way and they'd have fun protecting the palace as either couriers or royals. Everything was more fun with him. He'd been distant last night. He'd told her about Xeku being his father and he wasn't sure how to feel about it. She wondered if he were having second thoughts about staying because of him. Jak didn't join her for breakfast or hang out in her room, as he liked to do. He was still overwhelmed from learning he was an actual prince.

She entered the council chambers and found everyone there except for Prince Bashir and Princess Chiza. They'd been taken away to someplace safe. That was for the better. She glanced around the room and realized Jak was also not among them. She looked at Xeku and he shook his head once. Her heart sank and she felt it drop all the way to her boots. He'd gone, without a word to her. He'd just left. She bit back the hurt and anger and focused on herself. Rasha made her decision. With or without him she'd stick to her plan.

The Karmirian councilman, Gungbe, lifted a wooden staff and used it to hit the floor, signaling the beginning of the meeting. She'd learned most of their names and histories last night. If she accepted, she needed to know the council well.

"Have you come to your decision, Princess Rasha?" Gungbe asked.

"I have."

"What say you?"

"I will stand for the ten kingdoms as princess incumbent."

"Hear, hear." There were cheers all around the table and she got an approving smile from Xeku.

"We will begin the ceremony right away. There are many things that you must learn and are now responsible for," said the mermaid, who went by the name Keabasi.

"I have one request," Rasha said, as she held up a hand to stop them from scheduling any more of her time. "I must journey to the Twinlands of Tero-Joro in order to take my friend's things to his family. They are not aware of what has taken place and they should be told face to face."

Rasha gulped, realizing that it was her face that was going to be telling them.

"Understood. We will commence the induction ceremony upon your return then," said Keabasi.

"I'll return within the week."

"The council is dismissed." Gungbe picked up the staff and hit the floor with it.

Rasha walked out of the council chamber trying to hurry to her room, but Xeku caught up to her.

"I'm so sorry, your highness. I did try to talk him out of leaving."

"It's all right. He's a free spirit, and not everyone can fill this role," she said, choking back her feelings.

"He's a lot more like me than I care to admit." Xeku placed a light hand on her shoulder. "Give him some time."

"That's not something we've got a lot of. If he doesn't come forward, then Prince Bashir will have to stand with me. That will complicate matters when it's time for me to step aside and for Chiza to come forward. I know how these things work."

"Actually, no, we can find you another prince. There are several kingdoms with sons of age. Don't worry about that. But it will be hard to be rushed through a Choosing when your heart is already someplace else."

Rasha didn't want to think about her heart at the moment. There were much bigger issues. The savage beasts of the north could overrun the kingdom. They needed not only a princess, but a champion. They couldn't be worried about whether or not their champion was heartbroken.

"I'll be fine. Make the arrangements. I'll return shortly," Rasha said.

"As you wish." Xeku gave a short bow.

RASHA RODE for two days with Temi trailing behind her. He was the size of a large domestic animal and still seemed to be growing into his head and paws. He would dart off into the woods and would return with game for himself to eat when they made camp. She admitted that having the beastie with her felt right. He was a part of her life with Lu, and because he remained it was as if Lu remained. She figured the beastie felt the same.

When they reached Lu's home it was afternoon and heading towards dinner. Their hearth was burning inside. She saw the smoke coming out of the stack of the stone house. The straw roof was well insulated against the bitter winds from the north. Snow hadn't arrived this far south yet, but it was coming. She rode up, and the family trickled out one by one.

Rasha did her best to keep her face neutral but as they scanned around her and saw she was alone, it didn't take long for them to register why she was there. Lu's mother was already weeping before she placed his things in her arms. She clutched them and brought them to her face as she sank to her knees. His father held her up and took her inside. Lu's sister stomped off without a word. A moment later, the sound of things breaking could be heard all the way to the front of the house.

Lu's father returned and invited her in. Their home was a simple dwelling. The loft had belonged to Lu. As she entered and looked up the ladder a shiver passed over her.

"Rest dear friend," she told him silently.

"Thank you for coming, Rasha. Please tell us what happened to our Luduru." Lu's father sat down with his mother and waited.

Rasha cleared her throat. This was the part she wasn't looking forward to recounting. She didn't want to talk about her friend's belly being sliced open by the talons of a bird-man. How he died slowly enough to have last words. It made her stomach churn to think of how painful it must have been. Instead, she focused on Lu's heroism.

"He died saving the life of another. He could do no less or no more with his life. It happened upon completion of our last delivery. We found the kingdom of Adalu under attack by beasts of the north."

Lu's mother smothered a gasp, her large ears twitching with concern.

"They killed the king and queen, the prince, and all the princesses there for The Choosing."

"That's horrendous."

"Yes, a war with the beasts has begun. Lu leapt in front of a friend, saving them but losing his own life in exchange." Rasha let her eyes drop to the floor. She couldn't reveal the identity of Chiza and keep her secret.

Maybe they would assume she was the friend. "You should know his last thoughts were of you."

"He was a loyal and good friend to you," his father said, patting her on the back and wiping a tear from his face. His wife blew her nose in a handkerchief and nodded in agreement.

Rasha had tears of her own falling that she had to wipe away. She didn't have to say any more about it. They'd heard enough. His mother put Lu's things aside and returned to the hearth where she'd been preparing a meal.

"You'll stay the night. Dinner will be ready in just ten more minutes," she said.

"I guess we'll put your beasts in the barn. Does your domestic do well with other domestics?"

"I don't know. Temi belonged to Lu. He's fine with my mount, though. They can share a stall."

Lu's father didn't seem at all surprised by this knowledge and went to attend to the animals. Lu's sister remained in her room. She didn't come out for the meal or anything else. This also didn't surprise her parents. They were familiar with her moods and with something this big it was to be expected.

"She doesn't do well with change," Lu's father said.

"She adored Lu, admired him, more than she's willing to admit," Lu's mother added.

"I'll be off at dawn in the morning. I have much to attend to back in Adalu. Thank you so much for the meal."

"Thank you for coming yourself. I know it must have

been tempting to just send a message link or a messenger," Lu's father said.

"No, I respected Lu, and cared for him. I would never do his family the disservice of sending a message. This was something I had to do as much for myself as for you."

"The loft is yours. Sleep well," he said.

## 41

When Jak returned to the palace, it was as if he'd never left, all signs of the attack gone. The servants had cleared away the damage. It felt as if there'd been no atrocity here. He left his pack in the foyer and continued to the council chambers.

The chamber room and large oval table were empty. The guard let him in and promised to recall the councilmen. They entered one at a time, all noting his presence, including Xeku. He glanced at Jak before joining the rest of the council around the table.

Surprisingly, the Karmirian, Gungbe lifted his staff to begin the meeting. Jak didn't understand why they'd be starting without Rasha.

"Thank you all for joining me in the council chambers today. I'm here to give you my answer. Is the princess not here?"

"No, she is away on urgent business. Please, don't keep

us in suspense. What is your answer," Gungbe asked with his hands raised.

Jak nodded and took a step forward.

"I will stay and fight as Prince Jak Ostari Ameenu alongside Princess Rasha."

The council pounded their staffs on the stone floor in applause.

"Well done, Prince Jak. We welcome you, and are delighted you will be staying with us. There is much you need to learn about life here in the palace and your duties. We will, of course, allow you to rest from your journey and begin your extensive training tomorrow. Xeku, can you see to the other candidates and Prince Bashir?"

Xeku gave him a slow nod.

"Thank you all, this council is adjourned."

The group filed out but Jak remained with hands on the oval table. Xeku approached him.

"The conflict with the beasts against the ten kingdoms is imminent. I'm pleased you returned. Princess Rasha will need you at her side to defeat them."

Jak didn't respond.

"Is the other matter resolved?"

"No, not yet," Jak said through his teeth.

"We'll keep that between us for now then." Xeku lowered his voice and asked, "How's your mother?"

"Let's be clear about something. While I'm here, never ask me about my mother."

His father nodded once. Jak turned on his heel and left the room.

## 42

*R*asha prepared to leave at dawn as she'd said. Lu's mother had eyes red-rimmed from crying and still woke early enough to prepare some bread to take with her.

"You didn't have to." Rasha put a hand on the older woman's hand.

Lu's mother smiled and squeezed her hand in return.

"I want to." She wrapped the food and tucked it into a large handkerchief. She gave it to Rasha, who nodded and accepted the hug that came along with it.

"He didn't sleep. I'm sorry he can't be here to see you off," she'd said of Lu's father.

The night had been difficult for Rasha, too. Lu's old room seemed filled with his energy and smell. His small desk was as he'd left it, mid-project. There were gadgets strewn about in various stages of repair. She found herself half-awake most of the night, her dreams filled with memories of him.

"I understand. I'll collect my beasts and be on my way before the weather gets any colder," Rasha said.

"Safe journey, and don't forget us."

"I never could. Thank you." Rasha turned and walked out to the stables.

Temi yawned as she opened the stall and readied her mount.

"Oh please, you've slept enough. Let's go," he told him. He gave her a lopsided look as if he couldn't comprehend her.

"You understand, let's go."

She didn't make it far from the house when Temi turned and growled. Someone was running after them. They had big ears and big eyes, with long black hair. It was Lu's sister Ladi. Her eyes were as red-rimmed as her mother's.

"What do you want?"

"I'm coming with you." Temi sniffed at her, suspicious. Without taking her eyes off of Rasha she held up a hand for Temi to smell.

"No, you're not." Rasha turned away from her.

"Yes, I am. I'm taking my brother's place at your side. You and I both know it's my fault he took that fetch. He wouldn't let me go with him. Now he's gone and got himself killed."

"Because he knew better than to be dragging you around. You're untrained and unqualified. You can't just make yourself a courier. Besides, I won't be doing any courier assignments myself."

"Whatever my brother would have been responsible for, I'm willing to do. I'm almost as skilled as he was and I have a reputation for getting things that others can't get. You'll need me, I guarantee it."

"I don't need you."

"I'm coming with you," Ladi said she plopped along after her.

"And your parents? Haven't they lost enough? Shouldn't you be trying to figure out a way to help them?"

"This is the most honest job I know. They know I'm coming with you."

Rasha looked back at the house and frowned. The last thing she wanted was a kid running around after her.

"I'm the same age you were when you started as a courier," Ladi said as if reading her mind.

Rasha sighed. She had the same stubborn streak too.

"Where are we going?" Ladi asked when they stopped at a small inn.

"There's something I've got to do."

Ladi was quiet. She seemed torn between fascination and confusion.

Rasha entered the inn and found a table in the middle of the bar. She sat down and waited. Ladi looked around, taking in the dark furnishings and the poor lighting. This time of day people were either taking a late midday or early evening meal. The tables inside were peppered with tradesmen from all corners of the realm.

"Well, if it isn't the purple courier with the big fat secret." Silae sauntered in. "It's too early for drinks, girls."

"Not for the kind of drink we're here for." Rasha looked at Silae, her face serious.

Silae must have taken in Rasha's eyes and face before looking at Ladi and figuring out her relation.

"Oh no, he didn't."

Rasha didn't have to confirm it as her eyes filled again. They did that these days. She was getting used to it.

"Oh, Rash." Silae sat down next to her. "I'm so sorry."

Rasha let Silae take her hand. Then she stood up and went to the bar. She spoke to the barkeep and grabbed a bottle and three short glasses. She brought them to the table where Rasha and Ladi sat. Ladi watched her, eyes wide, as the barmaid poured the glasses for them.

Then Silae let out a cry that made the hairs on Rasha's skin stand straight up. The cry turned into a song about lost friends, lost loves and lost family. Tears streaming down her face, she held her notes and her voice never wavered, through the last heart-wrenching note. The entire bar was enraptured with her beautiful and sad song. Her voice died away and no one spoke for a full minute.

"To Luduru Moren, one of the best of the couriers we know. May your last delivery bring you peace." Rasha's voice was shaky with emotion.

"May your last delivery bring you peace," Silae repeated, the rest of the bar joining in.

Ladi let the tears fall as she watched a bar full of

strangers honor her brother. Then, as one, the entire room lifted their glasses and poured them out on the floor.

THEY WERE RIDING TOGETHER when they reached the palace. Ladi whistled at the sight of the building. Then her eyes landed on the figure on the steps. A man stood there, hair blowing in the wind and a long sword at his side. Both of them climbed down and Temi bounded to Jak and rubbed his head against him in greeting. Jak reached down automatically.

"Not bad," Ladi said. Rasha wasn't sure if she meant the palace or the man.

"Go inside, I have something to do."

Ladi walked past Jak, looking him up and down. "I'm sure you do."

"You're back." Rasha couldn't seem to take her eyes off of him.

"Yes."

"You left without a word."

"I had something that I needed to see to, personally." Jak held out his hands to her.

Rasha wanted to rush into them but held back. No, it wouldn't be that easy. She had learned not to be so free with her heart while he was gone.

"Look, I'm just as nervous about this new role as you are, but I stayed," she said.

"You're right. I'm not so good with the staying part, but for you I could learn to be," Jak said with a wink.

"Not good enough," Rasha said raising her voice an octave. "It's not just about you and me anymore. We've got ten kingdoms to answer to. I need to know you're going to stand with me for them regardless of *this*." Rasha said waving a finger between them.

Jak stepped closer. He wrapped his arms around hers. She struggled, but he forced her to look him in the eye. "I promise I'll stand with you, Rasha, until the end. You're the one they need, but we'll get through this together."

She saw the truth in his eyes when he said it and nodded.

Jak released her so they could start up the stairs. When they reached the doors, he turned to her.

"Oh, and this thing between us," he said, imitating her finger motion. "It might have something to do with this." He leaned down and kissed her until she melted against him. When he peeled himself away from her, he could barely catch his breath.

"We better go inside. We've got a lot to do." She took him by the hand and they walked up the stairs together. Jak pulled her to a stop and looked down at her, his eyebrows furrowed in confusion.

"Okay, but first, who's the green girl?"

"When those you love die, it's only you left to feel the pain."

The words of the councilwoman swirled in Chiza's head. They'd had to drag her down to the safe rooms with the Prince. Bashir had been angry at first as if the sight of her anguish reminded him of his own. He growled to himself instead of bothering to talk to her. Chiza sat in a chair in her room with her arms wrapped around her body, moaning in grief most days.

Chiza never slept without crying. The sight of food made her sick. Too much blood, death, and Lu. They'd thrown her along with Prince Bashir into the underbelly of the Adalu castle. It was to protect them from any more attacks and to rally the people behind Rasha as they prepared for war against the beasts.

It didn't bother her much that her father thought her dead. Rasha and Jak ruined his little scheme. He'd thought

he would somehow save his precious gems by holding
back his daughter from the Choosing. Something she'd
been looking forward to until she met Lu. The act of war
by the beasts of the north ruined the Choosing. Other
than Rasha she was the only princess left. It was no way to
start a bond. If she'd never met Lu, she might not
know the difference. She'd tasted real love and nothing else
would compare. Chiza couldn't imagine ever loving
anyone else. Since there was no one left, it would force
them to marry. That was the law. But she could never love
him. Instead of attempting to know him she spent most of
her days in bed.

They designed the secret compartment of rooms it
seemed for just this kind of event. A bedroom on one end
with a bath joined to a larger sitting area with another
bedroom and bath on the opposite end. The rooms held
minimal decoration, nothing like the rooms above. Ornate
rugs in blue and red covered the floors.

There were no family pictures on the stone walls only
decorative rugs depicting various kingdoms of Bolaji, their
castles, and their landscapes. Her own land of Sidoa, new
to the kingdoms, was not yet featured. It was just as well
as she didn't want the reminder of her home.

When she ventured from her bed she was freezing
cold. The lands to the south were sunny and warm until
the rainy season. Her first winter in Adalu hadn't gone as
planned. She didn't want to imagine enduring another
winter here.

In their evacuation, they had grabbed nothing for

themselves. The guard retrieved their clothing and personal items. But she had nothing from Lu, nothing to remind her of their short time together. He'd loved her, they'd wanted to marry. Had she known he'd die she'd have run off with him instead of going to Adalu. To the garbage with her crooked father's wishes, anyway.

The first few weeks Chiza didn't leave her room. Her large four poster bed had white linens with small blue flowers decorating the quilts. The walls in the bedroom had more landscape paintings of Majiwa, Vol, and Karmir. There were no other personal items on the nightstand or in the closet. These rooms had been unused for many rotations.

Three times a day they sat down at a small table in the sitting room to take their meals. Chiza didn't enjoy eating but knew must. They sat in silence staring at their plates of food with no appetite and no conversation. Bashir seemed no more inclined to talk than she did. He sat stiff as stone staring at his own plate. However, the sound of her rumbling stomach one evening seemed to break him out of his thoughts.

"You should eat something."

His voice was rough with disuse.

Chiza's took a sip of her tea but her stomach rumbled again.

"Please, I insist."

Bashir smirked as he pushed her plate with the edge of his own. It was the closest thing to a smile she'd seen in over a week.

"Come on, if you will I will."

Chiza shook her head.

"Why should I care if you eat? Why do you care if I do?"

Bashir used his spoon to scoop up some of the beti and held it out for her to eat, like a babe. She stared at it trying to keep any interest from her face and holding her stomach to prevent more growls of protest.

It didn't work.

Her stomach roared, and he pushed the spoon toward her face and laughed.

She couldn't resist smiling back before taking a bite. There was nothing wrong with the food. In fact, it was delicious. She picked up a spoon full from her plate and put it to his lips. He took the offered bite with relish. She wanted to laugh but the memory of Lu flashed into her mind and killed her mirth.

The moment passed and they finished their meals in silence. This time she left only a few morsels of food behind.

"I'm so bored. I think it's the worst part of all this," Bashir said. "How can we mourn when there's nothing to do but think about what happened?"

Chiza only nodded in agreement. He put down his spoon and stroked his naked chin.

"I'm thinking we should have books, games, a place to record our thoughts. I know they won't bring us comms but something," he said.

Bashir stood up. He decided they needed entertainment. He called for the guard to send their request to the council. Within an hour the guards brought in a small library of books, and several board and card games. When he caught sight of the digital comms his eyes grew wide. Chiza saw the look and wondered what they'd done wrong.

"Comms?" He asked the guard referring to the digital pages he gave to each of them.

"We've removed The transmission parts, Your Majesty, no one can track you here. There are pre-recorded films and a digital journal," the guard said, trying to determine how best to organize the items on the shelf.

"We'll take it from here. We've got nothing else to do. Thank you," Bashir said giving them a wave of his hand.

Chiza stroked the digital page with wonder. She hadn't considered writing down her thoughts and now, she wanted nothing else. Ignoring the games she input everything she'd been feeling over the last week. By the time she finished, it was dark, and Bashir was preparing for bed. He organized the books and the games in neat rows on the bookcase. Her mood was lighter and she vowed to play a game or two with the prince. She figured they both needed a friend.

Despite the books and games, the months passed in slow monotony. She'd read several of the books and they played one game together after every meal. Sometimes they'd take turns just walking around the rooms for exercise. Bashir even spent some of his morning doing muscle isolations in his room.

Chiza walked in on him one morning. She'd gotten up early to swap out a book from the library. His door was ajar and she saw him hanging from a metal bar, lifting himself into the air. The muscles of his back pale and strong with each movement. When he leaped from the bar and turned he caught her staring at him. Chiza dropped her gaze and returned to her room without a word. It was only on the other side of the door she realized she had forgotten to trade her book for another.

News of the battle outside trickled to them in bits and pieces. In war, there is little good news to convey. Chiza knew Rasha was doing her best and would never quit. It would make her a great leader if she ever chose such a life. Jak, her friend and perhaps more, would be there to protect her until the end. He was like Lu in that way.

Chiza paused at the thought. It was the first time the memory of Lu didn't make her cry. The ache was still inside but her tears seemed to have dried up for now.

As the days passed, Bashir did his best to keep them entertained. Chiza laughed and giggled more and more at his humor. She even shared with him thoughts she used to only put in her journal. It was difficult not to, they did almost everything together. They spent more time in the common room, playing games, watching the same recorded films, or reading side by side.

Often when one character in her story did something she disapproved of she made a sound in her throat. He'd lean in and ask her for more details and agree with her.

When he laughed out loud at something in his book, he'd explain it and they would both laugh at it together.

Then one day he did something that changed everything.

"Chiza have you read this book yet?"

Bashir held up a copy of The Hunter and The Fairy.

"Actually, I have. It's a lovely story though the ending is tragic."

"I thought we might read it together. We can change up the voices and make it our own."

Chiza liked the idea. It seemed far more enjoyable than reading the book straight through by herself. They divided the characters between them. He agreed to be the narrator. They lounged on the two-person chaise to share the book. Bashir sat down and Chiza settled in beside him. She felt his arm come around to hold her while he held up the book in one hand for both of them to read. They laughed over some humorous lines and changed the sound of their voices to give it even more variety. But there was one part of the story she'd forgotten.

Bashir read the narration.

*"The handsome young hunter fought his feelings, but it was no use. He'd fallen in love with the fairy and knew he would do her bidding good or evil."*

His voice dropped, and she saw his head turn to look at her. His gray eyes seemed to pierce her soul. They were a breath apart.

"Your line is next," he said still holding up the book.

Chiza tore her gaze away from his face and stared at

the book. The words blurred together. She couldn't seem to find her place so he repeated the line. Which only made her insides awaken in a flutter. His finger guided her to the missing line, and she swallowed hard before reading the part of the fairy.

*"Dearest hunter, you have given me something more precious than I could have ever imagined. Your heart is more valued than all the magic in all the world. I would gladly give it up to be with you forever."*

She'd forgotten to do the voice she'd chosen for the fairy. Chiza's eyes fell on the next lines. They both read them in silence. Bashir as the narrator seemed unable to speak them.

*The two of them realized they shared a love too big for their war-torn world. They sealed their vow with a kiss. A kiss that changed their worlds for the better.*

Bashir's arm tightened around Chiza and he lowered the book to his lap. He placed his hand on the side of her face. His mouth found hers and her whole world fell apart. His lips light on hers was a sweet kiss full of hope. Chiza couldn't help but think of her first kiss with Lu. In that moment she lost herself. When Bashir's kiss deepened though, there was a hunger, and a need she couldn't answer.

Chiza pulled back and found her voice.

"No."

But his arms still engulfed her. Their legs entangled around each other in the heat of the moment. He rested his forehead against hers his breath fast against her face.

She couldn't say what she needed to say with his arms still warm and welcoming around her. She detangled herself from him and moved to stand beside the seat looking down at him.

"Please, never do that again."

The words choking her as she spoke them. Chiza knew she'd hurt him. She let the tears fall down her face. Would it hurt him any less if he knew she'd caused herself more pain than him? She wasn't sure. Either way, she couldn't stand the broken look in his eyes and ran from the room.

Alone she went over the last days, weeks, months. When had she started to like him? She couldn't remember. It had just happened. Chiza wouldn't betray Lu's memory so soon. Wasn't one young man's sacrifice enough? The war wasn't over. If anything happened to Bashir, Chiza knew she wouldn't survive it.

# THE COURIER'S CONFLICT

## BOOK TWO

1

THERE WOULD BE BLOOD today. That was Rasha's first thought when she woke up to the sound of the battle horn. The beasts of the north had been making her world a living nightmare. She hadn't slept well since the beasts stormed the palace three months ago and slaughtered the princesses from eight of the ten Bolaji kingdoms. The fight at their front doors increased in frequency and intensity as the beasts grew impatient to conquer the ten kingdoms of Bolaji. Rasha threw off the covers and didn't flinch when her feet hit the cold floor.

Temi paced at the door, growling and ready to join the fight. He'd never been allowed on the battlefield before. Her bedroom door was a scratched and defaced testament to the fact he'd been locked inside. She was dressed for battle in minutes, her swords in their sheaths before Jak knocked on the door. She left Temi tethered to the bed and slipped out the room to join Jak.

A servant raced to catch up with them, carrying a tray with hot bazil and biscuits. Rasha refused the offered food, but Jak grabbed a mug and shoved it into her hands before taking his own. The biscuits he slipped into a bag at his waist.

"Thank you, Fisa." He drained his mug and handed it back. "Did you sleep well?"

"I did, Your Highness." She flushed and smiled, delighted he'd noticed her. Rasha wondered how he remembered their names.

"How is your mother? Is she still fighting the cough?" he asked.

"She's much better. The remedy you suggested worked quickly. She sends her regards."

Rasha listened to the exchange with amazement. How did he know so much about everyone? She'd fought side by side with so many whose names she never learned.

She handed her mug off to Fisa, trying with all her might to memorize the girl's name for next time.

"Thank you, Fisa," she said. The girl dropped a curtsy and left with the tray.

"How do you do that?" Rasha asked Jak.

"What?"

"Remember everyone's name and story?"

"I don't know, people tell me about their lives, I remember it."

Rasha huffed.

"What? Fisa and Margaret make your bed every morning. Are you telling me you've never spoken with them, princess?" He emphasized the title with a smirk on his face, teasing her.

Rasha rolled her eyes. They didn't have time for their usual banter. The horns sounded again. The fighters had gathered, awaiting their orders. This duty fell to her as the princess incumbent. Jak, as prince incumbent, had no royal education, and they deferred to him only when Rasha was unavailable. Which didn't bother him.

---

WITH ONE OPENED hand held high, Rasha signaled the soldiers on the northern cliffs to hold. She waited for the beasts to trigger the new electrified grid. With luck, many would fall after the charge was released. Her archers would pick them off as they could. They'd have to fight the rest hand to hand. Most of the beasts had the advantage of strength and size. Some were able to fly. The beasts with the ability to speak made no attempt at negotiations or discussions with the ten kingdoms. Their purpose was clear from the start. Take down the first kingdom of Bolaji, and the rest would fall to them.

Rasha scanned the forest's northern edge, then double-checked the monitor for signs of movement. The fighters on the ridge, many of them raw recruits, would wait for her signal. The ranking officers, the generals and their captains, were another story.

They'd met with the council after the attack on the

palace to discuss their military strategy in the official council chambers.

"Why should we take orders from a child?" The general from Karmir asked the council. "She's never seen battle."

"What does she know of military strategy?" The Vol captain asked.

"She's your princess incumbent and future queen of Bolaji. You will follow her into the depths of Q should she demand it of you." Tobi, the councilman from Chilali said.

"Tobi is right, though the theatrics aren't necessary." Keabasi spoke with the serenity her mermaid race was best known for. "She is our leader, and with this council behind her she will succeed. The same won't be said of any who stand against her."

It had silenced them for a time but remained a sore point for all, especially Rasha. She hadn't been feeling very confident, though she pretended that she'd led hundreds of armies into battle. That was how she coped with their cynicism and doubt.

On the battlefield, Jak took his place on her right. A true friend and confidant, he never faltered when she needed him. He blew hot air on his gloved hands and rubbed them against his legs for warmth.

"They're taking their time," he said. "Guess they're not in a hurry to become barbecue."

The winter snow had arrived in the night and continued to fall. Fighters from the southern kingdoms

suffered; most had never seen snow before. The people of
Adalu rallied on their behalf, making jackets and winter
coverings for any fighter lacking the winter essentials.

Jak was from Winaka, the seventh kingdom. His
people had joined the battle early, once they learned the
truth of Jak's origins. Willing to fight alongside their
newly found prince, they were the first in need of winter
wear and snow preparation.

Jak wore the new title and took on his role with ease.
He didn't like playing incumbent any more than she did,
but he seemed to handle it better. He was gracious and
kind, putting doubts to rest when people saw how well he
handled command. Rasha admired his easy manner and
hoped that she could someday master both his confidence
and his grace.

A group of startled small birds took to the sky from
behind the line of trees and she knew it was time; she
signaled again to the ridge.

A wave of roaring, screeching beasts emerged from the
tree line. The ground in front of the beasts lit up in a grid
of white lights and hit the beasts charging at full speed.
Beasts coming behind them hopped out of the way and
staggered back. Their leaders fell to the ground, twitching
from the shock it delivered. The beasts backed away from
the grid area with wary snorts and nervous growling. Bull-
men drove the animals forward with whips and prods, but
the animals resisted. Bird-men and dragons took to the air,
flying over the grid. Rasha held up a fist, and the archers
behind her shot down as many of the bird-men as they

could. Most of them dodged the arrows and landed only a few feet in front of Rasha and the front line. The charge on the first grid was down already. It lasted only a few minutes. She whistled for the swordsmen to press the attack while they scrambled into formation.

"I need that second charge," she yelled.

"I know, I know, I'm working on it," Ladi said. She turned to the grid control system and began tapping furiously.

"No time. I'm going in." Rasha drew her two short swords and charged the nearest beast, a bull-man. Jak drew his longsword, taking on a large wolf that tried to attack her from behind. Surprised by his attack, the wolf turned to face him. Jak's longsword came down across the face of the wolf and it staggered toward him before falling flat to the ground.

Rasha slashed at the bull-man until he doubled over and she could deliver a blow to the base of the neck. The bull-man fell with a thud, and she used his back as a springboard to leap onto the back of a bear that was mauling a fallen fighter. Her swords made quick work of the beast, and it collapsed. She rolled it over to check on the soldier, but he was already dead, his sightless eyes fixed on the sky.

"Ladi!" Rasha yelled.

"One minute." Ladi picked up the device with both hands and took position near the fighting. "Got it." She said. She pulled out a wooden whistle and blew a signal, loud and long, that carried over the din.

The fighters dropped to the ground at her signal. Without missing a beat, Ladi sent a burst of energy that carried an electric shock out in front of her four feet above ground.

A soldier dressed in the military colors of the eighth kingdom of Vol was fighting on the back of one brown bear when it took an electric shock. It propelled him into the air and the bear across the field. They both landed hard on the ground and Ladi ran to help the soldier. She found him laying with his eyes wide and no heartbeat. The stun for the beasts was far too strong for humanoids, but Ladi came prepared. She administered a lighter secondary charge, which restarted his heart. His eyes blinked and he gasped for breath, clutching her arms.

"You're going to be okay," she said as he looked around. Two of his fellow soldiers had come up behind her and helped the man to his feet.

The rest of the beasts retreated back to the north with the dragons and flying bird-men.

The remaining fighters went to the fallen, searching for any survivors, before they assembled to leave. Rasha was helpless to do anything but watch as the dead were carried away. Jak patted her shoulder. "There's nothing you can do. We should go."

She turned away from the battlefield, her heart heavy with the losses. It was becoming harder and harder to put away the images of all their faces. They came back to visit her in her sleep.

"Anything on long sensors, Ebere?" She asked. Courier

Central had automatically dispatched Ebere to be her new partner after Lu died. When she'd explained to him that she was in the middle of a war, he hadn't returned to Central as she'd expected. He chose to stay and fight with them. Despite his shy manner, Rasha found herself liking him for his bravery and let him stay and fight. They needed the numbers anyway.

"No, nothing, we're all clear," Ebere said, then gathered his gear and followed them.

"What happened to my secondary charge?" Rasha asked him.

"I prepared it, but when I went to set it, the parameters had been changed. My guess is Ladi was experimenting again."

Rasha and Jak stopped and waited for Ladi to catch up. Ebere went on ahead.

"What happened back there?" she asked when Ladi joined her.

"Did you see that? I mean the timing was a little off but the effect was out of this world." She spoke in rapid bursts. "Exactly what I was looking for. Total carnage would be better but we don't want to kill our own people, right? Next time bigger grid, better result. I'm on it."

Jak shook his head, stifling his laughter. Rasha glared at him and turned back to Ladi.

"No, I mean, why did you tamper with the secondary charge Ebere set?"

"It wasn't good enough."

"We've been through this. I don't want you practicing

on the battlefield! We have to be able to rely on our methods. Put your feelings for Ebere aside and focus on what you're supposed to do. Don't risk any more lives," Rasha said.

"I don't have any feelings for Ebere. Uck! Are you serious? He's such a snork."

"He's also within hearing distance," Rasha said and stopped, forcing Ladi to turn to look her in the eye. "He's a trained courier, something you aspire to become. You could learn from him."

Ladi huffed and stormed off without looking back.

Rasha squeezed her eyes closed and pinched the bridge of her nose to fight off the headache she felt coming on. She hated having this conversation with Ladi. It was like pleading to the winter wind for more sun.

Ebere joined them. "I'm sorry, I try to stay out of her way."

His smallish eyes darted in Ladi's direction for a split second.

"No, you did your duty, she didn't. Enough said."

"Go get some rest," Jak said with a pat on the young man's back.

Ebere had been given a room in the palace, a luxury that none of them took for granted. Many of the fighters were forced to depend on the hospitality of people in Adalu who opened their homes to the fighters and their families if they brought any. Others had erected temporary dwellings sturdy enough to protect them against the wind, but no more than a place to sleep.

Rasha and Jak wouldn't get either food or rest until they met with the council. Their first duty was to discuss the outcome of battle, prepare for the next, and then address the ten kingdoms of the week's events. Food was the last thing on her mind as they climbed the marble stairs to the foyer. Jak took her hand and held it in his calloused one.

"You did well today." He used a thumb to clear a smudge of blood from her face. He always seemed to find a reason to touch her these days. Rasha pulled back and out of his reach.

"Leave it. I want them to see what I've been doing all day."

"I know. I didn't get it all." He pulled her back and brushed a light kiss on her forehead. "I'm with you."

Something in her heart eased back towards him. When this was all over, she wondered what their days would be like. If she were being honest, she thought about it far more often then she should.

THEY ENTERED the council chamber together. The council banged their staffs on the floor to herald their arrival.

"Where were my soldiers today? You promised me you would speak to the mermen and get me reinforcements," Rasha said to mermaid councilwoman Keabasi.

The Karmirian councilman Gungbe was a stickler for procedure and banged his staff for order.

"Let the council convene," he said with a pointed look at Rasha.

"I'm sorry, Your Highness," Keabasi said, "I've sent word to the mermen but I haven't heard how many fighters we can expect. It's a difficult time of year to reach them; they don't winter in the northern waters."

"I need those men. We're getting slaughtered out there."

Falasad from the ninth kingdom of Buku said, "Perhaps we need to consider turning over the command to someone who can help us win this battle with the fighters we have,"

"Hold your tongue. You're speaking with the incumbent, or did you forget?" Tobi glared.

Keabasi raised her hands. "Please, gentlemen, the princess can only do so much with the resources she has. We must do what's necessary to help her."

"Yes," Rasha said, "and since none of you are on the front lines fighting, it's up to us to get things done while you're getting your daily massage." She looked directly into Falasad's eyes until he looked away. Then she turned to go.

"You need to rest, Princess. We'll re-convene in the morning," Gungbe said to her departing back.

## 2

FTER THREE MONTHS OF living in the palace, Rasha still hadn't learned how to get up with the sun like everyone else.

The morning after the battle she was awakened by a rapping on the door. She groaned. After a couple of half-hearted attempts, she managed to poke her head out from under the thick blankets. The knocking persisted, and Temi growled in annoyance. Once he'd growled at the sun on her behalf when she wasn't ready to get up.

"Princess. The council has gathered. They're waiting for you." When the door opened a crack, Temi lunged, and it closed with a bang.

Rasha sighed. She yawned and looked at her communicator to check the time. The message light flashed frantically for attention. She ignored it as she had since taking on the role of princess incumbent. She was late—it was close to half past the hour. She figured she might as well skip the whole thing.

The next person who came to the door didn't knock. Rasha's hand went to the knife she kept between the bed and the frame. As the door swung open she threw the knife. It stuck in the door, quivering at head height. She pulled the blankets back up, and Jak strolled in with one eyebrow raised. He pulled out the knife and closed the door behind him. Temi, moved away from the door and did nothing more than rub his head against Jak's leg as he passed. Jak gave him a pat and moved to sit on the edge of her bed.

"Sleeping late, are we?" He clucked his tongue at her and shook his head. "Lousy aim, but I trust you slept." He put the gem-studded gold knife on the table beside her.

Rasha groaned.

"I'm tired."

"I know."

"I'm not even dressed yet."

"You'll want to be. They frown on that kind of thing in the council chambers," Jak said, grinning as he leaned back across her legs, pinning her there.

"Isn't one locked up princess enough?" she asked. She started inching away, keeping the blankets up to her chin.

Rasha slid out a tentative foot and touched the floor. "Oh!" She hurriedly pulled it back under the blanket.

"Come on now, you can't have it both ways. Either you're coming out or I'm coming in there after you."

He pounced on her, trapping her under his weight.

"Get off!" Rasha said. "You need to lay off the dessert tray."

"But the caramels are so good." He nibbled her ear, making her squeal.

Another knock at the door, and Temi growled.

"Coming," Jak singsonged in falsetto.

"That doesn't even sound like me." Rasha gave him a knee to the rib, and he got off of her.

"Thank you, Princess," The voice behind the door replied.

Jak laughed as she rolled her eyes.

"Get out."

"I'll wait in the hall, but if you're not out in five minutes, I'm coming back. And I'll dress you myself if I have to." Jak winked and moved to the door.

"You can try, but you'll be pulling my knife out of a major organ." Rasha flashed him a smile and wriggled her throwing fingers at him.

He closed the door behind him, and she leapt from the bed. Rasha was dressed and ready five minutes later. Jak was leaning against the wall, waiting.

"Oh."

"What?"

"I like when you do that to your hair, it looks good pulled up."

"Whatever that means." She ignored his open appraisal and the flutter of her heart as she walked away.

He'd let his facial hair grow into a patchy beard, and it was strange to see him so changed. She couldn't decide if it suited him. He looked a little wiser and older. She'd be eighteen herself in a couple of months, but she didn't feel like it mattered. When they made her the princess incumbent and pinned their hopes of defeating the beasts and saving the kingdom on her shoulders, girlish pleasures seemed insignificant.

## 3

*L*ADI BOUNCED UP TO meet them on their way to the council chambers.

"Good morning, all," she said, giving Jak a long, slow look. "You're looking handsome this morning."

"Thank you," Rasha said, misunderstanding on purpose. "We're late. Can I help you with something?"

Jak choked back laughter.

"You can," Ladi replied. "Listen, I'm sorry about yesterday. I overstepped."

"Yes, you did. Ebere is a licensed courier, and you're not."

"Yes, I understand."

"Not that he doesn't have room for growth." Rasha stopped and turned to face her. "I'm tired of your jealousy. Put it away, Ladi, or I'll force the issue, and you can go home to your very kind and loving parents."

Ladi bit back whatever it was she was planning to say

and crossed her arms. Rasha and Jak left her standing there and went on to the council chambers.

Jak put his hand on her lower back.

"You've got this," he whispered in her ear.

"I know, but thanks for saying so."

"They're not going to like Temi coming in with us."

Rasha looked down. She hadn't even realized Temi was there. He looked up at her expectantly.

"He's the only one who can detect the beasts. They'll have to get used to him some time." Rasha stormed in, Jak beside her and Temi behind her.

## 4

WHEN RASHA AND JAK arrived, the council was discussing the growing population and the need for more resources. Rasha interrupted and asked the only question that mattered to her.

"Where are my fighters?"

"The call was sent. We await the reply," Keabasi reminded them.

"And in the south? The seventh, eighth, ninth, and tenth?"

Xeku said, "Wanaka has sent more men. They should be there in a day or two."

"How many?"

"Approximately two hundred."

"I want to be informed the minute they arrive."

"Your Highness." Xeku gave her a slight bow.

"Sidoa and Vol promised reinforcements weeks ago. Where are they?"

"They were stranded by weather at the Chilali border, Your Highness."

"How many?"

"Fifty, Your Highness."

"Fifty each? What do they think this is, a schoolyard spat?" She looked pointedly at the councilman from Sidoa.

"No, that's fifty in total. They're small and don't have as many men to call on," Xeku said.

Ummo, the councilman from Sidoa, looked away, embarrassed. He recognized that for the weak excuse it was. Hard feelings and spite were the real reason.

"They are sending beasts by the thousands, and we are still scraping together a few hundred fighters at a time. Is it any wonder we're losing this battle?" Rasha couldn't understand their shortsightedness. They would rather wait for the fight to reach their homelands than to stand with Adalu now.

"What is the latest report from the scouts?" Rasha asked.

"The beasts have pulled back. We expect it will be several days, at least, before they strike again."

From the corner of the room, Temi's booming growl filled the chamber. The councilmen covered their ears.

"The council feels that for now, royals should return to the palace and duties of state that cannot be delegated, such as addressing the realm," Gungbe called over the din.

"We have already discussed this. Jak and I cannot waste time attending balls and waving at crowds. We need to be at the front, defending the kingdom." Rasha was furious.

"Our combined forces will break up into factions. They won't take orders from other kingdoms. They are rallied behind our leadership," Jak said. "And furthermore, we can't make the necessary split-second decisions watching the battle on a screen."

Keabasi banged her staff to get their attention again. "The palace and your realm need to be your priority."

"I'm not staying up here and playing princess while the beasts take down our people." Rasha said, her voice climbing an octave and several decibels.

"The role of incumbent princess is only temporary. You'll be replaced soon enough. For now, you must keep up appearances."

Rasha found the whole thing demeaning.

"Let's be clear about something. This whole thing was your idea. I don't want to be here any more than you want me here. However, since I am here and we all have a job to do, what I need is support from all of the Bolaji kingdoms. I refuse to be a figurehead and stand by watching the kingdom fall to its knees. I'm not going to smile and wave from behind the palace walls, I'm going to fight. Are the rest of you willing to do the same?"

Rasha didn't wait for an answer. She called Temi and stormed out. Jak went after her.

"You handled yourself well in there. You didn't hit anyone this time," Jak said, giving her a poke in the ribs.

"Stop it." She slapped his hand away. "That was an

accident. Sort of like the one you're about to have." She shoved him hard in the shoulder but he barely moved, instead shifting his weight and pulling her in by the waist.

"Hey, come on now. Let's go get in some practice time, put all that mad you're carrying around to good use."

"Princess Rasha, may I have a moment of your time?" Ebere was standing shyly behind her, holding something she didn't recognize.

She was in no mood for another discussion. "Can it wait?"

"This will only take a minute," Ebere said insistently.

"What is it?"

Ebere looked up at her, his brownish-green eyes serious. He was an excellent second. He didn't talk too much, and his large ears were always alert. He could hear things that even Temi didn't catch.

"Remember how you asked me to try and find a way to capture and trace messages between the beasts and our kingdom?"

"Yes, I remember. Have you found something?" Rasha's eyes followed Xeku as he approached his son. They stepped to one side, and their voices were too low to be heard.

"I have, and you're not going to like it."

## 5

"*I* HOPE YOU'RE WELL," Xeku said to his son.

"I'm fine, thanks. I'm actually on my way somewhere. Did you need something?" Jak rolled his shoulders back. He glanced over and saw Ebere leaning in and saying something to Rasha.

Xeku cleared his throat. "There is a problem in the palace."

Jak looked at him quizzically.

"I hesitate to bring it up here, because there are so many ears," Xeku said, watching a servant with a tray passing nearby.

"Bring up what?" Jak asked impatiently.

"I believe the attacks on the Bolaji kingdoms were in fact orchestrated from inside the palace."

"Are you sure?"

"There's no physical evidence. Only after analyzing the battles did it become apparent. Someone from the palace is relaying our every move to them."

Jak didn't respond right away. He was deep in his own thoughts. If someone within the palace was giving their strategies to the beasts, they had to have access to their plans. The only people outside himself and Rasha with access were Ladi, Ebere, the council, and the military leaders. Jak noted Rasha's posture had changed. She looked ready to pounce on someone. She must have felt him looking at her; she looked up and nodded toward the gym. He nodded and turned back to Xeku.

"She still doesn't know? The real reason you left that night?" Xeku asked.

Jak tilted his head and gave Xeku what he hoped was a bored smirk. "I'll tell her in good time. Don't worry about that."

"You shouldn't wait too long. She'll discover the truth on her own, or someone else will tell her. It should come from you."

"Are you speaking from personal experience?".

"In fact, I am. You may not want to hear this, but I regret leaving your mother."

"She doesn't regret your leaving. After having met you, I can't say I'm sorry either. You're a coward." Jak spat out the words.

"I gave up everything to do my duty and serve the ten kingdoms."

"You sit around the palace instead of fighting for what's right. You send a girl to do the work for you. How long have you known there's a spy on the council?" He held up a hand when Xeku started to speak. "Don't worry, we'll take care of it like we always do." Jak spun on his heel and went to catch up with Rasha in the gymnasium.

## 6

"*I*T'S MOST LIKELY SOMEONE on the council," Ebere whispered.

Rasha wanted to punch someone. All of this, everything she'd done, was a sham? She was supposed to be the face of the palace. The incumbent princess and her prince playing heroes, while they plotted against her from the inside the entire time. Her pleas for reinforcements, delayed or even ignored.

Jak stepped into their small circle and said quietly, "I've just heard from my father there might be spy."

"We have proof," Ebere held up his device.

Rasha said, "We should stop discussing our strategy with the council. Shut them out. If they don't have our plans they can't give them to the beasts."

"No." Ebere and Jak replied in unison.

"Why not?" Rasha asked.

Jak nodded to Ebere.

He explained, "If there's a spy on the council we don't want to alert them we're aware of their presence. We'll never catch them that way."

Jak continued, "The more confident they are the easier it will be to catch them. In fact, let them hang themselves with misinformation."

Ebere nodded. He'd been thinking the same thing.

Rasha felt like a fool. She wanted to throw their lies in their faces. How could she trust anyone on the council? She looked up at Jak and asked the question.

"Can we trust any of them?"

"I doubt the traitor would tell us there's a spy, and Xeku is the one that warned us. Although he doesn't have a reputation for being forthright."

"Keep your personal feelings to yourself," Rasha said, rolling her eyes.

"And you don't do the same? A second ago you were ready to disband the council based on Ebere's word." Jak poked at her ribs, but she deflected it with a swat of her hand.

"I'm stating a fact. When it comes to your father you're a little biased."

Jak bit back a response when a servant stopped in front of Rasha and whispered something to her.

"Yahtz!"

The servant didn't wait for a reply. Rasha hung her head and, without a word, followed her.

## 7

"CAN THIS DAY GET any worse?" she muttered.

"What's wrong?" Jak and Ebere were trotting to catch up.

"You two go on ahead to the gymnasium. Ladi should be there. I need to take care of some family business," Rasha said. Temi watched the group split and followed Rasha. He preferred to stay at her side when they were in the palace.

Rasha had been hungry all morning, but the sight of the dining room made her lose her appetite. The princesses being devoured here left a scar on her memory that wouldn't heal. She had nightmares about it still. Of course, the room had been cleaned and painted, but it didn't matter. She could smell the death and carnage clinging to the walls. Temi didn't like it in any more than she did. When she opened the doors, he entered reluctantly and sat down near the door.

"Ah, there she is! Good morning my little princess!" her father said. The King of Chilali was attired as usual in his royal blue cape, wearing his crown. He was seated at the head of the table as if Adalu was his own kingdom. His wife was resplendent, and sat on his left. She stood up and made to embrace her daughter, but stopped short when Temi growled.

Rasha didn't correct him. She was annoyed and didn't care if it showed. They'd come here to the palace far too many times since she'd been named incumbent. Their visits had long since grown tiresome. They were always looking for another tidbit. Something they could take back to Chilali and spread as palace-insider news. Rasha couldn't contain her embarrassment at her parents, transparent pursuit of prominence.

"Sit down with us, darling." Her mother gestured to the seat next to hers. "You look so pale, I'm sure you haven't eaten."

Rasha looked down at the spread of delicacies and had to swallow the bile that rose in her throat. She couldn't understand how no one else could smell the blood spilled in this room. But she did as her mother bade her and sat. Her father continued beaming at her.

"This place suits you more than I could have ever imagined," her father said, looking her over and nodding.

"You know I never intended to come here, so let's not pretend this was something I wanted to do."

"The Universal has blessed you. Accept it for what it is

and enjoy it," he advised in the tone you would use to speak to a child.

"I'm sorry, but the slaughter of eleven people to raise me to princess incumbent isn't a blessing from the Universal. I stepped in because I was needed. Nothing more." Rasha started to rise, but her mother stopped her with a gentle hand.

"Where's your young prince? It's not often we see you without him," Her mother asked, trying to change the subject.

"Mother, please, don't. We've already discussed this."

"I can't want the best for my child? Tell her, dear," she said and looked expectantly at her husband.

"Your mother and I believe it's in your best interest to come home. Our army can protect you," He took a bite and, with his mouth full, continued, "and your friends, of course."

Rasha's jaw dropped. Then, as an enticement, her mother added, "We have all the best courtiers, you know. And the finest fabrics. We can make you something new, to your liking. It doesn't have to be a dress."

Rasha shook her head with disbelief.

"You expect me to leave the front, in the middle of a war, and hide under the bed?" She asked. "What would even make you think I'd consider it?"

"You're the princess incumbent. You need to be protected for the sake of the people. You can't do that playing solider at the front," her father said with finality.

"Playing?" Rasha felt her face getting warm.

Her mother must have sensed the danger, because she rushed in to correct her husband's mistake. "What your father means to say is that this war should by fought by soldiers, not princesses. You have diplomatic duties to attend to."

"Diplomatic duties? Don't forget, it's the soldiers that keep you safe in your precious castle. Please show a little respect for those laying down their lives for you." Rasha stood up. "Let me remind you of something. The reason you still have an 'army' is because you haven't sent many men to the front. I am disgraced not because I fight, but because my own kingdom won't help me end this war."

Rasha stood up quickly. "If you'll excuse me, I have diplomatic duties to attend to." Her father sputtered, and her mother's mouth opened and closed like a fish.

She stalked out of the dining room, and Temi followed her, looking smug.

WHEN RASHA REACHED THE GYMNASIUM, she found her team practicing with weapons. Ebere was watching intently as Jak instructed Ladi in the longsword. The tip of the blade dragged on the ground as she as she tried to get familiar with it. Once she had a firm grip, she was able parry as he moved to attack. Jak had a beautiful grace that always caught her eye. It was for that reason she didn't notice the other person there watching them. Her Aunt Sochi was waiting for her. A welcome sight after dealing with her parents.

"Aunt Sochi!" she exclaimed. They embraced and her aunt took her aside.

"When your parents decided to visit, I thought you might need a little extra support, so I came along. I hope you don't mind."

"No, of course not. You're always welcome here." Rasha smiled.

"I can tell that something's bothering you. What is it?" Sochi asked.

"I'm just a bit rattled."

"You've always allowed them to affect you like that. Tell me, what else has you so upset?" Her aunt took her hand.

"Other than insulting me, just the usual. Why aren't I married? I should give up playing soldier and come home where they can protect me and show me off to all of their friends at their royal parties and functions. Suitably dressed, of course."

Her aunt sighed. "Rasha, listen. You're a smart and strong young woman." She turned Rasha toward her and looked straight into her eyes. "The best defense against that is to continue to be the person you are. They'll come to accept it."

Rasha nodded, feeling herself lift a little at her aunt's words.

Sochi reached for a longsword and grinned wickedly.

"Now, let's see if life in the palace has made you a soft little princess."

---

## 8

*L*ADI LOVED THAT JAK didn't take his eyes off of her when they fought. It was the best thing about sparring with him. His eyes stared a challenge into hers, daring her to flinch when Rasha arrived. Ladi didn't flinch. That wasn't her style. Flirting with someone who wasn't interested in her wasn't her style either, but her fascination and attraction for Jak grew anyway. When he held his sword at her throat, just inches from killing her, she dropped her own sword in defeat.

"No, don't give up. You haven't lost, you just don't know how to get out of it yet."

He pulled his sword back and put a hand on her shoulder, giving it a friendly slap. "Right, now, you come at me the same way and put the sword to my neck, and I'll show you what I mean." He dropped to one knee and let go of his sword.

IF SHE WERE BEING HONEST, she'd have to admit she loved when he touched her to demonstrate something to her. She often pretended to be more exhausted than she really was, or that she didn't get something in order to get him to do just that. Why couldn't Rasha see how amazing he was? If Rasha were smart, she'd snatch him up and make it public. That's what she would do if she had those stormy blue eyes of his looking at her every day the way he looked at Rasha. She didn't even mind the beard he was trying to grow.

Ladi's arm trembled as she held the sword to Jak's neck. He turned his head to one side, as if she had him. The he swiftly leaned back, bending a bit, and picked up his sword. With a practiced twist, his sword knocked hers away. It gave him enough room to get up from the floor and face her again.

"See what I did there?" he asked.

Ladi nodded.

"Now you." Jak put Ladi in the same weakened position he'd been in and waited for her to try the technique. He heard Rasha and glanced up. She was speaking loud enough for them all to catch her frustration with her parents. Ladi waited a beat for him to return his attention to his task. When he didn't, she used his move against him, and he stumbled back with genuine surprise as she rose to her feet.

"Yes, good. Just like that," he said.

Ladi needed the training. She knew it could save her life. And before Ebere came along, she'd come up with some excellent tactics for tracking the beasts of the north and their movement toward the first kingdom. The fighting part was necessary because Jak and Rasha weren't always there to defend her when things got intense.

"Ebere, come here. I want you to take over for me," Jak said over his shoulder.

Ladi groaned. For all of her love of training and learning technique with Jak, she hated being paired up with Ebere. He hardly ever said anything. When he did, he insulted her.

"She's exhausted, and it's not even a fair fight," Ebere said.

Ladi raised her longsword and clenched her jaw. "I'm not too tired to take you on."

"Your sword could slip through your hands and slice off your foot."

Those were the kinds of things that irritated her.

"I'm not worried about my feet. You worry about your own," she said and pointed her sword at them.

He looked down, and she lunged at him. Jak smiled at her distraction tactic. He nodded as if to say, 'well done,' before he turned to watch Rasha parry with her aunt.

Ladi, watching Jak, almost missed Ebere's return and had to jump back, swinging her sword. Ebere pressed the attack until he had her backed against a wall. She ducked and, with a spin, had him on the defensive. His next thrust was wide, and she nicked his arm. He pushed her back with his forearm and swept her feet out from under her, and the fall knocked the sword from her hand. Ebere didn't stop. He straddled her chest, trapping her arms, and held his sword to her neck.

"Get off," Ladi yelled.

"Maybe next time, when you're not so tired," Ebere said calmly.

He stood up and went to hang up his sword. Ladi stayed on her back a few moments longer, catching her breath. He was such a fangledort.

## 9

*A*FTER PRACTICE, RASHA GATHERED her team to explain the situation. She trusted them much more than the council.

"In spite of my repeated requests to the council, it doesn't look like we're getting the help we need. I pushed my parents to send more from Chilali, and we've asked the mermen send more. Both have been slow about providing fighters. I'll be honest, it still won't be enough. There's one place, however, we haven't tried."

"I thought we'd contacted Chiza's father," Jak said.

"Not the tenth kingdom. I'm talking about the Wilds."

Ebere remained silent, as was his way. Ladi looked to Jak. It was Jak whose expression changed. He laughed.

"They'll never join us in this fight," he said.

"Why shouldn't they? Aren't their lands in just as

much danger as ours? There's much more for them
to lose."

"I can promise you they won't join us. It doesn't matter
to them how many royals are lost."

"I want to send messengers to the Wilds. My hope is
to gain their support. I can't follow your gut this time, Jak.
We need help from the Wilds to win this thing. We are
badly outnumbered by the beasts. This is the only way.
Unless you can give us a better idea."

"I'm not disagreeing with you to be obstinate. I grew up
there. They're not likely to let your messengers live, much
less listen to them," Jak said. "The wilds are lawless, Rasha."

"What could I offer them to get them to listen?" Rasha
asked.

"I don't think it matters. Joining the kingdoms of
Bolaji is the last thing they'll agree to."

"They wouldn't have to. We'd be working together as
allies on this. I wouldn't demand they take the oath and
become a kingdom or anything." Rasha said.

"Maybe you should," Aunt Sochi said.

"What? No, bad idea," Jak said.

Aunt Sochi replied, "The Wilds are independent
because they don't believe they'd be happy living under our
rule. But you should understand that people want to live
in peace. We don't threaten their freedom, and together we
can end the threat to both of our homes."

"Yes, exactly," Rasha exclaimed. "Then if they choose
to, they could be recognized as the eleventh kingdom."

Jak shook his head.

"You don't understand. They won't agree to help, no matter what you're offering. They don't trust the ten kingdoms."

"There was a time when there were no kingdoms at all, just feuding tribes that feared each other. That changed because of some innovative young people who saw that coming together, the inclusion of all people, would make their lives better. They created the First kingdom and named it Adalu. A new nation made up of many nations. Who's saying the same thing won't be true in this case?" Aunt Sochi said.

"An autonomous nation under the banner of the first kingdom. It's not unheard of." Rasha said.

"How do I make you understand? They don't want you, and they won't help you. They've spent centuries ignoring, avoiding, or robbing the ten kingdoms," Jak said.

"It might work," Ebere disagreed. "We should do some scouting. If we find something they want, we can offer it to them. Make them our ally, based on mutual benefits."

Jak was shaking his head.

"We should look at other options first," Ladi offered. "Jak's right, you can't force the Wilds into civilization."

Rasha bit back a retort. Ladi always sided with Jak. She tried to remember that the girl was just fifteen and had a lot to learn about boys and life. No wonder her family had such a hard time keeping her in line. It was times like this when she wished Lu were there to roll his eyes with her. She pushed the nostalgia away.

"I appreciate all of your input. I considered all of these points before I sent the messengers. They left a week ago. I expect to hear from them today or tomorrow. That information doesn't leave this room. There's still a spy, and we need to move with caution."

"What?" Jak said with disbelief. "You contacted them without consulting me?"

Ebere inched away from the circle. Ladi followed his lead.

"Headstrong girl," Aunt Sochi said in Chilalian, shaking her head. She stood up and found her way to the door with Ebere and Ladi on her heels.

"How could you?" he asked angrily.

"I did it for the sake of our kingdom. We need fighters, and there are none in the kingdom even half as good as you. So, I figured why not go right to the source?"

Jak pinched the bridge of his nose.

"I'm not upset you had the idea, or that you acted on it. I'm just wondering what I'm doing here. I'm just here to keep up appearances?"

"No, of course not." Rasha said. She realized her mistake. She'd been thinking he would disagree with her. Instead of facing him she'd gone behind his back and informed him after she'd already acted.

"Not only did you do this behind my back, you waited an entire week to tell me." Jak stormed to the and almost collided with a guard hurrying in with two others behind him.

"Your Highness," the guard panted, "the messengers have arrived from the Wilds." He flapped a hand at them.

Jak turned away, but one of the messengers called him back.

"Wait, Your Grace, this concerns you too."

## 10

*J*AK TURNED BACK TO listen, but didn't join Rasha. She hurried closer, anxiety and anticipation making her stomach clench. She willed herself not to look at Jak.

Both of the messengers seemed out of breath and tired from riding hard.

"Bring them water, now," she told the guard.

"I'm sorry Your Highness, we bring you bad news," the Karmirian messenger said. The other had light green skin and small ears, which suggested he was something other than Tero-Joro. "We waited for days and tried everything we could think of to get an audience. They refused to even see us."

Rasha nodded and patted his shoulder. "It's all right. I suspected they might not listen to us. You've done well." The water arrived a moment later, and they drank thirstily.

The other messenger turned to Jak.

"Your Grace," he said. "We also bring news of your mother. She is unwell. She's begging your speedy return."

Jak grabbed the messenger, demanding, "What ails her?"

"They don't know, but it seems her recovery is unlikely."

"Thank you," Jak said, releasing the man's shoulders.

Jak turned to Rasha, his eyes pleading.

"You should go," she said gently.

"I can't leave you here to face the beasts alone."

Rasha shook her head and tried to give him a reassuring smile. "I won't be alone. She's your mother. She needs you."

"I wish—" he began, but Rasha held up a hand, then laid it gently on his arm.

"Don't. Just go. I'll be here when you return."

Jak nodded "Perhaps you can spare Ebere?"

"Of course. He may be of help to you. The knowledge of healing among the Tero-Joro is legendary."

Rasha was reeling at the news. Why now? Why him? Rasha needed and wanted him, but she wouldn't even consider letting him stay. He couldn't know she was lost without him. It wouldn't help him to take care of his mother, and she needed him more. She opened her mouth to speak, but no sound came out. Something in his face changed. He came back, and, without a word, kissed her senseless.

Did she moan, or was that him? She couldn't be sure. She could feel the warmth of his chest on her palms as his arms were wrapped around her. His mouth was hungry and hot, demanding a response from hers, and she gave with the same desperation. Jak pulled back, gasping for breath. Not ready to let go, he rested his forehead against hers. When he released her, she felt the cold his absence brought.

"I hate this," he whispered.

"Me too."

And with that, he was gone. Rasha was left staring at the door.

The Karmirian messenger cleared his throat. Rasha was startled to find she'd forgotten the messengers were still in the room.

"Can we be of more help to you, Your Highness?"

"No, you can go." She waved a hand at them. "Wait! His mother, what's she like?"

They looked at each other and both shrugged. "Strong," they said in unison.


When the fighters from the south arrived shortly after, the council gathered again and sent for Rasha. She felt like she spent more time in council meetings than she did fighting the beasts.

"How many?" she asked.

The guard cleared his throat.

"Out with it," she said with a hint of impatience.

"Fifty."

"Fifty in total?"

"Yes," he said.

Rasha wanted to scream. How was she supposed to win a war for them when none of the kingdoms would send enough fighters? She said as much to the council, but they had no good answers.

"We can send for more," Tobi, the Chilalian councilman offered.

"No, begging for more hasn't worked. I'm quite sure they'd see the need if the battle was on their borders instead of on ours," Rasha said.

Mindful that there was a traitor among them, Rasha watched all of their faces carefully, looking for any reactions that seemed suspect.

"The mermen are sending us more fighters," Keabasi said.

"When?" Rasha asked.

"They'll arrive within the week."

"How many?"

"At least two hundred."

"That's better. I just hope it's enough. We have no idea how much time we have before the next attack."

"Well, if the past is an indication, we can expect the next attack to come within the next few days. And there are more of them every time," Gungbe from Karmir said. "I don't want to be an alarmist, but they will outnumber us very soon. Our borders could be lost. We must consider moving the prince and the princess."

"I already have a plan for that. Let me worry about it," Rasha changed the subject quickly. She wasn't going to tell her plans to a corrupted council. There was an almost imperceptible nod from Xeku. He approved of her cautious answer.

"One thing we must do is the organize the chain of command. There's been debate about how to allocate our men and women in battle. The fighters are reluctant to take orders from an officer that isn't theirs. If they fall, the soldiers lose confidence or don't understand any of the other leaders well enough to be effective," Tobi said.

"I'll work on that with the captains and leaders myself. Schedule a meeting with them in the morning to discuss it further. Tell them to meet me at the east field."

"Would you like me to represent the council at your meeting, Your Highness?" Keabasi asked. That was strange; she'd never showed any interest in tactics and strategy before. She noted it, and Keabasi went higher on her mental list of potential suspects.

"No, I will represent both the royalty and the council in this matter," Rasha said firmly, meeting everyone's eyes. She waited for someone to object. They remained silent. With a nod, she dismissed the council and left the room.

"Is Jak unwell?" Gunge asked.

Rasha caught Xeku's eye as she said, "Jak is on his way to the Wilds. His mother is ill."

It was as Rasha suspected. Xeku didn't know. His shock was genuine, she was sure.

"Oh dear. I didn't know. If you'll excuse me, Your Highness. I must speak with him before he goes."

Rasha nodded, then headed for the palace herself. The

idea of getting a glimpse of Jak before he left filled her stomach with agitated, sharp-beaked pikos. His kiss had left her bewildered. She'd had no time to process it before the council had gathered. These feelings she had about him were too new and not wholly welcome.

## 11

*J*AK SADDLED HIS TUSKIN and brushed off the dust of the beast before leading him out of the stables. His pack was slung over his shoulder. Ebere was right behind him, leading his own tuskin.

"Ready?" Ebere asked.

They both noticed Xeku standing on the path.

"I need a minute," Jak said.

Xeku stood in front of his mount, stroking his nose.

"Your mother is unwell," Xeku said. It wasn't a question, and he didn't expect an answer.

"I'll be back as soon as I can. Rasha will be on her own with the spy while I'm away."

"She'll be looked after. No harm will come to her."

"She's not ready to accept it yet, but I'm in love with her."

"Then you must tell her the truth."

Jak shook his head. "I can't tell her now, not like this. It will keep until I return."

Xeku nodded, but not in agreement.

"You believe she'll be less likely to run you through with her swords the longer you keep your secret?"

"No, it's just that it won't make that much of a difference."

"I thought the same once about your mother. It didn't go well."

Jak remained silent at first, looking down at his pack. "I'm not you," he said, his voice even.

"I never married because my heart always belonged to your mother. It still does. Don't let this one lie divide you for a lifetime. You deserve to be happy together."

Jak rolled his shoulders as if he were shaking off the guilt he felt.

"I have to go."

"Of course." Xeku stepped back, allowing him to lead his tuskin away.

Xeku said something to him in Winakan.

Jak stopped, and without looking back, nodded.

Ebere was already on his mount, waiting.

"What's wrong?"

"It's just something Xeku said."

"What?"

Jak didn't answer. Instead, he urged his tuskin forward. As they passed the palace, he looked back and saw Rasha standing there, with Ladi at her side. She was the most beautiful creature he'd ever seen. Her hair whipped around her face in the wind as she watched him leave. She didn't smile or blow him a kiss. She raised a fist to her heart and bowed her head slightly in his direction. He did the same. It was the closest thing to a declaration of her feelings that she'd allow. It warmed his soul as they put the wind to their backs and traveled southeast to the Wilds.

Jak couldn't imagine anyone more different from Lu than Ebere. The guy could go hours without speaking. Jak didn't love being alone with his thoughts, but he liked even less holding up all the conversation. He rode without speaking, letting his thoughts wander.

"Do you wish that Rasha had come with us?" Ebere asked over their campfire that evening.

"I do. I'd rather have her with me than not in almost any circumstance."

Ebere nodded.

"She's needed at the palace or I would have asked her to come."

Ebere agreed with his silence.

"I've been wondering though, when are you going to tell Ladi that you can't stand being away from her?" Jak asked.

"What?" Ebere turned greener, if that was possible.

"A heart in love beats to the same rhythm as a heart in love," Jak quoted the proverb.

Ebere didn't reply. They were lying down for the night

before when he said, "Were you in love with the girl you married?"

Jak had been ready for sleep to take him, but Ebere's question was such a surprise, he sat up and stared at him.

Ebere's voice didn't change as he continued, "I found out, and so could Ladi. She's young, but she's smart and motivated. She wouldn't hesitate to tell Rasha."

The two girls fought like two slithering stolkens in a basket, but Ladi would never keep a secret like this from Rasha.

"I know." Jak lay back down with his hands behind his head.

"You never answered my question."

"There was once a young boy who thought the prettiest girl in the world lived on the nearest ranch. She was older and knew so much of the world he thought he would be a fool not to marry the beautiful and smart girl. His feelings burned like a fire that couldn't be quelled. Their parents warned them of the trap of first loves. They decided, to the grave with their parents for not seeing how perfect they were for each other. So they married in secret."

Jak stopped speaking, and Ebere sat up to see if he'd fallen asleep in the middle of the story.

"Then what happened?"

"The young boy learned of the world outside his own backyard, and before long the burning fire he'd once felt for the girl died out."

"Is it the same with Rasha? The burning I mean."
Ebere asked, leaning on one elbow.

"No, with Rash, it's like the molten core of our planet.
Ever present and constant."

"How do you think she'll take it?"

He meant Jak's wife.

"I'm not sure. But she'll hear it from me, when the
time comes."

"Why? Do you think she's likely to take it better
coming from you?"

"No."

## 12

RASHA LEFT THE BATH of the royal suite still wet, wrapped in a long, soft white robe. She was brushing at her wet hair and stopped short when she saw Ladi lying on her bed. Temi was trying to get her attention. Rasha shooed Temi away from the bed and sat down facing Ladi. There was only one reason she'd come here: she wanted to talk about something privately. The guards were outside the door, but the room was large enough to have a conversation without being overheard.

It was the safest room in the palace, as Temi would dispose of anyone entering the room without her, and she kept the room locked when she left. Temi had a strong nose, and he hadn't reacted to anything in the room so far. Rasha had learned long ago, if all else failed, Temi had the amazing ability to sniff out the danger in any room.

Ladi hadn't changed into her nightclothes yet, choosing to keep her boots on as she lay on top the bed.

Rasha glared at the boots, and Ladi hastily swung them off of the bed.

"I have an idea," Ladi said without preamble. "It's about the spy here in the palace with us."

"Yes, I've been concerned about that too. I'm watching the council for any changes in their behavior, but it's difficult. People react differently during a war than they would normally, anyway." She thought of Keabasi and hoped she was wrong about the mermaid councilwoman.

"Yes, but there's one thing a traitor can't resist," Ladi said, leaning forward.

"What?"

"New information. Anything they can feed their allies. It has to be something big. Something that will propel them into action. We'll try to catch them passing information to the beasts. We know they're using some kind of covert communications. Something we can't track."

"What could they be using that we can't detect?" Rasha asked.

"I don't know. But it's worth a try."

Rasha nodded.

"Put it into action. I meet with the captains tomorrow morning. Let's lead them where we want them to go, instead of letting them surprise us."

"Agreed," Ladi said, but she didn't get up to leave.

"Is there something else?"

"Yes, it's about Jak."

Rasha wanted to roll her eyes, but she tried to keep her face neutral. Ladi looked down at her lap.

"What about him?" Rasha asked, her patience waning as she waited.

Ladi took in a deep breath and sighed, then looked at Rasha's face.

"He's married."

## 13

"*H*OW COULD YOU, JAK? I thought I was special, I thought we might be something." Rasha asked. She felt the rage building inside of her. An uncontrollable rolling in her stomach that made the room spin. He stood with his palms up, pleading with her.

"Try to understand, I was young, I was foolish. She means nothing to me now," Jak was trying to explain to her, he reached out to touch her arm but she pulled away from him.

A woman, not unlike Silae, entered the room. She had a wide smile on her face and belly heavy with child. The woman eyed her smugly.

Rasha turned back to Jak, who was staring as if he didn't recognize her. His mouth was open and his head was bobbing as he searched for something to say.

"I've heard enough."

Jak reached for her again. This time he put both hands on her shoulders, forcing her to look at him.

"I don't love her anymore, I haven't for a long time! I love you."

Rasha knocked his hands away and reached for her swords. With a cry, she lunged at him. The sword in her right hand, Cutter, plunged into his stomach. She let go of the sword. He stared down at it in disbelief.

"No, no." Rasha was crying and shaking her head. She hadn't meant to stab him. She'd only been angry and hurt.

"Murderer! You killed him!"

The woman that looked like Silae screeched and took an unsteady step toward Jak. She had Blade in her hand and she walked with purpose, toward Rasha. "You'll pay for taking him away from me."

She swung the sword across Rasha's neck. Shocked, Rasha tried to hold the wound together, but it was too late. The warm blood poured through her fingers, and she fell to her knees next to Jak's body.

"Your Highness!" Someone was shaking her awake. She woke with a start, eyes wide, until she realized she was looking at the maid. There was another behind her. Temi had his large paws on the bed staring at her face.

"Are you all right? You were screaming in your sleep." It was Fisa.

Rasha looked down into her purple hands. There was no blood anywhere. She'd been dreaming. The bed coverings had shifted to the floor, and she'd perspired through her nightgown. It was sticking to her. Fisa dashed into the bathroom to get her a cold cloth.

"Here, lie back and put this on your forehead. You've got the fever."

The other maid was putting the bed back to right. She arranged the sheets and blankets so that they covered Rasha to the waist.

"I'm fine, really."

"You're not well. You should rest today." The older servant—her name was something strange like Margaret—was looking at her with sympathy.

"I can't," Rasha said. She threw back the covers and climbed out of bed with shaky legs.

"Are you sure, Your Highness? Fisa said.

"I'm sure. Thank you, Fisa. I'll dress, and then the room is yours." She hoped she wouldn't fall to the floor and curl up into a ball. Not in front of the maids, anyway.

With the bathroom door closed safely behind her, she allowed herself to shudder.

She'd dreamed she killed Jak and been killed in turn by his wife. His wife. What excuse would he give for not mentioning it? Is that why he'd run off in the night after they'd asked him to become the prince incumbent? His strange behavior made sense now. Had he dissolved the marriage? No. If he had, Ladi would have found that out, too.

Ladi didn't seem happy to tell her the news, but Rasha wondered if the she might be gloating inside. Her infatuation with Jak was obvious, and her constant attempts to flirt with him exasperated Rasha. In her childish way, she'd been testing the strength of Jak's feelings for Rasha, but none of it mattered now.

Why couldn't things ever be simple? She'd had a job to do: collect a package take it to Adalu. It turned out that the package was a princess. That had been almost a rotation ago. With the real prince and princess in hiding, she and Jak had stepped in to help preserve the kingdom. Except Jak, her prince incumbent, was already married to another woman. If it became known, he would be ousted. No prince of Adalu had a wife and a betrothed. Not that Rasha had intended to marry Jak, she hastened to assure herself. Once this war was over, she planned to go back to her real life. Possibly a life without Jak.

RASHA LEFT the palace to meet with the captains at the easternmost part of the palace grounds. She'd left her cloak open, despite the biting cold. They were waiting for her near a dense line of evergreen trees.

THE MEETING DIDN'T HAVE an auspicious beginning. The ranking officers of the kingdoms had earned their authority over lifetimes of service. Being asked to place themselves and their men under someone else's command was disagreeable to almost all of them.

"We can't all have different plans of attack!" Rasha was exasperated.

"It's worked for us in the past," the leader from Karmir said stiffly. He'd been decorated many times, and wore his decorations proudly. For the last hour, he'd been adamant that his strategies and plans had never failed.

"We bring our battalions and lead them. We all know our own strengths. It confuses the enemy and ultimately leads to victory." He was looking at the captain from Vol, the eighth kingdom. It had been less than a hundred rotations since Vol joined the ten kingdoms. Before that, they'd been defeated by the Karmir many times. It was no secret the two nations were still holding grudges.

Rasha raised her hands before they decided to revisit the past right there in front of them.

"We're not here to revisit the past," Rasha snapped at them. "We will work together or we will lose this war. Let the beasts decide which of you tastes better for breakfast, if it suits you. But we will fight under a united command."

There were a few smiles at her comment, but everyone nodded

"Your Highness, we speak different languages," an officer from Buku said with concern.

"I'm aware of that. Nevertheless, we will find a way to work together and drive this threat from our kingdoms."

"I don't mean to be contrary, but you're quite young. How many battles have you won, that believe your counsel is better than mine?" It didn't surprise her that the Chilalian would be the one to give her the most trouble. He was a good friend of her father's. He gave her the same supercilious looks.

"My age is irrelevant. My status is not. Do you challenge my right to the throne?" To his credit, the general didn't back down as she stepped forward into his space. It was unheard of to challenge a royal because even thinking it was treason. The penalty for which was a long life in the dungeons—or a swift beheading.

Rasha stood ready to draw her swords.

"I've fought many times against many opponents. Just not the kind where you get shiny medals and a parade."

He measured her words, taking in the determination on her face. Rasha's hands itched to be holding her swords. It must have shown in her eyes because he finally conceded.

"No, Your Highness, I would never presume to challenge you or your authority."

Rasha nodded and turned back to the others. Rasha knelt down in the grass and they gathered around her. Using a handful of pebbles, she outlined her plan.

"I need three groups here. She pointed to what was the south of the kingdom. I need another three to the west and the other three to our east. Well make them come to us. Right here, we surround them, and then the battle is ours."

IN THE TRAINING ROOM, Rasha took up a longsword to continue Ladi's training. Rasha wasn't blind to the fact that Ladi preferred sparring with Jak because she had a crush on him. Jak either hadn't noticed or didn't care. He seemed to have that effect on women. They fell all over him.

She pressed an attack at Ladi, and she stumbled back. Rasha hadn't meant to drop her that fast, but she was having a difficult time controlling her feelings. Ladi was getting pummeled.

Rasha admired how Ladi shook it off and came at her again. She'd improved markedly since beginning her training. She'd be even better if she went to the Courier's Keep for a proper education.

"You should consider formal courier training."

"I don't need the training. I'm living the life."

"No, you're not. You're here helping us because the war has left us shorthanded. What will you do when it's over?" Rasha's temporary status was a closely held secret. Bashir and Chiza would return to their kingdom when the threat had ended. Rasha had been looking forward to leaving the palace life and working with Jak. He'd been a legendary courier himself. She wouldn't need Ebere when the authorities reinstated Jak. Not that there was anything wrong with Ebere, he just wasn't Jak, she mused, then realized she was doing it again—making plans for the future with Jak. Wouldn't he need to be home taking care of his long-lost wife? Rasha swung the longsword hard and fast, throwing Ladi off balance.

Rasha used her strength to push back and knock the sword from Ladi's hands. It landed with a clank. Ladi marched over to pick it up.

"Whoa, where did that come from?" Ladi asked.

"Sorry. I'm just somewhere else today," Rasha said, shaking her head.

"I know where your mind is. just forget about it. Who cares if he's married? He wants to be here with you." Ladi shrugged a shoulder.

Ladi picked up her sword and came at Rasha with renewed vigor. This time Ladi finished with her face pinned to the mat by Rasha's foot. Rasha offered her a hand up, and they started again.

"Oh, you mean ignore that he's married to someone else. Dream about him being with me the way you do?" Rasha swung the sword, punctuating her words with the clash of steel. She spun away from Ladi's next attack.

Ladi let out a war cry as she threw her sword with all her might at Rasha. Rasha had to move fast to avoid it. Ladi was angry now, too. Angry at Rasha. They continued practicing hard, throwing taunts at each other for well over an hour.

"Good." Rasha said as she returned her sword to the wall.

"Thanks," Ladi replied, still breathing hard.

"You'll be better after you graduate from the Courier's Keep."

"I've got a criminal record. If I put in a rotation with you, they might consider making me official." Ladi said with a shrug.

Rasha laughed. "That's what you think? Working with me will get you a license? You have a wild imagination. No wonder crime comes so easily to you."

"It's not always easy, but I've learned how to turn a no into a yes."

"We'll see when you're dealing with the robot at Courier Central. Without credentials, they won't consider you. They won't even acknowledge you exist without training. You should go to the academy while you can."

"What does that mean?" Ladi asked, sitting up straight.

"I mean we're losing this war. I don't know how much longer we can hold out against the beasts. We're badly outnumbered, and we may not survive the winter," Rasha said grimly.

LADI SEEMED SOMBER as she considered what that might mean. Then she brightened.

"But if we find the traitor, we might get ahead of them for a change. They won't defeat us again."

"Perhaps," Rasha sighed. "We're running out of time and options."

"If my brother were here, what would he say?" Ladi asked.

It was like that sometimes with her. She'd be laughing or talking about something, and her brother entered her thoughts. Rasha recognized it; it happened to her sometimes too. She'd see someone that looked like him, or hear a familiar laugh, and, for an instant, believe it was Lu.

"He'd say we're going to defeat those beasts and win this war, but not sitting around on the floor."

311

Rasha stood up and put out a hand for Ladi.

"Is everything in place?"

"Yes. The trap is set, and I'm just waiting for our false friend to take the bait. He's going to bite."

"He?" Rasha asked.

"I don't think a woman would do this."

"I'm not so sure."

"You have a suspect in mind." It wasn't a question.

Rasha nodded. "I think it might be the mermaid."

"Keabasi?"

"She's part fish. It's not beast, but an alliance between them wouldn't surprise me."

"Exactly." Ladi shook her head. "It's too obvious."

Rasha hoped it wasn't her, but if it was, she'd need more evidence to prove it. Either way, whoever was betraying them would pay. Her nightmare, Jak holding his hands over his bleeding belly, flashed in her mind. She had to shake of the foreboding that accompanied the vision.

## 14

RASHA FINALLY SLIPPED OUT of her boots at ten that evening. She'd done her best to prepare the fighters for the new tactics. She craved a long soak and dipped her hand into the waiting bath with a sigh. Rasha thanked the Universal for the hot water. She was loosening her vest when Temi's menacing growl got her attention. She cracked the bathroom door open to see Temi pacing.

"What is it?" She talked to Temi as if he'd reply. Lu had started it, and she'd grown accustomed to it.

Temi pawed at the bare floor, pushing his nose to the small crack under the door to the corridor. He snorted and growled again.

"Who's there?" Rasha wondered if anyone would answer. Temi grew more agitated.

"Okay, we'll check," she told him as she retrieved her swords. "Let's introduce Blade and Cutter to some new friends." Temi stepped back, allowing Rasha to ease the door open. As soon as it was wide enough, he bolted past her and down the corridor.

Rasha let out her own growl and raced after him. Servants screamed and leapt out of the way as he charged down the hall, snarling. A full tray of food ended up on the floor. She leapt over the food and broken dishes, cursing her bare feet. Temi turned down a second corridor Rasha recognized as belonging to the councilmembers. The floor got even colder, and she felt the biting cold of an open window. Skidding to a stop, Temi growled and whined to get at something on the other side of a door. She heard the sounds of a loud argument of some sort.

Temi scratched and pawed at the door. *When had his paws gotten so big?* she wondered. He'd scratched off much of the door's paint before someone answered.

Kyuk. The councilman from Buku. He replaced Bashir's father, the king, on the council.

"Hey!" Temi plowed past him and into the room.

Rasha had barely registered the man's silky pajamas before Temi reached the balcony doors and burst through them.

"Temi, wait!"

Temi was growling, his teeth latched on to something. Then came the sound of wings beating frantically and a screech that echoed through the night air. Through the open door, Rasha saw a birdman in flight. Temi blew out a mouthful of red, green, and blue feathers.

"There!" she called to the archers and pointed at the

birdman. The archers scanned the sky, but the birdman had made good his escape. Rasha turned her attention to the traitor.

Kyuk was backed against the wall. Temi was low to the ground, ready to pounce, snarling savagely.

"Good boy, Temi," she said. She drew her swords and crossed them in front of the councilman's neck.

His skin was light pink, a blending of Chilali and humanoid. His hair was more yellow than white and hanging in his sweaty face.

"I didn't do anything."

"You consorted with the enemy, and that's treason."

"Rasha!" Xeku entered the room with Keabasi and Gungbe.

"What's going on here?" Gungbe asked.

"Rasha, no!" Keabasi shouted.

Everyone was speaking at once, their voices creating a layer of noise that faded away into Rasha's memories. The blood-covered dining room she no longer ate in. Her best friend dying on the floor in a pool of his own blood.

"You killed them," she said her lips twisted in a snarl. Kyuk whimpered as her swords dug into his neck.

Xeku put an arm around her shoulder and broke the spell she was in.

"That's enough, Rasha. We'll take it from here," he said in an even tone.

Rasha stepped back, and Buku slumped with relief. Keabasi yelled, "Guard!" and two guards came running. "Please escort councilman Kyuk to a cell."

They dragged Kyuk from the room in his silk bathrobe, weeping.

Rasha started to calm down as soon as he left the room.

"Are you all right?" Keabasi asked. "I thought you'd taken leave of your senses for a moment."

"I'm fine," she replied.

"Tell us what happened. What did you see?" Xeku asked.

"I followed Temi here. He can smell the beasts, you know. He tore out of my room in this direction. When we got here, he tried to claw his way through the door. When Kyuk finally opened it, Temi ran into the room and out to the balcony. He got a piece of the birdman before it escaped."

"It would seem Kyuk was the traitor," Gungbe said.

"Perhaps," said Xeku. He didn't sound convinced.

"We found him with the birdman in his room," Rasha said.

"The birdman was on the balcony, you said." Xeku reminded her.

"Yes, but—"

"He must be questioned," Keabasi said.

"Why don't you believe me?"

"It's not a question of believing you. We have procedures to follow, young one. We can't just go around killing everyone we suspect is a traitor." Gungbe laughed as if he'd said something funny.

His laughter grated on her frayed nerves.

Xeku said, "You should rest. You look like you're not getting enough sleep. Tomorrow will be a busy day. I suspect that the birdman escaping is bad for our plans. We'll need to decide on strategy before dawn, in case the beasts attack."

Rasha swallowed her anger.

"I should be the one to interrogate the traitor."

"That's not the best idea, I think," Keabasi said condescendingly. "Without Jak around you seem, shall we say, more volatile."

Rasha glared at her.

How typical of them to expect results from her while dismissing her ideas. They'd caught him, so why didn't they make an example of him? What did Jak have to do with anything?

"I don't give a flying fig about Jak." Rasha had enough and went off to her rooms.

## 15

AS JAK GOT CLOSER to home, the change in the air and the familiar terrain beneath his tuskin's hooves filled him with nostalgia. The old way of life that his mother clung to was in evidence all around him. Everything fit together and belonged, including himself. Ebere had been quiet most of the journey, but now he seemed to want to talk.

"The grassy plains are yellow here. I like it. The way the ground meets the sky, making you feel small compared to the world around you."

"It's because we are small," Jak said. His childhood home looked small too. Smaller than he remembered. Every time he returned it seemed a bit shabbier. The roof needed work. The door still squeaked on the hinges. He'd have to deal with that sometime.

The interior of the house was dark, just a thin ray of light streaming in from the kitchen window. But his mother's room was bright. Someone had pulled back the window coverings to let the light in.

Jak dropped his pack at the door, and in just three long strides he reached his mother's bedroom door. He opened without knocking, and she opened her eyes.

Jola Ostari had once been a beauty. Even as sick as she was now, lying in bed, wasting away to nothing, her high cheekbones and blue eyes drew you in.

"Mother, I'm here." Jak knelt at her bedside and picked up her hand.

"Jak. My sweet boy." Jola coughed for a long moment. "News of you travels far and wide. I heard about your new status, and your betrothal."

Jak glanced back and saw Ebere had not followed him into the room. In fact, he'd quietly closed the door, giving them some privacy.

"Mother, I must tell you, everything is not as it appears."

His mother reached out and took his hand.

"You can be whatever you want to be. I never meant to —" She stopped to cough again. Jak stood up and found her water on the bedside table. She drank it all and asked for more. Then drank half of the second one. When she'd caught her breath, her voice was raspy and weak. "I never meant for you to live the life of a wanderer. Only to prevent them from trying to control you the way they did your father."

"Them?"

"His parents," Jola said. She squeezed his hand hard

enough to take him by surprise and pulled him closer. "About your father."

"He's not my father," Jak said.

"Listen. You need to hear the truth. I loved your father, and he loved me too, once. It wasn't what you were led to believe."

"Why? Why didn't you tell me before?" he asked.

"My stubborn pride." She coughed for a half minute. "At first I was angry he'd chosen the council over me. Then when I got sick, I didn't want him to come here. Better he remember me as I was." She half laughed and coughed again.

"You're beautiful, Mother, as always." Jak rested his palm on her cheek.

She continued, "I knew I was dying. It wouldn't have been fair. He's a good man."

Jak didn't want to listen to any more of this. He must have rolled his eyes because she squeezed his hand even harder.

"Don't punish him forever, the way I did. It was a mistake."

Another painful coughing fit. When it eased, she dropped his hand and closed her eyes.

"So tired."

"Yes, rest now," he said. He adjusted her pillows and pulled the blanket up to her chin to stop her shivering. The water was low, and he left to refill the pitcher.

Jak found Ebere seated at the kitchen table scanning one of his devices.

"I'm sorry, I didn't mean to leave you like that."

"Don't trouble yourself. I'm fine. How is your mother?"

"She doesn't have long," Jak said. "I'm just glad I'm here."

"Someone's coming," Ebere said, his head tilted and his eyes on the door.

Jak waited a moment, the glass pitcher still in his hand. The door swung open.

"Duna."

"Jak."

Duna walked in as if she lived there. She put the bag she was carrying on the table.

"What are you doing here?" Jak asked.

"What do you think? Someone had to be here for your mother. Took your time coming, didn't you?" she said with a disapproving click of her tongue. She assembled the ingredients for a meal.

"I came as soon as I got word," Jak filled the pitcher at the water pump.

"She hasn't been well for some time, as you know."

"I did."

Duna's pinched expression added nothing to her overall appearance. She'd pulled back her hair into a severe ponytail low on her neck. Her thin cheeks and hollowed eyes made her look as if her own life had been hard and long, much longer than the twenty-four rotations she'd lived.

He remembered how happy they'd been as children.

Things should have ended there, but Jak's lack of a father and Duna's longing for a mother drew them together. He had thought himself in love with her, but now, as he watched her moving around the kitchen, he couldn't remember why. They'd both changed so much over the last few rotations. They no longer resembled the boy and girl who'd carved their names into the tree between their ranches. Jak had so much he wanted to say to her, but there was only one thing that mattered.

"Our marriage is over," Jak said.

"Yes, of course." She pulled out the jeweled bracelet he'd given her and placed it in his hand.

Ebere looked from one to the other with wide eyes at their civil exchange.

"I wish you happy and safe," she said.

"And you." Jak slipped the bracelet into his pocket. He waited for her to go back to the stew she was preparing before he continued. "I can't thank you enough for being here for my mother. If you should ever need anything, I'll be there to help. No matter what."

"Thank you, Jak."

## 16

*K*YUK CONTINUED TO PROCLAIM his innocence through an entire night of interrogation. The weary council met the following morning to discuss what they should do next.

"He refused to give us anything." Gungbe began and held up a hand when Rasha tried to speak. "Before you ask, we implemented a variety of… forceful techniques. We did not go easy on him."

"We found him with the birdman. It's the best way to get them information without the signal being traced or their movements tracked. This is how he's getting it to them."

"We've got guards watching the skies for any more visitors from the north," Keabasi said.

"Let me question the prisoner." Rasha banged a fist on the table.

"Not one of your best ideas," Xeku said. "Be patient,

Your Highness. It's going to take some creative thinking to get the information."

"I can make him talk," Rasha said.

"That won't be necessary," Keabasi said. "Let us deal with this, Your Highness, while you work with the fighters. They weren't supportive of your original plan, less so now that the spy has gotten a message out."

Rasha groaned as she remembered the heated discussion among the captains and leaders. They had to work together, or they'd fail.

"I'll see to them right away. If there's nothing else?" She glanced around the table at each councilperson and wondered what they might be hiding. If they had one traitor, then there could be others. Maybe she was just being paranoid. She missed having Jak there to offer an opinion. She shook off her confused feelings.

Prince Bashir might be of some help. The palace had been his playground as a child. Who better to help them navigate its secrets? He'd also grown up with most of the present council, Kyuk excluded. She made a mental note to arrange a meeting with Bashir at his earliest convenience. The council wouldn't like it, but at the moment she didn't care.

RASHA MADE her way to the field. The sky wasn't holding back; fat flakes of snow were falling and sticking to the ground. Rasha reached the captains and listened as they argued about how best to avoid implementing her plans.

"May I speak?" she said. The idea of listening to them bickering with one another again annoyed her. "My overall plan is sound. We need to figure out a new way to implement it. If you continue to refuse to listen to me you'll be sending your fighters out there to die. I've seen enough to recognize our traditional ways aren't effective against them." How many had she helped bury? She'd stopped counting when she'd reached three digits, and that was ages ago.

One of the younger men from Adalu spoke up. "I agree. Many of you are new to your commands. My fighters have been here for months, and our numbers dwindle. We've tried it your way. Are we too scared to try it her way because she might be right?"

Rasha was grateful for his opinion and wondered why she hadn't noticed him before.

"Young man, who are you to speak? You're no captain. I've never seen you before," a leader from Buku said. His lean face and long nose made him look like a piko.

"I was promoted after my captain died last week." The young man squared his shoulders, daring anyone to contradict his right to be among them.

Rasha felt it was the perfect time to make her point.

"What is your name?" she asked young captain.

"I'm Hamisu. They call me Ham."

Then she addressed the older men but kept her eyes on the leader from Buku. "Well, perhaps you are too scared to listen to what I have to say. Never mind. When we collect your bodies from the battle field, I'm sure your replacements will be much more willing to listen, like young Ham here."

———————

IT HAD TAKEN another hour to convince them that combining their fighters and techniques would benefit them all. The next half hour was spent deciding who would be where and implementing which technique. Rasha was still grumbling about it to Ladi two hours later. They'd forgone training that morning to deal with more pressing matters.

Ladi listened when Rasha mumbled about the royals insisting they hold their annual winter ball, as if they weren't in the middle of a war. Ladi didn't understand it either. As if there was nothing to do besides putting on fancy dresses and praying they weren't eaten in them by some wild beasts. The council gave in for the simple reason that it was easier than having to deal with them.

"I'm sorry the original plan was ruined," Ladi said. "I understand now it wouldn't have worked anyway, since they were using the bird-men. I wouldn't have guessed that in a million rotations."

Rasha nodded but said nothing. That's how it was with her these days. Her temper was more volatile and her moods were unpredictable. Ladi was careful not to push, as she wanted Rasha to let her go ahead with her new idea.

"Rasha, there's been a new development. I think I can help this time."

"Well?" Rasha asked.

"I reached out to some friends of mine. Friends with connections in some interesting circles. There are rumors that not all the beasts are volunteers." Ladi smiled.

"So? They fight, so what difference does it make?"

"Don't you get it? The collars they wear deliver some kind of shock. If they're not fighting because they want to, then we might be able to get them on our side."

Ladi was so excited her hands were waving as she described her idea.

"How would you do that?"

"I'd show them that there's another choice. They might fight for us against the bird-men. Getting to their camp won't be hard. I already have the coordinates. I'll figure out a way to deactivate the collars. I just need to get close enough to one that's still alive to see how they work."

Rasha didn't reply. She just stared at Ladi.

"Well?"

*J*OLA OSTARI DIED THE following morning. It was as sunny day as the one before. Jak felt betrayed by the weather. Why wasn't it raining? They buried his mother, and he stood with his jaw tight and tears streaming down his face. Ebere was on his right side, and his ex-wife stood on his left. Duna was racked with sobs as neighbors helped put his mother into the ground.

She'd told him to forgive his father. On her deathbed she'd made him promise. He didn't want to think about Xeku. This day was for his mother, and he wasn't ready to think about anything else. She'd protected him and cared for him his entire life, and in the end only asked that he forgive his father. He wouldn't begrudge a dying woman her last wish. Before she took her final breath, she added something. The words that echoed in his mind even on this day.

"The princess, Rasha. You care for her." It hadn't been a question but a statement.

Jak didn't need to reply.

Jola nodded, as if he'd spoken. "You understand what it means to love someone now. She's already changed you for the better." Jola swallowed hard. "She's the one."

She'd gone into a coughing fit a moment later. When he lifted the pitcher and found it empty, he rushed out to get water. He hadn't meant to let it get that low.

"You seem so sure, how do you–?"

Jak knew the moment he saw her, she was gone. Her last words echoing in his heart.

After saying goodbye to his mother Jak's thoughts returned to Rasha and what she meant to him. He realized he'd already decided on Rasha. She'd become his closest friend, and he loved being the one she turned to when she needed to talk. If he was being honest with himself, he could say he'd found her attractive that first day, and his desire for her increased every day. Rasha had a fierceness and strength that drew him to her. Having his mother's blessing only meant he'd do whatever it took to keep her.

Rasha might forgive him for being married, but he'd have to return with more than his heart in his hands. He needed to do what none of her messengers had been able to. He would bring the Wilds into the war against the beasts. They had the numbers and fighters needed to tip the scale. He only hoped they wouldn't kill him on the spot for what he was about to suggest.

JAK AND EBERE ventured to the city center, where what passed as leadership for the Wilds gathered. Communities that came together because they didn't care for government and lived without laws didn't have formal leadership. Jak pulled up to a local bar called the Hub. Most of the men who had any kind of influence met there to discuss business, trade, and entertainment.

Today was no different, and near the end of the workday it was busy. Jak chose a table near the back of the room with an exit door nearby and a view of the bar.

Many of the men who dealt with the banks and commerce sat at the bar. Their jovial personalities made the bar a lively one. The merchants were a mixed group, some with smiles and handshakes while others were somber and serious.

The most interesting thing about the traders, Jak remembered, was their generosity. They were the ones buying drinks and sharing their meals. A typical day at the Hub.

"I found your exchange with your wife very interesting. Should I expect something similar here?" Ebere asked. He was leaning forward in his seat with his elbows on the table. There was a light in his eyes that Jak had only seen a few times—when Ebere looked at Ladi. She never saw it because he shut down the minute she looked his way.

"Like I said before, we married young. We mistook innocent infatuation for love."

Ebere sipped his vegetable drink. It had a green tint and an orange stalk he stirred it with. Jak gulped down his fermented fruit drink and hoped that he had enough courage to do this. He focused on Rasha and imagined her fighting alone on the front.

"Well, Jak Ostari, or should I say Prince Ameenu?" A man with purple skin wearing a business suit greeted him. Jak smiled back at Mr. Waza, a banker he'd had occasion to deal with before.

"Mr. Waza, let me introduce you to my friend Ebere," Jak said, ignoring the question. Like Rasha, he neither liked the title and was happy it was temporary. The only good thing to come with it was her.

"A pleasure, young man. If you need to do any bank business while you're here, I'd be happy to attend you, personally." Mr. Waza held out a meaty hand to Ebere.

Ebere shook it and then discreetly wiped the sweat off on his pants.

"I bring important news from Adalu, Mr. Waza. Is there a chance I might have an audience?"

Mr. Waza looked around and laughed. "You want an audience to discuss the Adalu? You've come to the wrong place. These people are not interested in what happens to the ten kingdoms."

"I must speak with you, it's urgent," Jak insisted.

"I heard about your mother."

Jak bit back the sadness that gripped his heart at the mention of her.

"She reminded me of something before she died," Jak said, leaning in towards the older man. "She asked me to stop holding on to the past so I might have a better future."

"Wise words from a wise woman."

"Which is why I'm here today. The Wilds have been living in the past long enough. It's time to move forward together." Jak's voice carried above the bar chatter. A few of the patrons stopped to listen.

Mr. Waza wasn't laughing anymore. His purple face looked at least a shade darker, and the sweat dampened his suit. He looked around the room at other prominent members of the community, then shrugged.

"Ladies and gentlemen, it appears the courier-turned-prince, Jak Ostari Ameenu, has something to discuss with us today. Shall we give him an ear?" Mr. Waza made the announcement and glasses stopped clinking and people stopped chatting to hear what Jak had to say.

Jak cleared his throat. He'd never spoken at the Hub before. He'd listened to their debates in the past, and they got heated at times. The last thing he wanted was to make things worse for Rasha. He took another swallow of his drink and then cleared his throat.

Ebere sat with his eyes closed. Maybe he was praying to Mat`ka of Poda, the nature goddess, for help. Unlike Lu, Ebere seemed to take his religious beliefs seriously. With the whole room watching, Jak couldn't ask him.

"Ladies and gentlemen, I bring you news from the First Kingdom of Adalu."

There were groans around the room and a few audible

discontents. Maybe he shouldn't have brought up Adalu. There were still bad feelings there.

"As most of you know, I'm Jak. Just Jak," He added with a sideways glance at Mr. Waza. "I grew up here, and most of you know me.

"Our way of life has always suited us just fine. We don't get involved with the ten kingdoms of Bolaji, and they don't bother us."

"Live free, die free," someone called out. The roar of applause was overwhelming.

How was he supposed to reach them? What he wanted was diametrically opposed to the people they were.

"I won't bore you with the details of the war that's happening on the borders of Adalu with the beasts of the north. I know you don't care about that." Several of the community members vocalized their agreement with that statement. "Let's talk about something you do care about: your livelihoods, your homes, your future, and the future of your children." Jak paused and waited for them to take that in.

"I don't want to try to persuade you with fancy words or shower you with pleas from the council or their royal representatives." He smiled, understanding how many considered him a lackey for the council. "I'll speak to you the way I was raised to speak here in the Wilds: with truth. The war is not going well. People from every nation and kingdom are being slaughtered. It's only a matter of time before they're snarling, slashing, and feasting at your front door."

The room grew silent again as they listened.

"These creatures show no respect for borders or people. How long do you think it will take them to figure out this land is ungoverned and unprepared to defend itself?"

"We've fought off kingdoms before," someone shouted.

"They don't call this the Wilds for nothing," a woman's voice agreed.

"Let them come!"

Jak nodded. It was the exact response he'd expected. They were indifferent, and they couldn't see the danger coming.

Ebere stood up and spoke.

"Many of you understand my people to be a neutral intelligence-gathering people. I would like to say something on behalf of them. When the beasts come and kill off all the other kingdoms, you'll have only yourselves with whom to trade. Communications all over Bolaji will be down. Trade will cease in every corner of the realm. No one is safe unless we come together. Please, for the sake of your own family and friends, reconsider."

Jak waited a moment. He hoped they would listen, but he didn't believe they would. He was right.

"What's in it for us?" Mr. Waza asked.

Ever the banker and businessman. It all came down to this.

"How about saving your people?"

"Not good enough. Sorry folks, I have a way off of this

rock if I need it, and it's a lot cheaper than a war." Several others agreed with him.

"What do you want?" Jak asked.

"Something your council would rather die than give us," Mr. Waza said.

"OUT OF THE QUESTION," Rasha said. "Are you a complete pumseed? You expect to just walk into their camp, and then you think one of their beasts is going to let you touch their collar long enough to disable it?"

"Not exactly. I'd do surveillance. Just give me a chance to—"

"Isn't it enough that your parents lost one child? You would risk your own life and leave them childless?"

"I haven't been a child in rotations." Ladi crossed her arms over her chest. "This is a solid plan. If I can get one to trust me, we could learn more about them and win some of them to our side."

"No. We don't have the manpower right now to send a team, and I won't risk them getting killed."

"I can go myself. I'm good at getting in and out of places unseen. They'll never even know I'm there."

Rasha snapped.

"No. I won't bury another partner. Sorry, you're stuck here in the palace with me. Why don't you help get these royals off of my back about this winter ball?"

Ladi fumed. Rasha was just like everyone else. No one ever took her seriously. She didn't want her parents to suffer, but she also didn't want the beasts to conquer the first kingdom and go after the Twinlands. It was better to take the risk herself than to lose her brother and both her parents. Rasha didn't understand. This was their only chance.

"Dragons!" A guard shouted. Rasha pulled her swords and ran.

It was true. The bird-men had arrived, and on the backs of the dragons were bull-men. They landed on the grounds and destroyed anything in their path. Ladi was ready for them this time. She'd already set up the pulse.

Ladi held up the remote trigger, and Rasha nodded. She sent word to the fighters to keep them from harm when the pulse went off. The dragons required almost three times the charge to do any damage. Their people would need to stay clear or they could be killed.

Rasha signaled to Ladi to get ready with a three-finger count down. When Rasha reached two, Ladi put her finger on the trigger.

Some of the bull-men on dragons took to the air again. The pulse was ineffective if their feet weren't on the ground. The beasts hovered above the grounds, picking them off. The small individual shocks and defense tactics didn't penetrate their thick skins. Rasha signaled their people back, and, in a haphazard fashion, they moved back several paces. It was clear to Ladi they needed to do more drills.

Ladi hurried over to Rasha.

"We need wire ropes," she yelled.

"Now is not a good time to try taming the beasts."

"No, for the pulse to work they have to be within the pulse grid!"

Rasha thought for a moment then yelled behind her to the guard.

"Wire!"

They gathered the wire and the archers attached them to their arrows while keeping them securely connected to the grid. The countdown began again, and Ladi waited with her thumb over the controller.

Rasha gave the signal at last. The archers fired their arrows, and they sailed over the beasts as if they'd missed. As the flying beasts struggled to untangle the wires that touched them, Ladi pushed the button, sending the pulse up the wires. The beasts howled and cried out, many of them falling to the ground.

The fighters cheered as the last of the beasts limped away.

Ladi approached an electrocuted dragon. It looked up at her with sad brown eyes.

"What are you doing?" Rasha asked when Ladi rolled

out her bag of small metal tools. She picked at the collar, trying to get it open, her hands moving with lightning speed.

"This collar is on a remote mechanism, but I think I can override it." She smiled when the collar opened with a hiss.

"We'll be faster next time," Ladi said, stroking the dragon. It heaved a loud sigh before it closed its eyes for the last time.

"Interesting." Rasha said, taking note of the way the animal seemed to welcome the permanent sleep.

"The rumors are true. Half of the beasts they're using are wearing these collars. Meaning that if we can figure out a way to get them off, they really might be eager to turn on them.

"You have a sound argument."

"That's why I want to go to their encampment. There might be a faster way to get the collars off, but I need to see them at work."

"What's it going to take to get it through your thick skull? You are not going off to the beasts' encampment alone. Maybe when Jak gets back, I can go with you."

"I'm not a child."

"Good, then I won't need to explain to you again why you can't go."

Rasha sheathed her swords and followed the rest of her people back toward the palace.

*L*ADI GLANCED AROUND THE room one last time, looking for anything she might have forgotten. Her bag felt light on her back as she mentally rechecked the contents. She'd packed a pulse, her hand tools to open collars, and items that might help on her trek through the woods. She placed a note on the bed, folded in half.

Rasha would be angry. The others probably would be, too. They still looked at her like a rebellious little girl. They didn't understand that this could end the war. Why didn't they at least want to try? Her life for the lives of thousands, if it came to that. Wasn't that exactly what Lu would have done?

The guards patrolled at regular intervals. She listened at the door, and their heavy boots marched by ten minutes ago. She slipped out her room and into the deserted corridor. Being on the main level afforded her easy access to the grounds.

She sucked in a breath of cold air when the winds hit her face. Her feet crunched on the icy ground as she made her way to the north wall. The archers would be the hardest to avoid. She had to creep along behind the trees and bushes, then, when she was clear, broke into a run. She readjusted the bag on her back. When she cleared the palace grounds, she'd have to keep up a steady pace to reach the encampment by morning.

A HIGH-PITCHED WHINE came from the trees just to her left. Temi poked his head out of the bushes before his body followed, placing himself directly in her path.

"I'll be back. Don't worry."

His head tilted to the side and he snorted as if he didn't believe her.

"What do you know? I'm going to do something more than sit in this palace waiting for the war to end."

He whined again as she turned to go.

Ladi turned to Temi and reached out her hand, stroking his soft head. The Tero-Joro had a strong connection to small beasties that lived on their lands. Ladi herself often found it easy to connect with them. Maybe that was the real reason she needed to go. Either way, she was even more determined when she faced the wall again.

"Take care of the others," she said over her shoulder.

Then she hauled herself up and over using the thick vines growing up the wall.

When she dropped on the other side, her enhanced vision and hearing kicked in. Being from Tero-Joro did have its advantages at times, like when traveling in the woods at night. Ordinary night sounds, insects and rustling leaves were all she could hear. No sign of anything worse ahead.

Ladi plowed through the forest, making her own path toward the coordinates. It would take her several hours to get there. She continued zigzagging through the dense trees. The distinct reek of contained animals reached her nose long before she reached the designated location. She wondered that everyone in the realm didn't have their position. Their smell permeated the air and everything around them.

Ladi swallowed the bile that rose in her throat. The stench burned her nostrils. She found a good place to watch and settled in. She could see a multitude of cages within an enclosure that spanned thousands of feet. She couldn't see the end of the maze of metal fencing from her hiding place. Most of the animals were locked into individual cages. Only a few held more than one beast. Some of the larger beasts looked too big for their cages. Ladi climbed a nearby tree to watch the animals and wait for an opportunity.

She peered intently, trying to count the ones wearing collars.

She wasn't surprised to see beasts wandering the main

encampment. These had to be the beasts that were with the bird-men. That meant all beasts in cages were there against their will. She should go back and tell the others what she'd discovered. With reinforcements, it would be easy to free the beasts and turn them against the bird-men and bull-men.

She knew that she should only do reconnaissance. Ladi thought about it, but going back and having Rasha tell her no again would only infuriate her. No, she wasn't going back without results. She'd stay, and maybe figure out how to communicate with them. Any advantage might help them. She told herself she wanted this for Lu. Maybe his death would mean something. If it got her commissioned as a courier with field status, that wouldn't be so bad either.

Ladi remembered the look on her father's face when she left their home. He and her mother seemed so defeated. They expected her to become a criminal master-mind and ruin their lives. Wouldn't they be surprised? She'd only ever done those other things because she'd been restless. Bored and broke to put it more simply. Each risky job made her easy money and cured her boredom for a time.

This mission didn't bring in easy money or kill the monotony. She needed to do this. Ladi wouldn't sit on the sidelines and let Ebere and the others take all the credit for saving the kingdom. She wanted her place in it.

Now the hard part: not getting caught.

## 20

"YOU WANT TO BECOME the eleventh kingdom?" Jak asked. It didn't seem possible. The community as a whole never showed the least inclination to want to be a part of the ten kingdoms. Hadn't he said as much?

"Not just the eleventh. We are larger and more independent than any of the kingdoms. Why shouldn't all things royal and governmental be here?" Waza said with a grin as he spread his arms wide.

The other tradesmen and businessmen in the room were transfixed. They were listening with eyes wide and mouths hanging open.

Jak took in their reactions and realized what Waza was doing. He didn't speak for the leaders of the Wild; he wanted to test Jak's resolve.

Jak ran a hand over his chin. He tried to keep his expression neutral.

"Well, Mr. Waza. You do aim for the stars, don't you?"

"Is there any other way to aim?"

"I suppose you're right. Well. I'd be happy to take your conditions to the council. But I don't want to leave you in suspense, so how about we shake on it right now? I'll guarantee you a favorable decision in exchange for two thousand fighters ready to move on the beasts of the north tomorrow." Jak put out his hand.

It had never crossed Mr. Waza's mind Jak would call his bluff. His mouth opened and closed, and his face was white. He scanned the room.

The reacting around the room was mixed. Some wide-eyed and hopeful, wanting to join the ten kingdoms, their businesses legitimate overnight. Some outraged by the idea of compromising their principles. A few looked around with shifty eyes and nervous hands. Their business dealings would be put firmly outside the laws of the ten kingdoms.

Mr. Waza tried to play it off and finally laughed as if Jak had told a joke that he found especially amusing.

"Did I say something funny?" Jak asked. "Or are you actually considering this amazing limited time offer?"

"The offer is a good one," Mr. Waza agreed, wiping a tear from his eye. "But it's not solid."

"What do you mean?"

"You're an illegitimate, bottom of the barrel, prince incumbent trying to pull off a deal he hasn't the authority to offer or honor." The energy in the bar changed as the business owners and leaders of the community understood what Waza had done. They turned back to their drinks and their conversations.

Jak had lost their attention and their respect.

"Sorry, boy. You're wasting your time here. You'll have to drum up soldiers elsewhere." Waza gave Jak a hard slap on the back before he turned to a table of businessmen in casual attire and having their after-work drink.

Jak looked at Ebere and shrugged. He didn't know what else to try. The Wilds had the resources and the people, but they weren't motivated to join the fight. He had to figure out a way to show them that his offer was real, and to their benefit, before it was too late for Adalu.

Jak did what he always did when he was feeling low. He tried to cheer himself up by being the plucky, attention-getting charmer he'd always been. Later in the evening, there were three girls at the table with them. Ebere, looking more uncomfortable than usual, seemed more inclined to escape out the door than to stay and listen to another song. Jak was belting out an old folk song of the mermen that got him cheers and another round of drinks from a yellow-skinned girl. Her dark green eyes never left Jak's face, but he barely noticed her.

In his heart, every song he sang was for only one person. When he thought of Rasha, he had an intense ache and a feather-light tickle of excitement that started in his stomach. His voice cracked twice during the last song. He had to lay off of the fermented fruit juice or he wouldn't be able to walk out of the bar, let alone sing more songs.

When he finished, the girls at the table stood and clapped enthusiastically. He sat back down next to Ebere, who kept motioning with his head to the left. When Jak looked to the left, a tall, winged man was watching him from the bar. He was dressed as one would expect in the Wilds, rugged and dusty clothing. His hair, though, was dark and long like the Karmirians, but his skin pale. The fact that the man had wings and was making no effort to hide them was what unnerved Jak. When had he ever seen a winged man with his own eyes? He wasn't sure he ever had.

Jak caught the man's eye and nodded toward the door. Then he slapped a hand on the table.

"Ebere, time to go."

The girls groaned and complained as they stood up.

"Sorry, ladies, maybe another time. Ebere wanted to stay with you, but we've got an appointment."

Ebere's face turned dark green as he glared at Jak. "What appointment?" he asked.

## 21

_R_ASHA WAITED ALL morning in the training room for Ladi. The girl had the infuriating habit of being early when you needed to sleep late and being late when you needed her to be on time. She practiced alone. She'd dreamed about Jak and Duna again, and it left her rattled. What was taking him so long? He'd sent news of his mother's death days ago; he should be back by now. She worked through her moves again. She heard someone clear their throat at the door and she stopped.

"Where is she?" Rasha demanded at a guard with a paper quivering in his hands.

"She's gone."

"What?" Rasha snatched the note from his hand and he retreated a few steps. He had a scar on his face. He must have been in one of the battles.

"You're free to go," she said without looking up.

Xeku came in and the guard almost ran into him headlong.

"You're in a mood this morning," Xeku said. "I see you've gotten the letter."

Rasha balled up the paper and threw it across the room.

"I told her she was not to go. She's so stubborn. I should have sent her home to her parents a long time ago."

"She's headstrong, and she thinks she's invincible. She reminds me a little of you."

"Ha!"

"You don't see it?"

"I didn't run off and get myself thrown in jail at every inconvenient opportunity. I attended the Courier's Keep and forced them to let me train. Being legitimate mattered to me. Without a proper education she'll keep finding trouble wherever she can."

"She wants to prove herself to you because she admires you. At the same time, she wants to prove that she's good enough to work alongside you."

"Did you know?"

"That she would run off? No." Xeku tilted his head to one side. "Why would I have any knowledge of that?"

"When Jak left–well, maybe you caught Ladi leaving too."

"Jak is my son, and he had some... unfinished business to see to."

"His wife, Duna." Rasha said. She picked up a longsword.

"He told you?"

"No."

"Oh, I see." Xeku picked up her short swords and rolled his wrists, testing their weight.

Rasha raised an eyebrow, and he answered the unasked question.

"Just because we serve on the council doesn't mean we don't use this room." Xeku said and smiled at her.

"How long have you known?" she asked.

He took up a defensive position and waited for her to attack him. "I've known almost everything of significance in my son's life since he was a boy."

Rasha wished now she hadn't taken the longsword. She'd given herself a disadvantage. Xeku didn't seem out of practice with the short swords as he threw them up over his head and crossed them in front of his face.

"You found out about Duna. That's why you've been so angry," he said.

He did a quick turn that forced her to drop her sword to defend her middle.

"I'm not angry. He can do what he wants with his wife."

She lunged, and he deflected her.

"You are, and you have every right to be, but I beg you not to worry overmuch about Duna."

"I'm not." Rasha grunted as she executed a spin combined with a thrust that failed with a crash. He'd been ready for her.

"Jak hasn't seen her for rotations. They parted amicably as I understand it, and she's already moved on."

"I don't care." She rolled to the side and out of the way of his attack.

They sparred for almost an hour.

When he knocked the sword from her hands and held her own swords to her neck, she yielded.

"Is that any way to treat the princess incumbent, Ameenu?" Her aunt arrived and lifted a sword from the wall, then took a defensive stance. "Why don't you come over here and pick on someone your own age?"

Rasha saw the feral smile on her aunt's face. Xeku was in for a beating. He'd already been going with her for an hour. There was no way he'd be able to keep up with Sochi.

"Sochi, you lovely thing. I wouldn't dream of hurting you."

Sochi let out a playful laugh. "As if you ever could."

Rasha watched with rapt attention as they sparred on the mat. Neither of them seemed to remember that she was in the room.

"I heard you told your son the truth." Sochi lunged, but Xeku turned away just in time. He brought his sword down hard on hers. "I suppose he didn't take it very well."

"No."

"Children are complicated."

"Yes, they are."

Sochi let his next blow push her back and she stumbled as if she were tiring. He lunged, and she brought her

351

sword down almost on top of his hands. He dropped the short in his left hand, and she brought her longsword up to his neck before he could make another move.

"I admit I wasn't at my best when we began," he said, trying to catch his breath.

Sochi was also breathing hard.

"Your best isn't enough." She gave him a light slap on the back. It made Rasha wonder how they knew each other.

"Have you known each other long?" she asked.

"Yes, ever since—" Xeku began but Sochi cut him off.

"Yes, before the last choosing." She gave him a look that Rasha didn't miss. There was something there that Sochi didn't want her to know. What secrets had she been hiding all these rotations?

"Some of us had a life before we took the responsibility to run the kingdom. Both sides are important. You need to find your balance between both."

"How does one become a secret fighter for the council? Leave your family and take on an advisory role in the palace? That way you don't get your hands dirty," Rasha asked, trying her best to sound unimpressed.

"Rasha Indari!" Her Aunt Sochi looked ready to strike her and Rasha flinched when her hand lifted into the air. Her aunt merely ran a hand over her own head.

"Xeku is a good man. You should show a little respect and remember that not everyone is like your parents." Sochi turned to Xeku. "I'm so sorry."

Xeku waved a hand in the air.

"I've earned it, haven't I?"

Rasha looked at them with astonishment, then amazement as Sochi reached for his hands and held them in her own. "No, you haven't. Be well, and may the Universal light your path."

He turned to Rasha. "Please, consider the message and not the messenger. Find your balance." He bowed and handed her Cutter and Blade. She sheathed them, and by the time she looked up, he had gone. Startled by his disappearance, she looked toward the door and caught only a glimpse of his robe as he turned the corner.

"I never dreamed I'd live to see the day you'd become the self-righteous princess your parents wanted you to be," Sochi said. She put her sword back on the wall with the others.

Rasha didn't even have the words to respond and felt her mouth moving wordlessly.

"I'm not the one who left his son without a father," she said to her aunt's back.

Sochi whirled around, and this time she gave Rasha a shove with one hand.

"He didn't leave a son. He left a spoiled little girl used to getting her way. Who, like a child, ran off with their son and hid him until he was almost five rotations old."

Rasha flushed. "I didn't know."

Sochi reached up and stroked the side of her face. A gentle stroke and then a soft pat on her cheek.

"Give them time. They need to heal on their own." Sochi sighed. "I'm not saying you shouldn't support Jak.

He's your friend. But be mindful, he only knows one side of the story. I want you to keep your own judgment reined until you know Xeku."

"What is it with you two? How did you meet each other?"

To Rasha's horror, Sochi shook her head and her eyes filled. What had she said?

"Not yet, but someday I'll share with you the story and its horrible ending." She shook off the memory and they walked out of the training room together. Temi was waiting outside the door and popped up to follow them.

"I wish I had been here for you when you lost your friend," Sochi said. She leaned down and gave him a pat. Temi's tail waved back and forth with happiness. He purred at Sochi and rubbed his head against her.

"Does he remember me and my little cottage?" she asked.

"I wonder what our little Temi knows at times, myself. I've still never seen another of his species," Rasha said, looking at him. "Lu was the only one that really understood him."

At the mention of Lu, Temi stiffened and sniffed the air before he settled with a sigh. The beastie was an enigma.

"What about his sister?"

"She's taken off to end the war with the beasts of the north on her own."

They passed the guards went and out into the gardens. The cold air whipped at her hair.

"That one's a lot like you."

"She's nothing like me, and I'm tired of people saying so. Ladi would rather remain a criminal than become a legitimate courier." Rasha picked a small twig from a nearby bush and broke it into pieces. "She's so obstinate."

"That was the quality of yours to which I was referring," Sochi said with a laugh.

Rasha mulled it over for a moment. It made sense. They were both willful and headstrong. Rasha had never learned how to accept 'no' as an answer, and Ladi had the same tendency.

"If she pulls it off, I'll be the first one to congratulate her. If she fails…" Rasha's voice trailed off. She didn't want to even imagine it. She looked at her aunt, remembering now that she hadn't been expecting her. "Why have you come, Aunt?"

"I'm here to fight. What else?"

---

## 22

*L*ADI PLACED HER pack on the ground and pulled out her tools. She'd need to get close enough to one of them to remove it. She communicated easily with the creatures of the wood near her home. But these beasts were different. She hoped they understood her benign intentions.

Her superior eyes and ears picked up most of what she needed to learn about the collars and how they worked. She watched as a dragon stomped and growled at a bull-man who was trying to lead him in the opposite direction. The dragon refused, and his collar lit up when the bull-man remotely electrified it. The beast resisted, and the bull-man turned the shock level up. Then again until the animal lowered his head in submission and obeyed. Ladi had already seen what the highest voltage could do on the battlefield. A painful death.

Ladi had several different tools to try since she hadn't

been sure what she might need. She hadn't been able to test a working collar. When their wearers died, the collars burned themselves out.

What a horrible existence these beasts had. She imagined the joy they'd feel once they were free. They'd thank her and her own people would praise her for bringing peace to the entire realm. The bull-man with the controller left the enclosure. Ladi made her move.

## 23

RASHA NOTED A distinct change in her status when her aunt Sochi arrived to join the fight. Her aunt Sochi added some kind of credibility to everything she said and did. It was as if Rasha had only been playing princess incumbent until her aunt arrived. Rasha wasn't sure how to feel about it. Of course, she was glad her aunt was there to support her, but why were the others acting so different around her now?

"THE BEASTS ARE ATTACKING from the west!" A guard exclaimed. Rasha met her Aunt Sochi running down the corridor toward the fight. They quickly joined the captains. Several nodded in acknowledgement to Sochi.

"The beasts are here, on our west flank. We have to push them to the east. We have scouts in the area, and I want to give them some breathing room," Rasha said. She waited for the normal resistance that came with her orders, but none came.

"I can lead a charge from the east edge of the palace and push them back, Your Highness," Sochi said. Rasha hated the title from anyone else, but when her aunt Sochi said it, the words seemed filled with such pride she couldn't help but smile. The look her aunt gave her said she was just as happy to say the words.

"Do it."

"I'll flank them from the north, so they can't break in that direction," said the captain who'd been her biggest opponent.

The plan of attack came together, in large part because of Sochi. The captains couldn't object or refuse without looking like fools or cowards.

"My people will push north. The rest of you circle around them and attack their flank," Rasha said.

After the captains departed to muster their fighters, Sochi turned to Rasha and said, "You're a fine leader."

"It's never gone that smoothly before. I feel like it's because you're here."

Sochi shrugged one shoulder. "It's easier to follow someone if they already have loyal followers. Loyalty by example."

Rasha only had time to give her aunt a quick hug before they ran for their positions. A dark cloud was coming from the north, and she wondered if they'd have a storm to deal with as well. Then the cloud broke, moving both east and west. It wasn't a storm cloud.

It was a huge number of flying beasts. As it drew closer, she saw bird-men, dragons, and some other smallish bird she'd never seen before. They were half the size of the bird-men with no fur and sharp, chopping teeth. They screeched and howled as they got closer. The sound of their wings on the cold air filled her ears.

The new beasts dove on fighters, biting and using their talons, tearing at faces, and slowing them down. Rasha was ready for the aerial attack, spinning her swords and cutting them down. The dragons were the worst. Their size and relative indestructability allowed them to land in the middle of the fighters, scattering them in all directions.

As the battle went on, she didn't understand how her brain managed to miss Jak. When she turned and saw of another graceful fighter making their way through the fray, all thoughts of Jak left her mind. Aunt Sochi's technique and skill with the blade bordered on legendary. Rasha had always admired her. She fought her way to Sochi's side, and the two fought back-to-back, bringing down beasts.

"There's too many of them, girl!" her aunt yelled.

Rasha grunted as she fought off two of the smaller beasts. She noticed a dragon getting closer. The collar around his neck caught the light. He hesitated, not closing in on them. His head began whipping around defiantly. Ladi's theory flashed through her mind, and she scanned the fray. She found him. The birdman amped up the charge, and the beast took another step toward Rasha, his huge amber eyes staring at her. An idea formed in her mind, and she didn't hesitate. Turning away from Sochi, she started running toward the birdman, and the dragon followed her. When the birdman realized she was running at him, he started to take flight.

Out of nowhere, one of her captains caught his leg and yanked him out of the air.

"Hold him," Rasha yelled, and her swords made quick work of him. The controller dropped from his dead hand. She snatched it from the ground and held it up, waving it at the dragon. The beast made a noise, his snarl melted into a whimper.

Moving slowly and deliberately, Rasha put the controller on the ground between them and took a step back. He watched her curiously, tensing when she raised her sword. She lifted Blade and hacked at the device until the sparks died out. Then, holding her sword to one side, she lifted her arms up. Did he understand she didn't want to fight him? Would he try to kill her anyway? The dragon's head tilted, then with a growl he leapt into the air and flew away from the battle.

Rasha looked around and realized their mistake. They were fighting the wrong beasts.

"Go after the bird-men! They're controlling the beasts," Rasha yelled to the men nearest her. She ran across the battlefield, spreading the word.

As soon as the bird-men and the bull-men figured out that the soldiers were going after them instead of fighting the beasts, they used the only defense they had. They used the remaining beasts to get off of the ground and away from the battle. The smaller, sharp-toothed birds continued to fight. They didn't have collars. Rasha looked for the source of their agitation and couldn't find anything.

Sochi was fighting back-to-back with another fighter, and she recognized the tall, elegant man as Xeku. They were fighting off a beast with a collar. Rasha searched until her eyes fell on a bull-man who hadn't left with the others. Rasha raced at him, but he held up the device and pointed it at the beast. She understood what he'd planned to do, but it was too late. She drove Cutter through him, he pressed the button and the beast dropped to the ground at the same time as bull-man.

"No!" Rasha yelled. Xeku and Sochi turned and saw her anguish. "They're fighting against their will. Get the controllers and the beasts will stop fighting."

"But if we don't stop them in time, they'll just kill the beasts," Xeku said, realization dawning on his face.

"What about the swarm?" Sochi asked as the beasts continued to fight.

"I don't know what's controlling them, but I'm sure something is driving them. Find it." Rasha raced to tell the others. The swarm was moving toward the palace, driving a pack of beasts. The bull-men and bird-men hadn't retreated. They'd only changed their target.

"The palace!"

## 24

*L*ADI CREPT ALONGSIDE the encampment. The beasts inside of the cages were quiet. She reached the back of the enclosure and crouched down, careful not to make any noise. She suddenly realized if she ran into trouble she might lose her tools. Maybe it would have been smarter to convince a beast to come with her and work on removing the collar outside the camp. It was too late now. She'd committed to doing this, and if a beast killed her, her tools would be useless to them, anyway.

The gates of the enclosure were open. Apparently there was no fear of the animals getting out of the cages. All the better for her. An eruption of cheering and shouting started behind her. The bull-men and the bird-men were up to something. She glanced behind her, then back to the enclosures. She'd come this far. She wasn't going to fail by getting distracted by something else.

The reek of feces and urine assaulted her. The cages were on legs that kept them off of the ground and allowed the waste drain out. From the grime and potent smell, they hadn't been concerned with making the place comfortable or clean. She didn't have to go far to find the beasts; their cages lined every inch of the fences. A smaller row of stacked cages took up most of the middle.

She went unnoticed at first, but eventually but her scent reached some of the beasts, and they clawed at the bottom of their cages. Their agitation was contagious, spreading from one cage to the next. As she crept along she had to avoid touching the cages. She made her way to the back, as far as she could get from the gate. It was much quieter there. These animals were maimed and scarred, some of them matted with dried blood. They watched her with defeated eyes.

Ladi crept up to a cage holding a wolf curled in on himself. He didn't even look at her when she touched the cage and whistled softly. He sighed, refusing to acknowledge her.

"Don't get angry. I'm here to help you escape. I've been working on something that might get that collar off of your neck."

Ladi sensed a change in the air behind her. She turned slowly and locked eyes with a bear, sniffing at her from the other wall.

The white bear's fur was matted and bloodied.

"A little help wouldn't go unappreciated. You might be

next," Ladi said. She leaned out to make sure the coast was still clear

Satisfied there was no immediate danger, she put her pack on the ground at her feet and pulled out her tools. She took out her device and held it up for the wolf.

"See, I can't remove your collar from there. I need you to come a little closer."

The animal continued to ignore her.

"Listen, I can't help you if you don't come to the edge of the cage at least. I'm trying to help you."

The gate creaked and Ladi whirled around. This time the animals in the cages didn't make a sound. She could hear heavy footfalls. The bull-man was coming in her direction, and there wasn't another exit. She reached into her pack and pulled out her knives. They weren't long, but she'd been practicing with Rasha and improving her technique. If the bull-man was carrying a sword, she might be able fend him off.

He didn't bring a sword.

The bull-man was near her, sniffing at the air. Ladi remembered her pack and slid it under the nearest cage with the toe of her boot. When he came around the corner of the cage and spotted her, she was standing with her arms crossed over her chest. She leaned against the wolf's cage, trying her best to look bored. She yawned loudly.

The bull-man approached, and she jumped away from the cage. She spun and stabbed him with each of her knives. He screamed in pain.

"There's more where that came from," Ladi said. He

retreated a few steps, until he hit the wolf's cage. Why didn't the beasts help? Surely the wolf could reach him. None of the beasts made a sound, not even when someone snuck up behind her and shot her with a sleep dart.

Ladi slapped at the sting on her neck and pulled out the dart. Her vision clouded over, and she staggered toward the bull-man. Still holding the knives, she threw one, and then the other. One of them must have hit him, because as she closed her eyes the beast's plaintive cry echoed off the cages.

## 25

SHE'D FAILED. THAT'S all Rasha could think as she raced for the palace. The beasts were already attacking the small group of guards left behind. Sochi and Xeku joined her.

"Round up the rest of the council."

"Are you sure?"

"What about the prince and princess?"

Rasha hated to admit it, but that's where they were now. She regretted never meeting with Bashir and getting his opinion on things. Now it was too late. This was the brink of defeat, and they needed to get everyone out of the palace.

She nodded. "Yes, we need to evacuate the palace."

Sochi reached up and put a hand on Xeku's shoulder. Rasha still didn't understand the relationship, but she didn't have time to ask questions. They needed to hurry if they were going to help.

"Sochi, I need the Tero-Joro inside, now."

"How many?"

"Whoever we have left," Rasha said.

SHE FOUGHT for a time that seemed endless, but it couldn't have been more than a few minutes when she got to the palace. When she ducked inside, the palace was empty. It felt like an abandoned tomb. As she looked around, she became aware of an incessant scratching sound. The small beasts were clawing their way in.

Rasha stood under the spot they were digging through and listened. There was something there, something urging the small beasties to fight without the collars.

Sochi arrived with a young man from the field. He had gangly limbs and eyes and ears larger than any Rasha had ever seen, even on someone from Tero-Joro.

"Where are the others?" she asked, looking behind them.

"He's the only one," Sochi said, pushing the young man forward. He flinched under Rasha's scrutiny.

"One?" Rasha groaned. "What am I going to do with one?"

"We could start with turning off the thing making that noise," he said.

"What noise?" Rasha asked.

"You probably can't hear it. The little flying beasts are being drawn to that high-pitched tone. Maybe it's imitating a predator or something."

"I don't hear anything." Sochi turned her head to one side, and then the other.

Rasha shook her head. She couldn't hear anything either.

"Where is it coming from?" Rasha asked, but the boy was already on the move. He had his face to the wall and then the floor.

"It's below here."

"I'll run down and see if I can find it." Rasha turned for the kitchens where she could access the stairs below.

"No," he said.

Rasha turned back to him, her swords twirling in challenge.

"No, what?"

"No, Your Highness." He was still crouching down with his head to the floor.

Rasha wanted to pull her out her hair. Not only did she have a Tero-Joro with her, but he had to be the slowest one she'd ever met.

"I meant, why not?" She rolled her eyes at Sochi.

Her aunt looked ready to giggle. Then she looked up at the ceiling where the persistent scratching continued, and a frown replaced the smile.

"The device is here. Not far. Just underneath these stones." He tapped on them until he got to one that echoed. "There."

Sochi thrust her longsword into the crack between stones. It wiggled, and she used her sword as leverage to free the stone. When they removed the stone, the sound increased, as did the scratching. The device underneath the stone was no bigger than the palm of a hand. The young man reached in and pulled it out.

"It's amazing. The vibration and tones are in perfect harmony to make it irresistible to the beasts. I'm not sure if they want to attack it or if they're drawn to protect it."

"Turn it off," Rasha said. Then she raised her eyes to the widening hole in the cupola. She raised her swords, ready for whatever came through.

"The design is intricate and delicate. Oh, that's interesting."

Rasha watched with horror as one beast got through and then another.

"Turn it off!"

The young man was turning it over in his hands.

"That's what I was trying to tell you, it's on a remote trigger, but it can't be far away. Whoever set this up inside the palace did it a long time ago."

Sochi took it from him, dropped it on the floor, and crushed it with the heel of her boot. The animals that were struggling to get in seemed confused now, flying around in haphazard circles. She and Sochi chopped down three that had gotten in.

"What would a remote for that thing look like?" Rasha asked.

"Probably no bigger than your finger. Could be a disk or oblong shape. It wouldn't need much power but it wouldn't have good range. The person had to be standing almost here when the device was triggered," he said.

"Someone inside the palace, just now, did this." Rasha wanted to be certain.

"Yes," Sochi said.

Without a doubt, the traitor was within the walls of the palace, and it hadn't been the traitor they'd put in a cell. What if he'd been innocent all along, as he'd claimed? Rasha's stomach churned and flipped as she realized that if she'd had her way, the man would already be dead.

"You didn't know. You can't blame yourself." Her aunt placed a light hand on her shoulder, reassuring her. Rasha stared at her. Did she look as guilty as she felt? Rasha shook off her distress.

"Sochi, I need you to make sure the palace is clear in its entirety. Evacuate everyone. Don't forget Temi. He's locked up in my suite. Make sure to take our prisoner with you. You know where to take them," Rasha said. There was only one place that would be safe enough.

"Yes, Your Highness, I do." Sochi gave her a slight bow.

Xeku burst in. "You're with me," Sochi said, and he followed her down the corridor without question.

The young man watched them leave, and then looked up at Rasha. His large green eyes searched her face. She had an idea, and she said a silent prayer to the Universal that it worked.

"How fast can you make a bomb?"

## 26

THE WINGED STRANGER met them outside and seemed to glide over the ground as he walked. Jak and Ebere had trouble keeping up with him. When they came to the edge of the woods, he slowed down. There the winged man stopped in a small clearing. He turned to Jak and Ebere.

"I think we can help each other," the winged man said.

"You're from the far reaches of the Wilds. I don't think I've seen your kind for over a decade." Jak said, looking him over, resisting the urge to tug at his feathered wings.

"Yes, well, we made ourselves scarce on this side of the Wilds as more of your kind started coming. Are your eyes broken? You're staring at me, green man."

Ebere had been staring. In fact, so hard and so close he had to step back. "I apologize. I've never seen anything like you in all ten kingdoms."

"That may soon change," he said. "My name is Tarrik.

My people are the Wola. We would like to consider your offer."

"What offer?" Jak asked.

"The offer you made to the banker. We will claim the eleventh kingdom."

Jak was dumbfounded.

"I'm not sure I understand," he said slowly. I made that offer to the businessmen of the Wilds because they're the ones who have the power to influence the rest. We need fighters."

"The Wola will fight with you. But the eleventh kingdom will be ours. The rest of your kind will have to leave or submit to our governance." Tarrik waited for Jak to process his this.

Ebere looked at Jak with wide eyes. It was bad enough he'd made the offer without the approval of the council. Now, he'd have to explain that not only had he committed them to this new kingdom, but those of Bolaji living here would be subject to Wola law. Jak thought for a moment. He knew what he had to do, but wasn't sure anyone other than Rasha and the Wola would like it. They'd have their fighters, and the Wola would be able to enforce their laws.

"How many fighters can you bring?"

Tarrik smiled as he looked up into the trees surrounding them. Jak followed his eyes and saw that the trees were filled with Wolans. Men and women with big, white wings smiled down at him. They carried swords and bows. They filled the trees as far as he could see. There had to be hundreds of them. How could there be so many when in his eighteen rotations he'd only ever seen one?

He put his right fist to his chest and held up his other hand up to Tarrik. Unsure, Tarrik just looked at it. Ebere assisted by repeating the gesture and nodding to Tarrik. When he lifted his hand, Jak closed the distance between them, placing his palm on Tarrik's. When he tried to step back, Tarrik wrapped his wings around Jak and leaned in until their foreheads were touching. When the wings had released him, Jak smiled and slapped Ebere on the back in congratulations.

Turning back to Tarrik, Jak said, "We need to get to Adalu right away. Any chance we can have a lift?"

## 27

*L*ADI'S HEAD FELT like someone hit her with the blunt end of an axe. She couldn't make out which way was up. She rubbed her eyes, trying to adjust to the dark. At last, she was able to make out they'd put her in a cage. It was small and cramped. A collar was heavy around her neck. They'd caged her not far from where they found her. She put her face against the door and looked down. The white bear was across from her. That meant she was in the cage just above the wolf she'd been trying to save.

"Wolf, wolf! Can you reach my pack?"

"Leave it be, greenie girl," the bear growled in a distinct but feminine tone. Although it was guttural, Ladi could understand her. Which meant they'd been able to understand everything she'd said before.

"I won't. I'm trying to rescue you."

"Some rescue. You got yourself captured."

Then she laughed, a throaty rumble. She slammed her hand against the door, and it rattled, but didn't give an inch. What did she expect? The animals didn't trust her. So far, she'd only managed to get herself caught and collared.

Reaching up, she put a finger between the collar and her neck, testing the edges.

"I wouldn't if I were you." The bear leaned against her own cage. "The last beast ended up with his head exploding all over the bars."

"Why didn't you tell me that before?" Ladi asked.

"You were too busy rescuing us." The bear snorted, and the oversized wolf cackled. "What a terrible ally your kind would make. We're better off eating you." The bear's sneer fueled the flames of her anger.

Ladi thought of her brother. If he were here he'd have come up with a plan already. He'd recounted dozens of stories to her family about his daring escapes with Rasha. What would he do if he were stuck in a cage with a collar? Ladi closed her eyes and took a deep breath. It didn't make her gag this time; her senses were adjusting to the smell. She blocked everything out for a moment. When she opened her eyes again, she examined the cage, every edge, every inch, looking for any sign of weakness.

And she found one.

A weakened link in the links of the cage. She pulled out her hairpins. They were actually small knives, designed for a woman to conceal in her hair. She used one to wear the link down further.

"Still trying to save us, green girl?" the bear said, watching her work.

Ladi stopped to listen for any movement. It was quiet, and she went back to her work.

"You won't survive the competition."

"What competition?"

"Why do you think we're all in here?" She let out a guttural laugh. The surrounding beasts joined in. It was strange, talking with these animals. They had higher reasoning skills and spoke the common language, albeit a bit growly.

"She'll see, she'll see," a small beastie in a cage beside her said, with hysterical hissing laughter. He grabbed the chains and rattled the cage violently. The disturbing little beast didn't say anything more, but his strange manner and excitement unnerved her.

Ladi continued to work at the chains until she heard the distinct sound of hooves approaching. Four bull-men returned with a beast laid out on a makeshift stretcher. The faded blue of the material was indistinguishable from the animal's blood that saturated it. They carried the beast to the far corner of the enclosure. He was already dead— that, Ladi could see for herself. The mauled beast was a wolf once, but now was a pile of torn up fur. Whatever had killed him, it had been thorough.

A soft howl began near the front of the enclosure. A sad and plaintive cry that brought tears to her own eyes, and she mourned with it. The mourning howls carried from cage to cage in waves as the animals inside the enclosures joined in mourning their dead. The old wolf below her cage took part in the grief song. What had happened to the beast? Where had they taken him? Ladi used the sound as cover for her cutting and continued to work on her escape.

When the howling ceased, Ladi put down her small knives. Her hands were cramped and aching. She'd made some progress, though. She leaned her head against the door and noticed the bear was looking at her.

"You know what happened to him, don't you? The mauled beast," Ladi said, keeping her voice low.

"He had to compete today. Entertainment for the birds and the bulls. He was defeated by his opponent," the bear replied, her brown eyes full of sadness.

"Why did they bring him back here?"

"A warning for the rest of us. Another will be chosen to fight tomorrow. Every day another dies."

"I don't understand why you won't fight back. Together you're stronger than they are. I could help you. In my bag there's a device that will help me to remove your collars."

"Can you remove them all at the same time?" She smirked as best a bear could.

"I don't think so. I've only taken off one so far."

"Then it won't work."

"Even if the biggest of you were free? I can't believe you would all rather die."

The wolf below her growled.

"Stupid green girl," he barked quietly. "You think you

know something about what's happening here. You know nothing." He slammed his head against his cage. "We fight because we must. They have collared our mates, our cubs. They've killed entire families in an instant for the pleasure of watching us die."

Ladi, stunned into silence, didn't say another word. It wasn't the collars that kept them subservient, but the hostages. The bull-men and the bird-men captured the families and used them for sport. A disgusting and wicked practice, but one that if she helped end could turn the entire war with the beasts around.

"If I promise to get you and your families free, will you help me?"

Ladi had to wait a full minute before she heard the softest response yet from the female bear.

"Why would you help us?"

"Because we need your help. The battle is going badly, and now that we know you're being forced to fight we don't want this to go on."

"Among your kind, are there others like us?"

"No, not like you. The animals in our realm are not as intelligent as you, nor as strong, but we would never treat them this way," Ladi said.

After another long pause the bear replied, "Yes, I'll help you. I can't speak for the others. They have reason to distrust your kind."

"I'll need my pack."

"Can you fit your arm through the cage?" the wolf growled below her.

"Not far, only up to my wrist."

"Good enough." He grunted and clawed at something. When he got what he was after, he tossed it up toward Ladi.

Her hand caught the pack. She couldn't get the whole thing inside of the cage with her. She would have to break down the components. She tied the bag to the chain link and pulled out her gear one piece at a time. The mechanism needed one of the command remotes to get the correct signal to release all the collars at once.

"Aren't you finished yet?" The bear's voice was anxious in the dark.

"I'm working in the dark without all my tools. I still need a controller."

"Leave that to me," the wolf said with a growl.

## 28

RASHA RAN THROUGH the palace with the young man from Tero-Joro. They set the bombs in key locations around the palace. The last one would be at the main door. It had to be open for the plan to start, but he was still fiddling with the bomb.

"Hurry," Rasha said, holding her swords at the ready. Several of the small beasties had already entered. She fought them off, but more were coming. "We're going now."

"One second. I've got to make sure it's in under the bearing wall or it won't work."

"No time!" Rasha grabbed him by the back of the collar and dragged him away just as a full-sized dragon charged through the doors. She half ran, half dragged him to the council chambers. Inside was the door to tunnels leading away from the palace.

Temi was outside the chambers, and he growled when she arrived. It was clear he'd been waiting for her. He'd gotten away from the others and wanted to go after the beasts.

She wouldn't let him. Rasha pushed the green boy through the door and called Temi inside so she could close the door behind them. They ran to another door. She used her code to let them in, and locked it again behind them. There was no way the beasts could get through the metal doors. They hurried through the tunnel and out into the forest.

"Now," she said.

He didn't hesitate. She respected that about him. He pushed a series of buttons and triggered the explosions. They brought the palace down on top of the beasts. It was rubble in an instant. She'd been tasked to protect the kingdom. The palace was a symbol of government and stability, the pride of the people of Bolaji. Now it lay in ruins. Even though the royals and the councilmen were safe, Rasha felt like a failure. She'd lost the entire first kingdom of Adalu to the beasts. She didn't know how many of their people survived, or if the battle was over.

The only thing she knew for sure was that she and the green boy had gotten out alive. When the sound of cracking twigs came from behind them, the green boy took to the trees faster than a bird, and she pulled her swords. Temi leapt in front of her and growled at whatever made the noise. When a low growl answered Temi, the green boy called out to Rasha to join him in the tree.

There was no place to run. From the brush, a large head emerged and peered out at them. A head that looked like Temi's. The two animals circled each other, smelling the air and clawing at the ground. Then Temi sat down and waited. The other seemed to agree this was an acceptable choice, and they sat together for a moment before nuzzling each other's necks.

"Temi found a girlfriend," Rasha said.

"I'm not so sure." The boy said. "I think he's a male."

Rasha shrugged. When the two finished their visit, the new creature yipped. Temi spun in a circle, then sat next to Rasha.

"Temi's made his choice beastie, you better go before these beasts of the north get a whiff of you," Rasha told it.

The animal sniffed at the air as if he understood, and then turned to go. Temi sighed softly behind her, and she wondered how close he had come to leaving with the other. They were the same species, and they were very rare. It was unlikely either would find another.

"Are you sure?" Rasha asked. Temi didn't budge. "Well, that's clear enough." Rasha took one last look at the burning ashes of the palace and started into the woods toward refuge.


"WHERE ARE WE GOING?" the green boy asked.

"The safest place I know." Rasha said. "By the way, what's your name?"

"I'm Chigo. I'm a direct descendent of Poge of the first kingdom."

"Good for you. Let's go. Without a tuskin we've got a long way to walk."

## 29

THE RUMBLE FROM the first kingdom reached the animals' encampment. There were cheers coming from the bird-men and the bull-men outside.

"What's happening?" Ladi asked and sat up.

The beastie in the cage next to her squeaked out an answer.

"The battle is won."

Ladi shook her head. "That's impossible. There's no way they took the first kingdom."

She tilted her head and tried to listen but couldn't distinguish their words. Then she heard it.

"Adalu has fallen!"

Ladi didn't want to believe it. If the palace was destroyed, then they'd lost. Rasha would never let that happen. Where were Jak and Ebere? Had they returned from Wilds yet? Was anyone in the palace when it was destroyed? Ladi kicked at the door several times before she moved to the corner of her cage and buried her head in her knees.

"I'm sorry, little green one," the bear said and went to the back of her own cage.

The morning came too soon. Ladi hadn't finished the device when the bull-men came for her. She didn't have to wonder what they were going to do with her because the little beastie beside her wouldn't stop shouting about the competition. Ladi didn't want to fight and kill any of the beasts. It would undermine her plans. They wouldn't form an alliance with a potential enemy.

When they opened her cage, she pushed her pack to the back. She didn't wait for them to snatch her out. She hopped out, landing on her feet in front of them. Startled by her sudden movement, they delivered a shock that weakened her knees, and she had to fight to keep herself upright. They didn't bother to close the door. Ladi whistled a tune as she was pushed along and out of the enclosure.

Ladi held up a hand to block the sun as she stumbled in front of the bull-men. She could hear a crowd shouting somewhere ahead of her. She studied the layout and the place they were heading toward. Another enclosure, but the inside of this one was an arena. The crowds were loud, almost overwhelming to her sensitive ears.

The floor of the arena was a mixture of hard, compact dirt and sand. The pungent odors of exertion and death had seeped into it. This was a place of certain death.

She was the first to arrive. She guessed they'd bring something for her to fight. Ladi's mind raced as she tried to think of a way to avoid the fight and not get them both killed.

The tools she'd used to open the first collar were hidden in her clothes, but it wouldn't stop them from using the pulse. She wouldn't be able to save them both.

When her opponent arrived, Ladi wanted to cry. The crowd laughed and started to applaud.

A white female bear growled and swiped at the bull-men guards with her long claws. When they took too long to get out of her way. The crowd of bull-men and bird-men seemed to enjoy that, too.

The bear that had just agreed to peace if Ladi could get them all out didn't seem at all surprised. Without a controller, Ladi didn't have any way to end the fight. Now more than ever, she wished that she'd listened to Rasha.

The bear looked worried as she approached. Ladi made a wide circle around her. She growled and roared at Ladi.

"We must fight," she growled

"Give me time. I'll think of something." Ladi circled the bear in the other direction, looking for anything to stop the fight.

The roaring of the crowd turned to jeers when neither of them moved forward to strike the other. The collars around their necks delivered a sustained pulse that made Ladi's teeth clamp down on her tongue until it bled. Her knees buckled under her, and she had to hold out her hands to keep her face from hitting the dirt.

The female bear shook her head and pawed at the ground.

"Do something," she pleaded.

Ladi got up and ran at the bear, then jumped on her back as if to tame her. The bear flung her into the wall. The crowd erupted in cheers and applause. They both moved more slowly than necessary and pulled back their blows. Ladi was able to duck or pretend to be hurt. Their stall didn't work for long. The bird-men caught on, and, instead of delivering another shock, a set of doors opened.

The she-bear howled in protest.

Ladi stopped and turned her back on the bear to see what was behind her. They rolled three white bear cubs in a cage out to the center of the arena. The crowd urged the guards to hurt them.

"I'm sorry," the bear said, her voice low enough for only the two of them to hear.

The she-bear delivered a ferocious swipe across Ladi's back that left three bloody lines. Ladi cried out instinctively, falling forward and away from her. The crowd roared to life again and cheered with more enthusiasm.

Ladi saw them roll out another cage. A large, collared dragon roared from inside. The dragon, it appeared, would take the place of whoever fell taking on the survivor. She scrambled up from the ground to avoid the bear's next swipe. Ladi circled the arena, looking for any escape. Fighting the bear wasn't an option, but neither was death. The doors they pushed the cages through were still open. If she managed to lead the bear that way, she might be able to move fast enough to escape through them.

"No games," the bear growled. Her eyes darted between Ladi and her cubs.

Ladi feinted, but she was too slow, slipping on the loose sand. The bear clamped her jaw on Ladi's leg and swung her further into the arena. She slammed against the cage where the cubs cried for their mother. Ladi was injured; she couldn't move her legs. She used her arms to push herself up from the dirt. Around her, the shouts of the crowd grew louder. The she-bear looked at Ladi's crumpled form, then back to her children. What came next, no one saw coming. Least of all Ladi.

Another dragon dropped down from the sky and set down in the center of the arena. The beast without a collar roared at the crowd, who had no power over him.

A small beastie, hissing with laughter, flew into the ring, carrying something in its mouth. It was the crazy animal that had been in the cage next to her. How had he escaped? It dropped a bag in front of Ladi. It was her pack. Ladi turned her head and heard the sound of many cages opening. The bull-men and the bird-men didn't appear to notice.

The pack in front of her had the device she'd modified. She reached inside and pulled it out. The weight of the pack was off; there was something else inside. She reached in and felt a controller. With a few more modifications, and the dragon distracting the others, she could use the controller the way she'd planned. Her legs wouldn't move, but her hands flew as she focused on the sensors. The she-bear was standing in front of the cage now, blocking her from the view of the guards. Blood on her hands made the tools hard to hold, but even as they slipped, she worked. When she had it ready, she hesitated for just a moment. If she was wrong, she might kill them all. They would use their controllers soon, and they'd all die, anyway. She had to try. Her thumb found the small indention, and she pressed down.

The collars around their necks hissed and snapped open at the same time. Ladi stared as the she-bear attacked the guard that stood between her and her cubs. With one paw, she knocked him to the ground and then rushed to open the cage and free her babies. More animals streamed into the arena and attacked the crowd. Bird-men tried to take to the sky in all directions, but they were no match for the freed dragons. The old wolf joined her a moment later.

"Little green girl, can you run with us?"

Ladi smiled. "I can't. Will you help me?"

"I will."

"Will you join the fight?"

"We already have," the old wolf said and knelt down so she could climb onto his back.

## 30

*J*AK RETURNED TO THE hub with the winged man. The place was as quiet as a tomb. Everyone's eyes were on their communicators or on the vid screen above the bar.

"What's going on?" Ebere asked.

A woman near him put a finger to her lips and shushed him.

"The beasts destroyed the palace," she said.

"What?" Jak pushed his way through the crowd and watched as the Tero-Joro reported on the activity in around the palace that day. The explosion could be seen for miles, and the aftershocks felt throughout Adalu.

When the news ended, a few of the patrons caught his eye. Jak took it as a signal to speak.

"Do you see now? This isn't just a Bolaji kingdom's problem. It will be a problem for you soon enough. The winged men from your eastern border have agreed to join us." Jak gestured to Tarrik, who gave a solemn nod. "They make up the majority of the Wilds territory east of here, and they will become the eleventh kingdom of Bolaji."

The entire bar was riveted. Some grumbles came from the table where Mr. Waza was.

"There are thousands of them, and we're only too happy to welcome them into our kingdom. Details and paperwork pending, their requests have been agreed to." Jak made eye contact with several of them as he spoke.

"What about us? We have demands too!" A woman in the back corner who'd scoffed earlier stood up to speak.

Jak smiled. He'd been hoping for this reaction. "I apologize, I'm merely a representative of the Adalu kingdom. I cannot speak for Tarrik, who has assumed the role of Wild's representative. Address your questions to him."

Tarrik stood up and waited, but the bar remained silent. Most of them had seen little of the Wola. They'd be having a lot more dealings with them in the future.

"We Wola don't want to disrupt the community you've created here, but we are lawless no more. We have plenty of time to discuss the details of the agreement later."

Mr. Waza stood up. "That's not the way we do business around here Mr. Tarrik." He glanced around.

Tarrik took a threatening step closer to Mr. Waza.

"No, you don't do business here at all unless we say so. This land has belonged to our people for generations, and we've grown tired of your lawless ways. I suggest you get used to a new way of doing things.

"However, in cases of emergency, I'm sure we can make an exception."

There was chatter after that, but the general malcontents didn't argue.

"We need to hurry. The situation at the palace is dire. With your help, we may change things," Jak said.

"It may be too late," Tarrik replied. He glanced at the monitor. "But we've agreed to your terms. Let's see if there's anything we can do."

FLYING with the winged men wasn't as comfortable or as convenient as Jak imagined. The position of their wings meant Tarrik could only hold him facing the ground or embrace him face to face. Both felt too intimate for their short acquaintance, but he decided that looking out over the landscape would be better than not seeing what was coming.

Jak watched as the sky went from black to purple and then orange. The sun was rising behind them. When they reached the third kingdom, Jak yelled, "Wait, I see something. We need to go down there."

"This is not the first kingdom," Tarrik said.

"No, but I believe they've moved the government officials here."

"Why would you think that?"

"The princess. This is where she's from. We need to check."

"As you wish." Tarrik changed course, and the Wola went with him.

There was too much activity here for it to be a regular day at the castle. He'd been there and seen their routine. They banked toward the castle, and the guards, two lines of men dressed in purple, loosed arrows at them before Jak could explain who they were. He understood their confusion: they could be a new kind of beast. But where was their leader? Rasha had a way of telling the difference between beast and humanoid.

The Wola outmaneuvered the arrows with ease. Tarrik put Jak down right in front of the line. At the sight of Jak, the archers paused.

"Hold your fire!" Jak put his arms up. "These are the Wola. They're here to help us fight the beasts. Lower your weapons."

The head of the guard dropped his bow and nodded to his men.

"What's going on here? Where is the Princess?" Jak asked. The Wola stood behind him.

"I beg your pardon, Your Grace. I am Kufre, captain of the guard. The Princess hasn't been heard from since before the palace fell." The guard turned and led them back to the castle.

Jak looked up at the foreboding castle and reminded himself he was the prince incumbent. He still had a job to do.

"The council. Where are they?"

"They are somewhere in Chilali, but we don't know

exactly where. No one knows. We have orders to shoot any beasts and await the Princess."

Jak felt something heavy in his chest. What if she'd been inside during the explosion? He reached up and touched the mermaid necklace.

"Temi, the animal she travels with, is he here?"

"No, Your Grace."

That was something. Temi wouldn't leave Rasha if she were still alive. He wouldn't leave her if she was dead either, but he pushed that thought away before it could take root and worry him.

"The king and queen will wish to meet with you," said Kufre.

"I'm sure they will." Jak remembered his last visit. He'd been chained up and locked in a cell. To Tarrik he said, "I need to speak with king of Chilali. Will you be all right here with Ebere?"

"We'll be fine. Patrols can be extended, and additional eyes on the sky and in the trees may be of help."

Kufre looked the winged man up and down. He was only about half the Wola's height. Anyone else would have been intimidated by their muscular physique and large, white wings. Kufre stood up straight and nodded. "Good idea. Get your people where they can be the most help. Just let me take the Prince to the castle, and we'll coordinate from here."

Tarrik gave him a brisk nod and turned to Jak. "I will have my best people coordinate the patrols and report back to the guards. I will join you, Jak, after your council with the king." As he spoke, the nearest Wola nodded.

"When I conclude my business, I'll meet you both back here."

Ebere nodded.

"This way, Your Grace." Kufre gestured to the steps leading to the upper levels.

Jak laughed to himself. "Of course," he said.

The large doors swung open, and the guard motioned Jak inside, but didn't follow. The king and queen, adorned with crowns and fur-trimmed robes, were sitting on thrones.

"Please, Your Highness, you're welcome here." Rasha's mother's eyes gleamed as he entered. He didn't have a clue what was going in her head, and was grateful he didn't know.

"How very nice to see you," Rasha's father said through gritted teeth.

Jak noticed that, aside from Rasha's parents on their thrones and their personal guards behind them, the room was empty.

Jak bowed to them.

"You have brought the Wola." The King's voice was expressionless. That's where Rasha got it, he thought.

"Yes. They are willing and able to help us on the front lines against the beasts. I was hoping to find Rasha here with her people after what happened in Adalu last night."

Rasha's mother let out a squeak as she held a handkerchief to her mouth in distress.

"She has not returned home. We expect that she might have been delayed, but guards have been sent to retrieve her and bring her here," the king said.

"When were the guards sent?"

The king's color deepened. "An hour ago."

"An hour?"

"At the moment, protecting the kingdom from the beasts must be our priority. Many from Adalu have sought shelter here, and we must attend them."

"I see." Jak worried his lip, wondering what to do. Her parents seemed less than concerned for her safety, and the northern border still needed protection. Without Rasha, he wasn't sure which plan to execute. Perhaps he should go and find her himself. The Wola might be willing to spare a few for the search. If she was injured, or worse, the guard might not find her in time.

"Is there anything else we can do for you?" the King asked. Jak noticed that he refused to use his title. He didn't seem to like being subservient to the young prince. Jak would have found it funny if he wasn't so preoccupied with Rasha.

"Not at this time. It is the priority of the first kingdom that we be prepared to face the enemy. It is my personal responsibility to find the Princess, and I will." He looked at the queen of Chilali and gave her what he hoped was a reassuring nod.

She mouthed a thank you, and he excused himself.

"Young Prince," the King called to him before he reached the doors. Jak turned back. He stood from his throne and walked over to Jak. He wasn't as tall as Jak, but he managed look down on him as if he were an insect.

"Let me be clear about something. My daughter may be the last princess alive, but you are not the last prince. I will see that my daughter has The Choosing at her earliest convenience."

Jak nodded and left. If he'd been wondering about her parents' opinion of him, he didn't have to wonder anymore. The king was letting him know not only that he wasn't good enough, but they didn't trust that Rasha had chosen him herself. He didn't concern himself with their opinions. Instead, he wondered how he was going to get Rasha. Her aunt had been among the fighters. He would coordinate with her in order to track down Rasha. Besides, he was pretty sure that Sochi had a better opinion of him than her brother.

31

———————

*W*HEN RASHA AND Chigo reached Chilali, she didn't go in the direction of the castle. She turned instead in the direction of her Aunt Sochi's home.

Rasha opened the door to the small cottage, and a warm gust of heat welcomed her. They stumbled inside, both blue from the cold.

"I thought maybe you would have started a fire and kept yourselves warm until morning," Sochi said as she pulled them inside.

Temi walked in behind the others, shaking the cold off of his fur. He walked to the fire and sat himself down.

"T-too cold, and wet. B-better to keep m-moving." Rasha's teeth chattered as she spoke.

"Look at you both, cold, tired, and starving." She pulled out a chair for each of them. "Sit yourselves down.

I've got breakfast on." She bustled around the kitchen, preparing their bowls.

She put the bowls of porridge in front of them, and they ate hungrily. The warmth of the fire seeped into Rasha's bones. She felt herself nodding off and sat up sharply.

"I need to meet with the council and discuss what is to be done now that the…" Her voice trailed off, and her eyes fluttered closed as she fought sleep.

"Right now, you're not going anywhere. Off to bed with you."

Sochi took Chigo by the hand and led him to a small cot near the fire, where he curled up and fell asleep in seconds. Temi lay near his feet and hadn't moved from the fire since their arrival.

Sochi shooed Rasha along to the bedroom. Sochi's room was filled with books and candles, and was a quiet sanctuary. She kept her current reading and keepsakes near the bed, along with a vase of white flowers. There was a desk and chair in the corner nearest the window. Rasha lay down on the bed and felt her body sink into the mattress. The last thing she remembered was her aunt humming as she removed Rasha's boots.

When Rasha woke, the sun was high in the sky. Her throat was dry and scratchy enough to force her out of the heavy blankets. She sat up and saw a glass of water on the table and drank the entire thing. Sighing, she put her boots back on and went into the other room.

Chigo was already awake and eating another bowl of porridge.

"Good morning, again," Sochi said. "Come eat."

"I'm fine. I need to meet with the others. Are they here?"

"Yes, I've given them something to eat and they are awaiting your orders, Your Highness."

"You don't have to call me that anymore. I think you know that."

"Until you are officially replaced I'll respect your role as we all should." Her aunt gave her a significant look.

Rasha nodded and went to the door.

"Temi, stay here and watch Chigo."

Temi made a half circle behind her, and then sat looking at Chigo.

Chigo said, "Rasha, wait, maybe I should come with you." Rasha was already out the door. The meeting she had planned couldn't include an ordinary citizen of the ten kingdoms. The real princess and prince would be there.

Rasha made sure no one was watching when she went into the barn. In the last stall on the right, she pulled a loop of rope, revealing a set of stairs leading down. She could see a faint light emanating from the rooms below.

Rotations ago, when she'd gotten into some trouble and needed a place to hide, Rasha had come here. Though it was three rotations ago, it seemed like another life now. Things had changed so much in such a short time. But Aunt Sochi hadn't changed at all. She'd always stood by Rasha.

Rasha followed the familiar tunnel until she reached the main room, two guards alert at their post outside. Each of them took a knee and bowed to her.

"Is the council ready?"

"Yes, Your Highness."

Rasha went in and found the council waiting, as promised. This room was nothing like the chamber in the palace. The council sat around a long wooden table. There were only twelve high-backed chairs, leaving Rasha to stand. Everyone stood as she entered. It was just habit she knew, because when the council stood, Prince Bashir and Princess Chiza looked up with confusion. A few councilmen sat back down. The real prince and princess incumbent were in the room; they shouldn't be looking to her anymore. Why did that bother her?

Prince Bashir was the first to speak.

"Princess, we are so glad to see you are well."

"Thank you, your grace. I bring news, none of it good."

The Prince stood, yielding his seat at the head of the table to her and moved to stand behind Chiza's chair. It afforded all at the table a view of him, except Chiza.

Rasha sat down and told the council and the royals what had transpired the night before and why.

"What gives you the right?" Gungbe the Karmirian asked. He slammed a fist against the table and his skin turned an even darker red. "You failed to protect the first palace from the beasts, and then you destroyed it."

Rasha knew this might happen. They had been evacuated and didn't grasp how dire the situation had been.

"Are you sure it didn't work?" Chiza asked, her voice a soft and calm contrast to Gungbe's.

Rasha nodded.

"I'm sure. By the time Chigo and I escaped, there was nothing left of the palace, and the beasts were dancing on the ashes."

A general unease rose at the table, and several of them grumbled in response to this news. She'd destroyed their home, hoping to take down the beasts, but it hadn't worked.

"We must retaliate. Send the beasts a message!" Gungbe raged.

"How can you speak of retaliation when our forces are down to nothing?" Bashir asked him with outrage on his face.

"What if we go into hiding?" The mermaid Keabasi was looking around the table. "I know this isn't what we wanted, but perhaps we should consider saving ourselves. The kingdom is lost. Now is the time to run."

"I don't think it'll solve the problem," Ummo from the tenth kingdom said.

Soon they were all speaking over of each other. No one was listening to anyone else anymore. This seemed like a good time for Rasha to interject. Instead of raising her hand she stood up.

"Rasha has a plan. I think we should hear it," Tobi, the Chilalian shouted, then looked at her.

"I'm sorry. I don't have a plan, not without hearing from Ladi and Jak. We can't move forward until we know what we're working with. The best thing we can do now is gather our forces and bring them to Chilali's northern border to regroup."

"I don't like it," Gungbe said. "You're only telling the beasts where we are. What's to stop them from coming here and attacking Chilali?"

"Nothing. But we can't sit by and wait for them to enter a less defended kingdom." Rasha took a moment to look at every pair of eyes. "We have resources. We only need to gather them. I believe we can track down our people and prepare ourselves."

The table grumbled again. The Prince cleared his throat this time. Once all eyes were on him, he spoke.

"Princess Rasha has been leading this war from the start. Now is not the time to abandon her. Do as she says, all of you. We may not have much time. The more time we sit in this room arguing, the less we'll be able accomplish."

Bashir spoke with such a natural authority; it was no wonder they listened to him. She saw the respect in their eyes, a kind of respect they'd never shown her. Perhaps it's because he always knew he would be king someday. The easy way he wielded his power had come with time and practice. After the council meeting ended, Rasha decided to track down the others as soon as possible. Jak's delay was worrying her. His last message implied he was working on something that could help turn the war. She'd received no other communications. When thoughts of him together with his wife entered her mind, she pushed them aside. She didn't have any energy to give to the situation.

Xeku caught her before she left. "He'll be here soon." Xeku's eyes, so like Jak's, seemed to see right through her.

"I'm worried what he'll be coming back to."

"You're doing your best. Don't doubt yourself now. You did what you could."

"It wasn't enough." That's what bothered her the most. Her leadership hadn't been enough, not from the start. The role of princess incumbent hadn't been enough to give her authority. She wasn't enough. She wished that Lu was there. He had a way of helping her see the way out of things. They'd been in several tight places and had always come through. She wondered, as she often did, if he were still alive, what would he do right now?

"It has to be enough." Xeku reached a familiar arm around her shoulders as he spoke in her ear. Intimate in a way that made her want to shrug him off until he said,

"The traitor is still among us."

Rasha had forgotten all about the traitor. The one that had placed the trigger that brought the little flying beasts to the palace. They were still hiding in plain sight and trying to undermine everything they had done to save the first kingdom. She glanced at Kyuk. She'd thought him the traitor, but he'd been safely locked away until they evacuated him. He sat with the others as if he'd never been accused. Rasha nodded at Xeku, and then turned to go.

Being in the same room with a traitor made Rasha want to crawl out of her skin. All of their lives were in danger as long as the traitor lived.

The sound of swords being drawn in the corridor had the council backing away, and Rasha stepped forward, her two swords raised. She raised her voice above the commotion.

"Everybody, get back."

*L*ADI SAT BY the edge of a riverbank, watching the mother bear speak in low growls and whispers to her three undamaged cubs. The scars and matted fur borne by the mother from her terrible ordeal were jarring in comparison. The beasts had stopped to rest and get water here. There were hundreds of them, and they helped each other as they raced for the first kingdom of Adalu. Each of them bore the scars of life as a caged slave.

"I never got your name," Ladi said to the mother bear.

"My friends call me…" She growled, and Ladi shook her head, unable to imitate the sound. The bear laughed. "Yes, I know, hard for your small throat to make those sounds. I will give you something easier. Call me Osa."

"Osa. I like it. My friends call me Ladi."

"Ladi." Osa struggled some with the 'l' sound, but it

was understandable, and much better than Ladi could do with the bear's real name.

"These are my babes. I thank you for saving us."

"I didn't just do it for unselfish reasons, I'll admit that. I just hope it's not too late."

"You are right, we should go. Come." Osa made the call to gather, and the other beasts assembled and began the trek toward the first kingdom again.

Ladi had regained some feeling in her legs, but not enough to walk. The old wolf, Browl, as he called himself, had grown tired and charged one of the dragons with her care. The one that had saved her in the arena. Many of the animals—including the dragons—couldn't enunciate well enough to use the common language. They would have to find a name for him later. He scooped her up, and they took to the skies. It wasn't long before they reached the ruins of the palace. Rubble and ash were all that remained in the place where the palace once stood.

Ladi's heart sank at the sight of it. It was worse than her imagination had conjured up. The black stain against the snow still on the ground around it suddenly reminded her of Osa's scarred skin against the white it should have been. She pointed to the ground, and the dragon sat her down in the middle of the grove facing the palace.

The smell of charged earth and building materials was faint as the winds here were strong. Using a large stick she'd found for balance, Ladi limped among the charred remains. She scanned the ground, looking for something, anything, that might give her a clue as to where they would have gone. There was nothing. She was about to give up when Browl signaled them to the far east end of the palace.

"There are a lot of tracks heading this way." He pointed with his nose in the direction of Chilali.

Ladi looked at the snow-covered ground. Despite the fresh fall and the wind that blew some of the snow around the tracks were unmistakable. It was the best lead they had to finding the others.

"We'll follow them. They lead to Chilali, the birthplace of the princess incumbent. She may have sent everyone there to regroup." Ladi wondered if Rasha had made it or if someone else was leading the charge now. Although she was worried, she couldn't imagine anything happening to Rasha. She had to be alive.

"Let's go. Tread carefully, there may be some frightened people along the way who don't know that we're on their side now."

THE DOOR OPENED, and a guard with a message came in.

"Prince Jak, Ebere, and a guest, Your Grace." He looked at Rasha, then looked past her and bowed again toward Bashir and Chiza.

Rasha put Cutter and Blade away as Jak entered the room. She tried to keep her face neutral. He looked at her for a long moment, as if he were committing her to memory. His eyes looked tired, but he held his shoulders back.

"Hey, Rash," he said.

She stared back at him, so many feelings and thoughts rushing at her at the same time that she couldn't decide which one she wanted to express first.

"Prince Jak," Bashir said, stepping around a tongue-tied Rasha, and regarded the giant winged man with surprise.

Rasha shook off her emotions and spoke.

"How did you find us?"

"Your aunt. I'd planned to go in search of you but she directed me here," Jak said.

"What news do you bring, along with your winged friend?" she asked, looking up at the Wola.

"Mostly good news. Let's sit with the council, for this concerns them as well." Jak moved past them to the table.

Rasha heard Xeku ask him in a quiet and mild tone, "Your mother?"

Rasha watched as Jak shook his head, eyes on the floor. She regretted she'd never get the chance to meet her. Xeku nodded and went back to his seat at the table, his own shoulders slumped.

Jak waited for the council to take their seats.

When all eyes were on him, he took a deep breath and started to speak. "While I was in the Wilds on a family matter, I made a second approach to the leaders of local trade and commerce. They rejected my offer. However, the winged men—they are called the Wola—were willing to listen. Tarrik and the others have agreed to join us, with one condition."

Bashir looked pleased. "What is their condition?"

"Ishola will become the eleventh kingdom of Bolaji."

The silence in the room only amplified their uncomfortable fidgeting.

Tarrik took a step forward.

"Is there a problem?" Tarrik asked.

"There is no problem. As the prince incumbent, I have

committed to this course of action on behalf of the ten kingdoms," Jak said, looking at Bashir.

"You should not have done that," Bashir said, his mouth in a grim line.

"Won't you even consider the prospect?" Jak asked.

"How many winged men do you bring?" Rasha ignored Jak's question.

Tarrik answered her, "We are two thousand fighters, but there are a thousand more guarding Ishola, where another three thousand women and children take refuge."

The council was quiet for a moment as they considered the implications.

It was Gungbe who broke the silence. "This is an outrage! You can't just go around making deals with whoever you like and offering them a kingdom." Gungbe's face turned dark red.

"You have overstepped your authority," Bashir said to Jak. "We cannot offer these men a kingdom."

"Why not?" Jak asked.

"We know nothing of these people," Keabasi interjected.

"They lived in the Wilds long before our discontented people ventured there to live outside of our rule," Jak said.

"That doesn't mean we should trust them," Tobi said.

Rasha stood and joined Jak.

"They have offered to fight at our side in a war we're losing. If there's some doubt of that, please look around and remind yourselves where you are," she said. "Ebere, what do your people know of the Wola?"

"Very little. They were something of legend for a long time. Sightings confirmed their existence, but nothing more."

"May I speak?" Tarrik was polite but firm. He took their silence as consent and continued. "The Wola have long believed contact with other species would be detrimental to our bloodlines and genetic code. We feared the loss of flight after prolonged contact and mixing with your races. When those of your kind moved into our lands, but kept to the edges, we allowed it. Now they are venturing further and further east. Their lawless attitudes and ways disturb us. We would rather join the Bolaji kingdoms than deal with your wayward people on our own."

"A sound and reasonable argument, and one we must consider. In this war we need all the help we can get. We must consider all options," Xeku said.

Bashir thought for a moment, then said, "All right. I agree this matter is urgent, and we must consider all possible solutions. The council will discuss your request. Jak, Rasha, Ebere, and Tarrik, you're free to go until a decision is made."

"Wait, why Rasha and me?" Jak asked.

"You are only prince and princess incumbent in my absence. I am here now and will assume my royal duties. Chiza will remain as she has no biased interest in this manner and I require her council."

"Yes, but—," Jak protested, then stopped himself. He bowed, and led the others out of the room.

Rasha had mixed feelings about being dismissed as

413

well, though she couldn't imagine why. She'd never wanted the responsibilities in the first place. But now they'd been taken away so abruptly she didn't know what to think about it. Did Bashir expect to lead them into battle now as well? She doubted that very much.

Temi was outside growling at the sky when they exited the barn. Rasha drew her swords.

"Did you bring any men with you?" she asked Tarrik.

"Yes, but I sent them out looking for you," Tarrik said.

"The beasts. They've found us."

A dark cloud of flying beasties was headed in their direction. Rasha remembered something.

"Wait here."

"Wait here and what? What are they?" Jak asked. "Rasha—"

"I'll be right back." She dashed into the house.

Sochi and Chigo were chatting at the table.

"They're here."

Sochi jumped up and went for her sword.

"Who's here?" Chigo asked.

"Remember the little beasties that were controlled with that device?"

"Yes."

"They're coming."

"How can that be? We destroyed the device." Chigo got up from the table and looked into his pack for the tracker.

"Yes, I know, but the traitor is here with us. They must

have put another one here or in the barn," Rasha said with agitation.

"If they have, I can find it." Chigo turned on his tracker and went outside.

Ebere and Jak saw him and then followed as he searched.

"What are you looking for?" Ebere asked.

"A resonant sound amplifier. It's putting out a steady signal that irritates the small flying beasts," Chigo said without looking up. He went into the barn, everyone trooping behind. He stopped at the last stall.

Rasha opened the door, and he headed down the steps. She nodded to the others to stay. "Keep them away from this door."

She followed Chigo to the council chambers. The guards stopped them from entering.

"You cannot enter now, princess, the council is in session."

Rasha heard the angry and impatient voices, but this couldn't wait.

"We're under attack. There is something in this room drawing the beasts here. The traitor must be inside. Let us pass."

"I cannot."

Rasha pulled Cutter and Blade from their sheaths.

"I don't want to fight you, but I will. The lives of the royals are at stake."

He moved to block her, but she deflected him and his

spear fell to the ground. Rasha held her swords to his neck as he backed away from the door.

Chigo opened it, and, without looking up, wandered into the room, following the tracker.

"What matter of insult is this?" Gungbe demanded.

"You cannot enter here, we are in session!" Bashir exclaimed.

Keabasi asked, "What are you doing?"

Rasha cut them all off. "There are beasts are on their way here, and soon, to this room. The traitor has put a calling device in here. We must find it and disable it before the beasts are upon us."

"Here! It's strongest here." Chigo said from the corner of the room, looking at a wooden display case next to an armchair. "I think it's behind here." Then he seemed to see the room for the first time. "Oh my, Your Highness, I apologize." He knelt down to the floor with his eyes on the ground.

Bashir raised a hand, waving away the indiscretion.

Chigo returned to searching for the device while Rasha monitored the reactions of the council. Xeku looked at the chair, and then to Gungbe. Keabasi did the same.

"Who was sitting in that chair?" Rasha asked.

Ummo turned to Gungbe, as did Tobi.

Tobi was the first to speak. "It was Gungbe. He was sitting there with his head against the case."

Gungbe got up, but Rasha was ready. She had her swords in his face before he took a step. She felt Jak behind her, but her focus was on the Karmirian.

"Rasha, wait, don't kill him. We need him," Xeku shouted.

Rasha made a low growling noise in her throat. All she could think about was Lu bleeding out on the floor of the palace in front of her. She felt a light hand on her shoulder.

"He has to answer for his part in all of this." Chiza's voice was soft and calm.

Of all of them, Rasha knew Chiza understood. Lu had been her lost love. Rasha lowered her swords, and Jak moved in to bind his wrists. She turned away. The sight of him made her sick. Ebere and Chigo were working frantically in the corner.

"Is it disabled?" she asked.

"No." They kept looking for the right connections.

"Tell us how to stop it," Jak said, holding his knife up to Gungbe's narrow neck. Gungbe clamped his mouth closed.

Rasha snatched the caller away from them.

"Let me see." She dropped it and crushed it with the heel of her boot. "How's that?"

"That'll work too," Chigo said as he reached for the broken device. The wires were exposed now, so all he had to do was cut them. The sound ceased immediately.

To the council, Rasha said, "I hope you've decided in favor an alliance, because the fight is at our doors."

"We have ruled in favor of the eleventh kingdom," Bashir said.

"Then take care of this traitor. The rest of you, let's go. We've got beasts to take down."

*R*ASHA RODE THE tuskin to the border of Chilali and Adalu with the Wola flying overhead. The small beasties had been diverted, and no other beasts had appeared, so it was time to take the fight to them. What was left of their forces would join them on the border and prepare to move on the beasts. Rasha was in command.

When they arrived at the border they regrouped, mixing their men with the reinforcements as much as possible. While they were arranging themselves, Ebere approached her.

"What about Ladi? Aren't we going to look for her? What if she was successful?" he asked.

"Ladi is on her own until we can secure the border. We lost Adalu to the beasts. I won't lose Chilali too. Stand your ground and wait for orders."

"She's just a kid! Don't you realize she might be

injured or lost?"

Rasha's anger flared, and she pulled her swords out and twirled them once. "Are you implying that I don't care about her? Because I want to be clear with you. I've known her and her family since she was knee high to a gump. I helped bury her older brother and took the news to her and her family. So if anyone cares about her, I do. But I think we have more than one person to worry about, don't you?"

Jak stepped in and pushed Ebere back and out of harm's way.

"He's a boy in love. Don't blame him for being worried," Jak said in her ear.

Rasha dropped her swords. She did understand the sentiment, but right now she was stretched to the limit, and they were on the brink of defeat. She couldn't go running off to find the little pumseed. Ladi made her choice when she snuck off in the night chasing a rumor.

"Get him away from me," she said between her teeth.

When a dragon was spotted approaching the west border, she barely had time to ready the bowmen. They awaited her signal, but she never dropped her hand. On top of the flying beast was a green girl with long, dark hair waving her hands wildly at them.

"Stand down," Rasha shouted to her fighters, and to Temi, who'd appeared at her side, ready to leap in front of her. Here, there would be no place for her to lock up Temi. He'd joined the fight, and she'd have to let him.

Ladi and the dragon landed on the trampled snow in

front of them. She eased off and, still using her stick, limped toward Rasha. Out of breath and half laughing, she threw her arms around her.

Despite everything, Rasha laughed too.

"What happened to you? Ebere was about to lose his neck over you," Rasha said. Ebere stood to one side, waiting to be acknowledged. He was so shy. Rasha felt bad now for lashing out at him.

"I found one of the encampments, and I was right. They were being forced." Rasha reached up and ran a light finger around the young girl's neck. A dark pink line remained from the collar they'd placed there.

"They took you? What happened to you?"

"It's a long story, but I'll shorten it. I helped the beasts escape. The entire encampment." She gestured with her head behind her at an enormous number of beasts approaching.

Rasha's fighters were anxious and ready to fire.

"Hold!" Jak called. There were so many of them his hand instinctively reached for his own sword. Temi was low to the ground and growling at the beasts as well. There were more than a hundred of them.

They burst through the trees. Bears huddled together, wolves in packs, and others as well.

Rasha noticed something. Fear. They were afraid. They also wore no collars. Ladi limped back toward a white bear with three cubs. Rasha and Jak exchanged a look and followed. The bear put a protective paw over the cubs as she waited for what Ladi had to say.

"This is the prince and princess of the ten kingdoms. They will grant you asylum."

"What?"

"Asylum?"

Jak and Rasha spoke at the same time. Neither corrected Ladi about their new status.

"Yes. They agreed to come here, but only if we grant them asylum from the birdmen and the bull-men. They were tortured and their families were held captive to force them to fight. We have to help them."

Rasha pulled Ladi away from the bear and her cubs.

"We are in the middle of a war we're losing, and you expect us to defend them over our own people?"

Ladi worried her bottom lip with her teeth.

"No, I thought they could stay here with us behind our lines."

Rasha ran a hand over her face and looked at Jak. He shrugged. They'd just gotten the winged Wola into the eleventh kingdom. Now they'd be going against the beasts' masters and beasts from other enslaved encampments.

"I need more fighters, not more victims. What am I supposed to do?"

"How did you get the collars off without killing them?" Ebere asked, Chigo nodding behind him.

Ladi switched into Tero-Joro and explained it to them. They nodded and added their own tech vocabulary to the exited discussion.

"Will someone please tell me in the common language what the yahtz you're talking about?" Rasha asked.

"Oh." Ladi looked surprised. "I have a way to disrupt the collars."

"That means we can turn any beasts they bring against them," Chigo said, his eyes wide and bright. Rasha wondered now, seeing him Ladi and Ebere, how old he was. He'd seemed ordinarily small for a Tero-Joro before, but he was even smaller than Ladi. He couldn't be more than thirteen. How had he ended up on the front lines of this war? Before she could ask, Jak said, "Can you gather the strongest of the beasts together? Any who can fight will be welcome to join us. If they have any ideas on how we can defeat their former masters, we would be delighted to hear them."

Ladi nodded and turned to go, but Ebere grabbed her hand, his eyes full of unspoken emotion. Ladi looked down at his hand, a confused expression on her face. She had no idea what he was doing. Rasha didn't have time for this.

"She's only fourteen, let her be," Rasha said.

"No, I'm fifteen now," Ladi corrected her, still looking at their joined hands.

"I'm happy you're well." Ebere dropped her hand after another long moment and turned away. Chigo followed him. He hadn't left Ebere's side since they'd met.

Rasha turned to Jak. "Asylum?"

Jak smiled. "It could be worse."

"How?"

"We could be dead?" Jak shrugged.

"There's still time for that."

## 35

*T*HE BATTLE BEGAN at dawn. The sun was a sliver on the southern horizon when the first of the flying creatures arrived. Rasha and her battalions were ready. She'd divided them into groups of a hundred and deployed them in a U shape on the border of Chilali. Rasha was at the front, mounted on a tuskin. She preferred fighting from the ground, but being atop the tuskin allowed her signals to be seen. The dragon she'd saved in the battle of the palace stood beside her, pawing at the ground in impatience. The tuskin, feeling the nervous energy, struggled to stand still.

"Steady," she muttered and held up a hand. The fighters behind her held their weapons ready.

Jak's group held their position on her right. Ladi, along with the bear and wolf, was on her left.

The snow was thick on the ground. Rasha didn't take her eyes off of the northern horizon when she saw the beasts coming. They'd come in high and low, their typical attack pattern. This time they wouldn't be divided by the beasts. Instead, the charge formed an arrow that would split whatever formation came their way. She waited until the nearest beast was within range.

Rasha dropped her fist and started the charge.

"Now!"

Most of the flying creatures had gone to either side of her, leaving the bull-men. She picked off a few, and then jumped off her mount and hit the ground, running for the nearest bird-man. He squawked in challenge at her. It hopped from foot to foot, trying to distract her from his powerful wings.

She didn't hesitate to clip them. He was down in a scant minute. The battle raged. As it became clear, they were winning this fight. The bird-men came out with their controllers. As expected, they had brought unwilling combatants. The beasts fighting for both sides hesitated as they faced each other. Mother against son. Father against daughter. The shocks that the bird-men delivered brought many beasts to the ground. The dragon that Rasha had spared bellowed in anger at the torture.

"Ladi!" Rasha ran toward the girl, Ebere right behind her.

"Where's Chigo?"

"He's with me," Ebere replied.

Ladi was fighting a large, scarred up bear. Rasha could see the bull-man controlling it.

"Fire that pulse as soon as it's ready," Rasha yelled to Ebere as she ran full tilt at the bull-man.

In her haste, Rasha missed the bird-man flying just above her. Talons came down on her shoulders and lifted her three feet off the ground, then dropped her before she could swing her swords. She had to roll to avoid breaking a leg and dropped Cutter in the process. Lying there on the ground, the bird-man was on top of her in seconds. She'd swung with her now-empty right hand and used her left to stab at him with Blade. Rasha felt the talons digging into her skin through her leather coverings. She grunted when the beast picked her up and threw her down, knocking the breath out of her.

She rolled over and looked up in time see the amber-eyed dragon, her friend, yank the bird-man off his feet.

"Are you all right?" Jak had seen what happened, but wasn't as fast as the dragon.

"I'm fine. How are we doing?"

Jak looked around for Ladi. When he spotted her, he smiled.

"See for yourself." Jak helped her to her feet. Her head was spinning a bit, but she was able to look around.

In that moment she couldn't be prouder as she watched Sochi and Xeku defeating beast after beast. Ebere fought with a ferociousness she'd never seen from him. The battlefield was filled with their fighters, mostly winning, thanks to the beasts and the winged men that fought beside them.

Three winged men had removed a collar from a

dragon, and all four of them took to the sky against the remaining bird-men. But it didn't matter, because Ladi sent a new pulse directly at them. This one wasn't lying in a grid formation in order to hurt the beasts, but was focused on the technology. The pulse reached its marks, shorting out the controllers.

Nothing that used any kind of technology could survive that kind of pulse. The bull-men were just realizing something was wrong when the beasts turned on their former masters with slashing claws and ripping teeth. The bird-men and bull-men and various beasts who'd chosen their side fled.

Some of their fighters started to give chase, but Rasha called them back. There was no need to pursue them. They had defeated them and freed their captives. The roars and howls of triumph from one and all echoed in her bones. She said a prayer to the Universal for the losses, as she did after every battle before letting in the joy of victory.

## 36

RASHA WOKE WITH a start. She'd been dreaming that a large beast was sitting on her chest. She looked down and saw Jak's arm stretched over her. They were both still dressed from the night before. The battle was won, and the reign of terror that the beasts had wrought had come to an end. He'd walked her to her room, and then they'd talked of all that went right that day and a few things that had gone wrong.

The sun was high in the sky as she rolled over and out of bed. Jak still slept, his beautiful face turned away from the sun streaming through a crack in the curtains. They weren't exactly where they were when he'd left, but they were still friends. He hadn't mentioned his wife, and Rasha hadn't spoken of her either. It didn't seem like the right time.

In the room of her childhood—all pink and disgusting —she wanted one good memory at last. She went to the closet and pulled out the least offensive-looking gown. A blue dress, cinched in the middle, but otherwise flattered her purple skin. She bathed and changed. When she reappeared in the bedroom, Jak was gone. A stab of disappointment cut through her.

Rasha had been hoping for some encouragement. She'd dressed up to eat breakfast in her own house not only to avoid an argument with her parents. Their anger at learning of the deception and that their daughter would not be queen was bad enough.

If she were being honest with herself, she could admit it felt strange. Rasha realized she'd worn the role so well she'd fooled herself. Her life as a courier waited for her, but now she wasn't sure how she felt about it. The incumbent title hadn't been as bad as she'd imagined. The responsibility had weighed on her: the lives of the fallen fighters, losing the palace. Those were the things that had been the hardest. She'd miss being taken seriously and having her ideas listened to. As she walked to the dining hall, she hoped that they'd all eaten earlier and the table would be empty.

It wasn't.

Seated next to her parents were Prince Bashir and Princess Chiza, both wearing royal white, and on the opposite side, Jak. He'd gone somewhere and gotten cleaned up. His hair was still damp, and he'd found something to wear besides the clothes he'd fought in. With his hair pulled back in a low queue, she could see the markings on the base of his neck. When would he tell her about those? Maybe when he told her about his wife, she mused.

There was an empty chair beside him for her. Ebere and Chigo sat side by side next to Chiza, and across from them and next to the empty chair was Ladi. She had been given a dress to wear as well, and looked stunning in the light pink gown. The rest of the council filled in the seats around the large table. They appeared to be in some kind of debate as they talked among themselves and hadn't even glanced in her direction.

Rasha went to the empty chair and made a small curtsey to both her parents and the incumbents. They nodded in her direction, and a servant pulled out the chair for her to sit down.

"Don't you look lovely this morning," her mother said to her.

"Thank you, Mother," Rasha said, putting on her polite face.

Jak leaned over and whispered in her ear, "Stunning." He let his hand rest on her thigh.

"You overslept this morning. You missed all the latest news. The council didn't sleep much last night. They were up late trying to come up with something to do about the beasts," said Prince Bashir. He swallowed a bite of food and continued. "It's been decided that for now they'll be free to live where they choose. It's best they not all live on the same hunting grounds."

Rasha nodded. She hadn't even considered that. They'd need more room.

"What about Gungbe?" She asked.

This time Jak answered. "He's already admitted to helping the beasts in order to gain the throne for himself. He thought that if he helped them they would allow him to save his Karmirian family and rule one of the kingdoms."

"He'll be brought to justice for his crimes as soon as a suitable punishment may be devised," said Prince Bashir. "Enough of that business," He waved a hand in the air, "I slept better than I have in months. I trust you did as well."

"Yes, thank you, Your Highness," Rasha said.

A few moments went by before Ladi spoke.

"Are you going to keep your dragon?" Ladi asked.

"What? Who?" Rasha asked, as Ladi was looking directly at her.

"Your dragon, the one who let you ride him."

"I hadn't thought about it," Rasha said and took a sip of her milk. It was the truth, she hadn't. "The beasts are not something to be possessed. He will go where he chooses I suppose. What about you, are you ready to enroll at the Courier's Keep?"

"I want to." Ladi was looking across the table at Ebere. He smiled and dropped his gaze when he noticed Rasha had looked at him too.

"Well, since we've lost our titles and our jobs, you're fired. So, you won't get more legal courier work until you finish your training." She gave Ladi a smile and she bit into a piece of bread.

"I know. I have a few things to take care of at home

431

before I go." Ladi pushed the food around on her plate. Rasha wasn't used to seeing Ladi so unsure of herself. It was disconcerting to know she'd matured so much in the short time they'd been together.

"The Prince was just telling us about their plans for the palace," Jak said, pulling her back into the conversation.

"Yes, we've come to a formal agreement with the Wola. Thanks to Chiza's father's generous gift, the new palace will be in the former Wilds. Its new name will be Ishola."

"What about Adalu?" Rasha asked.

"Too many bad memories there. It's time for change." Bashir patted Chiza's hand. "Speaking of change, I'm glad you're here, because I wanted to continue our conversation about changes we planned for the Choosing. Since the winter ball has been cancelled, we need to make a decision on this quickly."

Rasha tried to remember what they were talking about before their whole world had been turned upside down.

Bashir continued, "Rasha and I discussed this before the first attack on the palace, and we thought that the Choosing should change. My proposal to the young princes and princesses of the kingdom will be that instead of the traditional Choosing, we will try something new. The Choosing will be open to one eligible princess or lady from each kingdom and one eligible prince or gentleman. In that way, more than just the future king gets a potential mate."

"What a delightful idea!" Her mother clapped. She clapped. What was she doing? Rasha looked at her father, who was watching her with an intensity she had never seen before. He would say something she wouldn't like. She held her breath waiting for it.

"How will you preserve the royal lines?"

"If you mean the pure races, that's an archaic idea that I'm happy to see fall to the wayside. We are now eleven united kingdoms. It's time that we started to act as one empire."

"Making yourself the emperor. You are ambitious." Her father sneered.

"Rasha and I need to continue to work out more of the details later. I promise you'll be informed of the official changes. Let's enjoy our lovely breakfast for now." Bashir lifted his orange juice in salute. Chiza looked at Rasha. Her eyes seemed sad. Why did she look so defeated?

A guard entered the room and leaned over to speak in Rasha's ear.

"Princess, your beastie."

He didn't need to say any more. Temi's behavior was often beyond description. He hadn't followed her inside, and she'd assumed he'd needed to take care of necessary business. The only way the servants could handle him was to call on her to interpret his strange behavior.

Rasha stood up from the table to follow the guard. Jak had a strange expression on his face when she bowed to her parents and the incumbents. She couldn't read him. Was she just tired, or was everyone giving her strange looks that morning? The guard directed her to the front steps of the castle, but before he turned away, she had a message for Chiza.

"Please give Princess Chiza the discreet message that I will meet with her this evening in her rooms."

The guard nodded.

Temi was at the castle steps, whining and spinning in circles. The minute he saw her, he wiggled ecstatically. Then he dashed for the trees.

"Temi, wait!" Rasha ran into the wood after him. She realized her mistake after she'd tripped for the fifth time. Why had she worn the pumseed slippers instead of her boots? It wasn't as if her feet could be seen underneath the layers, anyway. She stumbled through the trees, using her sleeves to ward off the branches that threatened her face.

Rasha stumbled out of the trees into a clearing. Temi howled into the air. They both listened until, for the first time, she heard an answering howl. She retreated back to the edge of the tree line and waited to see what would happen.

Temi was almost vibrating with emotion when the undergrowth parted and Temi's friend, the beast of his kind they'd met near the palace, appeared. Temi seemed a little small in comparison, but he might not be full grown yet. Isn't that what Chigo had said?

Temi and the other beast circled each other for a moment, and then walked away together. Rasha started to go after him, but stopped herself. When he reached the opposite edge of the clearing, he sat down. He growled at his companion, then turned back to Rasha. He trotted to her and nuzzled his head against her thigh.

"That's all right you rotten beast. Go on."

Temi sat in front of her and whined.

"No, I'm fine. Go." She ran a hand through his fur and pushed him toward his new friend.

Rasha reached up and touched her amulet as she watched him walk through the opposite line of trees with his companion. Her face felt hot and tears stung her eyes as she turned back to the castle.

## 37

*L*ADI WATCHED RASHA get up from the table, and her eyes met Jak's. Why couldn't he look at her the way he looked at Rasha? She sighed. It was clear he didn't have those kinds of feelings for her. Then there was Ebere, who wouldn't take his eyes off of her. Where did that come from? Had he been that worried about her? What the yahtz was happening around here?

"I'm planning on attending the training at the Courier's Keep myself," Chigo said, interrupting her thoughts.

"How old are you?" she asked.

"I'm thirteen."

"They've never accepted anyone younger than fifteen," Ebere said without looking up from his plate.

"Yeah, and I'm sure they told her the same thing, before she became the youngest." Chigo grabbed his third piece of bread. "They may not let me work right away, but they'll train me."

"Well, maybe I'll see you there," Ladi said. She waited less than a heartbeat for Ebere to look up and make eye contact. Why hadn't she noticed that smolder before? She reached up and put a hand over her exposed neck and suddenly felt underdressed.

They'd always fought, and now all of a sudden, he filled her stomach with fluttering piko wings. Ladi thought back on her own behavior. She'd been obsessed with Jak. She glanced over at Jak again, who stood up from the table to follow Rasha. He was in love with her. Ladi hoped for his sake that Rasha had forgiven him. She stood up from the table and faced the royals.

"It was a lovely breakfast, Your Highness." Ladi gave a short curtsy.

"Where are you going?" Ebere blurted out the question.

"I have some packing to do." Ladi turned on her heel, not waiting for him to say anything more.

Ladi had reached the stairs before Ebere caught up to her.

"Ladi, wait," he called. She stopped, and before she turned, took a deep breath. She might only be fifteen, but she wasn't completely inexperienced.

"Yes?" She crossed her arms over her chest.

Ladi saw it coming. His eyes bore into hers. His lips slightly parted. She steadied herself, expecting something soft and sweet. Ebere wrapped his arms around her and kissed her senseless. His warm lips were forceful and sure. When he stepped away from her, she felt her arms drop. When had she wrapped her arms around his neck? She couldn't remember. Ladi swayed from being let go and had to take a step back.

"What was that all about?" She asked, trying to catch her breath. Her fingers lifted to her lips, tracing the outline of where his had been.

"A lapse in judgment." He backed away and then turned to go.

Ladi giggled before she called out after him.

"Can I hope there will be more lapses in judgment in the future?"

THE NEW INCUMBENT ceremony for Prince Bashir took place on the steps of the castle in Chilali. And it was not what anyone had expected. Rasha's parents had insisted it was the best place. That way they could sit in their balcony as usual and watch over the proceedings. Rasha stood beside Chiza and Jak stood beside Bashir. The council was behind them in a semicircle of support. Tarrik of Ishola stood among them, not yet an official member of council. It turned out they'd been reluctant to accept the Wola for that very reason, but things would get resolved. Rasha didn't have any control over how things went forward. She'd done all she could.

Rasha looked out over the crowd, most of them Chilalians. She caught her Aunt Sochi's eye, and her wink bolstered her to nod and square her shoulders with pride. There would be a vid recording sent throughout the kingdoms with the announcements in the following order:

The war against the beasts was won. The enslaved and abused beasts were granted asylum. The traitor Gungbe would be prosecuted for his crimes against the first kingdom and for the death of the princesses. The eleventh kingdom of Ishola was established, and would be the future site of the palace of royals. Prince Bashir's survival of the beasts' first attack, along with one other princess named Chiza from the tenth kingdom of Sidoa. Rasha and Jak, were thanked for their service in protecting the royal family line. Finally, the Choosing, in its new form, would begin as soon as the Ishola palace construction was complete.

The new Choosing caused a stir among the kingdoms. All the eligible princes and ladies would be invited to live at the palace, a building that promised to be double the size of the former with gardens four times the size. Due to the desert conditions of their new location, Bashir demanded a shaded pool near the palace for easy access in the hot summer months.

Everyone seemed shocked that the prince hadn't chosen Chiza or Rasha as the last available princesses. No one looked more disappointed than Chiza herself. The other evening, when Rasha went to meet with Chiza in her rooms, the doors were locked and there was no answer from inside.

What had happened to them while they'd been in hiding? Did her mourning for Lu keep Bashir from wanting to even attempt to be with her? Rasha watched the prince carefully. His attention had veered toward her at one time. Was he hoping to win her heart? She prayed that wasn't the case. The last thing she wanted was to become queen. Besides, hadn't she already picked Jak? Before she'd learned the truth, she was sure she had. Now, she wasn't so sure.

Jak removed the incumbent necklace from around his neck and handed it to Bashir. Rasha, with help from Chiza, removed the leather band from around her wrist. Chiza passed it to Bashir, who stood beside her. Then, Bashir held them both up in front of the crowd.

"The old ways served us well, but now with our tragic losses and our triumph in war, it is time to usher in a new way. We are the eleven kingdoms of Bolaji. It is time to unite our empire in a way it never has been before. Our kingdoms have been allowed to mix for hundreds of rotations. Shouldn't our royalty also represent that same unity?"

The crowd erupted in cheers, and Bashir smiled back.

"Then I, along with the other royals, will guard these symbolic bonds until the future queen of the empire has been chosen, whoever she may be." The crowd cheered, and Bashir led the others to the palace.

When the ceremony ended, the council was buzzing with excitement over Bashir's new approach to the Choosing.

"Thank you for your support, everyone, and I look forward to seeing you all in Ishola for the new Choosing once the palace is complete." He took Rasha by the hand

and leaned in, "Don't even think about disappearing. I need you." Then he released her.

Rasha looked around for Chiza. She was alone for the moment, and Rasha wanted to talk to her, but Jak stepped in her path, blocking her way.

"May I speak with you?" he asked.

Chiza departed quickly, making her way up the stairs to her rooms. Rasha would have to run to catch her. In her slippers she'd probably fall in front of them all, so instead she turned to Jak.

"Of course."

"I saw your face during the ceremony. You looked disappointed to be losing your title."

"I admit, I was getting used to it, but I don't mind leaving the weight of the responsibility behind," Rasha said. She realized in that moment that she meant it.

Jak took her hands. "I hoped that—," he didn't get to finish his thought.

"You were brilliant," Sochi interrupted, rushing forward to throw her arms around her niece.

Xeku came up and gave Jak a slap on the back. He seemed to be better around his father now. He wasn't overly friendly, but more civil.

"Thank you," Rasha said. "I guess now I get to be whatever I want to be again."

Her aunt eyed her with some confusion. "I doubt that, since the prince has told the world you'll be living with him in the palace as one of the Choosers, as he's called you all."

Rasha almost exploded. She wanted to strangle the prince. How dare he commit her to this thing? She had no intention of being paraded around or having others paraded in front her.

"Don't worry yourself about it now, it won't be for some time. I think you ought to see to your dragon. He's been pacing around the grounds, wearing a path outside your window."

"He's not my dragon, we just sort of helped each other."

Her aunt leaned in and said in her ear, "Well, don't tell him that, it looks like he's attached."

After an hour of shaking hands and speaking with the subjects of Chilali, Rasha wanted her bed. She was halfway to her room before she remembered Chiza. She ran up the steps and down the hall to where Chiza slept the night before. Rasha tapped on the door of the suite.

"Come in."

Chiza was sitting on the vanity chair staring out at the window.

"I'm sorry if I'm disturbing you."

"You're not," Chiza said without turning around.

Rasha joined her at the window. The sun was climbing. It warmed everything, but the snow remained.

"You seem unsettled," Rasha said after two minutes of complete silence.

Chiza sighed. "I tried." She didn't look at Rasha. "I did. I wanted to like him—to love him as I'd planned, but I couldn't. He's not Lu."

Rasha watched as a tear ran down Chiza's face. Rasha reached out and touched her shoulder. She debated whether or not patting her back would be appropriate, but then Chiza continued.

"He tried too. I'll give him that. We both did. There just isn't enough love in my heart to give him. Especially when he deserves so much."

"I'm sure he understands."

"I don't think he does." Chiza turned to Rasha at last. "He fancies himself in love with you."

"What?" Rasha's hand dropped from Chiza's shoulder as if she were on fire.

"He kept every single report from you. Then, when that wasn't enough, he wanted more. I overheard him speaking with one of the servants. He'd been asking for more intimate details about you."

"Intimate?" Rasha's mind raced over the past months as she wondered what Bashir had been told.

"He wanted to know what you liked to eat. What you wore was always a question. He asked about your relationships with your family, Ladi, Ebere, and Jak."

Rasha couldn't imagine anyone ever thinking of her in that way. Anyone other than Jak.

"I think it's the real reason he's changed the Choosing. He's hoping to convince you to stay."

"I'm not going to the Choosing, so he'll have a hard time of it," Rasha scoffed at the idea.

"You can't take this so lightly. He's named you as one of the Choosers. Other than me, that is. We must attend.

It's a royal command, and since he's announced it to the entire world, it's law."

If Chiza had said that she had a hidden eye on the back of her neck Rasha couldn't have been more surprised. But forced into the Choosing? She'd rather die, but if she defied the future king of Bolaji, her death wasn't in question. It was certain. Why couldn't Bashir and Chiza have just fallen in love with each other while in hiding? Was it so much to ask to be free of the whole thing?

"You would make a fine queen."

"Queen?"

"Did you know that when you're nervous you answer questions with questions?"

"What—" Rasha stopped herself.

"The only good I can see is that at least we'll be there together."

"If he doesn't love you, and you don't love him, why is he forcing you to stay?"

"I am to choose one of the other princes." Chiza rolled her eyes. She looked as enthusiastic as Rasha felt. "I know nothing about any of them. All of my study and focus was on Bashir and the other princesses. This whole thing will be a disaster."

Rasha felt that too, but she didn't want it to be her fault. She'd have to find something else to keep her busy and far away from the Bolaji palace.

"We'll get through this," Rasha heard herself say, although she had no practical idea how.

RASHA HEARD THE scratching as soon as she entered her room. She went to the window and looked down. Below her, the dragon with the amber eyes and scarred tail had ruined the flowering bushes under her window and worn through the snow and into the dirt in a large circle.

"What in the world do you want?"

The dragon sat down and tilted his head.

"Go on, you don't have to stay here anymore, you're free." She flapped her arms and pointed at the sky. The dragon misunderstood her. He flapped his massive wings, kicking up dirt and leaves into the window and right in her face. He perched himself on the edge of her balcony. It pulled away from the window under his weight, but held.

He was offering her a ride. Rasha looked down at her gown and thought about changing, but decided it hardly mattered to the dragon if she were in a dress. She grabbed her cloak and pulled it tight around her neck. Despite the changing of the seasons, it wasn't quite warm enough to go out with only a dress. She used his leg to help lift her onto his back. Before she adjusted her seat, he launched himself into the sky. Rasha struggled to hold on as he swooped up and back down again. She screamed with delight and wondered how the dragon would respond if she saddled him.

RASHA WAS STANDING in the gardens overlooking the pond when Ladi found her. The water was no longer frozen, but still very cold.

"I don't like goodbyes," Ladi said.

"Nor I." Rasha looked up into the sky where the dragon had disappeared. "Besides, we don't need to say goodbye. We'll see each other again."

Ladi gave her a brisk nod and tossed her bag over her shoulder. She didn't get two feet before she turned back to Rasha and threw her arms around her waist. Rasha had gotten used to her showy displays of affection. She could even hug her back. Ladi let go, and, without another word, walked away. Rasha hoped she'd go straight to the Courier's Keep and get her training. The sooner she was legitimate, the better.

The cold night air was starting to seep under her cloak and dress. She rubbed her hands over her arms and tightened the cloak around her.

Jak came out before she could go in, and she wanted

447

to crawl into a hole. In all the commotion, she'd forgotten they'd been interrupted.

"I saw you riding on that dragon and I hoped I'd find you here."

"Yes, he was determined to take me out." She looked up at the sky again and wasn't sure if speck in the distance was a bird or a dragon.

"It's a girl by the way."

"Really?" Rasha looked at his face to see if he was joking, but he only nodded and looked into the sky himself. His face turned sad all of a sudden. She imagined he must still be in mourning. Those moments used to happen to her frequently after Lu had been killed.

"How are you? I imagine you miss your mother dearly."

"I do, but she's still with me, here," he said. He placed a fist against his heart as he'd done when he'd left Rasha to go to the Wilds.

"Will you stay?" she asked.

"For the Choosing?" Jak asked. He nodded with understanding. "Yes, I'll be there because you'll be there."

"I'm not—" she started to speak, but Jak raised a hand to stop her.

"Don't lie to yourself, even if you want to lie to me. The prince has required we all be there, but in particular he's interested in you," Jak said. He reached up and tucked a few strands of hair behind her ear. "But he doesn't yet know you. Not the way I do."

"What does that mean?" She tilted her head back to look up at him.

"It means I don't give up that easy." Jak took her by the arms and pulled her to him. His warmth enveloped her, as if he had a fire burning in his chest. She melted into him. His lips touched her forehead and each cheek before he tilted her mouth up to his. He held the back of her neck, winding his fingers into her hair as he captured her lips with his own. He didn't let her up for air until he was ready. Gasping, her eyes blurred as they sought his. The longing echoed in his eyes. The truth that could be believed beyond all else.

"I have to tell you something. It won't be easy to hear."

Rasha lifted a finger to his lips and shook her head.

"I already know about her."

Jak's eyes widened. "You know?"

Rasha nodded and smiled. "Ladi discovered the truth the night you left."

"That green vixen," Jak said. "Well, it's done. We parted as friends and I wish her well with her new life." He reached down and fiddled with her amulet.

"I know that we're no longer incumbents, but I hope you'll consider choosing a life with me as I've already chosen you."

It took a minute before she could speak a coherent sentence. She couldn't believe what he was asking.

"I'm not ready for anything like marriage, if that's what you mean. But I can't imagine my life without you." She looked into his eyes. "I hope that can be enough."

"It is, for now," he said as he tightened his arms around her.

He leaned back, looking satisfied with himself. Then he smiled and cleared his throat to sing. This time he sang the familiar song in a quiet whisper, slow, and desperate.

> "There was an old bard from hither and to
>> who traveled the lands meeting people
>> like you.
>
> He sang and danced and pranced around
>> gaily, but deep in his heart he longed
>> for a lady.
>
> A beautiful lady with long white hair, to
>> tell her his feelings he wouldn't dare.
>
> She'd sneer, and she'd snap cause that's
>> what they do.
>
> Purple girls who love an old bard, deep
>> down yes they do."

War and diplomacy were two games Rasha was tired of playing. She longed for a fetch and delivery. Central had reinstated her status after her delivery of Chiza to the palace and the death of Lu. She wasn't sure if it was guilt or obligation that convinced them to do it but Rasha didn't care. What bothered her was they'd assigned her a new partner.

"Isn't this great?" Jak bounded alongside her.

The sun was a sliver in the northern horizon and he was already as happy as a piko.

"Is it?"

Rasha couldn't figure out how he'd done it. Jak had gone from courier outcast to her partner in a matter of days. It was no secret, she liked Jak. Maybe even more than she wanted to admit. She enjoyed being with him every day but she preferred to work alone.

A couple of years ago, they'd forced Lu on her too and

look how that turned out. His life taken too soon. She still thought of him sometimes and how she'd grown accustomed to his easy manner. It might be that way with Jak too. Rasha knew in her heart she'd always miss Lu.

Jak was different. He liked to push her limits. No matter what it was he always pressured her beyond her comfort level. He loved a challenge. Rasha didn't mind a challenge now and then but two top ranking couriers made them targets. His reputation was notorious and the moment Central verified his reinstatement they were fighting off lower ranking couriers for deliveries.

Courier code dictated that only one courier could carry a package at a time. There was nothing written that protected a courier from having a package taken and delivered by someone else. As long as they were a verified courier it didn't matter who delivered the package. Confirmation of delivery would go to the new courier. It seemed as though every courier in the twelve kingdoms was competing for their jobs hoping to improve their rankings.

"We've got our first fetch, it's in Karmir and bound for Vol."

Jak laughed as he leaped in front of her to drive their road vehicle.

Her stomach lurched as Rasha looked up at the sky. She'd prefer to ride on the dragon that had claimed her. She was inconveniently absent at the moment.

"If you give her a name, she'll come when you call," Jak said as if reading her mind.

"I'm not going to name it. It doesn't belong to me."

"What about something like Safira?"

"Ew, really? That's the best you can come up with?"

"You could try something more Buku, like Tobi."

"Stop, I'm not naming it. It's not a pet."

Jak shrugged, but she knew better than to think the subject was over. The vehicle lurched forward and Rasha clamped her mouth closed. They made it to the second kingdom of Karmir without incident. However, Rasha couldn't shake the feeling someone was already following them. The second kingdom of Bolaji maintained a dominant population of red-skinned people. It made Rasha stand out even more with her white hair and purple skin. She pulled her hood up and tucked her hair inside. She walked arm and arm with Jak, keeping her eyes cast down.

"This is more like it," he said as he pulled her in close to him.

"Don't get too comfortable, we're trying to blend in. Even though I think we're being followed."

"Yes, I know."

Rasha's eyes flew to his face to read his expression. He was serious.

"How long?"

"Since we received the message," he said fixing a smile on his face. "They're not great at hiding. I'm not worried."

Rasha reached for her short swords. Jak put an arm around her shoulders and kissed her forehead. She was so surprised that she jerked against him.

"Keep Cutter and Blade sheathed. We won't need them."

Rasha narrowed her eyes at him. He seemed so sure. She slid them back in place. She didn't mind letting him take the lead. But when they got the jump on him she'd handle things her own way.

"This is the place," Jak said looking up at a local inn. The building's facade was made of large stones and there were black smudges as if it had survived a fire. The pattern of the burns, however, showed it was by design. They even made the interior furnishings out of carved stone. As if the owners didn't want their tables broken or moved. The chairs were a solid wood covered in a dark blue fabric.

The eatery was empty except for two figures sitting hunched at the bar. Rasha almost looked past them but Jak paused a moment longer than usual and it made her take another look. The two men were familiar. Two lower level couriers, no doubt looking to snag a fetch from two high ranking couriers like her and Jak. Jak nodded to a booth on the far side of the eatery and she followed him over to the table. They needed to stay calm until they had the fetch in their hands.

After several moments of waiting the barkeep came over to take their orders. He was fidgeting and his hand shook with nerves as he asked them if they wanted to know about the specials.

"No, we're only interested in the catch of the day," Jak said under his breath.

It was the pass-phrase and the barkeep dove into his

pocket as fast as lightning and pulled out his communicator. He scanned Jak's thumb to confirm fetch before tossing a small palm-sized box on the table between them.

"Run," he said between his teeth before bolting out of the eatery.

His feet hadn't hit the bottom steps before the two at the bar whirled around to face Jak and Rasha. Jak pulled out his long sword. Rasha held a short sword in each hand. He ran along the floor toward the two brutes while Rasha leaped from table to table launching herself at the largest of the two men.

The man saw her coming and braced himself but stumbled back as she landed almost on his toes. He used his long sword to fend off her attacks. Despite his size she dropped him in a matter of minutes. He landed hard on his back but held his sword up between them. She used Cutter to lift. With the tip of Blade, she nicked his hand and he dropped his sword.

Jak had already dispensed of the other one and used the butt end of his sword against the man's head knocking him unconscious. It would be bad form to kill another courier over a package. They just didn't do that anymore. The citizens of Bolaji had become more civilized over the last few hundred years.

Jak was laughing as they dashed for their vehicle.

"You were magnificent. I love watching you take those big guys down."

He grabbed her without warning and kissed her hard on the mouth.

"You weren't too bad yourself," Rasha said.

Jak often got caught up in the moment and showed his affection in public. Rasha pushed down the embarrassment and tried to enjoy it. Their time on the battlefield during the Beast Wars hadn't only made them better fighters. They'd been through so much. Rasha had come to rely on him in a way she never thought possible. When they were together, she felt near invincible.

"Wait, why aren't we moving?" She asked when he still hadn't turned the vehicle's power on.

"I don't know. It looks like they cut the power. This thing isn't going anywhere."

"We can't afford to wait," Rasha said leaping from the vehicle and racing for the woods.

"We're not going to run all the way to Vol are we?"

Rasha put her fingers to her lips and whistled hard. The dragon who'd come to her aid in the past was there again and she swooped down through the trees to allow Rasha and Jak to climb on.

It was Jak's turn to look uncomfortable. He held onto Rasha tighter than necessary. Rasha laughed when the dragon took to the sky and he let out a whoop. The dragon was twice the speed of anything on the ground and she smiled. Anyone following her would never catch them.

They reached Vol before the sun went down and they met the patron of a metal shop for delivery. The dragon dropped them on the edge of the forest as was customary. They walked the rest of the way.

"Let's spend the night over there. That inn looks better than most."

"I doubt it. That's fresh paint. They're probably trying to cover up something. My guess is a fire."

Jack looked at the inn and sighed.

"Why can't you be positive for once?"

"I'm positive it's a garbage heap," Rasha said. "Now, let's go make our delivery."

Rasha put a hand inside of her coat and felt for the familiar square package. She handed it to Jak as they entered the metal shop. The two fangledorts from the inn were already there. How could they have beaten them there?

Rasha was sure her mouth hung open because one of them mentioned it.

"Close your mouth, purple girl."

"What are you two doing here? We have the package," Jak said holding it up in the air.

"Do you?"

They both laughed then sauntered out bumping both of Jak's shoulders as they passed.

"Sorry, you two, I've already confirmed delivery," said the shop keeper.

Jak looked down at the package and opened it. The box held a worthless stone inside. He held it up for Rasha to see.

"What the Yatz? How did those two mukes get our package?" She asked.

"Could they have swapped the packages while we were in the middle of the fight?"

"Impossible, we were never close enough for a switch. We left them on the floor."

"Unless they had the package before we arrived," Jak said looking at her.

"The barkeep, he was nervous, remember? They must have threatened him."

"Yeah, he was worried we'd figure out he'd already given up our package to those twyllos."

"That doesn't explain how they got here ahead of us," Rasha said.

When she heard the distinct engine of a flying shuttle, she looked up. It was the two couriers heading back to Karmir.

"We need to get one of those," Jak said.

Rasha sighed.

"There goes our rating."

"At least we know how they got here so fast."

Jak draped an arm over her shoulders.

"We'd better get another fetch and quick."

Rasha shook her head.

"I knew this partnership would ruin me."

Jak pulled her close against him and planted a wet kiss on the side of her face.

"Come on my little purple princess. Call your dragon. We've got fetches to deliver."

Rasha pushed against him until he released her. She wiped her hand across her cheek to remove the wetness.

Then she grabbed him by the lapels of his coat pulling him up against her. She gave him her most seductive smile as if she would kiss him. When his lips parted in anticipation, she spoke low in his ear.

"Who are you calling little?"

# THE COURIER'S QUEST

BOOK THREE

## 1

*R*ASHA LAY PRONE ON THE roof, watching Jak on the ground below, wondering if he forgot the signal or had decided to audition for acting in the theater down there. The way he was dancing and prancing around, she couldn't make out what any of them were saying.

At last, Jak pulled out his sword, giving her the signal.

She whistled for her dragon, who swooped in with a screech and a roar.

Rasha climbed onto her mount and they descended, landing hard on the ground in front of the tavern. Inside, the men who saw the dragon scattered in all directions.

Jak came running out first.

"What the yahtz was that? I said come in quiet!" Jak leapt up behind her onto the dragon and pointed to the side door with his sword.

"Dragons aren't quiet! Or didn't you know?" Rasha directed the dragon to where he'd pointed.

As soon as they were close enough, Jak slid off of the beast and held up his sword, ready for the first of the men to come out. Two men charged him at the same time and he got between them. He knocked one back, giving him enough time to deliver a kick and disable the other. Their size and strength, however, made it difficult for Jak to keep up with both of them.

"I could use a little help down here," He said as he fought off two of the men. Rasha jumped down and took out the one at his back. Two more made their escape during the commotion. Her dragon caught them running and delivered a whip of her tail that sent both men flying backwards.

"That's why you bring a dragon," Rasha said to Jak.

She huffed as she deflected another man's sword in front of her. The two of them fought off the men until they were all down. Jak knocked out the last of them with the butt of his sword.

"Got it." She reached into the fallen man's pocket, but it was empty. "It's not here."

Jak reached down and felt inside one of the other unconscious men's pockets. After closer examination, they still didn't find a package on any of the men.

"Well, what happened to it?" Rasha asked.

A transport vehicle built for jungle and desert travel pulled up next to her dragon.

The dragon stumbled back out of fear and roared at the two men inside.

"What a delightful beast you have, Rasha," Gorg said from behind the wheel of the vehicle. His partner snickered beside him.

"What are you two doing here? Looking to lose at another game of Hand?" she asked.

The two had lost their last vehicle to her and her partner Lu. She never let them forget it. Gorg's face puckered in annoyance. Jak had heard the story and didn't mind goading them either.

"How old were you then, Rash?" Jak asked, feigning ignorance.

"I was seventeen and Lu was only sixteen."

"That's right. Well, enough reminiscing, what are you doing here?" Jak asked.

"Oh, nothing. We just like to watch you work for nothing. Since we've already fetched the package, there's no reason for you to be harassing these men," Gorg said as he flashed them the small package.

Rasha's blood boiled. There was no way they'd gone through all of that to come away with nothing. Before she could get the question out, he offered an explanation.

"We thought we'd come by early and relieve them of the package, then wait and see how you would have done it. The dragon's a nice touch." Gorg revved the mechanical engine, and the two raced off, kicking up mud and dirt behind them.

Rasha used her hands to brush at her clothes. She

walked over and patted the dragon on the neck. The poor thing, startled by the closeness of the noisy vehicle, had retreated further and only now ventured forward.

"There, there. Those pumseeds are gone now. You're safe."

Jak kicked at the dirt.

"That's the third one in two months," he said.

"Yes, once is a coincidence. The others make it a pattern. We need to find out why the Courier's Keep is giving them our assignments."

Jak put one arm around her shoulders and reached out with the other to give the dragon a pat on the neck.

"It's true, the dragon is a nice touch."

Their communicators beeped at the same time. Jak and Rasha both reached for their pockets.

"Priority level one," Jak read the message.

"Delivery to the Courier's Keep. Well, that's convenient," Rasha said, slipping her communicator into her pocket.

"We have to go to Poobari's stink hole. Should we take the dragon?" Jak asked, gesturing with one hand to the beast.

Rasha made a face. She hated Poobari's Tero-Joro prison.

"Yes, that way we've got a quick exit," she said as she climbed into her seat behind the dragon's neck.

"By the way, when are you going to name her?"

"I don't know what to call her."

Jak hoisted himself behind her. "You named your

swords Cutter and Blade," Jak paused, realizing he'd made her point. "True, you need to think of something more original than Dragon."

---

"Poobari, you mangy man, I thought you were dead," Rasha said. She and Jak entered the jail and found him sitting at his desk. The man's thinning hair—the patches that hadn't fallen out, anyway—had grown down to his shoulders. His thin mustache and beard looked like extensions of the greasy hair from his head.

"I heard you were a princess," he returned. "Can't believe everything on the feed." His middle jiggled and rolled with laughter. "You must be here for the delivery to Courier's Keep." Poobari leaned to one side of his desk and pulled out several square keys. He slipped them into his pocket as he stood up.

"Correct. If it wasn't so urgent we'd love to sit around here and–" Jak looked around the tossed room, at a loss for words, before turning back to him, "stare at the walls or whatever it is you do here."

Rasha stifled a laugh. She held out her hand and wiggled her fingers with impatience as she waited for Poobari to give her the package.

"Oh no, it doesn't quite fit in the palm of your hand." Poobari waddled to the door and used his blue key to unlock it.

"This way." He continued down the corridor, not

waiting for them to follow. "They told me they'd be sending the best, I had no idea they meant you," Poobari said as he continued down the dank corridor. The jail had the distinct odor of rotting flesh, urine, and feces.

Rasha leaned forward and took a whiff of Poobari, then leaned back again, letting him get several steps ahead of her. The rotting flesh might be him. They'd taken two turns before Jak spoke up.

"Where are you taking us?" he asked.

Poobari smiled but said nothing.

"You could have had the package waiting for us when we arrived," Rasha said as she avoided an outstretched hand from a prisoner inside one cell they passed.

"Nope, this one is special." He stopped in front of a dark cell and chuckled. "She and I are old friends. Aren't we, little girl?" Poobari pulled out an orange key and unlocked the cell door.

The prisoner sauntered up to Rasha and Jak with a huge grin, then put one hand on each of their shoulders.

"I'm so pleased to see you. Have you both been well?"

"Ladi?" they asked in unison.

## 2

*P*OOBARI STOOD HOLDING THE DELIVERY tag out to them, impatient to be leaving.

"Is one of you going to accept the fetch or do we need to call for someone else?"

Jak didn't respond, but he pulled out his communicator and accepted the package. Poobari didn't wait around after unlocking the door. He made his way back to the front near his desk. The sound of desperate inmates calling out to him as he waddled back down the halls didn't seem to bother him.

Ladi stood staring at the two of them as if she'd invited them over for a meal.

"What are you doing here?" Rasha asked.

"My final exam didn't go well. When things got worse, I ended up in here again with Poobari. He really is

a horrible man, but it's either here or someplace worse."
She shrugged.

*How could she just shrug?* Rasha wondered.

"No, I mean, how did you end up here? Aren't you
supposed to be completing your training?"

"It turns out that wasn't really for me," Ladi said. She
squeezed between them and lead them back up the
corridor.

Rasha looked at Jak who shook his head. What could
she be thinking? Why was she being so evasive? Rasha
didn't know what to think about it.

Jak held up a hand behind Ladi's back. He'd seen
Rasha about to lose her temper.

Rasha bit back her response and let him take the lead.

"So, you returned to a life of crime?" Jak asked.

"Not exactly," Ladi said as she reached the door to
Poobari's office.

"I'll be taking my weapon, package, and my communicator, now."

Ladi held out her hand.

Poobari ignored it and picked at his dirty nails,
looking at Rasha as he spoke.

"Young people these days are so disrespectful. In the
old days, as I recall, they used to be much more polite.
Not like these uneducated rangleforts."

Ladi put her hands on her hips.

"I don't have all day to fool around with you, old
man. Give them up."

Poobari laughed then Ladi leaned forward on his desk

and crooked a finger at him to come closer. He inched forward, wary of her, and she whispered something in his ear that made him swear. From underneath the wooden desk, he pulled on a drawer and lifted out a small package and a communicator chip. The sword was last, and he handed it to her blade first.

Ladi sheathed her sword before turning to Rasha.

"Shall we?"

"You know where we're going?" Rasha asked.

"Of course, the Courier's Keep will want to see me about this package. Let's go."

"See you again soon, my little green girl," Poobari called from behind her.

"Not if I can help it," Ladi said without looking back.

When they reached the outside and stood in front of Rasha's dragon, Ladi let out a whistle.

"You kept him."

"Her." Rasha gave the dragon a pat on the neck. "She wouldn't leave."

"Are you going to take me up on her? Please, it's been so long since I've been on a dragon."

Rasha put a hand on Ladi's shoulder and turned her around.

"Are your brains half cooked? We just picked you up from jail. You swore you'd never return there especially after what happened to your brother. You have to go back to the Courier's Keep to answer for the package you fetched but never delivered. What's wrong with you? Talk to me."

471

Jak took that moment to walk away.

Ladi looked away, her eyes filling.

"Don't. Don't do that. I'm trying to understand," Rasha said.

"You can't understand. You don't know what it's like to have to walk in his shoes."

Ladi's shoulders dropped. She'd obviously been carrying this for some time.

Rasha had struggled with her own feelings about Lu and his death. What could she say to get through to her? Ladi continued to blame herself for her brother's death.

When Jak moved towards them, she looked up and shook her head. She wasn't ready to end their conversation.

"You can't keep punishing yourself for your brother's death," Rasha said.

"They don't want me. They want him." Ladi shrugged away from Rasha. "All they wanted was for me to be more like him. Just like you. After a while, I couldn't take it."

Rasha took a step forward and turned Ladi to face her again.

"That's not true, I don't want you to be him. However, the job of the Keep is to train you to become the best courier you can be. Why did you feel you had to leave?"

"They wanted me to take the Courier's Oath, but I couldn't."

"Why not?"

"How can you ask me that?" Ladi asked, incredulous.

"To lie and say that I'm loyal to no kingdom. How did you do it and stand on the front lines of Adalu, killing the beasts?"

Rasha stopped short.

"What do you mean?"

"The oath: 'In service of the ten kingdoms, allegiance to none.' How could I say it and mean it after all we've been through?"

Rasha's hand dropped as she thought about what she was saying.

"Allegiance to none," Ladi said, waiting for Rasha to understand.

"Yes, but a courier just like a princess is still in service to the ten kingdoms."

"Not ten, eleven. Serving is not the same as allegiance."

Rasha hadn't even considered the oath since she'd returned to the job. She wondered what Jak thought of it. She'd have to ask him later. Ladi was too volatile now to consider the issue with reason.

"Listen, you have to stop thinking like this. No one is comparing you to Lu except you." Rasha put a hand on Ladi's shoulder and forced her to look into her eyes. "Do you want to be a courier or not?"

"I don't think I do anymore," Ladi said.

Rasha didn't know what to say.

Jak moved over to her but Ladi had already walked away.

Rasha shrugged and waved it off. They agreed it would

473

be best if Rasha and Ladi rode on her dragon to Adalu. Jak would have to make his own way there and meet up with Rasha to complete delivery.

THE KEEP WAS LOCATED in what was left of the first kingdom and the weather had already turned warm again. Most of the damage from the rotation before had vanished in most places. There was a scar left across the land from where the beasts and the ten kingdoms had fought. The ruins of the first palace was the only dark smudge among the greenery of Adalu. Rasha and Ladi arrived that evening at the Courier's Keep and for the first time since ending her own training, Rasha was allowed admittance.

"Welcome, Courier Jenchat-42769 how can I be of assistance?" The robotic assistant had no humanoid features on its metallic plate of a face, only a faintly recognizable humanoid anatomy.

"I request an audience with Courier's Keep to complete delivery of Fetch #456-257."

"Processing…"

Rasha twitched while she waited for the confirmation.

"Please follow the blue lighted signs to the Courier's Keep located on the fifth floor."

Rasha and Ladi didn't need the lighted signs to find the Keep. When they reached the imposing wooden doors of the Keep on the fifth floor, Ladi stopped short.

"What's wrong?" Rasha asked.

"I don't know if I can do this."

"We don't really have a choice. You have to give the package back."

Ladi shook her head and backed away.

"No, Ladi, don't even think of running."

"I'm sorry, Rasha, this can't go back to them."

Rasha watched in horror as Ladi bolted down the corridor. The doors of the Keep opened and Rasha turned to run after her.

"Wait, stop, there's no way out that way!" She ran after her but only made it as far as halfway down the hall before Ladi jumped through the window.

"No!" Rasha ran to the window but the only thing on the ground was the broken glass. Ladi hadn't landed on the ground. She was flying in the arms of one of the Wola, his arms clutching her middle as her legs dangled in the air. Rasha's hand came down on the window sill.

Rasha returned to the doors of the Courier's Keep. they were still open. She entered the large domed room, its eye-level windows letting in light from all sides. A man older than her father with a turquoise hue to his skin and blue hair stepped forward. His face was grim and disapproving.

"Rasha Jenchat, I told them you wouldn't be able to bring her in."

## 3

_R_ASHA STARED UP INTO THE face of her former courier instructor with as much sass as she could muster.

"That sour expression has aged you."

"I see you haven't learned any more respect being out in the world. You think your perfect record gives you the right to disrespect the couriers that came before you?"

"I'm only here to deliver a fetch, not to get into it with you."

The man lifted his sword and lunged at her. "Wrong, you'll leave when you're dismissed."

Rasha had only a half a second to pull out Cutter and Blade to defend herself. She countered his hit with one of her own. They danced around the Keep, avoiding students in the midst of their practice. A few stopped to stare at them, at first wondering what was going on. After the whispered comments made it around the entire floor, they encircled them, waiting to see the outcome.

"You're still dropping your left," he said.

"I'm not, but you're not as fast as you used to be." They sparred for several minutes before Rasha used the exercise equipment behind her to propel her into the air. She landed on top of him, his sword barely able to absorb the shock of her hit.

He raised a hand in surrender and the exercise ended.

Applause erupted from all around them.

Rasha sheathed her swords and shook hands with her trainer.

"Let me present Rasha Jenchat. She used to be the youngest courier we had ever trained."

"Rash," Chigo ran forward. He threw his arms around her and she had to hug him back or fall over. "I can't believe you're here. How is everyone? Have you seen Ladi?"

"That's enough questions for now. Back to your studies." The instructor clapped his hands, and they returned to their practice. Chigo did the same, keeping one eye on Rasha.

Her former instructor raised a hand, pointing toward his office. She knew it to be soundproof. No doubt that was the reason he chose it now. He'd want to discuss Ladi but not in front of the others in her class.

"Sit down, let me get you a glass of water."

He poured her glass and put it on her side of the desk. He lifted a large bottle and drank from it. Then he picked up a sprayer and sprayed his face and head, letting the water run down his neck. As a merman, he struggled with the time on land like most, but committed his time and life to training couriers.

"Tell me exactly what happened, from the beginning."

"Jak, my partner, and I received the fetch and agreed to pick it up." He nodded at the mention of Jak but didn't interrupt. "We discovered the fetch was a prisoner, Ladi."

"Did she explain why she took the package in the first place?"

"No, sir. She admitted that she'd dropped out of her training and that she had doubts about taking the oath."

"What kind of doubts?"

"She didn't think she could, in good conscience, say 'In service of the ten kingdoms, allegiance to none.' I reasoned with her, insisted she return the package, and she agreed we'd came here to clear up the matter."

"She agreed?"

"Yes."

"You used no force or coercion in any way?"

"I did not."

"Interesting."

"Why would she agree to come all the way here just to jump out a window?"

"She wasn't alone, then?"

"No, a Wola caught her mid-air and carried her off. It was planned from the start, from what I could tell."

"The package, did she give it to you, did you see it?"

"She did not. I didn't even see the contents. She kept it with her the entire time. We weren't together long."

"How did you manage that? She was in the Twinlands, was she not?"

"Yes, however, we traveled by dragon. It took only a matter of hours."

"Dragon? You ride on a dragon?"

"Are you avoiding my question?" Rasha asked. She put the water down and sat back in her chair, crossing her legs.

Her instructor took a deep breath.

"I don't know why she would bring you here," he said, avoiding her eyes.

"That's a lie, try again," she said crossing her arms and losing her patience.

"I don't know what she thinks you can do," he said looking her in the eye.

"She's the younger sister of my former partner and friend. I've known her for rotations. She trusts me. The question is why doesn't she trust you or the courier system?"

"She has no reason not to trust us. Her role is simple. You understood it at her age. You fetch and deliver, you don't ask questions and you don't deviate from your instructions."

"Are you saying she deviated from her instructions?" Rasha asked.

"She completed the fetch as planned but she did not deliver the package. To our knowledge, she still has the package in her possession which is paramount to theft and a betrayal to the courier's code and to the ten kingdoms."

There it was again, he'd said the ten kingdoms instead of eleven. That had bothered Ladi and now it was bothering her.

"What do you mean ten?"

"The Wola did not accept The Courier's Keep and our courier system. We only serve the ten original kingdoms."

There was something else there but she wouldn't get the chance to get it out of him as his communicator beeped and he jumped up from his desk.

"I have some other business to attend to you. Shall I see you out?"

Rasha stood up. She looked at her former instructor, measuring him with her gaze. He was hiding something. Something beyond this training program, perhaps for someone in a higher position of authority.

"No, I know the way."

Rasha took her time leaving the building. She reached the front desk and tried another tactic.

"Can you help me?"

"Courier Jenchat-42769, how can I be of assistance?"

"The Courier's Keep, who has direct oversight?"

"There is no direct oversight. The Courier's Keep must answer to all, loyal to none."

"Do you mean they answer to all the kingdoms?"

"Yes, they must answer or forfeit their diplomatic status," the robot answered.

"If they fail to adhere to a kingdom?" Rasha asked.

"Then they shall serve none."

"Who would provide the courier service for the kingdoms should this happen?"

"Answer unknown." The robot tilted its anatomically incorrect head to one side. "Do you need further assistance?"

"Yes, why are assignments given out to multiple couriers?"

"Please, clarify the question."

Rashsa huffed. She thought that was as clear as she could get it, but she rephrased it instead.

"Under what circumstances would two different courier teams be given the same job?"

"Processing."

Rasha waited for the whir of the machine to stop.

"Unknown."

"Really? It took you that long to figure out exactly nothing?" Rasha threw up her hands.

"Please clarify the question."

Rasha shook her head and thought for a moment.

"Here's a better question, have duplicate assignments ever been given before?"

"Processing."

Again, Rasha waited while tapping her foot with impatience. This time, however, the whir stopped fairly quickly and she was rewarded with an answer.

"Yes."

"Please provide details," Rasha said.

"That information is classified. Courier Jenchat-42769, you do not have the appropriate clearance."

That might be worth checking into, but first she had to focus on Ladi. She turned to walk away.

"Do you need further assistance?"

"Not at this time, thank you," Rasha called out over her shoulder.

"Courier Jenchat-42769, have a pleasant day."

"I wish I could."

## 4

*A*FTER WATCHING LADI FLY OFF with one of the Wola, it was clear she was working with them in some way. Rasha figured the fastest way to find her was to track her down. The mystery of the Keep would have to wait. If Jak followed the route they'd taken, he'd still be on foot and more than a day away. She called the dragon to her then climbed on, heading for his approximate location. They were already losing time and she only half understood what was really going on at the Courier's Keep. When she was close to where she thought he might be, she signaled him and flew down to pick him up.

"Did I miss anything?" he asked, taking in her facial expression.

"Only my first incomplete delivery."

"What? How?"

"She bolted. At the last second, she did a flying piko right out the window and into the arms of a Wola."

"The package?" Jak asked.

"Gone. She took that too."

"So, she went through the whole compliant thing to just leave you on the front steps of the Keep?"

"Not the front steps, the training door. I met with an instructor. There's something going on, but I'm not sure what it is."

"You look like you could use a ferm. Want to hit up Silae?"

"Not particularly."

"I'll take that as a yes."

They rode the dragon less than two hours to the pub where Silae worked. Rasha hadn't been there since she'd announced Lu's death to his sister. She'd been proving a point then, and now it seemed pointless to hang out in the place without him. Jak had been trying to get her back in there for months but she'd refused. Seeing Silae would bring the memories back and she wasn't sure she would ever be over that. Silae, as it happened, wasn't bothered at all. In fact, she was more excited to see Jak than she'd ever been to see Lu, which only irritated Rasha more.

"Welcome, Prince Jak Ameenu. Sit anywhere you like." Silae leaned forward enough to just brush his arm with her ample chest, then pulled him along, pointing out the benefits of one empty table over another.

"Seems sort of quiet for this time of day. Where is everyone?" Rasha asked, looking around at the bar.

"Sick. It's that time of year so, not unexpected. With the changing of the seasons from cold to warmer, it happens. Seems like more people than usual are dropping like pikos, though," Silae said.

"I think the small table in the corner will do just fine." Jak smiled back at her. He would because he was that kind of guy, the guy who girls fell on top of themselves for whether they had a chance or not.

"Could you get us some drinks?" Rasha asked.

Silae ignored her and continued to fawn over Jak. She'd worn her hair down today, in the Karmirian style. The black waves reached her lower back and her skin, a chestnut red, had a glimmer as if she'd used some kind of body make-up.

"So, I hear the Karmirian traitor will be sentenced for his crimes," Silae let Jak sit, then squeezed in beside him. "He might even be executed."

"That's more than he deserves," Rasha mumbled.

"He was doing it to protect his own family and king-dom. Can you really blame him for making that choice?" Silae asked.

Rasha's fist came down hard on the table.

"That muke put the whole of Bolaji in danger, not to mention he supported the torture and brutality of those animals. If it had been up to me, I would have taken a piece off of him for everyone who died because of that war."

Silae tossed her hair to one side as if they'd disagreed on the weather and changed the subject.

"Anyway, the prince will be inviting some eligible princesses and princes to the Ishola Palace in a few days.

Are you planning to attend?" She slid closer to Jak and wrapped her arms tight around his right arm.

"I hadn't planned on it, no," Jak said, his tone casual and almost dismissive. "Is there any reason I should change my mind?" He gave Silae a wink and a smile that made her giggle.

"Absolutely," Silae said.

"Ahem," Rasha said clearing her throat. "Do you mind?"

"Not at all, you're excused," Silae said with a wave of her hand.

Rasha was not amused. She was beyond annoyed and heading toward full on furious. What was Jak doing? Silae was incorrigible. She had no shame and no respect for herself as she threw her breasts at anyone who dared to come into the establishment. Her apron covered more of her body than her clothes did. Rasha lost her patience.

Her right hand reached for her sword and Jak gave her leg a nudge with his foot and shook his head.

"Any interesting news come through here about the Courier's Keep?" He asked, an inch from Silae's nose.

Rasha watched as her smile grew. She tossed her long black hair behind her shoulder. Then she leaned into the table, looking at both Jak and Rasha.

"I hear Lu's little sister got herself into some trouble."

Rasha looked at Jak, amazed. This is what he'd been planning all along.

"What kind of trouble?" he asked without taking his eyes off of her.

"The Couriers have a code, as you know, and she didn't deliver. They say it has something to do with the package itself."

"Does anyone know what's in it?" Rasha asked.

Silae leaned back in her seat.

"No one seems to know that bit. She's not even supposed to know what's inside, but she found out without opening it. At least that's what they say."

"She didn't open the package?"

Silae shook her head.

"Then how could she know?" Rasha asked.

Silae shrugged.

"The yahtz if I know." She looked over at Jak and put a hand on his chin. "You look thirsty. Let me get you something to drink."

She bounced up from the bench and worked her way across the room like a master. Silae spoke to regular customers, greeted new guests, and cleared up dishes as she moved among the patrons. She did it all with that wide smile and the short skirt that emphasized her swinging hips.

"We need to find out what was in that package," Jak said.

"It might be easier to find Ladi and ask her," Rasha said.

"I doubt it."

"Why?"

"She's just like you, she won't tell anyone until she figures out how to handle it or gets caught again."

487

Rasha rolled her eyes. He was referring to when she hadn't told him about her royal status. He'd found out when she got them all arrested by the Chilalian royal guard for refusing to go to the Choosing. She'd been made princess incumbent anyway and ruled for the months they were at war with the beasts of the north. After prince Bashir came out of hiding and took his throne, she'd immersed herself in the courier business along with Jak. They hadn't given the palace another thought.

"What are you going to do if he comes for you?"

Jak's thoughts must have followed hers. He was thinking of the New Choosing that Prince Bashir had announced. He'd all but said the whole thing was her idea. If the prince demanded she attend, she wouldn't be able to get out of it. In fact, she might even have agreed to go if he hadn't tried to force her to go. The majority of the idea was his but if she were being honest she liked the concept. Instead of choosing from the eligible princesses, he would host several gatherings to encourage all the royals to meet and choose among themselves. This worked well in this case since most of the eligible princesses had been killed by beasts at the former palace the rotation before.

Rasha still couldn't erase all the gory images from her mind. She and Chiza had been the only princesses to survive. Lu sacrificed himself to save Chiza, and forced her into hiding with Bashir. The prince expressed interest in Rasha but she'd shrugged it off at the time. It had been over a rotation already since he'd told her how much of an impression she'd left on him at ten rotations old. The attack from the beasts had interrupted the rest, but it lingered in the back of her mind and, she believed, Jak's as well.

"I'll do what I must," Rasha said, and he seemed satisfied with that for the moment. Her gut told her it wouldn't be long. The prince would call for her and she'd be forced to go. The only good thing about it was that Chiza would be there, as would Jak. They'd handle it together.

Silae returned with their drinks and this time didn't sit.

"Any other news?" Jak asked before she could twirl away.

"Just be mindful of your hygiene. That horrible flu going around is taking all my best customers and you don't want to get yourselves sick," she said then dashed off to deliver more drinks.

## 5

*L*ADI REACHED ISHOLA WITH MERRICK by nightfall. Right away, they welcomed her. The rest of the Wola who walked the grounds around the cabin where Tarrick took residence acknowledged her with smiles and nods. The small, unassuming building was just a cover for the underground caverns underneath. Around the grounds, Ladi gazed up at the trees filled with Wola who preferred to avoid being on the ground. They built up their perches with small tree homes where they could rest free from wanderers who might stumble upon their location.

They entered the cabin and when the floor opened below her feet, Merrick led her down a set of cavern stairs. Moments later, she reached the underground chamber, Tarrick's office. He had a large wooden desk where he stood and worked. He'd explained to her before that it made room for his large wings. Ladi had learned she probably wouldn't like them as much as she once thought. However, she did like the wide rooms and tall workstations that accommodated their wings.

Merrick stood at the door as she approached Tarrick. He embraced her in his Wola way with his wings surrounding her, and she touched her forehead to his. Then they took a step back, and she lifted her fist to her chest and he did the same in the way of the humanoids.

"How did it go? Did they believe you?" Tarrick asked. As an ambassador and council member for the Wola, his opinion mattered most.

"I left her at Central. I couldn't risk them getting this back." She held up the small package.

Tarrick sighed.

"I'm not sure you're going about this the best way. I don't understand why you don't just tell her."

"You don't understand, it goes against everything she knows about the Courier's Keep. I can't just walk up to her and say the couriers are being manipulated or, worse, that they're involved in a conspiracy against the beasts of the realm."

"I don't see why not. She seems much more reasonable. She's no longer the princess incumbent. Plus, you are a close friend. She cares about what matters to you."

"No, she doesn't." Ladi looked down at the package. "She cared about my brother. Everything she does for me is really in memory of him. She's just like the rest of them. She won't understand unless she can see it for herself."

Tarrick nodded to Merrick, who left them alone. Tarrick motioned for Ladi to sit down.

"Sit down, you're wearing a hole in the floor with your pacing."

"It helps me think."

"It helps you worry. Now, please." He gestured to the gray, low-backed seat. He sat down beside her and turned to face her, allowing his wings to expand behind him in their natural resting position.

The feel of the soft cushions did wonders for her as she sank into them. She was worried and it was showing.

"You have the Wola."

"Right now, I just need for Rasha and Jak to understand. When they realize what's going on, I think they will be on our side." Ladi bit down on her lower lip.

"How do they feel about the eleventh kingdom?"

"They don't understand the discrepancy the way we do. The prejudice against the beasts is very high. Most of our fighters and soldiers were in the war, but not everyone saw how the freed beasts came to our aid," Ladi said. She ran a hand over her face.

"If your brother were here, what would he do?"

"He'd trust Rasha."

"Do you trust her?"

"I think so, yes. I know her and Jak would do anything to protect the kingdom, she said as much when I spoke with her. Once she's convinced of the threat against your people and the beasts, she'll act."

Tarrick nodded.

"That is also my perception of her and Jak." Tarrick leaned forward and took her hands. "What now?"

"I need to go to where the worst of the prejudice is happening and find out if the rumors are true. If the beasts or Wola are in danger, someone needs to do something."

"I will give you all the help you need. But first, you should rest and bathe. I believe it's been too long since you've touched water." Tarrik's nose scrunched up.

"Poobari's prison isn't the place to get clean. I'll attend to it right away, Ambassador." Ladi stood up.

Tarrick allowed Ladi to leave with Merrick and one other Wola. They were to investigate what was happening with the beasts who had travelled south of Tero Joro and into Vol, Buku, and Winaka. Merrick was seeing another Wola, her name was Erima. She accompanied them and took turns carrying Ladi. They reached the border of the southern kingdoms before dark, where she asked to be let down. There were several small towns on the way, but the beasts would stick to the outskirts. That's where the Wola followed her as she marked tracks and followed trails she thought might belong to beasts.

Ladi lifted her ear to the wind and away, listening for any sounds out of the ordinary. She heard growling and snarling a short distance ahead of them and lifted a hand to signal the Wola to stay back as she tracked the sound.

She soon caught up with the source and saw a large patch of grey in the shuddering brush ahead. In front of her, the grey stopped moving long enough for her to make out the figure.

"Ladi, I'd know your scent anywhere," growled Browl.

Ladi parted the thin branches and stepped through the leaves where she found Browl surrounded by a litter of grey and brown cubs. The interruption didn't bother the cubs as they continued to launch themselves at their father, nipping and tugging on his ears and tail.

"Well, someone has been busy." Ladi laughed and went to scratch him behind the ear. But a sharp high-pitched bark had the cubs retreating behind him and to his left.

"It's all right, she's a friend," Browl said to the brownish figure in the trees.

The female wolf whined and he growled back at her. She stepped out of the woods, nipping at her cubs to stay behind her.

Ladi raised a fist to her chest, saluting in the Tero-Joro way.

"I'm Ladi Luduru"

"SHE WAS OUR FREEDOM FIGHTER," Browl said, giving his mate a reassuring push forward with his nose.

The female nodded but remained silent.

The trees behind her shifted as Merrick and Erima stepped through.

The female hunched down growling at them and gathering her young.

"Merrick and Erima are with me," Ladi said gesturing to them. The Wola didn't move forward but bowed their heads.

"The Wola helped fight off the masters," Browl said nudging her with his nose.

"Grella is my mate." He used his teeth to gently pull a pup off of his tail. He then plopped him unceremoniously in front of Ladi.

Ladi bent down and scratched the cub behind the ears, but Grella's back stiffened. Seeing the change in her, Ladi straightened deciding it was best not to upset the nervous wolf with any sudden movements.

"I've come to find out how the beasts are living here. Have you run into any trouble?"

He looked up into the trees and sniffed the air. "Come," Browl said. "Let's not talk here, it isn't safe."

Browl and Grella moved through the trees and Ladi ran to keep up. The dense brush hung too low to allow the Wola to fly unseen, forcing them to run alongside her. They came to a small clearing where a large river with sparkling blue water ran in their path. The roar of the falls nearby was tremendous. Little would be heard above it. Several other beasts drank from the flowing stream. Ladi saw a family of white bears, two dragons, and another family of grey wolves who all looked up from their drink and noted the humanoids. The other family of wolves moved off, but the dragons stayed, as did the bear family. Ladi recognized the white bear. It was Osa and her cubs.

Ladi waved to them with a smile. They moved in her direction. Out of captivity, the bear cubs had healthy white coats, and the two looked happier than she'd ever seen them. She reached out and they welcomed her with several bear cub licks and rubs.

"Boys, enough," Osa said as she sat down on the river-bank. She looked from Ladi to the Wola. "Friends?"

"Yes, these are the Wola. They were a huge part of the effort to end the war and they have been good friends to me ever since."

Osa nodded to each of them. Despite her sons' curiosity, she kept her cubs within reach.

"There have been rumors of trouble. We're here to investigate."

Osa said nothing but looked to Browl.

"Yes, here it is less rumor and more fact."

"What have you seen?" Ladi moved so she was sitting between Osa and Browl while their cubs moved off to play together nearby but out of easy listening.

"Not everyone accepts us," Osa said.

"They prefer their own kind," Browl said. "As do some of ours." His eyes never left Grella as she watched over the young cubs. She showed no interest in discussing matters with Ladi and the others.

"Hunting has been difficult." Osa's voice was soft and quiet. "We can eat fish and berries. Many cannot."

Browl hung his head and shook it from side to side.

"It is difficult to know the domestics from the prey."

Ladi understood their dilemma now. Many of the beasts were hunters like Rasha's Temi. Their relocation forced them to learn which animals were acceptable to hunt and which were domesticated and cherished by their owners.

"There have been accidents," Osa said. "However, not all have been forgiving."

Ladi's heart sank. She'd hoped that her effort during the war would bring the beasts and the humanoids together to the same side. Now, it seemed that despite her sacrifices, the beasts still struggled.

"That's not all of it." Browl moved closer to Ladi. "They have taken some of our kind."

"Whole families disappearing in the night," Osa said then smiled as her sons returned to her side. "Sleep is difficult when you can only close one eye."

Ladi understood the sentiment and wondered what to do about it.

"Have you told anyone?" Ladi asked.

"Yes, we've spoken to those from our encampment and warned many others, but we're not sure it's enough," Browl said.

"Have you told the humanoids, Prince Bashir?"

Osa and Browl looked at each other, the confusion clear in their expressions.

"We don't know this Prince Bashir, but we know you. We would have sent word of our troubles sooner except we had no way to reach you."

"I blame myself." Ladi shook her head. "I thought I was doing the right thing by going to the Courier's Keep for training. Now I know better. I believe they may be part of a conspiracy to cause you harm and I plan to stop it."

Osa moved closer.

"Ladi, we aren't defenseless, you know."

"I know, but I also wouldn't turn my back on a friend in trouble. Someone doesn't want you to be a part of the Bolaji kingdoms. Even the Wola haven't been fully welcomed."

"We are partially to blame," said Merrick. "We've chosen to remain independent in many things and made ourselves autonomous. So, some view us as competition when providing similar services and products."

Ladi didn't see the logic in that. They all should learn from the Wola, not compete with them.

"Our hunting is more cunning than most are used to. It frightens them," Browl said.

"Proper hunting grounds are needed, but that's no reason to do you harm. Do you have any idea where they are taking them?"

"No," Browl said, shaking his head.

Osa shook her head too, then said, "I fear for my little ones, and I don't have to tell you what I'm willing to do to protect them."

No, she didn't. Ladi remembered all too well how she'd fallen after she'd been slashed across the back by Osa. The bird-men and the bull-men masters had forced Ladi and Osa into a grand arena to fight for their entertainment. When Osa had refused, they'd threatened her children.

Ladi still bore the scars and the dreadful memory. But now she only nodded.

"There is talk that the beasts may have been taken further south. But where they may have gone from there, we can only guess. Perhaps back to the territory of the masters." A growl behind Browl had them all turning toward Grella.

Ladi sniffed the air and she caught a hint of something metallic, something not from nature. The others scattered into the trees without a word. They would defend themselves but they wouldn't start a fight or risk a frontal assault with their young around their ankles. Ladi nodded to the Wola who took to the sky to get a better view.

In seconds, something shot through the sky above them and lassoed around the wings of Erima. She cried out but her cries were cut off as she was pulled back down to the ground.

Ladi raced through the trees to catch up to those who had taken her. Merrick followed from above, reaching them before Ladi could. She arrived just in time to watch them throw another lasso around Merrick's wings. They dragged him down to the ground and into a separate cage

"Looks like we're going to get two for one, boys."

Ladi watched the two men from the safety of the dense green trees around her. Merrick didn't let his lack of flight stop him from punching one man down and kicking the other, forcing him back. His mistake was taking his eyes off of them for a moment to reach for Erima's ropes. He had it in his hands when he stopped.

Ladi didn't see or hear anything amiss, but Merrick reached up to his neck and he pulled out a small dart.

He watched it fall to the ground before he toppled over.

Erima yelled, calling his name, piercing the air. She, too, paused suddenly and looked down. A thin needle poked out of her leg, but before she could pull it out she collapsed as well.

Ladi strained to see what happened.

The younger man held something in his hands, some kind of thin tube he quickly stashed in the pocket of his vest. The two men groaned and sweated as they pulled and shoved the Wola into a large metal cage. It wasn't unlike the ones she'd seen before, when the bull-men and bird-men kept the beasts imprisoned and forced them to fight each other. The two men congratulated each other before getting into the motorized vehicle and moving off, pulling the cage on wheels behind them.

She'd never be able to keep up with them without transport, but she ran after them anyway. Whoever they were, they had the answers to what was happening to the beasts. Ladi was determined to find out who was behind it all.

She pulled out her communicator to send a message to Tarrick. He needed to know what had happened to the others. She wouldn't ask him to send more Wola, it was dangerous and she blamed herself for the two they'd caught. They were her friends, and they'd believed her when she told them that things were not as they should be for the beasts. Before she could send the message, she felt a sting on the side of her neck.

"Oh," she said as she watched the same small dart fall out of her hand. She felt herself falling and waited for the jarring ground to slap her in the face, but she never felt it.

## 6

---

*R*ASHA AND JAK MADE THEIR way back to Ishola together for the first time since they met almost two rotations ago. The last time Jak had been in Ishola it had still been called the Wilds and the Wola were in relative isolation. Now it was the center of all things government related. The council and the reigning prince lived at the newly built palace and the Wola roamed freely throughout the now eleven kingdoms of Bolaji.

Jak had been instrumental in bringing them into the fight those many months ago. He'd helped to seal their victory against the beasts in what they were now calling the Beast wars. It had been a difficult rotation to put behind them. Jak had returned home to bury his mother and she wondered how he felt now as they flew toward the place where they'd buried her. Instead of asking him she decided to ask him about something else that she'd always wondered about.

"What are those markings on your neck? Do they stand for anything?"

Jak's cheeks blushed. Was he actually embarrassed?

"It was from a long time ago, another life."

"Tell me about it."

"When I was still young, before the Courier's Keep, I was a part of a group of boys who sort of ran havoc in the streets of the Wilds. We had a bit of a bad reputation."

Rasha's eyebrows drew together.

"You were bandits?"

"I was young and impulsive, lashing out against my mom and the people who'd raised me. They were all boys around my age and they've got a history of sticking up for one another no matter what. At the time I needed that."

Rasha thought about it. Then realization dawned on her.

"You were a Triple B?"

Jak rubbed the back of his neck his cheeks still pink.

"You're looking at a former Bad Boy Bandit."

"They're notorious for being kidnappers and thieves."

"It's been many rotations since anyone has been kidnapped. That died out almost a hundred rotations ago. But the general thieving and mischief remained." Jak shook his head. "We started to mark ourselves over a decade ago to signify our allegiance to the group."

Rasha shook her head.

"I always wanted to be a part but they have that silly rule." She looked at him out of the side of her eye.

"Yeah, that no girls allowed rule. That's eventually why I left too."

"Traitor to the cause," Rasha said.

"Yes, it's difficult to get married and stay with the Triple Bs."

"I would think so. Who wants a husband who is a professional thief?"

"That was the rotation I enrolled at the Courier's Keep. I'd had a perfect record up until," Jak caught himself and then stopped.

"What happened? Why didn't you deliver that package all those rotations ago?"

"I suspect for the same reason Ladi won't deliver this one. I found out what I was carrying. There's a reason they don't want you to know. But I've reconciled myself to that now and my ideals have changed to a more realistic version of what they once were."

"Do you remember what it was?"

"Yeah, it was poison. The kings of Vol and Buku were still feuding. They were sending each other poisoned gifts in the hope that one of them would be stupid enough to accept the gift and die."

Rasha shook her head. The early tribal wars among the kingdoms hadn't been much different.

"I decided then and there that I wouldn't deliver poison from one kingdom to the other because it was disloyal to the king accepting it. I chose to be loyal to all and not to one. Eventually after several sessions the council and Keep agreed with me and I was exonerated despite my rebellion but it still tainted my record. The break from courier life helped me to regain my focus. I examined why I had become a courier in the first place. I refused to be an ignorant player in anyone's gang or war again. Then the king of Sidoa of the tenth kingdom chose me for a covert mission. I was to follow his daughter in a crate to make sure she made it to Adalu for the Choosing. That's when I met you."

Rasha must have had her mouth open the whole time he was talking. When she closed her dry mouth again the missing moisture returned.

"Well, I hope we get some answers about what Ladi found. Once we learn what she's got maybe we can more easily track her down."

Tarrick had a small cabin in the woods on the edge of the dessert lands and the forest lands of Wola. They'd grown too accustomed to the trees in the region to leave it, even for the luxuries of what now surrounded the palace. The arid desert was flourishing due to the constant addition of water brought in by the prince and his people. Rasha admired Tarrick's choice. The quiet understated cabin with an underground passage was something she often craved. Solitude followed up by even more privacy.

The Wola in the area noted Rasha and Jak's arrival but continued about their business. Several of them bowing in their direction. As the former prince and princess incumbent, people recognized them for their former roles as leaders in the war against the beasts.

When they reached the cabin, one of the Wola Rasha hadn't met yet came up to greet them. He had long blond hair and a thin graceful appearance. He wore the same loose fitting kind of shirt that the other Wola used to give their wings freedom of movement while bearing his chest. On his hilt he carried a long sword that slapped against his fitted trousers when he took a step forward. His long fingers he held up in the traditional Bolaji greeting.

"Welcome Rasha and Jak, I will inform Tarrick of your arrival if you will be so kind as to wait here."

"Yes, of course," Rasha said as she watched the Wola leave.

Jak shrugged his shoulders when she looked at him in question.

They didn't have to wait long as the Wola returned shortly to escort them inside.

As they walked down the corridor and steps, she broached the obvious question.

"I'm sorry did something happen to Merrick?"

"Oh, my apologies. My name is Ogene. I am carrying for Merrick's duties while he is attending to other matters in the south of the kingdom."

Rasha nodded accepting the information while at the same time looking him over.

"Tarrick will be here in just a moment, please be made comfortable." Ogene gestured to the chair with no arms and the two of them sat down.

After several long moments of waiting Tarrick entered the room from a door in the back and greeted them.

"My apologies, I was in another meeting. The council makes themselves a priority as you're well aware." He walked to them both and put his head to first Jak's forehead and then to Rasha's in greeting.

"Of course, we hate to intrude on your already busy day, it's just that we need your help."

"Anything."

"It's regarding our young friend Ladi. She has virtually disappeared," Jak said.

"The Courier's Keep has sent her to deliver a package and she refuses to deliver it," Rasha said. "Normally, that wouldn't be something we would bring to you obviously except she was last seen with one of the Wola fleeing from the Courier's Keep."

"We were hoping you could tell us if she's been here," Jak said.

Tarrick didn't flinch or falter when he answered.

"Yes, she's been here. On several occasions, actually."

When he offered nothing more Rasha and Jak simultaneously leaned forward. Then catching themselves, Rasha shook her head and spoke up.

"When was the last time you saw her?"

"She was here several hours ago, but she hasn't been back since."

"Wait, do you know what she's done and why?" Jak asked.

"Yes."

Rasha stood up and her hand flew to her hip before she remembered that Tarrick was a friend and she didn't need her swords.

"What has she told you?"

"I cannot reveal any of what was spoken as it was revealed in confidence."

"Confidence," Rasha mumbled to herself throwing her hands up and letting them fall to her thighs.

Jak held up a hand. "What can you tell us?"

Tarrick stood up and faced Rasha and waited for her to stop pacing before speaking.

"Your friend is in danger. She has discovered a very sinister plot but has no idea who is pulling the strings. The beasts of the north are involved and I fear it won't end there."

That got Rasha's attention and Jak stood up so they were shoulder to shoulder.

"I need to find her before it's too late, help us."

Tarrick shook his head.

"I cannot tell you anything more, however, we will stand with her no matter what happens. She will not be left on her own. Besides Merrick is with her now."

"Merrick?" Jak asked. "That must have been who flew her away from the Courier's Keep."

Rasha pulled out her swords and held them ready.

"You won't need those," Tarrick said holding up a hand.

Jak put a light hand on her shoulder but she shrugged him off.

"You need to tell me exactly what you know," Rasha said between her teeth.

The door opened behind her but she didn't flinch. Whoever was behind her must have had weapons because Tarrick held up his other hand and spoke up.

"Everything is fine, return to your post." When they didn't move he put his hands down. "Now!" Rasha heard the door close behind her and Tarrick turned his back to her and walked back toward his desk putting more distance between them.

"You won't hurt me. I'm the only one who knows where Ladi is and if something happens to me, no one will know where she's gone. We are looking after your friend, you don't need to worry."

"Don't tell me how to feel. Tell me where she is and I'll see for myself."

"At this time, I cannot. Even I must honor a word spoken in confidence."

Jak pulled on Rasha's arm until she realized he was holding her. Rasha shrugged him off and walked to the door.

"If something happens to her, you do realize that despite everything I'll come back here for you." She turned her head but didn't look over her shoulder.

"Yes, I'm aware," Tarrick said his features calm and neutral.

Rasha nodded and left the way they'd come. She didn't wait long before she felt Jak behind her.

"He's right about being a good friend," Jak said.

"Yes, that may be true. He's being a good friend to her but if it gets her killed, then what kind of friend is he?"

Rasha stopped and looked up at Jak and he met her eye. The wind had picked up and it blew his hair to one side of his face. The wind pulled it away from his growing beard. His hands came up and rested on her shoulders as she took deep breaths.

"We will find her. We know which way she went."

"What?"

"She's with Merrick and he's gone south. So will we. I can bet you any amount of credits she's not walking so we'll fly south too. Someone will have seen her. Now stop slowing us down and let's go." He dropped his hands giving her a little shove at the same time. They were in the air minutes later.

# 7

THE SMELL OF FOOD COOKING over a fire reached into her dreams and mind pulling Ladi from sleep. As her mind regained consciousness, she felt the dull ache at the base of her neck as if she'd been hit from behind. Then it started to come back to her memory. She'd been shot with something small that stung like a pollinating Zinger. She'd seen it just before she went down. She groaned and felt someone move to her side.

"Easy," said the familiar voice in the dark.

When Ladi moved her head to look at him she grimaced in pain.

"I said easy. Whatever they shot you with is going to leave a tail." Ebere looked down at her his eyes warm.

Ladi felt herself about to heave. Thankfully, her stomach was empty. When she was able to settle back down on the ground, she looked him over. He was stirring something in the small pot he often carried. The substance was as black as the night around them.

"How did you find me?"

Ebere smiled and glanced at her his large ears wiggled with the movement.

"You're not that hard to track."

Ladi, grit her teeth and then remembered that he'd kissed her once. He was probably teasing her.

"What are you cooking up?"

He scooped a small bit of it out of the pot and put it into a cup for her to drink. Ladi shook her head only moments ago her empty stomach had been a blessing she was hardly going to test the goddess' patience now.

"It will settle your stomach and ease your headache, I promise." He held it out and Ladi took the steamy hot liquid in her cold hands. She let the warmth flow through her for a moment before she tested the liquid against her tongue. It carried a mild flavor of flowers and something spicy. She sipped at it for a moment and the pain at the base of her skull began to fade.

Ebere grabbed his own cup and sat back to regard her.

"What do you think you're doing out here by yourself?"

"I wasn't by myself, for your information, I was with two Wola. They were captured by thieving mongrels. You still didn't answer my question."

"Didn't I?"

Ebere said with a laugh. There was something confident about him, she'd never seen him so playful. It was different as if their kiss suddenly changed him into the kind of guy she would have liked from the start. He was a little more cocky, a little more flirtatious, more like Jak. Then it occurred to her she was in the middle of sending a message to Tarrick when she fell to the ground.

"My communicator?"

Ebere lifted the remains of her communicator from the ground it dangled in three pieces.

"I was debating about whether to see if any of it could be salvaged when you started to stir. But from what I can see there's nothing left of it. Whoever knocked you out got the best of it."

Ladi wondered who it had been that snuck up on her. She looked around they weren't anywhere near the trail she'd been following. It was obvious from the line of golden trees where they sat.

"Where are we?"

"Not far from the trail you were following. I thought it best not to start a fire too close to their road in case they should double back to finish you off."

"If they wanted to kill me I guess they would have," Ladi said. She tried to shrug off the shiver that traveled down her back at the thought of dying out there in the woods alone. Without Ebere, she might still be lying out there unconscious. She took a few more sips of the drink Ebere made for her and the last of the headache dissipated. In a vehicle, the abductors had already gotten too far ahead for them to catch up.

"We'll wait for morning and then see if we can pick up

the trail where you left off," Ebere said as if he could read her mind.

Ladi watched Ebere tend to the fire while she settled back down her elbow propped on the make-shift pillow he'd given her. It was the blanket he used for cold nights while traveling. She recognized the material with the horizontal and vertical stripes in white and two shades of blue. After he'd stoked the fire, he looked up and met her eye. When did he become so bold to stare at her so openly? She found herself looking away as her face warmed at the intimacy of his gaze. A shiver crept down her spine and she shook it off.

"You're still cold," Ebere said standing up and moving to her side of the fire. He must have seen her shake off the shiver and misunderstood its source. "Come here." He sat with his back against a moss covered boulder. Ebere put his arms out to reach for her, pulling her in so that she could rest her head on him. Then he moved the blanket to cover them both. Ladi felt so comfortable in his arms she wondered why she hadn't done it before.

In fact, she glanced up to say something funny about it but when she saw the intense look in his eyes. Her joke faded from her mind and she found herself staring at his mouth. She didn't have to wait long before he shifted an inch to accommodate putting his face as close to hers as possible.

It was a question and demand as his parted lips waited a centimeter from hers. Ladi answered by breathing him in and pressing her mouth to his, claiming and being claimed by him. It was the second time, he'd kissed her, but he'd been holding back some heat before. This time he unleashed it and the groan that escaped her lips was uncontrollable and it lit something in him. His kiss deepened and his entire body was clutching her as if holding her kept him from falling off of a cliff's edge.

They parted only to breathe. Ladi didn't know how long she and Ebere were locked in that kiss. Was it only minutes her belly filled with the flames of passion or was it hours? The one thing that was clear to both of them was neither was letting go and Ladi shifted only enough to lay her head on his chest. Ebere didn't say a word about why he held back his feelings. Ladi didn't talk about his changes. Instead, they clung to one another until sleep took them both.

They held each other so tight that when Ladi woke, she was surprised that she was curled up on the ground again with his blanket underneath her head. Her eyes slowly adjusted to the sun rising in the south. Ebere wasn't there, she didn't know how she knew but she knew it. She rose slowly from the ground and looked around using her heightened vision and hearing to locate him. That's when she heard someone talking in the distance.

Ladi tracked the sound coming from within the trees just ahead of their location. She crept through the tall wood until she found its origin. Ebere was crouched low to the ground. But he'd stopped talking. He stood up and turned to face her.

"I'm glad to see you're awake, we can get moving. We'll eat on the way," he said as he moved to her side.

"Were you talking to someone? I thought I heard voices."

"No, I was mumbling to myself. It's a bad habit from when I used to travel alone." Ebere took her hand as casually as if they'd always walked together that way. "We should hurry, your friends could be in danger."

Ladi nodded unable to get over the warmth of his grip on her cold hand. He led her back through the woods to where they spent the night together. Her heart leapt into her throat as she realized this journey might be a few more days and they would be cuddled up together again and again. Did he crave the nights now as much as she did? She watched his face as he let go of her hand to put out the residual embers from the fire and gather his things.

When he was ready, he slipped the pack on his back and took her hand again and led the way back to the trail. The marks left by the large vehicle towing the cage were distinctive and easy to follow. Despite being tethered to each other by linked hands they moved with relative speed over the pebbles and rocks down the center of the path.

"How many were with them when they took your friends?" Ebere asked.

"Two men," she said, then she remembered she'd been taken from behind, "No, three. The third knocked me out with that sleep dart. You've seen them before." It wasn't a question, Ebere knew exactly what to give her to ease the dull headache she had upon waking up.

"Yes, I have. Not those exactly, but something like it. The substance when in contact with the skin can put you to sleep in an instant."

"Yeah, I noticed," Ladi grumbled the words. She was still upset about not hearing whoever it was that crept up on her and hit her with the dart in the first place. She had both excellent hearing and vision for a Tero-Joro mix there was nothing better. How is it she didn't have a clue about the third person until it was too late?

Ladi remembered that she'd been surprised before back when she'd been attempting to free the beasts in the enslavement camp over a rotation ago. That had been different. The sound quality had been skewed by the echo among the cages. Her vision had been limited as well with the unnatural darkness caused by the large enclosure. She'd also been fighting off one bull-man at the time. So when another arrived and clubbed her from behind it made sense. This was different. She wondered why she hadn't at least heard them coming. While she was lost in her own thoughts about what happened, Ebere was racing along the trail. When he came to an abrupt stop, she almost collided into him. If their hands hadn't been joined, she might have run right in to his back. He provided enough warning of what was coming with the shift in his body and hand.

"What is it?"

"The trail it's gone."

"What do you mean it's gone?"

"I mean gone," Ebere pulled her forward.

Ladi saw for herself the tracks of the vehicle disappeared right in front of them and instead of one path there were three different paths to choose. None of them bore any resemblance to the trail they followed up to now.

"That's impossible," Ladi said as she looked behind her at the trail they followed and now there was nothing. Worse there were multiple smaller paths but no indication as to which they followed.

"We've lost them."

"No," Ladi said as she pulled her hand away and climbed the nearest tree. They searched for some evidence of the vehicle. Even a slight bending of the trees. She was determined to find it. She reached the tree top and pushed aside the bright yellow leaves in order to see around them. With one hand over her eyes to block out the sun she scanned the area. Then she climbed back down to the ground. Ebere was waiting for her to say something but instead her shoulders fell and her eyes dropped to the ground in defeat.

"They're gone."

## 8

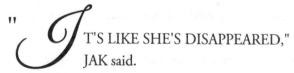

"IT'S LIKE SHE'S DISAPPEARED," JAK said.

"I don't get it. We should be on top of them by now. Someone should have noticed two flying men and a green girl traveling together." To the dragon she said, "come on Zele, let's keep looking."

"Zele?"

"Yeah, I kind of like it." She turned her head so he could see her smile.

Zele snorted and started to pull back.

"I do too, it fits," Jak said giving her a pat on the shoulder.

"What's wrong girl?" Rasha asked as the beast fought the direction they were headed.

"Either she doesn't like the name or there's something down there she doesn't like. Let's go down and take a closer look."

519

Rasha steered Zele the best she could to the ground. It was difficult since the dragon wasn't convinced that a bridle of any kind could tell her where to go. Instead, she usually went along with Rasha but today she was having none of it and she couldn't put them down fast enough. In fact, the moment they were on the ground she made two angry circles before going straight up into the air and flying off.

"I guess, that's it for our ride," Jak said watching Zele fly off.

"What's gotten into her?"

"I think we better find out. Let's keep on in the direction we were heading."

When they came upon a small village, they were hopeful that they'd find someone who'd seen Ladi. The area was too small to hide anyone for long. In fact, it was so small it was almost dead quiet.

"Did we come on a celebration day?" Jak asked in a whisper.

Rasha shrugged. Even though he'd whispered, she held up a hand to signal him to be quiet. The small village had no activity. The only thing moving were animals that had appeared to have gotten out of their pens and cages. Where were all the people? Just then they caught sight of a young girl. She was wrapped in peasant clothing and she had dark smudges on her face. The yellow of her hair caught her eye and she moved to speak with her.

"Excuse me, where is everyone?"

The startled girl dropped the bucket she'd been carrying and dashed off into the trees.

Before they lost sight of her Rasha called out to her.

"I promise we just have to ask a question, we're not going to hurt you."

The girl ran headlong into the woods and over a creek bed. When the trees opened to a small clearing, a log cabin home came into view. Rasha slowed down and Jak was right behind her with the girl's large bucket in his hand. Rasha looked down at his hand with one raised eyebrow.

"What? I'm not going to have her get in trouble for losing perhaps their family's only bucket on top of scaring her to death." He flashed her his killer smirk.

Rasha shook her head and couldn't resist smiling. He was the type to be concerned about the little fellow. Perhaps it was her upbringing in the castle but she always found it difficult to remember those things. She'd seen a lot of that in him while they were living in the palace and she'd improved but she could still do better. She took the bucket from him with a nod and walked up to the house and tried to put on her most non-threatening smile.

The front door was slightly ajar and instead of walking in she knocked on the front door. When no one answered she tried again. On the third knock Jak reached out and put a hand on her shoulder. He shook his head and indicated she look to their left. On that side of the house were two freshly dug graves. The mounds were still well above ground.

"What's going on here?" Rasha asked.

It was Jak's turn to shrug. He stepped in front of her and into the log cabin home. At first Rasha barely made out anything beyond Jak's shoulder but there in the corner were two smaller children huddled together. One was a mix of mermaid and Buku from the look of her pink ombre hair and the other child with jet black hair must have had Karmirian ancestry. Then the girl with the yellow hair that they'd seen earlier entered the room. The others ran to hide behind her even though she wasn't much taller or bigger than the two of them.

"Where are your parents?" Rasha asked the girl.

"They're dead," the girl said.

"They're all dead," said the little boy behind her.

Rasha caught Jak expression. It had changed to something she wasn't sure she'd seen before. Was it fear?

"How did they die?" He asked.

"They got sick and died."

"What kind of sickness?"

"They get the flu but when their lips turn blue, they go to sleep, and they never wake up." The girl with the yellow hair kept her face neutral and her voice flat and without feeling. "You can't stay here." She placed her hands protectively over the children behind her.

"We're not going to hurt you," Rasha said taking a step forward and raising her hands when they retreated a step. "I'm Rasha and this is Jak we're friends with the prince of the eleven kingdoms, we might be able to get you some help."

"No!" Her voice shrill. "Don't send anyone here. They just keep dying. I can't bury any more bodies, I'm tired."

"How many people from your village are left?"

The two younger children glanced up at the older girl with hope in their eyes only to be disappointed as she shook her head.

"You are the first people we've seen alive in over a week. I was afraid you'd try to take the children."

She was referring to the younger ones and they clutched at her dress as if daring anyone to separate them.

"It's not safe for you to stay here among the dead. You must leave this place."

"No, this is my home and I know how to care for them here. I can't protect them in the forest or on the trails," the girl said with defiance.

Rasha thought for a moment. It was true. Someone of her age maybe no more than twelve or thirteen wouldn't have the resources for herself or anyone else away from this place.

"Okay," Rasha took a step back.

"Okay?" Jak asked, turning to her.

"Stay here and we'll see what else we can find out. You'll need food and supplies, will you at least accept help?"

The younger children again gazed up with hope on their faces to see the older girl's reaction.

She nodded.

"Tell us, what is your name?"

"My name is Yinka."

## 9

"*T*HEY NEED MORE THAN THIS," Jak said looking down at the small pile of food and supplies.

"Yes, I know," Rasha said as she lay down the last sack of roots she'd gathered and dropped it on the on the doorstep.

The children huddled inside. After they'd walked out she'd locked them out refusing to let them back into the house. The fear in their eyes was real and valid. In their search they discovered lots of graves and no other people. Jak still had a wary look on his face and didn't appear to be very eager to be near the children or the village. Something strange was going on and it was more than a flu.

"We thought it was the beasts but, Zele didn't want to come here for a reason. It's possible she can smell the death here," Rasha said.

"I can smell the death here," Jak said as he dusted off his clothing.

"We need to find out if anyone else is dying of this new flu."

"I'm not going to like this next part am I?"

"Someone needs to stay here to look after the children."

Jak ran a hand over his hair and rolled his eyes.

"They don't want to be looked after."

"All the more reason, we need to make sure that they're okay and none of them get sick."

Rasha put a hand on his shoulder and gave him two pats. "I'll be quick."

Rasha dashed off into the forest on the trail towards the next town in the area. The sun was going down and she had to hurry or risk dealing with whatever beasts used this area for hunting grounds. The idea made her stop. They hadn't seen any beasts in the area. She wondered if like Zele they could smell death in the air and avoided it on instinct. It was a working theory at best but for now she had to get help for those children before she continued her search for Ladi.

The moment she stepped foot into the town she felt something was wrong. It was late it had taken her three hours to walk and the sun had long since set. The eerie glow of the two moons was all the light she could see. The pubs were dark the homes were dark there wasn't a single light on in a town of hundreds. She walked along until she saw a dim fire burning in the woods. But when she reached the fire, she realized they were cremating dead bodies. The man didn't hear her approach as he placed another dead body on the fire.

"Hello there," Rasha said getting his attention before the stench of the bodies overwhelmed her. She held up her arm to her nose but gagged whenever she took a breath.

He waved her upwind of the fire and they stepped to one side. He pulled the cloth down from his face and she noted the pink skin.

"What are you doing out here?"

"I'm came over from the village, looking for help. They've almost all died out from sickness over there and from the looks of it, you've got the same problem here."

"We can't be of much use, it's better to keep a tight quarantine anyway. We've started burning the bodies because it's too much to bury and we don't want to pollute our water."

"Pollute the water with what? What are they dying from?"

"The flu is as much as we can tell. They get the normal symptoms then their lips turn blue before they slip into a deep coma. Sometimes it's days sometimes its weeks but they always die at the end."

"What have you tried as a cure?" Rasha felt her heart racing in fear. If it was as bad as this, they would need to move the children to a safer distance.

"What haven't we tried? The two doctors were at one point working together but they didn't find anything that might even slow it down."

"The doctors, where are they? We need their help."

"Those are the doctors over there," he said pointing to the bodies on the fire. "They won't be helping anybody else."

Rasha had to hold back from gagging again as the wind shifted slightly in their direction.

"Look, there's not a lot we can offer any survivors. If they come in the day, it will be better for them since there will be people about doing their chores. At night, don't expect a warm welcome here. People are tending to their sick."

Rasha remembered then the young children and their pleas not to bring anyone else that they might have to bury. Could they be better off on their own as they'd suggested?

"Other than burning bodies, is there anything anyone can do?"

"Yeah, stay away," he lifted the cloth again and tied it back around his face before continuing to tend the fire, leaving Rasha staring after him.

Things were worse than she'd imagined. Rasha didn't bother looking for a place to stay. The man was right, a quarantine was better for everyone. If one is infected, they all were and she didn't want to risk bringing the disease to another uninfected area it would only spread the disease faster. Rasha tracked her way back in the woods, it was difficult with the lack of light but the well trodden trail between the town and the village was clear enough. It was early in the morning when Rasha reached the village again.

Jak was sitting at a fire he was still awake as if he were waiting for her.

"Well," he said before she reached the fire.

"The news isn't good," she said.

"What good news can come when people are dying from this and no one even knows about it."

"So, you think its contained here?"

"I wouldn't risk bringing the survivors anywhere else."

Rasha nodded. That had been her own conclusion. That meant only one thing. The children would stay and they'd stay alone. Rasha held on to her amulet and said a silent prayer for them. Jak caught her eye and he nodded to her amulet.

"I think you've got the right idea this time. It feels like we might be a bit over our own heads."

"Agreed, we need to inform the palace and let them know what's going on here. Besides that I'm sure the doctors in Tero-Joro can get to working on something."

"For all we know they could already be working on a cure," Jak said.

"True."

Rasha wondered if this thing would literally die out on its own or if they would have to help it along. How many would they lose before it was too late? She kept thinking about all the graves between the village and the town. It made her sick again just thinking of the stink of burning bodies.

"The children here will be fine on their own. We'll

leave at first light and get someone to come back here to bring them the cure once it's found," Jak said.

They curled up next to the fire. Rasha tucked her head into his shoulder and he wrapped his arms tightly around her. She dreamed of death and woke up alone.

The early morning sun was rising up in the sky and the two moons were fading into the distance. The fire was now only burning embers. Rasha looked around and didn't see or hear Jak nearby. She was about to get up and go to look for him when the door of the cabin opened and Jak came out.

"What's wrong?" Rasha asked him in a loud whisper.

"They're still asleep, I went hunting and skinned them some meat. It took a while to find a beast since they've all fled from these parts but I managed to get them something to keep them for a bit. It might help keep their strength up."

Rasha smiled at him. He was that kind of person. It made her warm inside to think of him caring for her in such a way if she should ever need it.

"Let's go," she said. Before she could get too sentimental, she kicked dirt over the fire and turned away. She looked back at the cabin once and she saw one little face staring out at them as they left. The sad little girl with dirty blonde hair with the look of determination on her face.

"May the Universal Eye keep watch over you, Yinka," Rasha said as they walked away.

## 10

*R*ASHA DIDN'T HAVE TO WAIT long after sending her message before the call from the palace of Ishola came. Prince Bashir sent her a private communication while she and Jak were traveling through the woods of the Twinlands.

"Prince Bashir," she said, trying not to show her discomfort.

"Princess Indari, it's a pleasure to see you."

"You received my message."

"Yes, and I have the council looking into it immediately. However, I'm calling in regard to some other business."

"Of course, how can I be of assistance, your highness?"

"No need to be formal with me, Rash. I'm not calling about anything so serious. We're having a little party tomorrow night and your attendance is requested."

"Tomorrow?" Rasha almost dropped the communicator and had to sit down on a nearby log.

"Yes, I'm sure that dragon of yours will be able to manage it. Come by early, we'll have some gowns available for you to try on. I know how much you hate that sort of thing so I took the liberty of preparing a few items for you."

It was a good thing they'd reunited with Zele. She'd been waiting for them well away from the village. She'd been pacing the ground, hoping for their return.

"Um, thank you?" she said since he seemed to be waiting for a response from her.

"Of course, we'll see you after breakfast." He signed off and Rasha sat staring at the device in her hand.

"Prince Bashir?"

Rasha looked up into Jak's kind blue eyes and nodded.

"He sent me a written message. I guess I didn't warrant a face-to-face communication," Jak said.

He smiled and took a seat beside her on the log.

"You hate this," he said.

"I hate this."

"Let's get out of here."

"And go where? Anywhere we go they can follow us."

"Not if we go off planet. Some of the couriers from other places are making their way here for trade. We could find a place where we're not royalty and no one cares who we marry." Jak's eyes lit up with excitement as he spoke.

Rasha loved the idea. She wondered why she hadn't thought of it before. Granted, she'd never imagined

531

leaving the planet on her own. But with a partner, she'd be unstoppable. They could live where and how they wanted. She thought about those she'd have to leave behind. A dragon wouldn't be easy to transport off world. Not that Zele would want to go, anyway. Then there was Ladi. It must have shown on her face because Jak put an arm around her shoulders.

"We won't leave, just yet. Let's get to the bottom of where Ladi has gotten off to and find a cure for this disease first."

Rasha nodded. Jak knew she wouldn't rest until they found Ladi. That mystery needed solving. They'd been all over the Twinlands looking for anyone with information on her. She'd disappeared. Rasha had been discreet when contacting the Morens to ask how they were doing. With the sickness going around, Rasha wanted to rule out her being at home. When they asked if she'd seen Ladi, it was clear they hadn't spoken to her either and neither of them had gotten sick.

"Why didn't she just tell me what's going on?" Rasha asked aloud.

"Maybe it's related to your very different beliefs about the Courier's Keep. Maybe we should go back there."

"It will have to wait. We're expected at the palace of Ishola tomorrow morning."

"Impatient fellow, isn't he?"

"I never knew anyone in such a hurry to be rejected."

THE PALACE of Ishola made the former palace of Adalu look like a small shack. When Prince Bashir put his mind to rebuilding, he didn't want it to resemble the former in any way. The palace extended in all directions, with over two hundred and fifty bedrooms and a hundred guest rooms designed to entertain every royal in the kingdom and some. Some thought it elaborate, with its sprawling garden design in the middle of the desert and a large enclosed pool with a retractable roof. However, during the construction of the new palace, Prince Bashir spoke of the loss of his family and the princesses. He dedicated so many of the rooms and buildings. People soon forgot the heavy price tag that the building carried.

Rasha and Jak landed on the stony path leading to the palace entrance. That left the dragon plenty of room to avoid the manicured lawn. The intelligent beast had learned that it displeased Rasha when she destroyed the shrubbery around a castle. She took the same precautions here, curling up under a tree and keeping her large wings and tail tucked in to avoid smacking the saplings.

The palace was full of activity this morning. The servants bustled about, hanging lights and baskets of flowers. Most of the plants and trees wouldn't flower their first rotation. By next rotation, though, the place would be covered in several hundred varieties of imported flowers. The servants carried trays and boxes from one side of the palace to the other. The kitchens in the back held a steady flow of servants dressed in pressed whites carrying trays and ready to work.

Four guards descended the front steps of the palace and stopped in front of them. Two guards on the ground and two remained on the second step, all of them dressed in their royal blues with tall hats and staffs at their sides.

"Prince Jak Ameenu of Winaka and Princess Rasha Indari of Chilali, you are most welcome. Please follow me to your rooms," the guard said.

Neither of them had been in the new palace before and the elegance had them both looking around the entrance with awe. A giant chandelier hung from the center of the peaked ceiling, lighting the entrance. The natural stone pillars and archways created a breathtaking vision. Jak gave Rasha a wide-eyed look of awe.

"They've been busy," Jak said.

The entrance divided into three directions. Two guards led Rasha to the right while two others led Jak to the left. Rasha glanced over her shoulder and caught Jak staring.

"I guess I'll see you later." Jak continued to watch her leave.

"Yes, of course," Rasha said, then turned to follow the guards who'd already gotten several feet ahead of her.

Photo recreations of the royal family over the rotations decorated the walls, filling the corridor. To the left of them, windows every few feet lit their way with no need for artificial lighting. Rasha looked out into the courtyard at the back of the palace and the beautiful trees and fountains that the small birds and animals had made their home.

When they reached a spiral staircase, she shouldn't

have been surprised that the stairs were also made of the beautiful stone, along with its chiseled banister. It was cold to the touch, but she held on so she could keep walking while looking at the paintings on the walls. There was a picture of each of the lost princesses. One every few steps. She paused when she saw the young Princess Osika. She'd been kind and also tragically one of the few Rasha had seen viciously devoured. A sight she couldn't forget no matter how hard she'd tried.

The guards waited at a respectful distance when she reached out and touched the framing of the picture. She was proud of Bashir. It was good and right that he'd honored the princesses here.

Rasha turned back to the guards and at her nod, they continued without a word. They reached the first landing but didn't stop until they'd gone up to the top of the stairs. The walls on both sides had doors. Rasha counted ten on the left and ten on the right. At the end, one of the guards opened the door on the left.

"Your rooms have been prepared but if there is anything missing that you require, simply ring the bell and one of the servants will attend you."

Rasha could do nothing but nod. The room spread out before her was bigger than anything she'd ever seen before. The guard bowed before leaving her and closing the door behind himself.

She threw her pack on the nearest high-backed chair and entered. The small sitting room was perfect for entertaining visitors to the suite. She found the bedroom and master bathroom behind a closed door to her right. The bedroom had three large windows that overlooked the front of the palace. As promised, she found the closet filled with gowns in an array of color options. The favorites had been hung together with a note from the prince.

Please wear one of these today. ~Bashir

Rasha looked at the gowns, one a beautiful royal blue and the other an emerald color. The one in front, her favorite, was a silver-grey color. She didn't like shopping for clothes, but she could appreciate his excellent taste. A knock on the door pulled her attention away from the gowns.

Rasha walked over to the front sitting area before calling out.

"Enter."

The door opened and Chiza walked in wearing a beautiful bright yellow gown, her signature and most suited color. Yellow didn't look as good on anyone as it looked on her. She closed the door then raced over to hug Rasha.

They embraced like the old friends they were then sat down. Chiza, a head shorter, had twisted her hair into an intricate design that sat on top of her head. Rasha was mesmerized by it and couldn't wait to find out how she'd done it.

"It's so good to see you," Rasha said.

"I'm so glad you came," Chiza said.

"How have you been?" Rasha asked.

"Lonely, it's difficult being the only girl here."

Rasha hadn't thought of that. They were the only two

surviving princesses, which meant that there would be a shortage until the prince invited more eligible young women to live at the palace.

"Your family, were they very disappointed?" Rasha asked.

"My mother wasn't, she still believes I have a chance with the prince." Chiza shrugged, "My father isn't happy about losing the crown and his gems, but they've found more so," she let her voice fade away. After learning of her father's plot last rotation to keep his gems and his daughter, Chiza hadn't been completely reconciled to her family. It had caused her more embarrassment than anything else.

"Things are so different here," Chiza said looking around.

"It's enchanting. The others will love it."

"The ball tonight should be spectacular, I've been looking forward to it. Most of the time I've been in my rooms or in the gardens. Speaking of rooms," she said, looking around, "I can see he favors you."

"What do you mean?"

"Your room is twice the size of any of the others."

Rasha looked around, taking it in again.

"It is?"

"Yes, you'll see when you come visit me in my room."

Rasha didn't know how she felt about that news. She didn't mind Bashir being nice to her, but she didn't want to be singled out, especially when the other girls hadn't yet arrived.

"What will the ball be like do you think?"

"I believe the only gentlemen joining us will be princes, so it's exciting. The girls will be invited tonight then, if they're selected by any of the princes, they'll be asked to stay at the palace. They'll be put on our floor, I imagine."

Rasha shook her head.

"For how long is he expecting us to stay here?"

Chiza reached out a warm hand to Rasha's cold one.

"Don't panic. We'll be here until he makes his choice and then we'll be free to go, I'm sure."

The prince could take as long as he liked for the Choosing. Even opening it up to other young women, there was no guarantee they wouldn't be there for months. Rasha couldn't help but panic. She stood up, needing to walk. The room was large enough to take several strides before she had to turn around again.

"I can't be here that long. I only agreed to this because I didn't want to embarrass the prince," Rasha said.

Chiza watched Rasha with a knowing smile.

"What?" Rasha asked.

"You," Chiza said, standing up. "You've been trying to get out of the Choosing from the start and yet here you are anyway."

Rasha wanted to scream but wound up laughing instead. She flopped back down into a chair with her feet spread out in front of her.

"What a nightmare."

"It won't be that bad," Chiza said "We have each other."

Rasha wished that was enough.

"Ladi's missing. I have to find her."

"Ladi? What's happened to her?"

"I'm not sure. She quit the training at the Courier's Keep and stole a package she was supposed to deliver."

"Why?"

"I wish I knew. She didn't tell me. I'm not sure what it is, but it has something to do with the reason she wouldn't take the oath."

"What oath?"

"The Courier's Oath. It basically says you'll serve the ten kingdoms of Bolaji and not put loyalty of one kingdom above any others."

Chiza looked thoughtful. "I'm required to be loyal to my kingdom above all others unless I'm wed to the prince, at which time I'd become loyal to all the Bolaji kingdoms. Isn't loyalty to none and loyalty to all the same thing?"

Rasha listened to her words and wondered the same thing. Hadn't she said as much to Ladi? The oath hadn't changed with the addition of Ishola, but hadn't that been a Wola choice? She'd also been overly concerned with Lu and the comparison between the two of them, but Rasha didn't feel it fair to mention it. Chiza had been so in love with Lu that she'd planned on renouncing her loyalty to her kingdom to marry him.

"I'd better let you get dressed. The prince will want to see us both for lunch." Chiza stood up and gave Rasha a kiss on the cheek before dashing out the door.

Rasha was left wondering how she was going to get

through a month of this royal tedium. Then she remembered the dresses. They were beautiful.

She moved to the closet to choose one, wondering
what Jak would think of them. A thought occurred to her
that had her moving to her communicator. Ladi was
missing and there was only one other person who cared
about her as much as she did.

## 11

*D*ESPITE THEM GETTING ALL DRESSED UP, they held lunch in the gardens underneath a large, floral-decorated gazebo. Rasha was the last to arrive. Prince Bashir and the other princes, including Jak, all stood when she set foot in the gazebo. Eight princes, one from each kingdom, all smiled at her and bowed. Chilali didn't have a young prince, nor did the tenth kingdom where Chiza was from.

Chiza gave Rasha a nod and a knowing smile as she moved to greet Bashir.

When Prince Bashir greeted Chiza, he fumbled with the cup in his hand. With grace, she managed to catch it then curtsy before moving to sit down. His shoulders dropped and his cheeks turned pink, but he recovered by the time he turned to Rasha with a huge smile on his face.

"You are a vision." Prince Bashir moved to take her hand and brought it to his lips.

Jak didn't wait long to move to her side. He placed a possessive hand on her shoulder that neither she nor the prince misinterpreted.

"Bashir," Jak said, dropping the title it seemed on purpose.

Rasha's eyes flew to his face as she wondered what was wrong with him to be so informal with the prince.

"Jak, it's been awhile hasn't it?" He held out a hand, waiting for Jak to drop his hand from Rasha's shoulder to take it. Jak looked from his hand on her shoulder to Bashir's outstretched hand. He must have felt the eyes of everyone else on him because he quickly moved his hand to take Bashir's. They shook once and as soon as he was released, Jak put his hand back on Rasha's shoulder.

Bashir only smiled as the others gathered around and sat. The servers brought out trays of finger foods as they sat around talking. One prince, a young merman, seemed to struggle with the common language and had latched onto Jak when he realized his skilled use of his native language.

Rasha loved the sound of Jak's lyrical voice. Prince Bashir seemed impressed by the exchange and would surely request that Jak help him when he wanted to speak with the merman. At his earliest convenience, the prince cornered her on the far side of the gazebo. Rasha saw him coming before he slid into the seat next to her.

"How are your rooms?" Bashir asked Rasha. When he spoke, Chiza excused herself with a quiet nod to the prince. The prince stared after her as she moved to the other side of the gazebo where the princes from Vol and Buku stood. Although shy, she seemed to be making an effort to speak with every prince. Rasha admired her. What would Chiza's father think of his daughter having interest in a prince from a kingdom that tried to take their gems and land only a rotation ago?

When the prince turned his attention back to her she answered. "The rooms are lovely, but, you shouldn't have singled me out."

"Nonsense, you're the hardest to impress." Bashir's smile was like that of a large predator.

Rasha tried not to smile but couldn't help it. He was so obvious. She looked around and noted that the eight men present, including Jak, had given the prince a wide berth. No one seemed inclined to interrupt the Prince and his pursuit of a mate. Despite their recent conversation, Chiza didn't seem to be over Bashir as she continued to watch him while four gentlemen competed for her attention.

"The dress really does look amazing on you," he said as he drank from his cup and offered her another.

"You have great fashion sense." Rasha accepted the cup and looked over the rim in Jak's direction. He'd turned to watch them but didn't move to interrupt them. She smiled at him. He didn't smile but he didn't turn away. "The other ladies will arrive tonight, I understand."

"Yes, and I can admit to you alone that I'm beside myself with nerves."

"Why? You're the prince. Of everyone here, you have the highest chance of finding someone."

"No, if my experience with you and Chiza is any sign, I'm no prize. I think that's my real reason for going through with this. If things had worked out with either of you, we wouldn't be doing this."

Rasha felt a wave of guilt. It was true if Lu had lived he would be with Chiza now. She wondered if she'd done all she could to keep Chiza from falling in love with him. Rasha had gone over it a million times in her head. Lu was a great guy, and he'd fallen for Chiza at first sight. She'd never seen two people so well matched. No, there wasn't anything she could do to stop what had happened that rotation. However, she could help the prince in her own way.

"I could be of some use to you," she said as she popped another cracker into her mouth.

"How?" He adjusted himself in the seat beside her to face her.

"You'll need to weed out some of the undesirables when they arrive. They won't all be showing off all their feather's colors when they get here. The ones intent on impressing you may put on a different face in private or among the other ladies. I'd be happy to relay anything I learn to you."

"That's amazing." Bashir tilted his head. "I can't believe you'd do that for me."

"I wouldn't, not without something in return," Rasha said.

"I see, and what is the price for this bit of espionage?"

Rasha smiled at the term. She would be his spy for a time.

"I'll give you my biased opinion of the ladies and any other pertinent information about their motives that comes my way. In exchange, you'll give me time away from the palace to work."

"You want to be a courier, during The Choosing?" Bashir's eyebrows shot up.

"Yes, as it happens, I'm in the middle of an assignment and I'd like to maintain my perfect record of fetches and deliveries."

"In the middle of an assignment? Now I'm intriqued."

"Well, sort of. My package was a person, she got away but I'm still looking for her," Rasha said avoiding his intense gaze.

"You are fascinating." Bashir smiled at her. "Not another princess I hope."

Rasha's eyes flew up to his and she hoped he could read the sincerity in them.

"No, she's a friend."

Bashir paused a moment and stroked his bare chin.

"If I agree to this, how often would you be gone?"

Rasha scrambled for an answer. She never imagined he'd agree to her offer at all. Now, it was in her grasp. She tried to calculate how much time it would take her to find Ladi and uncover why she's in hiding in the first place.

"Two weeks."

Bashir shook his head.

"No, if you'll be giving me valuable information you need to be here."

"Fair enough, give me three days a week."

Bashir stroked his chin for a moment. "Nights here in the palace?"

Rasha calculated Zele's speed. They'd be pushing it to return to the palace every night, but it would be worth it for freedom during her days to find Ladi. She nodded.

"Good," He said.

Rasha put up her left hand, raising a fist to her chest in a solemn vow.

"Not so fast. There is one other stipulation. Your partner must stay here," Bashir said with a nod in Jak's direction.

Jak straightened when he realized that they were talking about him. Rasha shook her head at the prince as much to Jak.

"No, I need my partner. We took the assignment together."

"No. I won't allow one of my prospects to spend three days a week alone with another prince, especially a formerly married one." Bashir looked at her in challenge.

"You know?"

"Yes. I'm upset he didn't tell me himself, but I wouldn't exclude him from all this and risk your wrath."

Rasha knew it must have taken Bashir awhile to accept Jak in the first place knowing how Jak felt about her. She couldn't be running around with Jak for all to see when the prince had asked them all to keep their options open for The New Choosing. Rasha nodded.

Bashir raised his left hand and put his right fist to his chest. Rasha was still reluctant, Jak wouldn't be happy about this. In the end, she put her right fist to her own chest and raised her left hand.

"Then we are agreed. I'm looking forward to tonight more than ever." Bashir stood up and moved to where Chiza stood.

Although they'd decided against each other, Bashir still kept up appearances by giving her as much attention as he gave Rasha. She wondered what had happened to them in the time they were in hiding. The battle she'd experienced with the beasts had been savage. However, it might be nothing compared to the torture of spending every day and night with someone you couldn't stand to be around.

Jak took the seat that Bashir had vacated next to her. He leaned in and spoke without looking at her, choosing to keep his eyes on the others.

"So, should I be worried he's already stolen you away from me?"

"Stop it, he can't steal something that doesn't belong to you," Rasha said. The words rushed out, but she hadn't meant them in the way they sounded.

Jak flinched as if she'd slapped him.

"That's not what I meant," Rasha said and reached out a hand. "It's not always about you and I."

"Even better," Jak said as he stood up.

"Wait, I need to talk to you."

"I don't think now is a good time." Jak stormed out of the gazebo and back toward the palace.

Rasha stared after him. What had gotten into him?

Chiza gave her a look in question but Rasha could only shrug. She needed to clear her own head. She stood up and found the quiet young man from Buku staring right at her, his dark green eyes curious under his mop of dark curls. She felt a jolt of something pass between them, but shook it off.

She curtsied to the prince and excused herself. Rasha needed to be alone, and the gardens were just as good a place as any. She was followed the minute she reached the garden maze. When they didn't reveal themselves, she ruled out Jak or Bashir. She kept walking, careful to stay ahead of her pursuer. Rasha rounded the next corner and reached for her swords, but she'd left Blade and Cutter in her rooms. With no time to curse herself for leaving them behind, she took her position behind the nearest hedge and waited.

Whoever followed her didn't come around the hedge as she'd expected. He reached through the hedge instead, grabbing her shoulder. Startled, Rasha tumbled forward, tripping over the long hem of her dress. The young man raced around the bushes. His hands come around her waist, catching her before her hands hit the ground. He lifted her with ease to her feet.

There was something familiar about him, but she couldn't place it right away. Instead, she gathered up her skirts and tossed them behind her as she took a step forward to confront him.

"Why are you following me?"

He didn't answer right away, only made a slight inclination of his head in her direction.

"You had better start talking or you're not walking out of these gardens, you'll be crawling."

He answered in a deep tenor, "As fun as that sounds I don't think that would be appropriate, do you, princess?"

The way he said 'princess,' it was more of a challenge than an acknowledgement or gesture of respect.

"Then why don't you tell me why you're skulking around in the bushes instead of getting ready for the ball tonight."

He laughed, a true and tickled sound.

"Even you know this is a farce."

"I'm sure you're mistaken," she said, unsure of what he was referring to.

"This is an elaborate cover up. The prince doesn't care to choose either of you, nor you him. This is just a way to get more options into the castle and make it appear that everyone is happy with the decision."

"Since you know so much, what are you doing taking part in such an obvious breach of your ethical standards?"

"Ethical standards?" He laughed out loud. "I like that. My reasons for being here are my own and they're none of your business. Just don't get in my way."

"You were the one following me. So, may I suggest the same? But since we're already here, let me remind you of something you seem to have forgotten. I'm the best courier in the ten, no, eleven kingdoms with the prince's ear. If you cross me, I'll deliver the bad news to the prince that you are no longer welcome here."

He nodded with a smile on his face that dared her to try.

"Don't push me or you'll be sent back to the rock you crawled out from under." Rasha stood up to her full height, just reaching his chin, and poked him in the shoulder.

A guard came around the hedge and stopped short of them. He cleared his throat and waited to be addressed.

"Yes?" Rasha said without turning.

"Princess Indari, there's a message, would you like to take it in your rooms?"

"Yes, I'll be there shortly." Rasha turned on her heel and followed after the guard, but she still heard the young prince's taunt.

"We'll be seeing each other again soon, princess."

She wanted to knock the entitlement out of his mouth but settled for ignoring him as she walked away.

During the day, Rasha had plenty of time to plot. She worried her lip. For a Tero-Jero, Ladi had proven herself more concerned with political affairs than she should be. None of her actions were consistent. She had to admit, Ladi had made drastic changes to her life since the death of her older brother. However, this new behavior didn't fit.

TONIGHT, she had to ready herself. She went to the closet and pulled out the first dress in the line. It was a cerulean blue that cinched at the waist and fell to the floor in a cascade.

THE DOORS OPENED to the first of the potential ladies at around six that evening. The entire palace was draped in lines of hanging lights. All the shadows and dark corners were brightened with paper art encased illuminators. The decadence wasn't lost on the ladies. They entered the palace with breathtaking oohs and ahhs.

Rasha and Chiza agreed to admire the competition as they entered from the upstairs balcony of Chiza's room. The palace doors were lit up and the guard lined the steps, leading the ladies inside. Each lady arrived at the gate, brought by carriage pulled by two tuskins to the main entrance. Chiza nudged Rasha as the ladies of the seventh, eighth, and ninth kingdoms arrived together. The young women were all wearing the old traditional ballroom style of gown in colors that complimented their colorful skin tones. They chattered among themselves, giggling with excitement over the evening to come.

The mermaid from the sixth kingdom arrived in a gown so fitted and like her skin tone, it seemed as if she wore nothing at all.

Rasha and Chiza saw the guards turn to gawk at her

backside. They giggled and were about to make their way downstairs when another carriage arrived. The door opened, and the guards helped a young Karmirian out and she took to the stairs. Her black hair cascaded down her back. She wore a night-black dress that fell in waves around her. She glanced up and smiled. Rasha's jaw fell open as Silae entered the palace.

"Do you know her?" Chiza asked.

"No, I don't think I do."

THE ARRIVING LADIES SENT THE princes into unmitigated excitement. Jak watched as one by one the girls entered the main ballroom area and each of the princes came forward to greet them. The prince himself hadn't yet arrived. He'd make a dramatic entrance, it appeared. The others believed, as they'd been told, that Bashir didn't want to upstage them by taking the girls' attention right away. Jak knew better. He'd seen Bashir with the princesses. Just because he chose one or two at the outset didn't mean he didn't have his eye on every single one of them.

Jak didn't have any interest in any of the ladies who arrived. They seemed young and silly compared to Rasha. The mermaid caused a stir with her skin-colored turquoise dress that shimmered when she shifted in the light. Her hair fell in waves of color, white, blue, purple, and pink. She smiled at them all and greeted everyone in her own chorus-like language before speaking in the common language. Jak smiled over the rim of his cup as he watched her circle the room. She took time to speak to each prince while keeping her eye on the door where Bashir would enter.

The last lady to arrive was a Karmirian with a darker shade of red skin. Her parents must have been from two different races. She wore her hair back, away from her face, showing off the four white dots all Karmirian received at birth. One braid starting from the middle of her hair accented her dots' perfect placement. She smiled and, ignoring the others, made a direct line to Jak before the mermaid had made it half way around the room.

Jak handed her something to drink from a tray in the hands of a servant standing to his right. She accepted it and took her position on his left.

"Well, what have we here, Prince Jak? I didn't think you'd stoop to this common event." She smiled before taking a sip from the cup.

"I wouldn't miss it."

"Liar."

Jak tilted his head to glance sideways at her. He understood now why Rasha liked her. She was honest. Sometimes too honest. Silae spoke her mind and wasn't bothered by the shocked reactions she sometimes received.

"You look lovely this evening. Are you hoping to get a prince or a king?"

It was Silae's turn to glance in his direction before turning her attention back to the room.

"I think you already know the answer or you wouldn't have asked me. Tell me about the young secondary options. The prince from Buku seems interesting." Silae was referring to the young man who stood off to one side, his green eyes taking in the ladies but not making any moves to anyone in particular. Not even the mermaid who seemed surprised when he didn't engage her more. The young woman shrugged and moved on to the next potential suitor.

"He's brooding, if that's what you mean. He seems to be plotting something, but of course I have no idea what it is. Unlike you ladies, gossip isn't something that a lot of men do. We talk about concrete things, business, trade, and sport."

"That is entirely untrue. You forget that I work as a barmaid. I know to you it might seem solitary and disconnected, but I get to hear what the men talk about when they come to my bar. They gossip as much as old women do. Just this week I heard two tradesmen ready to come to blows over a rumor about the prince being rejected by the two remaining princesses."

Jak put his cup down and looked up as the others did when Chiza and Rasha entered.

"That's not a rumor." Jak left his place beside the wall with Silae and moved to take Rasha's hand as she came down the stairs. He led her to the left. The prince from Vol did the same, taking Chiza's hand and leading her around the room in the opposite direction. When everyone had made their introductions, Rasha was face to face with Silae.

"I'm surprised to see you here," Rasha said, taking a moment to give Silae a light embrace.

Silae gave her a knowing smile. "No more surprised than I am to see you and Jak here. I was sure you'd be hunting down Ladi by now."

Rasha looked to Jak. They hadn't talked about Ladi since their arrival. She'd been intent on talking about something earlier. He regretted storming off because he wanted to talk to her alone and now wasn't the time. The prince entered, forcing them all to stand apart and welcome him into the group.

The ten ladies all curtsied as he entered and he acknowledged them all one by one. He started with the mermaid who'd been standing the closest. Then one after another he welcomed each of the ladies. He even had kind words for both Chiza and Rasha, whose hand he kissed. Jak felt his own hand clench in response. Why did he have to single her out? When Bashir made eye contact, he wondered if it wasn't out of spite.

Silae bowed her head to the prince in a slow, measured movement, giving him time to notice her. When she raised her head, he stepped forward and placed his four fingers over the dots on her forehead and spoke in the Karmirian language.

Jak understood it to mean, "You are welcome, Karmirian daughter, please accept me and my home as your own."

Silae's smile lit up her face and her eyes. Then she spoke in the common language.

"If I am to your liking, I look forward to both."

Bashir smiled and his eyes went wide.

Jak wasn't sure what kind of answer he'd been expecting but Silae had surprised him, that was clear. He hoped she'd be able to distract the prince from Rasha.

"Jak," Bashir said with a quick glance.

"Bashir," Jak said.

"I trust you'll let the rest of us have a chance at marriage as well?"

Jak felt his mouth get dry from gaping before he closed it. So, the prince knew. It was no doubt for that reason he'd been so cold to Jak, in addition to he and Rasha having an established relationship. Jak's hands closed into tight fists before he relaxed them again.

Bashir leaned in and spoke to a servant who bowed before lifting a staff and hitting it on the smooth stone floor to get their attention.

"To the ballroom, please."

Jak looked around and wondered how many of them would dance this early in the evening. He noted a wary expression on at least one face. The prince from Majiwa, a merman, had held back. The mermaid who'd introduced herself earlier smiled and took his arm, patting him in reassurance.

As Jak entered the ballroom, he noted it was filled with people. The council was present, as were many of the parents and families of the chosen princes and ladies. A general buzz ensued when the families were reunited. Interesting strategy, Jak noted. He'd assumed the whole idea was to distance themselves from the old way. Bashir had brought in their parents, whose ideas would no doubt conflict with the general premise of the evening.

Rasha moved to stand near her parents for a moment, the smile on her face vanishing. Her father and mother both wore forced smiles and stood on each side of her, whispering their instructions for world dominance it seemed.

Jak's own father moved from his place alongside another council member to join him.

"How is your evening progressing?" Xeku asked him.

"Fine."

"You and Rasha had a disagreement." It was a statement not a question.

"Not so much a disagreement as a misunderstanding."

"Do you care to discuss the matter?"

"No," Jak snapped. He did want to talk about it, but not with his estranged father. After the death of his mother, Xeku had changed, relaxed into his role as councilman and father to an adult. Jak didn't feel any pressure to speak but found himself doing so, anyway.

"I believed we'd made our choices clear to one another, but it appears I was mistaken," Jak said.

Xeku nodded and continued to glance around the room, scanning until he found Rasha.

"She looks enchanting this evening. The cerulean suits her very well. Did you happen to mention it?"

"I did, I-" Jak stopped, catching himself in a lie, "I planned to but I never got the chance."

Xeku turned to face him. "You are a skilled fighter and companion in your courier life. She values those skills and respects them. However, if you're ever going to be more to her than a friend and become more than someone she liked once, you'll have to give her a reason to choose you over the others."

"She doesn't even want to be here. Rasha is not going to participate in that way."

"But she is here," Xeku said as he and Jak both followed her movement from one side of the room to stand beside the prince. "If you pressure her instead of woo her, you're going to lose her."

Jak watched as Rasha listened and the prince spoke in her ear. What was he saying to her? Rasha didn't stay there long as she continued around the room and introduced herself again to the giggling ladies from the southern kingdoms of Vol, Buku, and Winaka. The three couldn't be more than sixteen as they hung on every word of Rasha's with wide eyes. Then they all in unison seemed to look his way, and he was caught staring. Rasha covered a laugh. The others all giggled before turning back to Rasha, their faces enraptured with what she was telling them. After a few sighs, he'd had enough.

The music started to play, and he needed to get Rasha alone. Dancing would be the easiest way. He wasn't fast enough. The prince from Buku beat him to her. Rasha had been looking at Jak and seemed just as surprised when the young prince stepped into her line of sight and held out his hand for a dance. She accepted, and they moved to the middle of the floor. Jak smiled to the young ladies who were now the only ones left, and they all giggled and curt-sied when he approached them.

"So, which one of you is the best dancer and willing to keep me company as I stumble around out there?"

## 13

*R*ASHA WATCHED AS JAK RECOVERED and moved to ask one of the girls to dance. They'd probably be delighted. Rasha had heard them talking about the rumors of how handsome and charming he was. They wouldn't be disappointed. She'd seen his charm first hand. The young prince of Buku annoyed her, and she didn't make any pretense of her feelings being otherwise. He fit into a memory she couldn't place but it was his abrupt and arrogant manner that bothered her most.

"You seemed more than a little bored so I thought I'd rescue you," he said.

"I don't need rescuing, but you will if you don't pay more attention to what's going on around you."

"I don't understand," he said furrowing his brows.

"That's my point. Are we going to do this again?"

"Do what?"

"Threaten each other without a proper introduction." Rasha glared at him and forced herself not to shrug him off when his hand cupped her back.

"I know who you are. You're Princess Rasha Jenchat Indari, daughter of the house of Chilali."

"Yes, I know my title. I have learned yours as well, Prince Omi Gonma, son of the house of Buku. That's hardly an introduction. Who are you?"

"I'm someone who's been in the shadows long enough. I'm ready to take my rightful place." His lip curled as he looked off to her left.

"Oh, I see. Mommy and daddy issues."

"What?"

"I've seen it before. You apparently don't know my story. It's a daily struggle," she said with a nod to her parents.

"Yes, I'm familiar with your story. You ran from the castle and intended never to return as I understand it. What brought you back?"

"I needed to help a friend."

"I don't have any friends to get in the way."

"That wasn't my point. I was saying—" The music came to a halt and the dinner bell rang.

Omi bowed to her and turned away before she could say another word. Odd was the only way to describe her encounters with the young prince.

Rasha's father grabbed her by the elbow as they entered the dining hall.

"You'll sit with your family this evening." He gripped

her arm until it bruised. She snatched it away and her mother took her other arm and gently put it over her own.

"Come, your father wants us to represent a united Chilali tonight."

Rasha bit back a response before letting her mother lead her inside. The table settings were labeled by family and they all took their seats. Bashir placed Rasha on his right, to her parents' delight as it placed them so close to the prince. Silae and her parents were across from them on the prince's left. Rasha felt the anxiety of the evening welling up inside of her as she looked for Jak. He and Xeku were placed at the far end of the table.

A purposeful slight on the prince's part. Shameful, she'd thought the prince better than that. Chiza was on that end of the table as well. Her parents sat like statues next to her. At least Jak would be there for her. The prince drew everyone's attention as he stood up.

"Ladies and gentlemen, I welcome you to the dinner this evening. The night, however, is for your children. They've already received rooms for the night and will, with your permission, be staying with me and the other royals for the New Choosing. Because this is a time of discovery and romance you'll be excused after dinner to return to your homes. I want to thank you in advance for your generosity and understanding of the new arrangement." The prince sat back down and leaned into Rasha.

"Here come the protests. Be ready."

Rasha didn't have to wait long to see what he meant. The mumbles and grumbles around the table grew as

563

the parents of the invited guests realized they would not be staying.

"I travelled from the western sea shore. I am expected to travel back again with no place for respite?" the merman king demanded. His long blue hair rested on his shoulders while he fidgeted in his seat.

It was true they would have a long way to travel. It wasn't fair for them to have to go all the way home. Of course, they couldn't stay at the palace. That would change the dynamic too much. She stood up and offered an alternative.

"My home in Chilali is one of the closest. If you need a place to rest, it is not along your route home but much closer. You are welcome to stay there."

Her father looked up at her, his face a dark shade of purple. Rasha wondered how he could be angry. This excellent arrangement ensured their contact with as many royals as possible. She saw no problem with the idea.

"We are not an inn for every passerby," her father said between his teeth.

"No but you are potentially hosting the parents of the new queen," Rasha said, looking at each of them in turn.

Rasha spoke up again. "My parents are very generous. They insist that you make the journey north and let the Chilalians show you hospitality fit for a king." The prince started the applause that broke out over the table, and he leaned over to speak to her parents.

"Your generosity will be rewarded." He bowed to them and her father bowed back to him.

Smug now, Rasha sat down and received a grateful smile from the prince and a knowing smile from Silae. What did she know? How did she get an invitation to this party? She was no royal and there were plenty of pretty girls throughout the realm. The mystery would persist until the moment arrived where Rasha could pull her aside and ask.

## 14

*A*FTER THE FAMILIES WERE SENT on their way, the night took a dramatic change. Prince Bashir had arranged for entertainment and more dancing. Hired performers did tricks and played games on one end of the large ballroom. The guests found drinks and snacks along each wall. The other end of the ballroom was cleared for those who wanted to dance. A juggler with a painted face tossed balls into the air, then plates, then knives. There was a fire swallower as well as two women with the flexibility and stamina to make almost any pose and stay that way long enough for people to appreciate it. A mime walked around, putting couples together and making strange faces. He'd matched Jak with the mermaid. There were some oohs and ahhs. Chiza's hand was placed in Omi's and everyone laughed at that.

Rasha didn't care for the mime. He'd taken her hand and placed it in Prince Bashir's hand, then made a show of bowing as if she'd already been chosen. The prince blushed as if he hadn't seen it coming. A few others laughed, but Rasha didn't. Jak didn't either. Chiza was facing in another direction and Rasha couldn't read her face, but her shoulders seemed to droop.

"Really, I'm not so bad, Rasha. I wish you'd give me a chance," Bashir whispered to her.

"I'm sorry. I want to feel like I have a choice," she said.

"You don't think you do?"

"Am I free to come and go as I please?" Rasha crossed her arms.

The prince nodded. "I see what you mean. But the option to make your own choice, whatever that may be, is still yours. I can live with whatever you decide, so long as I know you considered me."

"That's just it. I have to decide. What if I'm not ready to make that choice?" Rasha turned away, not waiting for the answer. There wasn't anything he could say.

Rasha needed fresh air, and she'd rather spend the rest of the night in her room than in the stuffy ballroom. If Silae hadn't stopped her before she made it to the doors, she would have.

"Don't," Silae said and moved to block the door.

"You had better get out of my way, right now, or I promise you'll regret it," Rasha said between her teeth.

"Don't leave, the others are watching you. It will look bad if you storm out after speaking to the prince." Silae folded Rasha's arm over her own as her mother had done.

"Let's take a slow walk to calm you down." Silae took a deep breath, urging Rasha to imitate her.

Rasha did and the blood flow reached her brain and she saw the curious eyes of the others watching her.

"What did he say to offend you?" Silae asked.

"It's not him. It's this whole stupid thing. This New Choosing is just the Old Choosing dressed up in different clothes. I'm not sure I can do this."

"You're eighteen, stop acting like a child. You have to do this. As the princess of Chilali you know your duty. Besides, do you think your options will be better when you're 80?"

"I'm not ready." Rasha stopped and looked at her. Silae had once again chosen the most revealing gown she could find, something the same color as her reddish-brown skin, and it clung to her every curve.

Silae gave her arm a pat and continued.

"Get ready."

"Don't bait me."

"I'm not," Silae said, looking sincere. "We often must do things before we're ready. The war proved that. You and Jak were incumbents for almost an entire rotation. In all that time, I'm sure you did things you never imagined you could."

Rasha was nodding. It was true. She'd felt so old after that war, now it was over and she'd gone back to her old way of thinking.

"I guess, I wanted things to go back to the way they were."

"You mean the way things were when Lu was alive?"

Rasha stopped short and turned to look at Silae. That's what she'd been trying to do this whole time. Yet, how could things go back without Lu? Ladi had filled the gap. Had she been forcing Ladi to take Lu's place the way she'd said? If she were being honest, she'd have to say yes.

"How did you manage to get an invitation to the New Choosing?" Rasha asked, changing the subject.

"You mean because my parents are of different kingdoms I'm so obviously not pure?"

Rasha shrugged. She'd implied it, but wasn't going to say it.

"Well, my father is pure born, as is my mother. They petitioned on my behalf. We're not royals but we're not backwards and our family lines are strong."

Rasha nodded. That made sense. Her beauty was a strong case in her favor, the reddish-brown skin and the long wavy hair the same color as her black almond eyes. Her children would inherit most if not all of those traits.

"Your turn. What is the prince giving you in exchange for tolerating this event?"

Rasha shouldn't have been surprised that Silae had seen through the façade, but she was. She'd thought that she'd been discreet but perhaps not enough.

"I'm gathering as much information about the girls here as I can so I can tell the prince the things he might not find out on his own. In exchange, I get time away from the event so I can track Ladi."

"I can help you with that. Since your last visit, I've been asking around."

"You have?"

"Ladi is the sister to a dear friend. Don't seem so shocked. Plus, she's young and impulsive. Better to find her sooner rather than later."

Rasha agreed.

"Our young friend might have gotten wind of a small uprising among the beasts living within the ten kingdoms. She may attempt to help them. The mistreatment of the beasts that moved south is rampant. Many people lost everything to those animals," Silae said.

"They were forced."

"Not everyone is ready to forgive."

Rasha saw it, though. She didn't want to believe her own people could be so cold. She thought of her parents. They hadn't welcomed the beasts with open arms. It seemed they tolerated them for Rasha's sake since she rode a dragon herself. They wouldn't deny them a place to nest. She wondered how the prince was dealing with that news. He had mentioned nothing to her, not that she was on the council. It might be better to speak with Xeku.

"There's someone I must speak to. Thank you for your help, as always, Silae. Next time, go with something a little classier."

"I'll take advice from you on how to dress when you stop dressing like a boy."

Rasha's head tilted as she looked down at her own lovely gown.

"Oh, so you fall into a dress one day and it makes you an expert. I'm sure you didn't even pick it out."

Rasha's cheeks turned deep purple and she glared at Silae.

"Princess," Silae gave her a slight curtsy and turned away.

Rasha glared at her a moment longer before she rushed off toward Jak. He'd know where to find Xeku. The council had residence in the palace somewhere. Jak looked up and saw her moving his way and dislodged himself from the young merman. He smiled as if he were about to say something when she heard a startled scream followed by another. Rasha changed direction and ran toward the sound. She reached down for her swords but they were tucked away in her room.

## 15

---

*I*T WAS TWO GIRLS FROM the southern kingdoms screaming. The third, the one from Vol was on the floor. The young Vol—white from the top of her head to her toes—seemed without life. Rasha was the first to reach her and remembered to check for a pulse. It was a fast but uneven pulse. Her skin was clammy to the touch.

"Get a doctor," Rasha said to the nearest person.

Jak joined her on the floor and checked her body for injury.

"Nothing," he said.

"No, look at her lips, they're turning blue. We need to get her to her room and keep her isolated from the others," Rasha said.

"I've taken care of that," Bashir said as two guards came through with a small cot and put the girl on it. They carried her to her room. The festivities came to a halt and everyone retired to their rooms. No one would forget tonight but not for the reasons that the prince had intended. He paced the floor at the entrance to her room.

Rasha and Jak joined him a moment later.

"I can't believe this," Bashir said over and over to himself. "The doctor says she's got that horrible flu virus."

"Oh no, I'm sorry," Rasha said, putting a hand on his arm.

"It gets worse. The entire palace and grounds are now under quarantine. No one can come and no one can go." He looked at her, waiting for her to understand the impact of his words.

"But I must. You and I had an arrangement." Rasha's voice grew louder with each word.

Bashir yanked her hard by the arm and pulled her to one side. Before Rasha could react, Jak's hands were on the prince's shoulders turning him around before pushing him back hard against the nearest wall. One guard standing nearby knocked Jak in the back of the knees dropping him to the floor before putting a sword to his throat. He only waited for the order. The prince recovered and straightened his clothing. He ignored the guard as if he weren't there and put his hand out for Jak. Bashir helped him to his feet and turned back to Rasha, speaking in a low tone.

"I'm sorry. I didn't mean to hurt you. I understand your feelings, only too well. But no one can find out we're under quarantine right now. It will send a panic throughout the palace and the rest of the kingdoms. For now, you must forget your mission and wait along with the rest of us. Please keep our arrangement to yourself."

"What arrangement?" Jak asked waiting for one of them to explain.

Prince Bashir raised an eyebrow at Rasha. He must have assumed that Jak had been told but Rasha hadn't had a moment to tell him. She shook her head. The prince bowed to excuse himself.

"I must see to the young lady. Please go to your rooms for now. It is best."

The guard who'd taken Jak down stood at the ready in case he should attack the prince from behind. Jak nodded to the guard and turned to Rasha.

"Let's go." He led her to the Princess Wing as they called the staircase leading to the upstairs rooms to the right. The princes were on the left of the palace. Bashir had taken the suites set aside for the royal family. Jak waited at the bottom of the stairs.

"I'm sorry, I pressured you and I shouldn't have."

She held out a hand and touched his shoulder. He'd been ready to take down the future king of the eleven kingdoms to protect her. How could she not care for him? Not that she didn't. She knew it had nothing to do with Jak. Rasha would have to come to terms with the fact she was old enough to decide, just as Silae had suggested. She wasn't a little girl anymore, rebelling against her parents' choices. She had to make her own choices and not choosing wasn't an option. Especially when someone's heart was involved.

"I've been wanting to talk to you all day, but you didn't give me the chance earlier. I wanted to tell you about the arrangement."

A guard rushed forward.

"Your highness, I'm sorry to intrude but it is urgent. Your beastie has returned."

"The dragon?"

"No, the other one."

Jak kept up with her as Rasha raced to the stables where Temi had been taken. They heard the crying before they entered the door. Two guards stood at the entrance, looking as if they'd rather be anywhere but there. The stableman was kneeling over Temi. Temi was panting and whining. When Rasha entered, his tail and body moved in recognition of her.

"What's happened to him?" Rasha asked, looking at the poor bloated beast. He looked like he'd swallowed a tuskin.

"Not him, her. She's about to give birth," he said.

If he'd said Temi would sprout wings, she couldn't have been more shocked. Temi was female. All this time, they had no idea.

Jak face broke out into a smile.

"What's the matter, Rash, you're not ready to be a grandmother?" He gave her ribs a poke.

She rolled up the sleeves on her gown and hiked up her skirts.

"What can I do?"

The stableman glanced at her. "I can handle this, your

highness. I wanted to send word, so you'd be aware of what to expect in the morning."

"I'm not leaving Temi, he — she's been a part of my life for a while now and she needs me. Just tell me where you want me."

"She'll want a good whiff of you, so come over here by the head and let her rest her head in your lap. It will be a little painful but she won't bite you, I think."

"Have you ever done this before?" she asked.

"Not with this kind of beast. Never seen one like her before, but the panting and crying I recognize from the tuskins I've birthed. I'm not sure how big her cubs will be, though."

"I have, they won't be big at all."

"I beg your pardon, your grace, but would you mind fetching blankets to help clean up the cubs when they come?"

Jak dashed out without a word.

The stableman turned back to her. "I don't suppose you know how many we might be expecting?"

"I don't. Temi was days old when we got her. She fit in a cup back then."

"A cup?" The stableman moved to her rear and prepared himself for whatever was going to come.

Rasha didn't know what to do, so she stroked Temi the way Lu used to and whispered soothing words to her.

"Surprised us all, you sly girl. But you knew where to come when you needed help. That's a good girl."

They waited another hour before the first cub arrived.

There were eight in all. Rasha couldn't have been prouder of Temi. She endured the whole thing and seemed to understand just what her little teacup babies needed.

"There's a good girl, all finished," the stable man said to Temi, giving her lower back a rub. He stood up and looked at Rasha. "I'm afraid your dress is ruined, we should get you cleaned up."

"Not yet, I'm not ready to leave her just yet." Rasha stroked Temi's head a bit. "You go ahead, I'll be along."

"No worries, after I've cleaned up I'll be back to watch over her and the cubs. No harm will come to any of them on my watch."

Rasha nodded.

"Thank you." She gathered up her skirts and watched as the babies clung to their mother for warmth and fell asleep.

## 16

THE NEXT MORNING, RASHA WOKE up with the sun. She felt more rejuvenated than ever. She couldn't wait to show off Temi's cubs to the palace guests. It would be something to take their minds off of the quarantine. Rasha didn't bother with a dress this morning. She dressed in her courier clothes and strapped on Cutter and Blade on her way out of the room. When she reached the front doors the guards at the entrance stopped her.

"You're not allowed to leave, your highness. I think you already know that." It was the same guard from the night before who spoke to her.

"I'm not leaving, I'm going to the stables. My beastie is there, and she had cubs last night."

He looked her over and shook his head.

"No, the prince said you might want to leave to do some courier work and not to permit you to leave."

"My clothes? Because I'm dressed this way you think I'll leave? I didn't want to ruin any more of the dresses that the prince had given to me. But if you insist, I'll change and head to the stables in one of those." She put her hands on her hips. Her swords shifted under her hands. A subtle hint she would use them if she felt inclined.

"One moment." He stepped to one side and informed the prince of the situation.

"The prince says you can do what you please with the clothes that were given to you, as long as you wear them."

"Are you serious?"

Rasha grumbled all the way up the stairs. Now, she couldn't be trusted to wear her own clothes. She'd have to have a talk with Bashir after she'd finished in the stables. The gown she chose was not the ugliest, but she wanted to make a point. She picked the rose colored one with the frilly touches along the short sleeves and hem. The bodice was an intricate lace that would be ruined while playing with the cubs. She strolled passed the guards with a toss of her hair and headed for the stables.

She heard the mewling of the cubs when she arrived. They'd been moved. The stable that Temi had been in was cleaned and empty while the cubs were alone in the stable across from it. They could barely see and when she knelt down, they curled into her lap, wanting to be near something larger than themselves. They were asleep in moments.

The stableman returned and found Rasha on the stable floor with the cubs in her lap. He smiled.

"I hoped you come and take care of them."

"Where's Temi? She should tend to them."

"I have some bad news miss, it seems she passed in the night."

"Temi's dead? No, he–she can't be." Rasha stood, but the babies started to cry and she sat down again.

"Some animals have that kind of cycle. They birth their babies and then die. That would explain how you came to have one so early in its life."

Rasha looked down at the babies who'd settled in to the first person to come along. It was like a mallet to the stomach. Temi had been loyal and faithful to Lu then to her. The only thing she'd asked for in return was for someone kind to take care of her babies. She'd come all of this way from where she'd been. Thankfully, the last moments of her life, she hadn't been alone. That was a blessing from the Universal. She reached for her amulet and kissed the stone.

"What would you like me to do with these cubs, your highness?"

Rasha thought for a moment.

"Get me a large basket and leave them to me."

The cubs were the success she hoped they'd be, and the young women were enraptured by them. The princes loved having them around too. She handed them out, letting the group give them the love and attention they needed. She sat down and realized that there was one left.

He'd been hiding in the blanket and had only just poked his head out to see where his siblings had gone. He cried a little until Rasha pulled him out and stroked his head as Lu had done to Temi that first day. She looked him over as he calmed down. She wasn't sure if this one was male or female.

Playing with the small cubs eased some of the pain of losing Temi. The others wanted to keep their beasties and since there was no one to care for them otherwise, Rasha agreed to let the cubs go. She only kept the one.

"So, you will name this one?" Jak asked as he sat down beside her. He watched the others cooing over the cubs and looked down at the one in Rasha's lap.

"I don't know what to call him."

"You'll think of something. You did well choosing for Zele."

"That's not the same. She doesn't belong to me."

"I doubt she knows that any more than this little guy." Jak reached out and stroked the little beastie and it mewed in her hand.

"I'd better go. I need to talk Chiza. She didn't come down this morning. I'll see if she wants one of these," she said holding up the basket. Chiza wasn't the antisocial type. If she hadn't come down with the others, there must be something wrong.

## 17

*R*ASHA DIDN'T HAVE TO REACH her room to discover the problem. Several servants were coming and going from her room, carrying bedding and wearing masks over their faces. Bashir had already been called. He paced outside the door, looking anxious. He looked up when he saw her coming.

"She's sick, just like the other young lady. I think we might have a bigger problem on our hands than originally thought."

"Is there a cure?"

Bashir shook his head.

"Too many people have died from this sickness already. I can't have the young ladies in the palace exposed. If they are sent home, they might spread it to their lands, if they've already contracted it somehow."

Bashir's normally put together facade was falling apart. He looked like he'd thrown on his clothes from the night before and his hair fell in unkempt wisps around his face. The alabaster skin under his eyes had colored into a faded purple.

"What can I do?"

"Nothing, I can't risk you leaving any more than the others."

"I'm not like the others," she said as she squared her shoulders.

Bashir turned away from her to rest his hand on the wall. It looked like he was holding up the wall but it was the other way around.

"I don't know what to do. Chiza is," Bashir's shoulders slumped, but he didn't turn around.

Rasha placed a hand on his shoulder.

"You care for her," Rasha said. He turned into her and she saw it then. The pain in his eyes made her bite her lip in sympathy. "Oh no, I'm so sorry. But it's not too late. Something I learned from spending a lot of time with Chiza is that she's stronger than she seems."

Bashir nodded.

"Even in mourning, she was stronger than me." He took a few steps away from his guards and toward the hall window. The gardens below were luscious and green. He smiled at a memory. "Did she tell you about our time together?"

Rasha shook her head.

"Of course not, she's a lady in every way. I just assumed since you were close she might have shared it with you."

"I didn't ask, and she didn't seem inclined to discuss it. It was a difficult adjustment."

"At first it was, we barely knew each other and we were both grieving. Difficult is a good word for it." Bashir turned toward her, resting his shoulder against the glass. "We lashed out at each other in every way possible until there was nothing left. Then somewhere in there, we'd become friends. We played games, we talked, we cooked, we walked. There wasn't anything we didn't do together. We read the same books then we debated about them afterwards. It was glorious right up until I kissed her."

Rasha watched the light go out of his face.

"She hadn't been ready. I'd been so excited to latch on to anything, anyone, that I'd moved too fast. After that, I felt her pulling away until she was out of reach. I demanded that she get over it. I'd done it, why couldn't she?"

Rasha shook her head, seeing what was coming.

"I have never seen someone shut down so fast. That moment, the words, the anger, I'd take it back if it were possible. I'd gone too far, I realized it, but of course it was too late. So, you see, it's only fitting that she die from this disease and leave me pinning for her as she once did for her lost love."

Rasha felt tears filling her own eyes as she listened. This couldn't be happening to people who really love each other. The Universal would never allow such an injustice. There had to be a way. Bashir reached out and took her hands in his. His were thin and cold. She wanted to breathe on them to warm them. He beat her to it. He raised their joined hands to his lips and kissed her fingers.

"Thank you. This has been weighing on me for some time."

"I hope I'm interrupting," Jak said from behind Rasha.

They jumped apart at the sound of his voice. Rasha turned, his eyes were on Bashir but his words were for her.

"When you didn't return with Chiza, I got concerned and wanted to make sure you two were all right."

"We're fine," Rasha said. She had to wipe a tear from her eye. "Chiza's sick."

"I saw the commotion. The girls are downstairs. They're concerned," Jak said and looked at Bashir.

The way the two measured each other made Rasha wish that Jak hadn't seen them holding hands. It might as well have been an embrace the way he was acting.

"Please excuse me, princess." Bashir brushed the back of his hand along her arm. An intimate gesture that fit the circumstances but that made Jak clench his fists.

"I'm sorry if I've disturbed you, princess." Jak turned to leave but Rasha grabbed him by the arm.

"Hey, what's going on with you. I did nothing wrong. We were just talking. We were both concerned about Chiza."

"I didn't ask."

"You didn't have to, your posturing is obvious and childish." Rasha opened the door to her room and put the basket with the now sleeping cub inside. She needed to get out of the dress and into her own clothes. The prince might not have any idea what he needed, but she knew what Chiza needed and that was a cure. She was the best courier in the kingdom. Who else would fetch the cure and deliver it in time to save Chiza?

Besides, Ladi was out there somewhere and she was dealing with something bigger than herself. The worst thing was to leave her to handle whatever it was on her own. Things were taking a bad turn with Jak. He paced her balcony while she changed. When she came back out in her courier's clothes, he looked her over. His eyebrows stretched toward the ceiling.

"Are you going someplace during quarantine?" he asked.

"Not yet, but soon. Chiza might die of this virus. They'll need someone to find a cure."

"And that's you?"

"Yes, in fact, it is."

"The prince is just going to let you walk out of here?"

"I believe he'll ask me to leave. I won't be walking out, but I'll be flying out."

He held up his hand to stop her.

"Flying out how?"

Rasha watched as Jak's lip curled in challenge.

"On my dragon, Zele." Rasha looked down at her

hand. She still held the basket with the sleeping cub. She shoved the basket at him. "Here, take care of this one until Chiza gets better. She'll want him or her or whatever."

## 18

RASHA HAD BEEN RIGHT. She didn't even have to wait that long before another two girls fell ill. The other two of the young girls from the southern kingdoms of Winaka and Buku. One prince had also fallen ill. The Joro prince was sick in bed and another, the prince from Majiwa, had been weakened by the onset of the disease. He was put into the pool to maintain his most natural form and fight off the virus. The mermaid kept vigil at his side, refusing to leave despite the recommendations from the doctors.

Bashir came to her room. Rasha was sitting by the window. She wasn't fond of reading but she'd found a book of Bolaji history and was reading it while she watched the sun begin its fall from the sky.

"I see you are prepared to go."

"There was the possibility you'd need me. I wanted to be ready." Rasha put her feet down from the windowsill and stood up to face him. His hair looked even more unkempt than earlier and the circles under his eyes darker. "I can get it, only tell me where."

"That's the problem. We don't know where. The Tero-Joro are working on a cure as we speak but I'm not sure how far they've come. Their communications there are down. I need to find out if they're close and what they've discovered. At this point, a cure is purely hypothetical."

"I've got contacts in Tero-Joro. I'll see what I can do."

Bashir put a hand on her shoulder, then brought his hand up to cup the back of her neck.

"I hope I don't need to remind you it is urgent you find it. This disease is sweeping the country. This news can't be contained any longer, the families will be informed."

"I understand."

"I want to give them hope. If you're out there looking, I'll have it."

"Jak?"

"Yes, your partner. Of course, you'll want to bring him. I'll allow it."

Rasha bowed to him in respect, "Thank you, Your Grace."

She left Bashir and went directly to Jak's rooms. The prince's wing had almost as much commotion as her own. They were wearing masks here as well. When she reached Jak's room, there were servants coming in and out. She asked one of them for directions.

"I must be in the wrong room, I'm looking for Prince Jak Ameenu."

"This is his room, your highness." The young maid bowed to her and bustled off.

Rasha's knees buckled as she walked inside. Two servants were cooling his brow with water as they'd done to Chiza. His face was a pale green and his eyes, though closed, had dark circles around them. Xeku stood hovering over him, cooling his feverish arms.

"He just collapsed. I don't know, we were talking and then…" Xeku didn't look up as she drew closer to Jak's bed. When the maid left to change the towels, she took her place on Jak's left. She grabbed his hand and felt the cold clamminess of the disease on him. His eyes fluttered open but the two blue pools wavered about as if searching the room and seeing nothing.

"I'm here." Rasha knelt down.

Jak's eyes fluttered closed, and he squeezed her hand. It was the only sign he'd heard her.

"I am leaving to find the cure, I'll be back soon. I promise."

Rasha's eyes filled as she realized at worst this could be the last moment they'd have together. How could she explain to him now what she wanted? When he'd asked her before but she hadn't been ready. She didn't like the idea of being chosen. Now it was all she could think about. Why had she been so foolish?

"I need to go, now."

"Yes, go and find the cure."

"I'll be back as soon as I can."

"I know." Xeku stood up. "Thank you."

Rasha's aunt stood up from the chair and moved to her side.

"If you need me, I'll come with you."

"No, I think you will be more needed here." Rasha looked to Xeku. "You two seem to have a connection."

"We've been friends for a long time."

Rasha wasn't sure what to say, so she didn't say anything. Sochi put her arms around her in an embrace.

"Can I ask you something?" Rasha asked.

"Anything," Sochi said and looked her in the eye.

"Is there something more than friendship between you two?"

Sochi looked over her shoulder back at Xeku, then back to her.

"Does the thought worry you?"

"No, it seemed that perhaps things had changed between you. I'm not sure how Jak will take it."

"He's not the only one we have to worry about," Sochi said more to herself than to Rasha.

Rasha thought of her parents, then of the council. There were many obstacles to an entanglement between the two.

"You should go, don't delay," Sochi said urging her forward.

She was right. This cure could be anywhere within the

eleven kingdoms of Bolaji and she needed to find it or she might lose Chiza and Jak.

"There's one small thing. I need you to take care of something for me." Rasha tilted her head in the direction of the basket with the last of Temi's sleeping babies on the floor.

## 19

ERO-JORO MADE THE MOST rapid changes in the time they'd become a part of the Bolaji kingdoms. Once a people who primarily lived among the trees and nature, they'd made technological advancement early, setting themselves apart from the rest as leaders in all things modern. It was that advancement that brought Rasha to their kingdom. Her best friend had taught her a lot about their culture and traditions.

Their belief in the goddess of nature was something she could understand. Lu put no faith in anything he could not see, hear, or touch. Ladi seemed similarly inclined. Rasha's own beliefs fell somewhere in the middle. Although not devout, she believed the Universal touched everything and everyone. She held up her amulet and said a quick prayer she might find the cure to help save her friends.

The city center of town, known as Q Prime, housed

their local government which had long stopped using the monarchical designation and had instead termed their leaders by their function. Rasha steered Zele directly to the scientific labs of Q Prime, a modern building made of glass and steel. It didn't have the warmth and charm of the castles she was used to, but it held some of the most modern of art.

The entrance, lit from the sun outside, had windows from floor to ceiling. Rasha entered the immaculate building and walked to the entry level reception area where three android robots sat answering questions via the communication switchboard. The one in the center noted Rasha approaching and, finishing its current call, was ready with an anatomically correct smile.

From the top of his head to his waist, he was formed to look like a Tero-Joro humanoid complete with enlarged ears and eyes and two-toned, green skin. When Rasha reached the desk, she saw that from the waist down their makers hadn't bothered with anything resembling a humanoid. A metal s-curved form held the android to a chair that swiveled but didn't seem to move any further.

"Hello and welcome to Q Prime Labs. How can I be of service?" The android spoke in the native Chilalian.

Rasha answered in the common, "I am Courier Jenchat-42769. I am here on urgent business for Prince Bashir. Rasha held up her communicator, showing her credentials. She waited for the inevitable resistance from this one. Androids were the one form of security measure she was thankful the other kingdoms hadn't decided to adopt. Rasha found herself often in debates with them over minutiae. The android scanned the information and within several unnaturally timed blinks, had relayed her request and received an answer.

"Please proceed to the elevators behind me and take one to the eleventh floor. Someone will be there to meet you."

"Thank you."

"Have a pleasant day."

The android seemed more relaxed but still artificial. She found the elevators and took the first one available to the designated floor. When the doors opened, another android was waiting. Despite its complete anatomy, the tilt of its head and fast scanning of her with its rapid eye movement gave it away as another machine. She rolled her eyes and followed the female android to the lab office. As they walked, they passed several glass doors and frosted windows that led to working labs with androids and humanoids on the opposite side, working without noticing or bothering to notice the visitor gawking at them on the other side.

"Right this way, Princess Indari."

She hadn't stated her given royal name, and felt the annoyance rise in her throat as the android addressed her by title instead of by her courier status.

They followed the corridor to its end where a double glass door led to another reception area. There was no one behind the desk and Rasha waited for the android with her to take her station. The android lifted the headset to her head and spoke into the microphone.

"Shall I send her back? Right away." The android looked back at Rasha, "You may proceed through the door on my right."

Rasha didn't bother thanking the android but walked to the door. It slid open without a touch. All the modern conveniences were available. When the door closed behind her, anxiety made the hairs on the back of her neck stand up. What if she hadn't walked all the way through or had hesitated? Would the door have crushed her? Shaking off the unease, she continued through the bright white space to the one and only humanoid working in the room.

The man's thinning hair and yellowish skin put him in his late fifties. His smallish ears and large eyes said he was more Joro than Tero. He kept one large eye focused on some kind of magnifying device.

"I know what you're here for, I only wish I could help you."

"The cure isn't ready,? Mr.–?"

"I'm Idobe, and we don't have anything like a cure. Nothing we've attempted so far has had any effect on virus. It's like nothing we've ever seen before."

"Any clue as to origin?"

"No, my people are starting to believe it is from off-world."

"What?" Rasha couldn't hide her shock. There were several implications if it had come from another world. "How do you know?"

"We've been in contact with people from two other worlds that have dealt with the disease."

"How did they cure it?"

"THEY DIDN'T." Idobe's face remained passive despite his devastating words.

"So, they just let their people die?"

"No, anyone with the disease was quarantined from the general population and then terminated."

Rasha couldn't believe what she was hearing. They'd ended the virus by killing the victims. It was so barbaric that she couldn't imagine a people willing to do that. She must have made a face.

"I see what you're feeling and I can't say I blame you. However, when a third of your population is already sick and you've got a wide spread epidemic on your hands, you're desperate for a way to save the other two-thirds. That was just the one case. The other was a sole survivor from a planet destroyed by a neighboring species who feared the disease so exterminated them rather than deal with the virus themselves."

"So, there's no hope."

"I wouldn't rush to that conclusion just yet. Our circumstances are not so dire." He looked up from the microscope again, but this time Idobe looked up at her, "You seem smart. Tell me, how long before all nine kingdoms showing cases will be rendered incapacitated?"

"Nine?" Rasha had assumed all the kingdoms had citizens that were affected.

"The Wola and the Majiwan have no cases within their borders. As far we understand, not one Wola has fallen sick. The Majiwan infected were outside of the water at the time and were quarantined on land."

Rasha wondered about what that might mean.

"I don't know what that means," Idobe said as if reading her thoughts. "It's only a place to start and not a place to give up. I believe through science we can find a cure, but we must keep working."

"But you're all alone here. Where are the others?"

"Some are sick with the disease. We determined it was best to work within independent labs. Every lab in the facility had dropped their work to focus on the search for a cure. We keep our contact with others limited in case of exposure, but all the science is put into a shared database until we land on the solution to this complex problem."

"What shall I tell Prince Bashir?"

Idobe thought for a moment. Then he looked up from his work with a sad smile. "Tell him to pray to the goddess Mat`ka of Poda we find a cure in time to save the Bolaji kingdoms. Otherwise we'll be forced to take more drastic measures."

Rasha understood now what he meant by 'drastic measures' and a chill ran down her spine. If the science labs at Q Prime couldn't manufacture a cure, they were lost. She left the building feeling less sure about her next move than ever before. If Jak was with her, he'd say something funny to keep her spirits up or sing a song. Instead, he was lying in a bed at the Ishola palace dying of an incurable disease. She missed him and wished more than ever that their last words had been different. She wrapped her hand around her amulet. He'd said to pray. That's exactly what she planned to do. Rasha wasn't ready to return to the palace empty handed, so she made her way home first.

## 20

---

*T*HE INTERNAL DEBATE ABOUT whether to contact Sochi for some kind of update on Chiza and Jak lasted most of the ride to Chilali. Rasha decided there was no use in worrying if they were worse or if they were too far gone. Sochi would have already contacted her if it were the latter. Rasha led Zele to touch down on the grounds out front where she was most likely to be seen. The guards rushed out to greet her and to see to her animal, though they were never quite sure what to do with the creature who shied away from their sharp staffs.

"Zele will be fine on her own, leave her," she said as they reached up to help her dismount.

"As you wish. Welcome home, Princess Indari," Kufre the captain of the guard said.

The six guards bowed in unison as she walked past them to the castle. How much things had changed in just a rotation. The entire castle had been improved upon during her nine months as princess incumbent. Her parents' status had been elevated again, and it showed in the improvements.

"Your parents are awaiting your arrival in their chambers. It is requested that you take all the time you need to ready yourself before you attend them," he said, looking her over.

It was the one thing that her parents still demanded. Her father refused to see her if she dressed as a courier. In his presence, she was a princess first and above all else. It would grate on her nerves, but she didn't have time to worry about that sort of thing. She ran a hand over her face.

"Your room has been prepared, and a bath drawn."

A bath sounded nice. She'd been a long time on Zele's back and she needed to seek their council. It wouldn't do her any good if she were tossed out for inappropriate dress. Rasha hadn't seen her old room since she'd gone rotations ago, but when she entered, she wasn't sure she was in the right place. The guard who escorted her broke into a smile at her reaction.

"Yes, your highness, this is your room. I'll inform your parents you will join them at your convenience." Kufre bowed again and left her to inspect the room on her own.

The pink bedroom with the ruffled curtains and nauseating feminine touches had been completely redesigned. The walls were now painted a soothing cream color and embellished with large paintings of oversized flowers in blue, purple and white. Her pink bed coverings had been swapped for a soft white lace overlay with rich royal blue and purple throw pillows made of a soft silk. Her vanity chair was recovered in the royal purple. The adjoining bath was decorated in black and white, including lace accents on the towels and window coverings that took her breath away. Rasha ran her hand over the purple and blue soaps in the dish beside the water basin. She sighed at the sight of the lit candles around her prepared bath.

It was such a drastic change, she couldn't wrap her mind around the reason her parents would do such a thing. She walked to the closet, hoping she'd find dresses more to her taste. The clothing that hung in the closet had changed little. There were two notable additions in more neutral tones but other than those, her wardrobe remained the same. Change came slowly, but she was happy for the small blessing.

She bathed and put on one of the new dresses. The fit was nice and the sleeves were short to go along with the warm weather. The silver of the gown complimented her skin, and she pulled her hair up and back, away from her face.

The king and queen were waiting in their chambers when she arrived. Rasha wasn't sure, but it looked like they'd been arguing about something. The table between them sat askew, as if they'd sat down in an abrupt manner. The chamber maid must have taken a step back, because she took a step forward now. Her father's temper was legendary, as she could attest. What had her mother said to anger him so?

Rasha bowed low before them and waited to be addressed.

"Welcome, daughter," her father said in a tone dripping with sweetness.

Unnerved, she rose again and stared at them.

"I hope your room is to your liking," her mother said with conspiratorial grin.

"It is, I love it. Thank you."

Her mother nodded and looked to her husband and waited. What were they discussing before she'd entered?

"Were you expecting me?" Rasha asked them, wondering what all the fuss was about.

"Sooner or later we had no doubt you would return. You may sit." Her father waved a hand, and the chambermaid lifted a small chair and placed it in front of her parents. They sat in a perfect triangle.

"Well, I don't want to waste your time so I'll get to the point," Rasha said. "I need information and I'm hoping with your many connections you can point me in the right direction."

Her father nodded and smiled. "We hoped you would consult us. That is wise. First let me say it is very generous of the prince to allow this without beheading you both."

"We were prepared for everything," her mother interjected.

Rasha was confused. How had they heard of her mission? Bashir wouldn't have told anyone.

"He's a fine boy but we think it would be prudent to keep your options open. A prince he may be but he's got no royal family line. The others of the kingdom have more of a legitimate upbringing."

The realization of what he was talking about hit her between the eyes like a dull axe. They were still concerned about the New Choosing. They didn't realize with all the commotion over there that the Choosing was on hold. Besides that, she wasn't there for the Choosing but to help the prince. Her father continued speaking while her mind filled in the missing blanks of their original meaning. It was Jak they didn't approve of now.

Rasha could feel the anger rising in her belly and turning her skin a darker purple. It was never ending with them. First, they were mad that she wouldn't attend the Choosing. Now they didn't like all the choices available. She hadn't chosen Jak, but he'd made no secret he'd chosen her. By law, he was a prince and she could choose him, but to her parents his upbringing in the Wilds away from his royal family made him unsuitable. The two of them were unbearable.

She raised a hand to stop her father's ramblings.

"Your highness," she used the formal speech to get his attention, "you mistake my purpose in coming here. I am here as a courier for Prince Bashir on behalf of the eleven kingdoms of Bolaji. I am not here to discuss the New Choosing. If you will forgive me, may I continue?" Rasha was so pleased by her own restraint she had to keep herself from smiling.

Her mother and father looked at each other then back to her. Without a word, her father nodded for her to continue.

"You may have heard of the deadly sickness that is sweeping the lands. The sickness has officially reached the palace and many of the princes and princesses are unwell."

"The prince?" her mother gasped with a hand to her chest.

"When I left the palace of Ishola, he was in good health. I have no idea how long that will last. The sickness is spreading far more rapidly than originally thought. Since it is already here, I wanted to discover if you've made any progress toward a cure."

Her father put a hand on his chin and stroked.

"No, our people haven't made any advancement in that area. We believe the Tero-Joro may have something. If they do, we'll do what we can to get the cure here as soon as possible."

"I have just come from there. They are hard at work on something but they do not have a cure. None of the other kingdoms are as advanced as they are in the sciences and they are struggling. I'm afraid if they don't find something soon, we will all be lost."

"What about the New Choosing?" her father asked. She wouldn't get out of that one so easily. The truth would be hard to hear but she wouldn't dash their hopes to the rocks yet.

"The New Choosing is postponed while the entire

palace is in quarantine." Their disappointment was no surprise. But her mother's next question floored her.

"And your Jak? How does he fare?"

The tears that sprang to her eyes almost blinded her as Rasha tried to speak. All she could see was his ashen face lying against the white pillows.

"He is quite unwell," was all she could get out. "If you'll excuse me. I must go to the temple."

Not waiting to be excused, Rasha dashed from the room and into the hall. She brushed angry fists over her eyes before taking measured steps down the hall. Rasha found her way outside the castle. The doors of the temple were open wide and welcoming, despite her father's decree they remain closed when not in use.

## 21

---

$\mathcal{T}$HE TEMPLE WAS AS SHE'D left it. The benches were polished, and the Eye sat at the front of the alter, glowing day and night. She knelt in front of it and poured out her heart to the Universal. She prayed for the life of her friend Chiza and for Jak. Countless more would be sick and could die if she didn't find an answer soon. Her shoulders slumped with the weight of the mission in front of her.

A soft shuffling to her left brought her head up. She saw an old woman coming toward the altar.

"I'm sorry, I need to be alone," she said, hoping that the woman would understand she wasn't trying to be rude.

The old woman didn't speak, but eased herself down to her fragile knees and bowed her head to the Eye, her purple skin already ashen and her hair black with age. Rasha turned away, then stopped short when she noticed something in her hand. An amulet identical to the one she wore around her own neck. The necklace had been a rare gift and the sight of it in the woman's frail hands gave her mixed feelings.

"I'm sorry, where did you come by your amulet?"

The old woman mumbled something before the Eye without looking in her direction. Rasha took the woman for too old to hear and turned back to the Eye and reached for her own amulet. It no longer hung around her neck. She felt around the floor around her and then within the folds of her dress, wondering how she hadn't realized it was missing. Perhaps the old woman had found it. She turned to ask but the old woman had disappeared.

"No," she said in a hushed whisper. She got to her feet and raced around the altar, looking for any sign of the amulet or the woman who'd been beside her just a moment ago.

The soft shuffle she'd heard before returned just a head of her. Rasha glimpsed the old woman's cloak as she turned the corner, and followed. Behind the altar there was a small door that whispered closed as she reached the corner. She had no idea where the passageway lead. This was a part of the temple she'd never dared to venture to before and hesitated out of respect for those who worked here. The shuffling on the other side of the passageway door was fading. How could the woman move that fast?

Rasha pulled open the door and entered the space. It looked like no one had been there in ages. There were wisps of webs all around the entry way and she could see her footprints in the dust on the floor. Where were the prints of the old woman, she wondered? Why hadn't anything been disturbed as she entered?

The small cackle of the old woman reached her ears and Rasha picked up her skirts and continued after her. The next corner was darker than the last. If it wasn't for the faint light ahead, she'd be lost. She moved toward it and at last she arrived in a small chamber. It was no bigger than a small changing room. Rasha looked up and caught the faint residue of fire marks, the kind made from burning torches. Four lit the upper part of the room. The old woman wasn't here. She had to be close, there was no way the woman could have beaten her speed. Rasha was huffing as it was and wouldn't be able to keep up the pace much longer.

A faint light moved to her left, and she found another small door. It was almost half the size of the door to the room. Rasha pulled the door open and it lead to a winding set of stairs. They were steep and when Rasha poked her head inside and glanced up, the light vanished. She reached up to her neck, wondering if she was daydreaming. Her hand came away empty, and she knew she'd race after the woman until the ends of the earth for her amulet. Rasha climbed the stairs, not bothering to rush now she realized that the nearness of the sounds of the old woman bore no resemblance to her actual whereabouts.

A whisper of fabric, another door, and she was standing on the peak of a steeple near the castle. She'd never needed to come here before but as she looked around, she took in most of the grounds and most of the kingdom of Chilali.

The view from up on top was breathtaking and Rasha took it all in. She noted that Zele had found a nice cool spot to sit underneath the cover of some trees near to the edge of the castle property. Rasha caught her resting close to asleep. After a moment, she turned in the other direction. She noted the guard performing various drills as they readied themselves for whatever might come their way.

"You move slow for one so young." The old woman's voice from behind her made her jump. Rasha's hands flew to her sides but her swords weren't there. It was becoming a horrible habit, her leaving her swords in her room.

"I want my amulet back, old woman."

A gnarled hand snaked out of her cloak and she held up the amulet for Rasha to take. Rasha grabbed it and checked it for a broken clasp. It seemed intact, which only made her wonder more how the woman had come by it.

"I have a gift," she said waving her hand in the air. She spoke as if she'd read Rasha's mind which only unnerved her more.

"What do you want with me?"

"You are the courier, yes?"

"I am."

"The cure is what you seek but cannot find."

"What do you know of the cure?"

"The entire kingdom is at the mercy of the plague. If we don't want to lose many, we must cure them all."

Rasha looked out over the trees. "The Tero-Joro are the closest to a cure."

"They have nothing." The old woman spat on the ground.

"How do you know that?" Rasha asked, turning back to the woman and examining her more closely.

"The cure is The Niramaya Tree."

"What is The Niramaya Tree? Where can I find it?" Rasha asked.

"It is a tree that grows and grows. Where it lives, nobody knows. The blossoms and the leaves upon it are red. If you do not find it we are all dead," she sang.

"I don't understand. No one has ever mentioned The Niramaya Tree before."

"It is as ancient as the land, long after the kingdoms will it stand. Many long to live forever, but the tree is much more clever."

"I'm not good with riddles," Rasha said, rubbing her temples.

"If you look on land you lose, it is underwater you must choose. Right or wrong, it stands for all. Once cut, the leaves and tree will fall."

The old woman lifted her voice and whistled. Zele lifted off the ground, responding to the call, and moved to the roof. Rasha held up her hands to stop the beast from trampling the old woman. But when she turned back, the old woman had vanished again, not leaving a so much as a shoe print behind.

THAT NIGHT, RASHA'S DREAMS were filled with images of the old woman and a mysterious tree. A large tree with white bark and magenta leaves. A color not found anywhere in nature. The tree swayed back and forth as if waving to her. Rasha woke feeling tired and anxious. Her sick friends didn't have much time. The lyrical message stayed with her long after the dreams had subsided. She hummed the lyrics to a tune from her dream while she dressed.

Over breakfast, she broached the subject with her parents.

"Have you ever heard of The Niramaya Tree?"

"Who told you about that?" her mother asked.

"Fantasy," her father said at the same time.

"A crone approached me in the temple and said it holds the cure to the plague that is sweeping the kingdoms."

"The Niramaya Tree is an ancient legend. I have heard nothing of it since I was a child." Her mother rubbed at her arms.

"Is there something wrong?" Rasha asked as she noted her mother's odd behavior.

"No, I had an odd feeling like we shouldn't be discussing it."

"Imaginings," her father said between bites.

"Either way, I need to ask around to find out if anyone has ever seen this tree," Rasha said and shrugged one shoulder.

"Waste of time," her father said.

He shook his head and muttered something about her getting married.

"Be careful, child," her mother said, reaching over and grabbing Rasha's arm with a death grip.

Rasha pulled her arm away and nodded. Her mother seemed so strange, so altered. The old woman had an unnerving way, perhaps her mother had seen her, but before she could ask about it a guard at the door interrupted them.

"There is a visitor for her royal highness, Rasha."

Rasha nodded and stood up to leave. She bowed to her parents and excused herself. Her mother's worried eyes followed her every movement. Once they were out in the corridor and out of range of her parents' hearing, the guard spoke again.

"A greenie, he refused to give his name."

"Do not refer to the Tero-Joro in that way. No doubt it is only Ebere."

Rasha realized then she should have contacted him a long time ago. He might have had an idea where to find Ladi. Ever since he'd kissed her, he'd had a new sort of confidence that was interesting to see. Rasha wondered what he would be willing to do to help her. When the guard reached the corridor, he stopped and stepped to one side, allowing her to see who'd arrived. The build on this person was too slight and the stance too casual. Ebere had a much more formal way about him. She glanced at the figure draped in oversized clothing and hair tucked into a large cap. It wasn't a man at all but a girl. It was Ladi. The recognition must have touched her eyes because Ladi gave a slight shake of her head before she bowed low.

"Your highness, I beg a moment of your time."

Ladi didn't want to reveal her true identity to the guards nearby. Rasha played along, unsure of the end goal. She raised a hand and gestured toward the gardens. As much as they needed privacy, she couldn't be seen with another man while in the middle of the New Choosing even if it was only pretense. She avoided the tall hedges and walked along the straight path away from the doors.

Ladi walked a step behind her and followed her into the tall hedges. The weather was warm this time of year, and she welcomed the breeze beneath her lifted skirts as she avoided tripping on them.

"Where in the name of the Universal have you been?" Rasha asked once they were out of hearing of the guards.

"I'll explain everything."

The large fountain in the garden would serve to mask their voices and Ladi's face. She couldn't sit down in the dress she wore and instead indicated with a nod of her head that Ladi should sit down.

Rasha looked her over again, taking in the clothes. They did look like something Ebere would wear.

"Why are you dressed like Ebere?"

"Why are you dressed like a princess?"

Rasha was about to say something and then looked down at her yellow gown. Yes, she did look a bit ridiculous with all the ruffles and lace but she had her reasons so she shrugged.

"Ebere loaned me these so that I could come to you without getting caught,"Ladi said. "I don't want anyone to recognize me. I need to maintain complete anonymity until the truth is revealed. "

"What truth?" Rasha's patience was wearing down. "You've yet to tell me anything of substance."

"I left you at the Keep, didn't you see what was happening there?"

"You didn't leave me much to go on. Things have changed little from what I could see."

"That's my point. Things haven't changed. The kingdom of Ishola has all but been ignored."

"Not by Bolaji choice. You forget they were the ones who demanded independence from the other ten king-doms and it was granted. We have a peaceful relationship but the Wola keep their own rules and laws to avoid any uncomfortable transition."

"That's not the point. They are purposely excluded, but that's not the worst of it," Ladi hissed. She pulled out a small package. The package she'd been tasked to carry.

Rasha stared down at the brown paper wrapping the box.

"What are you still doing with that? You shouldn't have it," Rasha said backing up from the thing.

"Look at this. Things aren't as they appear." Ladi stood up and pushed the package at Rasha, forcing it into her hands.

Rasha looked down at the small package. The light brown wrapping had shifted and the thin tie was loose. She removed the packaging and stared at the black device in her hand. Then she looked up at Ladi, who nodded in confirmation, her lips pressed together into a thin line, before sitting back down on the edge of the fountain.

Rasha turned the small black device over in her hand. She'd seen many like them. A controller used against the beasts, to control the collars. Most of the beasts had their collars removed. Some feared removing them even now due to how many died trying to do the same. This controller could force them into submission again.

"Who?" Rasha asked.

"I don't know yet, that's why I'm here. I need your help. I lost track of them and they've begun to take the beasts and they have two of my Wola friends and I want them back." Ladi's voice rose with her anger.

Rasha used her hand to indicate she was getting too loud and Ladi bit off her rant.

"How many of these have you seen?" Rasha asked.

"The entire graduating class at the Keep received a box of the same dimensions as mine. I was the only one to open mine."

"Yahtz," Rasha said under her breath. "Where were they going?"

"They were sent to the leaders of the kingdoms, from what I could gather. This one was going to Chilali."

"Interesting."

"Interesting? Is that all you can say?" Ladi stood again and paced in front of her. "The kingdoms could gather against the beasts, starting a war for no good reason."

"Not that," Rasha said and waved a hand again to get Ladi to calm down. "My father mentioned nothing about not receiving a package or expecting a package."

"I beg your pardon but is your father much on sharing his private business with his rogue daughter?"

Rasha didn't let the sarcasm bother her. "Not in particular but it is a courier matter. He wouldn't hesitate to mention that I wasn't doing my duty as a princess or in making deliveries. Plus, if he wanted to control the beasts himself he would be proud of it. Too proud to keep it to himself."

"So he doesn't know about it?"

"No, I don't think he does, which means most likely none of them know about it." Rasha put the device back into Ladi's hand. "However, they all came from one place and we need to go back there to get answers."

"I know, that's why I sent you," Ladi said with a roll of her eyes.

"Yes, as I recall, you left me at the Keep with less information than a newborn piko. No, this time we go in prepared. There's only one problem."

"What?"

"The plague is spreading, everyone is getting sick and Chiza and Jak have very little time."

"Oh." Ladi's mouth formed the word, and the sound was a whisper on the wind. "What if there's no cure?"

Rasha couldn't entertain the thought even for a second and shook her head.

"Your people are working on a cure. There may also be an alternative. It lies within a tree."

"Where?"

"The old woman didn't say precisely."

"The old woman?"

"There was an old woman at the temple. She gave me a riddle. I think it's supposed to lead me to this Niramaya Tree."

Ladi stroked her chin. It seemed to be a mannerism left over from the boyish clothes she wore.

"Tell me the riddle and let's see if we can't solve it together. The sooner we get the cure to them, the sooner we can get to the Keep and resolve this matter." She shook the device in her hand.

"There's an easy way to resolve this matter for the time

being," Rasha said, then she took back the device and put it on the ground to stomp on it. Her slippered feet did no damage to the device, but the device hurt her foot.

Ladi moved forward and, with her heavy boots, she stomped on the device then she gathered the pieces.

"Better keep these for evidence." Ladi gathered the pieces into the cloth and tied the package back together. "Now, tell me exactly what the old woman said to you."

Once Ladi had heard the riddle twice she smiled.

"What?"

"She told you where to find the cure. It won't be easy to get to, but I think we can have the cure before the end of the day."

"Where is it?"

"You might want to get changed into your regular clothes and grab your swords because you're not going to like it," Ladi said crossing her arms.

## 23

*T*HEY STOOD ON THE EDGE of the water. Rasha was pacing back and forth. Zele sat under a tree, watching her nervous movements with fascination.

"You have to do this," Ladi said for the fifth time.

"I can't. I don't like the sea. Drowning will ruin my day."

"You won't drown. The Majiwan will take you down using a breather. It'll be fine."

"Why don't you do this?"

"The old woman didn't talk to me, the prince didn't send me, and I'm not the one in love with Jak."

Rasha stopped and stared at Ladi. She was only fifteen, but she had her moments.

"Is it that obvious?"

"Only to anyone who isn't you." Ladi smiled. "The

best thing, though, is that Jak loves you back, and he has the patience of Xeku."

Rasha didn't know what to think about that. She did love Jak. Why was it so impossible to tell him? The idea being obvious to everyone except her made her nauseous. Although maybe that was partly the water too. She remembered why she feared the water. She had almost drowned once. The memory had faded, but the feelings remained. Standing in front of the sea now brought all of those feelings back.

"Better get it over with," Ladi said with an encouraging smile.

Rasha opened her mouth and sang the words Ladi had told her would call the Majiwan. The words stuck in her throat and she croaked out the tune. Ladi shook her head once.

"I better help you or we'll be standing on this hot beach all day." Ladi had retained her boyish clothing for the journey and Rasha's own courier clothes grew warmer against her skin.

Ladi joined her voice, and the two sang the words to the sea, waiting for the Majiwan to appear.

Two heads appeared in the water a hundred yards from in front of them and continued toward the beach. To males with staffs and stern expressions. From behind her, Zele stood up and roared at them. Rasha held up a hand to indicate Zele should be calm.

When their shoulders crested the water, Rasha spoke to them.

"I'm aware this is not how diplomatic meetings are arranged but I need to speak with your king. It is urgent that I see him."

Ladi reached out a hand and touched Rasha's arm.

"Not yet," she said in a low whisper as the men continued to walk toward them. When their feet touched the sand, Ladi gave Rasha a tap to start her request.

Rasha took a deep breath and started again.

"My name is Rasha Jenchat Indari, princess of Chilali, and I request an audience with your king. It is a matter of life and death."

The men looked at each other then back at her. They nodded in unison before turning their backs on her and walking back into the water.

"Wait, I cannot go in without help. I need a breathing thing."

They walked on and when their shoulders were touching the water, the one on the left held up a breather, a small clear mask that fit over her face and provided air for her to breathe. The magical device was a wonder. She'd never investigated further as she'd had no intention of going underwater by choice.

Rasha dared a glance behind her. Ladi gave her one last wave. The current helped carry her under the water, the two mermen doing the rest by tethering her to them. She'd missed the transformation of their legs to fins and decided she might want to see that next time.

Below the surface of the water, there wasn't much going

on. She noted the sun's warmth still carried even with her head well below the surface. She looked left and right but there was nothing here, no fish or anything. Further into the deep blue and greenish sea around them, she swam. Unable to keep up with their speed, they dragged her along while she kicked her feet uselessly behind her. Her ears, the first thing affected by the pressure, grew tight and she pushed the air out of her mouth, trying to keep the pressure equalized. The mask helped, but it wasn't a perfect fit. There was still some pressurizing she had to do herself.

They touched the sea floor at last and the mermen stopped to allow her to complete her pressurization. Her head ached but she could see all around her the Majiwan swimming in groups. A large group swam to her left and another to her right as she watched in amazement. She'd heard stories about the life of the Majiwan but this was something one had to see to believe. The array of turquoise, amethyst, and emerald seemed to be in everything and touch everyone.

Several of the Majiwan stared openly at her as she was led along. The kingdom of the mermaids had few visitors, especially someone from Chilali. Travel across the lands to other nations and kingdoms wasn't strong in either culture. Rasha and the mermen continued their swim to the entrance, to the large palace that dominated the center of their kingdom. Coral covered tall buildings without stairs. A green sort of seaweed covered the windows and offered a bit of privacy. The mermen swam with her through the large doors that stood open and into the underwater palace.

They reached the king's public chamber. He sat alone with an empty chair at his side. It was common knowledge that the king of Majiwa ruled alone since the death of his wife over ten rotations ago. His long hair, a three-toned blue, shifted with the movement of the water surrounding him. His grey eyes watched her with interest as she swam awkwardly toward him. The mermen remained tethered to her, keeping her from floating up to the ceiling.

Rasha remembered her manners and bowed to the king and spread her hands, requesting permission to speak. She sent a silent thanks to Aunt Sochi for all those kingdom etiquette lessons.

"You may speak and I will listen, you are as welcome as the stars that glisten."

He greeted her in the traditional rhyming of the Majiwan and Rasha's face went a deep purple. Their language wasn't something she'd mastered. She waved her right hand in circle as she tried think of a lyrical response.

"Please, you may speak the common language," he said after regarding her struggle.

"I beg your pardon, your highness, I've yet to master your tongue. I hope you will forgive me," she said, forcing the words out through the mask she wore over her face.

He waved it away and motioned for her to approach his throne made of a natural coral formed around a throne of stone. It didn't look comfortable, but he rested one elbow on the arm.

"I am Rasha Jenchat Indari, princess of Chilali. I come here as a courier on behalf of Prince Bashir of Ishola."

"Princess and courier. That is an interesting combination," he said before prompting her to continue with a nod of his head.

"The Bolaji kingdoms are in danger of being wiped out by a very serious plague." He didn't seem surprised by the news, he only listened as she continued. "I was told there is a tree, The Niramaya Tree it is called in the common language. It holds the only known cure. We hope you will grant us access to this tree and allow us to gather the needed cure from it."

The king's face changed, hardened as if he were angry. "I cannot allow it."

Rasha was expecting to be laughed out of the palace for even suggesting such a tree might exist. He hadn't denied the existence of the tree at all. Not only was he aware of the tree and its location, but he refused to let her see it.

Rasha's jaw tightened and her hand moved to her hip. The mermen lifted their staffs and pointed them at her throat at the small twitch. She relaxed her hands and raised them up in a slow measured movement from her sides. The king watched all of this with a stern expression on his face, but he didn't move.

"May I ask why you have denied a request that will cause you no harm and will benefit all of Bolaji?"

"The Niramaya Tree is not for the taking. Its use has always been limited and its location kept secret for genera-

625

tions. My wife could not even be saved by it. The Tree you speak of dies a little each time you take from it. What you're asking will destroy it and leave us with nothing. You have no right to ask us to do this."

Rasha couldn't believe he was refusing to help. Chiza and Jak were lying in beds dying while the cure was here in Majiwa.

"Your refusal could mean the end to us all. You must reconsider."

The king shook his head, his hair swirling around him.

"I cannot. You must find another way."

"There is no other way, your own people will die from this. There are two at the palace now in danger."

The king sat up and ran a hand over his face.

"My son. Yes, I know."

"You would let your son die of this disease rather than share the cure?"

"As I told you, to take from it now would mean the end of the tree."

Rasha turned to leave. She wanted to storm out, but she remained tethered to the mermen who'd brought her. She took a tether in each hand and yanked, getting their attention. They both looked at her and then to their king. The king waved at them and they turned to take her back. Rasha's mind raced to find an answer to her dilemma.

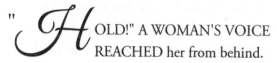"OLD!" A WOMAN'S VOICE REACHED her from behind.

"Mother, do not interfere." The king's voice managed to boom in the chamber.

Rasha yanked again, stopping the mermen from swimming off. They made a slow circle and when she turned around, she saw an old mermaid floating at the side of the king.

"I will speak, you tell half-truths to save what is already gone." She waved Rasha forward. "I am Queen Idara, mother to the king. I believe I can help you."

The queen squared her shoulders.

"There is something, however, you must do for me," Queen Idara said.

"Anything."

"You are a courier so I know this is well within your

ability. I will show you where to find The Niramaya Tree. It is said not all who cut from the tree do harm. You must be pure of heart, spirit, and motive. You cut for another, someone you love?"

Rasha nodded. She loved Jak. Chiza was a close friend, and she also did this for her.

"She may do it without causing harm to the tree," she said speaking to her son but not looking at him.

"If she is not pure of heart? The tree will be gone. Another will never grow in its place," he said.

The queen swam forward, and she put her hand out and touched Rasha's heart. A warm heat emanated from her hand. The heat spread from Rasha's heart through her chest. Queen Idara lifted her hand and tilted her head as she looked at Rasha.

"Who is the source of your information?" she asked Rasha.

Rasha shifted, uncomfortable with the question. She didn't want to sound crazy, but they insisted and she told them.

"A crone I met in the temple of Chilali. She seemed frail, but she wasn't and after racing after her she finally told me about the cure."

"Yes, if Yada trusted you that's saying something. She has the empathic ability." The queen looked Rasha over from head to toe. "I believe she will do. Come with me."
A wave of her hand had the mermen following her out of the nearest door.

Rasha looked back and saw the king's face. His eyebrows had drawn together and his mouth was turned down. She wondered in that moment what had happened to him and his wife.

The swim to the tree took much longer than Rasha expected. They'd been under the surface and swimming for over an hour. Her limbs were tired, and the mermen had to drag her along. The sun was setting by the time they reached the tree. As Rasha looked at it for the first time, she had no doubt that this tree held the power to cure.

The tree's bright white bark was iridescent in the dark water and had an inner glow that grew brighter despite the lack of light. The magenta leaves on the tree swayed back and forth with the motion of the water. It was as she'd seen in the vision that the old woman had shared with her.

Queen Idara stopped a good distance away and helped untie the tether from Rasha to the mermen.

"I'm not sure how much I need," Rasha said. She worried now of taking too much or too little.

"Let your heart guide you and take what will help your people."

RASHA HAD to fight the fatigue and swim hard to reach the branches of the tree. It was larger and stronger than she'd thought. She held firm as she used the branches to get as close to the tree as possible. A tree would be like any

629

other medicine she'd encounter, but she wasn't sure which part would hold the curative property. With her sword she cut from one branch that held two hands full of leaves. Then she moved to the trunk of the tree and used her sword to slice off some of the white bark. She clutched the pieces and placed them inside of her satchel and swam away from the tree hard and toward the mermen.

The three were watching the tree with amazement. Rasha turned back in time to see the branch she'd removed grow back in an instant. Even the leaves were replaced. The struggle to stay below the surface intensified, and the mermen tethered her again. The old mermaid continued to watch the tree. She opened her mouth and the softest song she'd ever heard came out. A song of thanks. The mermen joined in her song. Their voices created a harmony that sent a chill through Rasha's skin.

The three of them seemed to extend the glow of the tree. Inside her chest the warmth that the mermaid had placed on her heart grew again and Rasha let it fill her body. It warmed her inside out from her chest to the tips of her fingers and toes. The others must have had the same sensation because as they sang, they smiled at one another. Rasha lifted a hand to her face and stared at the glow pulsing through her. When the song stopped the glow faded. They nodded to each other and began the swim back the way they'd come.

"Thank you, Queen Idara, on behalf of the other kingdoms," Rasha said for a lack of better words as the king's mother swam alongside her.

"We should thank you. You have proven the legends correct. There will always be those who can cut from The Niramaya Tree. However, most should not venture near it, for fear they will kill the entire tree with their want." When they reached the beach where Rasha had entered, they ascended to the surface. Going up was much easier on her ears than it had been going down.

Before her head broke the surface, Queen Idara reached out and took her arm.

"You made me a promise, remember?"

"Yes, what would you like me to do?"

"My people, as you know, were one of the first to rule the kingdoms of Bolaji. There is a necklace that belongs to my people. It has been passed on from princess to prince for almost one hundred rotations along with a leather bracelet that goes from prince to princess. We hold the claim on the necklace. We would like it returned to its rightful place."

Rasha knew the necklace and leather bracelet well. She'd worn the leather bracelet around her own wrist for almost a rotation and had placed the necklace around Jak's neck when they'd become the incumbents. There was little doubt that the prince would agree to exchanging the necklace for the cure. Rasha nodded in agreement. She'd deliver the necklace without fail.

"You have my word as the princess of Chilali," she said and did her best underwater floating bow.

"Your word as a courier means more," the queen said with a wink.

Rasha felt her eyes open wide in surprise "You have it."

Rasha returned to the surface with the satchel full of pieces from The Niramaya Tree. She was more determined than ever to get the cure into the hands of those who'd know what to do with it.

HE SUN WAS FADING FAST when she climbed out of the water. Looking back over her shoulder, she saw only the tops of the mermen's heads as they dipped below the dark blue water. Ladi wasn't anywhere to be found. Rasha called for Zele. She'd left the dragon under a nearby tree. Zele didn't need to hunt very often and she normally never strayed far when Rasha needed her. Both of them missing from the beach triggered a warning signal in her mind.

Would Ladi take Zele and go up against the Courier's Keep on her own? No, she hadn't made any impulsive moves other than opening the package. In hindsight, all of her actions were focused, her attempts to help had been calculated. What if something had happened to them?

Rasha paced the edge of the beach as she watched the sun set in the north. She looked down and saw something she hadn't noticed before. A distinct pattern on the sand of something being dragged along. The evenly spaced mounds in the sand could be Ladi's legs. They marked one end of the beach to the other. Zele, however, couldn't be dragged off. She made the call again. But the normal sound of Zele's large wings didn't answer. Rasha grew more concerned when she noted a distinct slash of claw marks in the bark of one of the trees. Zele had struggled against something.

Rasha pulled out her swords and walked south, following the tracks on the beach. She turned her head to listen for sounds on the wind that blew lightly against her face. The normal sounds of the night reached her. The creeping and crawling things that were only awake during the evening hours. With the cure in her satchel and no way back, she used the light from the moon already showing itself above her to make her way after Ladi and Zele.

A fight somewhere in front of her broke her stride, and she crept up behind it using the trees as cover. The swords clashing took on a more rhythmic tone. She wasn't so sure anymore it was a fight. It sounded like training. Rasha glimpsed the firelight from a campsite and two men hitting their swords together in a slow attack and counter. One faced her and the other had his back to her.

A large cage sat furthest from her position with Zele inside. She wore a shiny new controlled collar and slept at an odd angle. She hadn't curled up to sleep; they must have used a chemical to put her to sleep. Ladi was tied to a nearby tree by her hands with her feet left dangling. Her head lolled to one side and her eyes were closed.

The man whose face she could see was the weaker of the two. She didn't recognize him. He seemed young and inexperienced as he practiced a more complicated defense. The other lead him along until the final blow and, at the last moment, changed things, putting himself on top.

The young man didn't seem annoyed by this, only challenged. He began again. He spoke up this time.

"Next time, I'll win."

"You don't know enough about fighting to win yet," his voice carried a familiar lisp.

"I know enough," the young man said, goading him on.

The other shook his head and turned his back on the young man, leaving himself open. Rasha caught the man's smile and recognized him immediately. But what was he doing out here in the woods with Zele and Ladi? He'd left himself open on purpose, hoping that the younger man would attack and, like all predictable things, he fell in line.

Rasha's hands tightened around her swords as she waited. She didn't wait long as two more men she recognized came into view.

"You have them, I doubted your ability," the man said, his back still turned.

"I've given you no reason to doubt me. Make sure you hold up your end of the bargain. I'm not leaving here without the antidote," said Gorg. His partner stood a step behind him, scanning the trees.

"We shouldn't be out in the open like this, she'll come for them," said Gorg's partner. Rasha couldn't help but feel a sense of pride at the thought that the man was afraid of her.

"Let her come." The other man turned at last and she saw his face for the first time. Prince Omi Gonma of Buku pulled out a small satchel and tossed it to Gorg.

"What do you plan to do with these two?" Gorg asked as the youngest scrambled to his feet and away from Omi.

"She'll get the dreaded sickness and the beast will be an example for the others."

Rasha couldn't believe what she was hearing. It was too much to believe. How did Omi get his hands on the disease and why would he recapture the beasts? Whatever he was up to, it involved using Gorg and his sick family. She almost felt bad for him. Until he walked over and gave Ladi a kick in the hip to wake her. Ladi's head rolled to the other side, and she moaned. Rasha noticed a small twitch in her leg. She wasn't unconscious.

The sound of Rasha pulling out Cutter and Blade made all three men look in her direction, as she'd hoped. Ladi used her legs to attack the young man closest to her. He didn't even see it coming. Close enough now, she kept him restrained while he beat against her powerful legs to no avail.

Rasha rushed both the prince and Gorg at the same time. Gorg reached for his sword before she could. He held it out in front of him. The prince pulled his own sword.

"What are you doing here?" Rasha asked Omi.

"Never mind, I'm taking care of some unfinished personal business," Omi said with a ferocious smile dominating his features.

"You brought the plague. The disease will kill so many people. How could you do it?"

"I have my reasons."

"You'd kill that many people and you have nothing else to say, no message of self-righteousness, not even vengeance?" she said, goading him.

"The disease has yet to touch the people I hoped dead. Until they die, no one will get the cure."

"Well, that sounds like a threat. I have a better idea. Why don't we go after the people that hurt you instead of killing thousands, maybe more, to satisfy your need for justice? Doesn't that sound a little saner?"

"I won't be judged by you. You have no idea how hard it is to reach people in power when you have none."

"You're a prince," she shouted.

A short whistle brought her attention away from the prince. She saw that Gorg had his sword to Ladi's throat. The young boy remained crouched on the ground, clutching his neck. Gorg's partner had also used the distraction to get out of the fight as he dashed back into the woods.

"I'm leaving here with my bit of the cure. What you do with him is your business," Gorg said. Using a long stick within reach and moving the way Jak had taught her, Ladi swept the sword from in front of her. With the same stick, she delivered a hard whack to his hand that forced the sword from his hand and to the ground. Before he could move to get it, she stepped on it while keeping the large stick at his nose. Despite her hands still being bound together, she'd defeated him.

"I guess that leaves just you and me," Rasha said turning back to Omi.

"I've got the cure, you need me."

"No, I've got the cure, we don't need you at all. Give me one good reason I shouldn't run you through and deal with the consequences later, after everyone is well?"

Omi kept his sword in front of him as he circled Rasha. Once she was in front of Ladi, she didn't give up another inch, forcing him to pace in front of her.

"You were born to the privilege that should have been mine. I wasn't going to kill you, but if you get in my way, I may change my mind."

"Me? I was born to it but have never desired it. Your parents are royals, that makes you a prince."

"True, but my parents abandoned me and they'll pay along with everyone else who stole my rightful throne."

Rasha wasn't sure if she was dealing with a prince anymore or a raving lunatic.

"I don't understand what you're getting at. You have a throne."

"No, I don't. I assumed the identity of Prince Omi Gonma. That is not my real name. I wasn't even born in Buku."

"Who are you?" Rasha asked more confused than ever.

His face contorted in anger and frustration before he turned with a grunt and disappeared into the dark woods.

Rasha couldn't risk losing Zele or Ladi again. She let him go, this time.

"Yahtz," she muttered to herself.

"Do you mind?" Ladi asked. She nodded to her hands to be cut.

Rasha used Blade to slice through the rope and in an instant Ladi had Gorg's sword in her hands.

Zele made a plaintive sound as she woke up, shaking her head. Then she clawed at the collar around her neck.

"No, no, not yet. Let's get you out of there and we'll remove the collar," Rasha said holding up her hands to stop the beast's frantic behavior. She used Cutter to break the lock and Zele stumbled out of the cage, shaking her head.

"Ladi, can you remove it?" Rasha asked.

"I think so. Give me a minute to find my tools, do you have this one?"

"Yes, I'm pretty sure I can handle him," Rasha said looking at Gorg, whose eyes were on the ground.

Zele sat impatiently as Ladi worked on the collar. A moment later, the ineffective device lay on the ground between them. Zele shook herself and took to the sky to remove the rest of her unease.

Ladi came to stand beside Rasha as she dropped her sword and indicated that Gorg should sit down. He plopped himself on the log that Ladi had used to keep her propped up. He still held the satchel in his hand refusing to release his grip on it.

"I need to get to my family," Gorg said, his voice filled with worry.

"First, you'll answer our questions. Let's start with how you know Prince Omi?"

Gorg laughed.

"Omi is no prince." Gorg laughed before he continued. "He found us. We discovered a while back that he had the technology to tap into the Courier's Keep and get us ahead of the courier's deliveries. He wanted to give these little controller packages to the newbie couriers to deliver across the kingdoms of Bolaji. What did we care about that? Once that was done, we used you and Jak as target practice. That was our payment."

"Why did you agree to help him spread this plague?"

Gorg's eyes went dark as he glared at her. "We didn't." Then he shook his head. "We didn't know anything about it. When my family got sick, though, I knew it had something to do with this Omi and his plans. I came for the cure and he demanded that we help him with one last job. We snatched your little greenie and the dragon in exchange."

In that moment, Zele returned. Her eyes were clear and she had blood on her mouth. She must have eaten. The remnants of feathers remained in her teeth. Zele bent low and close to Rasha and sniffed in the direction of Gorg before roaring in his face.

"You're all right now. We'll stop this," Rasha said,

giving the dragon a pat on the neck. She turned back to Gorg.

"What do you know of Omi's plans?"

"What I told you is what I know. He didn't share with us his real purpose. But I have my own theories."

"Let's hear them," Rasha said, crossing her arms.

"I don't have all night to jaw with you, I've got to save my family."

"We've all got sick family so you should start talking, and fast."

Gorg sighed as his shoulders slumped.

"He got the plague from the bull-men and the bird-men. That's why he's shipping off the beasts to their part of the world. This time they're using boats off the coast of Sidoa so they don't have to travel over Bolaji lands."

"Sidoa is just allowing this?" Ladi asked.

"The king of Sidoa knows nothing but his people are running low on gems. For the right payment, anyone can be a friend, if you know what I mean," Gorg said.

"Where are the beasts now?" Ladi asked.

Gorg's mouth clamped closed.

Rasha's swords came up and crossed in front of his face.

"There's a shipment going out in the morning. They'll be in the water on their way to the bull-men and bird-men at dawn."

Rasha looked to Ladi, who nodded as if she'd already asked the question. They'd have to split up if they were going to save everyone.

Rasha noticed that Ladi rubbed at her raw wrists.

"Are you all right?" Rasha asked.

"Fine. I want to stop him before he gets to any other beasts."

"Yes, I know, but first we need to get this cure to the people who can best make use of it. Contact Ebere and let him know we're going to need his help."

"I wouldn't do that, if I were you," Gorg said.

"What do you mean?" Rasha asked as they both turned to look at him.

"That greenie isn't with you, he's with us."

Ladi laughed. She actually laughed out loud, holding her belly.

Rasha didn't laugh but she watched Gorg's reaction.

"What do you mean he's with you?"

"I mean, we had a courier on the inside. Besides, Omi needed someone with the chemical skills to help with distributing the sickness."

Rasha was calculating the likelihood of Gorg lying at this point, and what would be the benefit. She'd played cards against him at the tavern, and she'd worked alongside him. He had absolutely no reason to lie about Ebere. Ladi hadn't yet worked out the conclusion as she stopped laughing and turned to look at Rasha.

"You're not going to believe this lying twyllo, are you?"

"I'm not lying to you, little girl. How do you think Omi got the cure? He's got connections but he's not smart enough to make it himself."

"What, so now you want to help us all of a sudden?" Ladi held the sword up to his face again, but he didn't flinch or back down.

"I've seen enough death. How much are you willing to see before you believe me?"

Rasha used her own sword to push Ladi's down. With a nod to Gorg, she let him go. He dashed off into the woods on foot.

"What are you doing? Not ten minutes ago he had a sword to my throat," Ladi yelled.

"Think about it, Ladi, Gorg wouldn't know Ebere was a greenie unless they'd already met. Ebere hasn't done any courier work since he was assigned to me over a rotation ago and we spent that rotation fighting the beasts."

The realization of her words were getting through to Ladi, but she shook her head to fight it. Her eyes filled with tears.

"I need to go and help my friends. If we can believe anything Gorg says, they'll be in danger," Ladi said.

Rasha knew that feeling of betrayal, but she had no way to spare her friend from it. Ebere was most likely a traitor to the eleven kingdoms and regardless of their former feelings for him, he wasn't someone they could trust anymore.

Rasha leapt on top of Zele's bowed head and held out her hand. Ladi hesitated.

"You won't be able to travel faster than we can. We'll take you straight to the coast after we've delivered the source of the antidote to the Tero-Joro," Rasha said she stretched out her hand again.

Ladi took it less than a minute later and settled herself behind Rasha. With two long sweeps of her wings, Zele had them in the air.

## 26

THEY REACHED TERO JORO WITHIN
hours. However, due to the late hour of their
arrival, Rasha wasn't sure there'd be anyone at the labs.
She saw an illumination, an unnatural light on in the
buildings. The entrance was always bright and the robots
there always working. It didn't surprise her they recognized her. They didn't break stride to make it to the
mechanical lifts they used to get to the upper levels of the
shiny building.

Most of the labs, however, were dark but the robot at
the entrance assured them that someone would be available in the lab to help them. They stepped off of the
mechanical lift and on to the glossy floors.

"One word: sterile," Ladi said as she let her feet slip
along the floor.

"Efficient, and we need that cure *now*." Rasha
approached the double doors at the end of the hall as she'd

done before, and the faceless robot on this floor greeted her with a cheerful voice.

"I am sorry, Courier Rasha Indari and companion, you are too late."

"What do you mean?" Rasha asked.

"The laboratory is closed."

"We have just arrived here and the one downstairs said it was okay to come up."

"The lab is closed, there is no one here to help you."

Rasha watched the robot with interest. They were connected to the same network. Why would there be a difference in the responses?

"Show me."

"Come with me." The robot glided on the smooth floor with one wheel and to the lab with the light on.

"What is this?"

Rasha and Ladi looked from one lab to the next. All the rooms had lights on but only one had a technician slumped over the table.

"Is he dead?" Ladi asked.

"No, he is breathing but no longer conscious."

"Why is he still here?" Rasha asked. "He needs to see a physician."

"The first fell this afternoon. They have requested that no physician be called until one has reached the unconscious state, this is the last."

"When were you going to make the call?"

"The physicians were called five minutes ago. They have arrived and are on their way up."

"This is bad," Ladi said.

"Who else is working on the cure?"

"There is no one left."

"That can't be. There's no way they'd make it this far and have only the people in this building working on it. If they knew they would lose consciousness at some point, they'd have a plan." Rasha moved to the monitor, careful not to touch the unconscious man at the desk. "I need access to this unit."

"Only authorized personnel are permitted to access the network."

"I have the cure, let me in, now."

The robot's internal circuits whirred. "That is the correct response." The monitor came to life. "I need to attend to the physicians." The robot rolled away.

Rasha tapped one key at a time on the display until Ladi pushed her aside.

"Here, let me." Ladi's hands flew over the monitor and the screen changed in rapid succession in front of them. "Tell me what I'm looking for."

"Any communications between the lab and someone outside the building. Can you figure that out?"

"Yes, it'll take a minute."

"Hurry, there has to be someone there that can help us."

"Got it, oh," Ladi said.

"What? Who?" Rasha asked as she leaned over her shoulder to stare at the screen then swore. "Anyone but him."

"We can't give the cure to Ebere, we don't trust him."

"No, we don't."

ZELE DROPPED Ladi and Rasha on the front lawn of Ebere's family home.

"What if he's not here?" Ladi asked, fidgeting with her clothes and hair.

Rasha had felt the same way when she'd realized that Xeku was Jak's biological father. If she had met his mother before her passing, she imagined she might be just as nervous. But this was different. Ebere was most likely a traitor and even so, they needed his help.

"Are you sure you can do this?"

"Of course, if he gets out of line…" Ladi let her voice trail off. Either she was planning for the worst or she wasn't sure what she was going to do.

"Relax."

"I am relaxed. Why wouldn't you think I'm relaxed?"

"You've touched your hair twice in the last sixty seconds and you keep adjusting your clothes. I'm starting to wonder if you're going on a date."

Ladi's hands stopped midway to her scalp before she dropped them to her sides.

"He'll give us the cure or else," Ladi said, squaring her shoulders

Rasha gave Ladi one more warning glance as she knocked on the door in front of her.

A woman with an older version of Ebere's face

answered the door. She looked them up and down with a fair amount of suspicion before she spoke.

"Can I help you?"

"We're looking for Ebere. Is he here?" Rasha asked.

The woman's expression only grew in suspicion as she regarded both girls. A small head peaked out from behind her skirts. Boy or girl, she couldn't be sure.

"Who's asking?"

"I'm Courier Rasha Indari, and this is Ladi. Ebere was my partner."

The frown on her face changed from suspicion to recognition.

"Princess Rasha Indari." She bowed with a well-practiced curtsey that made Rasha's skin blush to a dark purple. "I'm sorry I didn't recognize you. Come in and excuse the state of our home. I'm Ebere's mother, Hema."

"Mama, she's purple," the little girl with short hair and her mother's face said. She'd refused to let go of her mother's skirts, even after her mother had turned in a complete circle.

"Hold your tongue," she said to the child. To Rasha she said, "my youngest, Yisha."

Rasha didn't bother to respond. Nothing made her more uncomfortable than the attention her royal title gave her. Comments about her purple skin didn't bother her over much. There were plenty in the eleven kingdoms who'd never seen purple skin.

"Ebere?" she asked again.

"I'll fetch him. Please sit." She detached the little girl's small hands from her skirts to dash off to find Ebere. The little girl wouldn't be left alone with them and scurried after her mother.

Rasha and Ladi each sat down on one end of a soft couch with hand stitched repairs on each end covered by white knitted doilies. The living space was about half the size of Ladi's home. The wood burning stove was close enough to feel the heat from dinner emanating from it. There were several family photos on the walls, most of them featuring an older man that looked to be Ebere's father. Ebere never spoke of a father and Rasha had assumed he'd died a while ago. The way Ebere's five-year-old self stared up at him, he must have been much admired. She looked over at Ladi and saw her glancing over everything too. Was she thinking the same thing? How could Ebere be a traitor with all this normal and sad stuff in his house.

Hema returned in a flurry, her apron tied around her waist she offered them both something to drink. Ladi accepted for them and as they sipped their cold drinks, Ebere appeared. He was still adjusting his clothes when he entered the room. Rasha noted the exhausted eyelids and the worry around his mouth. But when he saw Ladi, his entire face seemed to lift and lighten. Rasha looked at Hema, his mother. She'd noticed it too. Could he have real feelings for Ladi?

Ebere tripped over himself to see Ladi, ignoring Rasha all together.

"I hoped you were okay. I tried to contact you, but

you never answered. Did you find them?" He babbled off questions while Hema stood with her hands on her hips.

Rasha was probably the only person who noticed that Ladi's hand was on her sword. "We'll get to that later, we need to know if you can help us. You're the last person working on the cure with any connection to the labs."

"You've been to the labs? Why hasn't anyone there contacted me?"

"They've all collapsed. They have the sickness. There isn't one person other than you who was working on it," Ladi said.

"By the way, why are you working on the cure?" Rasha asked. "I wasn't aware that you had any kind of medical background."

"Oh." Ebere looked down at the floor. "I don't really, it's sort of my hobby. After Ladi and I parted ways, I kept in contact with the scientists to see if they needed help at the labs. I liked dabbling in chemistry once." He exchanged a look with his mother.

Hema's lips tightened and her gaze landed on a photo of his father on the wall to her right.

Ebere continued, "Not that it matters. I'm sorry, I've made little progress." He gave them a shrug.

It all seemed a little too well rehearsed but they didn't have much of a choice at the moment. They needed a way to distribute the cure. "We have." Rasha opened her satchel and pulled out the piece of tree. It looked as vibrant as it had when she'd plucked it. She didn't much like turning it over to a traitor, but with

Ladi there to watch him she hoped that it would be enough.

Ebere's eyes grew wider and his mother and sister both leaned forward.

"Now, what is that?" Hema asked.

"Someone said this might help us to make a cure," Rasha said, holding it out for Ebere to take. He cradled it in his hands as if he feared dropping it would damage it.

"It's not much. How will that little thing cure all the people who are sick?" Hema asked. She reached out and rubbed a thumb over one leaf.

"I was hoping Ebere could help us with that part," Rasha said.

He was shaking his head.

"You're our only hope. The palace is counting on you."

Ebere looked from his mother then to Ladi then back to his mother.

"You can do this," Ladi said and put a hand on his arm.

Rasha tried not to smile at Ladi's well-played performance as she waited along with the others for Ebere to respond.

Ebere looked down at her hand and nodded.

"I'll try."


RASHA PACED the living room floor, trying to figure out what to do about Prince Omi. He'd said he wasn't the prince of Buku but he was royal. She'd already sent word to the palace, but someone would have to stop him before he got out of control. When her communicator beeped, she hoped with all her heart it wasn't an update on Jak or Chiza. It wasn't. There was only one word on her device.

"What's it say?" Ladi asked.

"Come." Rasha gathered up her things and stood up. "I have to return to the palace. Are you going to be all right here on your own?"

"Yes."

"Don't do anything..." Rasha thought for a moment, "rash. Let me know as soon as you have something."

Ladi nodded.

Rasha wondered if Ebere would even give Ladi what they needed.

## 27

"*Y*OU'RE FAMILY IS NICE," Ladi said as she sat twirling herself in the seat beside Ebere. His small room was decorated with all of his passions: dangling science projects and half put together technologies. He'd cleared his desk to make room for the tree and his chemicals.

"Thanks," Ebere said. He placed a special pair of glasses over his eyes that enlarged them.

"What do those do?" Ladi asked.

"They make it so I can see down to the cellular level. This tree is amazing."

"What do you mean?" She moved closer, her hand on the hilt of her sword. She'd have to stop him if he tried to destroy the tree.

He slipped off the glasses and handed them to Ladi.

"Oh," Ladi said and slipped on the contraption then stared at the tree leaves.

"See how the cellular membranes are shifting?"

"Yes, is that normal?"

"No, not at all. Look down at your hand."

Ladi noted the scales of her skin and whipped off the glasses. "Uck! That's just gross."

Ebere took the glasses back from her, pulled out his wooden stool and sat down.

"That's our skin, Tero and Joro alike. But it's not shifting the way the cellular membranes are in the leaves of the tree."

"That is interesting." Ladi moved her chair back an inch from him. "How long do you think it will take to do something with it that will help the others?"

"It depends."

"On what?"

"It depends on how many times I have to explain everything to you."

Ladi scoffed and then shut her mouth.

"Why don't you get us some drinks?"

She didn't want to leave him alone with the tree but she also didn't have a good reason to stay. "Fine." She stood up and walked into the other room.

Ladi stopped short when Ebere's mother, Hema, looked up from her needlework with one raised eyebrow.

"Can I help you?"

"Um, Ebere wants something to drink. I was getting it for him."

"Just through there in the kitchen you'll find what you need. I trust you can find your way around one?"

Ebere's little sister Yisha snickered behind her hand.

"My mother wouldn't have it any other way." Ladi ignored the insult and bounced into the kitchen.

Ladi had no idea where to find anything in the kitchen. She opened one cupboard then another. Maybe she should have just asked for help in the first place, now she would look like a pumseed.

"Yahtz!" she swore to herself when she was about ready to give up.

"Yahtz!" Ebere's younger brother repeated loud enough for everyone to hear.

"Please don't use that language around the children." Hema came into the kitchen and urged her young son into the other room. She moved to the cupboard that Ladi had first opened and pulled the mixture. The dishes were in the bottom cabinets and she pulled out a pitcher and five cups.

"So, you're what all the fuss is about these days," Hema said as she added water to the mixture and stirred.

"I'm sorry?" Ladi wasn't sure she understood what the woman meant.

"My son may be shy but he's got people in his life that love him and will protect him. Do you understand?" The stirring spoon hit the table with a slam.

"I'm sure I don't," Ladi said crossing her arms.

"If you mean my son any harm, I advise you to think about choosing another target for your coy games."

Ladi's mouth fell open, and she had to snap it closed again. This woman thought she was the danger. She wondered what the mother of a traitor would say when the truth was out. Before she could speak, Hema put out two cups filled with the mixture before turning her back and pouring two more for her younger children. She had to help the youngest one who continued to swear with delight to his mother's annoyance. Ladi left the kitchen and carried the cups with care to Ebere's room and leaned against the door to close it.

"What took you so long?"

"Nothing," Ladi said. The last thing she wanted to do was tell Ebere how his mother had cornered her. She saw the tree root was where it had been when she'd left. "Do you have a cure yet?"

"Patience," Ebere continued working, then looked up at her behind the glasses that made his eyes grow to the size of saucers. "You could help me."

"I know next to nothing about scientific procedure."

"No problem, you can help me record my findings while I do trial and error."

"Sure." Ladi picked up the communicator and continued where he'd left off. "Can I ask you something?"

"I guess."

"Will you really be able to do this?"

"I'll be honest. I'm not sure, but I owe it to Jak and the others to try."

"Why do you care so much?"

"Why haven't you taken the oath?"

He caught her off guard. He meant the courier's oath. She stuttered and shook her head.

"I don't believe in it anymore," she said.

"Which part?"

"'Loyalty to none,' it would be a lie. I left Tero and stood for the first kingdom beside Rasha because she was the princess incumbent. We battled against enslaved beasts. I can't turn around now and say I'm not loyal to them."

"So, you're loyal to the first kingdom or to Rasha?"

"Well, Rasha, she was my brother's best friend and partner." Ladi was embarrassed. She'd never talked about her feelings toward Rasha. She wanted to be like her. It was the first time she'd told anyone before.

"Right, so not loyal to the kingdom or the land but to the people who live there."

Ladi thought about it a moment. True. She was loyal to the people. Was that the same as saying loyal to none?

"You cannot be loyal to one kingdom over another and still be loyal to all the citizens of Bolaji."

In one sentence, he clarified her dilemma. She could be loyal to all people yet loyal to no kingdom. Was that what Rasha and the others had been trying to tell her?

"I'll never let the boundaries of the individual nations that make up Bolaji keep me from my duty. That's why I care about its citizens so much," Ebere spoke as if he meant it.

If so, why let the beasts be taken and help distribute a disease that was killing everyone? Before she could ask him, he turned to her.

"So, when this is all done, are you going to tell me who gave me up before you kill me for betraying you?"

Ladi took in a couple of steadying breaths before she could speak.

"Should I?"

Ebere shrugged.

"Gorg told us."

Ebere hit his fist against his thigh. "Dirty ranglefort! I knew the moment you arrived something was off," he said, his voice an angry whisper.

Ladi didn't deny it as she stood there, watching him with amazement. Had she believed him capable of it until now?

"From the outside, I know how it looks," Ebere said as he stood up from his stool.

"Tell me, how does it look?" Ladi's hand went to her hilt again.

Ebere raised an eyebrow, then he shrugged again.

"It looks like I'm working with the enemy, supplying them information about how they can access the sacred Courier's Keep systems while helping them figure out a way to distribute a contagious disease that could kill everyone."

Ladi crossed her arms and stared at him, waiting. But he stopped speaking and continued to make observations of the tree and take notes.

"Well, you talk a lot about serving the citizens of Bolaji but you sure don't have a problem killing them."

"Not all of them, no. When Omi approached me, I knew what would happen if I didn't help him."

"What?"

"You mean after he threatened my family?" Ebere shook his head and stood up, taking two steps away from her. "He'd have done exactly what he said he would do. He'd find someone else to make it for him and make sure that me and everyone I loved were the first to get sick."

"So instead you secured your own family and stood by, watching the rest die."

"No, I agreed to help so I would be able to work on a cure. I knew they'd be the first to find one. The day we went our separate ways, I went to work on a cure."

"But you didn't think to warn us?"

"Of course I wanted to warn you, but Omi was clear that none of you could know or his entire plan was at risk."

"What plan?"

"He's after the Chilali throne."

"What? Why?"

"He didn't exactly make me a friend and tell me all of his secrets over a bowl of bazil."

"So, why did you stop me from finding them in the forest after they took my friends?"

"I was protecting you. They were going to kill you rather than risk you running back to Rasha with their location. I was traveling with them that day. When I saw you tracking us, I doubled back around and put you down with a sleep dart. Then when you woke up and saw me, I made up the excuse that I'd been following you."

Ladi felt her hand cramp. She'd been gripping the hilt of her sword but hadn't noticed it until now. Her hand released it and she stretched it out.

"If you spoke to Gorg then you already know I found the cure."

"Yes."

"You're wondering if I'll give it to you." Ebere shook his head. "I'd give you the moons if you asked me."

"Don't start," Ladi said as she took a steading breath.

"Why not? Do you think I could fake my feelings toward you?" He scoffed at her reaction.

"Of course you could. To say otherwise is to lie to my face. I'm not a pumseed."

"You are if you believe I'm capable of that."

He reached out a hand, but she took another step back. She was now against the door.

Ebere held up his two hands in front of him as if to stop her from leaving.

"I'll give you the cure, I'll give you the easiest way to distribute it. But I do want something in return."

Ladi held up a hand to stop him from speaking. Rasha had warned her that in the end he'd plead for something. He'd want his freedom, his family's freedom, his life. None of those things were in her power.

"I can't help you, I don't have the authority," Ladi said.

"You have authority over your own heart. Please, look

there and see if there's any way you could forgive me for my selfish actions."

"I won't promise to forgive you, you're a muke if you think I'd do that."

"No, I know you can't forgive me now. I'm only asking you to consider my actions and my reasons. Think about my feelings for you and in that vein, decide if you could give me any hope."

"Hope?"

"Yes, hope that we might someday be together," Ebere's hands fell to his sides.

Ladi's heart broke into a thousand pieces.

---

## 28

*E*VEN FROM THE OUTSIDE, THE palace had the appearance of death. The bushes and trees had no spring flowers on them that was expected. It was the apparent lack of attention from the grounds keepers. Untended grass and uncut bushes grew in haphazard patterns. Rasha ran up the stairs to the palace with no resistance. Without any guards standing at the gate or the doors, anyone could come and go as they pleased. She ran a hand over the chill on her arms at the sight of the abandoned place. It seemed no one was anywhere near the front door.

"Hello," Rasha called out. No one answered until she reached the second floor.

"Rasha, is that you?" Silae came out of a room and dashed toward her, gripping her hands. "Where were you? We've been worried sick."

"The prince sent me to help find a cure for this plague. I've only just returned."

"Did you bring it with you?"

"No, we're still working on it. Where is everyone?"

"Either sick or keeping to their room." Silae took Rasha's arm and tucked it under her own as they walked. "The prince hasn't left Chiza's side for more than a few minutes at a time. Xeku is tending to his son and most of us are helping each other as we can until we fall sick. I'm one of the few still unaffected."

"Thank the Universal," Rasha said. "Is my aunt around?"

"No, she left on urgent business. I suspect she didn't ask for permission."

"Why do you say that?"

"Bashir seemed angry that she'd gone. It caused a stir among the princes who were upset to learn that some had been allowed to leave while the rest were forced to play nursemaids." Rasha had a feeling about who'd be the ring leader of that group.

"Prince Omi, is he among them?"

"Yes, until today he was among the most vocal." Silae took a seat near the window so she could keep an eye on the doors. She glanced from one to the other, listening. Rasha remained silent while Silae listened for her patients.

"What changed today?"

"I'm not sure, but no one's seen him. When he didn't turn up for his rotation, the princes went to search for him. He may have found a way out of the palace."

Silae stood up and rolled her shoulders. "I better get back."

"An entire floor to yourself?" Rasha asked.

"We go in shifts now that there's so few of us. One of the other girls will be here soon. Most of the servants and royals fell sick days ago. There's only a skeleton staff in the kitchen so if you're hungry you have to go hunting up your own plate. The prince will be glad to see you."

"I hope you aren't too disappointed," Rasha said.

"About not being the future queen of all eleven Bolaji kingdoms? No, I'm fine. To be asked to the party, that was all I wanted." She flashed Rasha a playful grin. "Besides, you need someone to keep your partners busy."

Silae picked up her skirts and turned toward a door. Rasha couldn't fathom how Silae always managed to look amazing even while nursing the sick.

Prince Bashir would be in the room at the end of the hall and on the right. When she reached the door and raised her hand to knock, she heard voices. The prince's voice grew louder as he refused to listen to the person in the room. Rasha placed her knuckles against the hard wood and knocked before she slipped inside the room.

To say Bashir appeared altered and nothing like himself was being kind. His hair hadn't been combed since she'd left. He'd stopped changing his clothes as it appeared his white shirt had two different colored stains. His feet were bare as he paced the rug beside Chiza's bed.

"No, I won't accept that," Bashir was saying. Neither man had heard the knock at the door.

When Bashir caught sight of her, his face lit up and her own heart sank. She still didn't have what he needed, even though it was close.

"Rash, I'm so glad to see you. The cure, did you find it?"

"It's complicated. Can we sit? I'm tired."

"Of course."

She wasn't all that tired, but he was so it didn't matter. Besides that, she didn't want to sit too near the bed and risk seeing the death that seemed so imminent on Chiza's face.

"I believe I may have something." Rasha explained how she'd found Tero-Joro working hard on a cure until they'd all fallen sick. Then she explained about her encounter with the old woman that lead her to the mermen. He interrupted her before she could explain what they'd asked for in return.

"This tree sounds like some kind of magic, did you bring it here with you?"

"No, Ebere, my former partner, is working on a way to disseminate it to the kingdoms. He's a scientist, as it turns out."

"When will it be ready?"

"I'm not sure. We're close, Bashir." She leaned forward in her seat and put a hand on his knee. "Just a little longer."

He ran both hands over his face, then his head dropped as he nodded to the floor.

"There's more. I found the source of the disease. It wasn't an accident."

Bashir's head came up in a flash.

"Who?" The question was almost a growl.

"Omi Gongma."

"Prince Omi?"

"As it turns out, he's not the prince of Buku, he told me so himself. What's strange is that he said he did it out of revenge, only the people he'd wanted to hurt hadn't fallen sick."

"You didn't apprehend him?" Bashir jumped from his seat. "I'll take care of him myself." He started for the door.

"He's not here, your highness, he's long gone. If I hadn't been fighting off another, I would have brought you his head. My people are investigating him now. We'll track him but you needed to know."

"Speak to Xeku, he seemed to be uncannily familiar with the young man. He may know more." Bashir's shoulders slumped again as he turned back toward the bed. He didn't speak for a long moment, just stared at the bed that engulfed Chiza.

"The doctor says she may not last another night."

A stabbing pain cut into her as she caught his resignation. They were so close to a cure. She lifted her amulet to her lips and sent out a prayer to the Universal. It was time to see Jak.

# 29

THE ENTIRE FLOOR HELD THE smell of death. A young maid was dressed as a nurse and she hurried from room to room, caring for the ill in the West wing. Her mouth was covered with a cloth. Rasha's eyes dropped to the floor. She didn't have to ask where Jak was located. She'd never forget seeing him lying down in that bed for as long as she lived. She'd been running around the kingdom looking for a cure because she wanted to avoid this very moment. Xeku held the answer to her question, and she'd have to ask him. The burden weighed on her shoulders and she drew them into her chest before she knocked on the door.

She didn't expect an answer. Instead, she opened the door and slipped inside. The figure in the bed drew her eyes and she couldn't stop staring. Jak's skin had turned sallow and his cheeks had sunken against his teeth. He looked starved, though she was sure his father tended his every need. Rasha moved toward the bed, unable to tear her face away from the sight of him. Jak's eyes were closed and his lids were faint purple, as if someone had battered against his eyes to open them.

His father, Xeku, was resting near this son's hip, his eyes closed, a light snore the only indication that he wasn't affected by the disease. Rasha moved to touch him but instead her hand went to the side of Jak's cheek. He didn't stir when her hand brushed the clammy skin. Cold. He was too cold, she decided, and started to look for something to warm him despite the blanket that cradled his body up to the chin.

"I'm so sorry, I should have told you," she whispered and placed a light kiss on Jak's forehead and mouth. Rasha waited as if he'd open his eyes and give her that mischievous grin. He didn't move. His breath came in shuddering gasps. She was mesmerized, watching his chest rise and fall.

"There's been no change since he closed his eyes."

Hearing Xeku speak into the silence of the room was startling. It was like someone had yelled in her ear and she jumped.

"I thought you were sleeping."

"I nap, now and then, but I haven't slept since the day he became confined to this bed." Xeku took a damp cloth and wiped Jak's forehead. The curls at the front of his hair line stretched then bounced back as they dried.

Rasha was tempted to reach out a hand and touch them, but instead she tightened her fists.

"I need to speak with you, Xeku."

Xeku looked around then smiled at her. "I think we're alone. You may speak."

Rasha dropped her gaze to Jak's face then back to his father.

"I see," Xeku stood up from the chair and gestured for her to follow him as he walked around the room. He stopped at the window. "What's troubling you?"

"The prince is under the impression that you know the true origins of Omi Gonma." Rasha watched Xeku's sharp features went from soft to hard, the distinction so great that Rasha's left hand moved instinctively to rest on Cutter.

His expression changed almost as fast to exasperation.

"I can't get involved in this. I didn't want to be involved in the first place. I've caused enough trouble for your family."

"What does this have to do with my family? I want to know where this Omi came from and what his end goal is before he kills us all."

"What are you saying? He has something to do with this?" His expression hardened again.

"I'm saying he's behind this disease and he's after revenge. I need to know against who so I can get to him before he does even more damage."

"I have the towels— The voice came from a thin girl wearing a white apron over a faded pink dress. She wore her hair in a yellow ball at the base of her neck. The girl's eyes grew wider with recognition as she stared at Rasha.

"I'm sorry, I'm interrupting Xeku, I can come back."

"No, it's okay. This is Jak's—"

No one could seem to finish their sentences. Rasha didn't move from Jak's side. It was as if she were giving him up to allow the young woman to be close to him. Instead, they stood staring at each other without a word.

"Well, I guess introductions are in order," Xeku said as he stood up. "Rasha this is,"

"Duna," Rasha said. The word threatened to choke her. What was she doing here?

"Yes, and this is,"

"Princess Rasha Jenchat Indari. Yes, I'm aware." Duna put the towels down and gave Rasha a light curtsy. "You're probably wondering what I'm doing here, your highness."

Rasha didn't know why her official title should be so bothersome but she hated the sound of it more now than she ever had. Instead of acknowledging the curtsy, she turned away from her and looked down at Jak. She put a light hand on his shoulder, a caress and a nudge. The nerve of him to leave her here to meet his ex on her own. This wasn't right at all.

The room threatened to suffocate her. The dreams from before came rushing back to her as she stared at Duna's narrow frame and flat belly. She wasn't pregnant, but there was something in her expression that made Rasha want to guard her neck.

"I have to go. Excuse me," Rasha said in one breath.

"Go to your aunt," Xeku said with a heavy sigh. "She'll answer your questions. I can't."

Rasha nodded to both Xeku and Duna before rushing out of the room. She ran down the stairs and didn't stop until she was breathing the fresh clean air outside.

One of the little Temis was there, curled up by the door. He yawned before wrapping himself around her ankles. Then he yawned again. She was tired too. Her aunt knew something and she needed to find out what it was she was holding back.

If Lu were here, he'd know just what to say. The communicator in her pocket beeped twice, and she pulled out the transparent square and saw an image of Ladi's face.

"I've got the cure, and we're here but there's a problem," Ladi said.

"What happened?"

"He knows."

## 30

RASHA TURNED OFF HER COMMUNICATOR in time to hear a cry inside the palace. She ran, praying to the Universal it wasn't Duna. She found one of the servants, a young girl, on her knees with her hands over her face. Silae had her arms wrapped around her.

"It's one of the princes, he's dead. Chiza too, I believe," Silae said in a whisper over the girl's sobs. Tears streaming down her own face, she said, "Jak doesn't have much time left. Go to him."

"Ladi, she's here with the cure, we've got to get it to everyone, find her," Rasha said, already in motion.

Rasha's heart was in her throat as she ran up the west wing stairs two at a time. Where was Ladi? She said they were already here. She'd never run so hard or so fast in her life and was out of breath when she burst into Jak's room. It took her a moment to take in the situation. Duna held a hand over her mouth. She'd been the one to scream, Zele had startled her. Zele sat outside the window on the ledge looking as innocent as ever, and Ebere and Ladi were already in the room. She'd assumed Zele had curled up in the woods. Instead, the dragon had gone back for Ladi.

Ladi held a small vial of gold liquid in her hand and she placed two drops on Jak's tongue.

It took less than a minute for Jak's eyes to flutter open and focus on the room around him. Xeku laughed and hugged his son to his chest.

"You're alive. You're alive."

Duna threw herself across Jak's torso before Rasha could take two steps forward. She was so relieved and distracted that she didn't feel the tears streaming down her face until he whispered her name.

"Rasha, I need–," his voice was scratchy and barely audible, but something inside of her lifted at the sound of her name on his dry lips.

"I'm here," she said. Duna stepped back, making room for her, and she sat on the edge of the bed and put her forehead to his.

He lifted a hand to grab her face, and she clasped it in her own. His eyes focused on her.

"What, did you think I was going to let you get out of the New Choosing?" She laughed. "You've got too many hearts left to break."

Jak didn't smile or joke. Rasha didn't realize until now how much she missed seeing his confident smile. His eyes fluttered closed, his skin returning to its normal cream.

She remembered Ladi and Ebere then. Ebere eyed her like he would a rabid snake. He'd betrayed them all and yet he was here helping distribute the cure. She wanted to know why but there wasn't any time.

"We've got to distribute this to everyone with the disease. We've got lots more," Ladi said, making her way to the door. "Ebere's with me."

Rasha wasn't sure what that meant. Had Ladi already gotten the answer to this riddle? She could only hope as it was their only chance now.

Rasha nodded. "The princess, Chiza. She's gone. Go and help the others."

Ladi nodded and Ebere was right behind her with what looked like a bag filled with more vials. Rasha couldn't help but wonder how many would be killed in Omi's little scheme. She still didn't understand his end game, but since he'd disappeared she wouldn't be able to find him tonight. They needed to focus on distributing the cure. Now that Jak was safe, she felt she should go and pay her respects to Chiza. She'd been a good friend and would have made Prince Bashir so happy as his bride.

Rasha remembered how different they'd both been when Chiza came out of that crate. It seemed like a lifetime ago. She never imagined the young princess with anyone other than her best friend Lu. When he died protecting her, Chiza had to make her peace just like they all had. Would the Universal reunite them after death the way they couldn't be in life? Rasha didn't have that answer, nor did anyone. She dragged herself to the east wing of the palace and up the stairs to where Chiza lay across the hall from her own temporary room at the palace. It was quiet here, no doubt in respect of the prince.

The door to Chiza's room was ajar and Rasha pushed against it instead of knocking. Inside was the most astonishing thing she'd seen in her life. The prince sat on the bed. He and Chiza were locked in an embrace. He was kissing her face and murmuring to her.

"I love you, don't ever leave me again," he said into her soft brown hair.

Chiza's soft laugh came out in a rasp as she clung to him.

Before Rasha could ask what was going on, Ladi appeared behind her. She was out of breath and she waved Rasha out of the room and into the corridor.

"What's going on? They said she was dead," Rasha said in a whisper.

"She was, when I got here he was crying over her cold body. But after what you said about The Niramaya Tree, I thought it might be worth a try." Ladi took another breath. "I put a couple of drops on her tongue as I'd done the others. Her color came back and her heart started to beat again."

"We have to get this to the everyone else," Rasha said starting to pull Ladi along. But Ladi was shaking her head.

"It's already done, I contacted the Wola. We gave a vial to each and sent them across the eleven kingdoms."

"The beasts?" Rasha asked.

"They're unaffected by the disease. However, there are

still some of them missing. I believe that Omi was planning something, but Ebere and I will reach the coast before dawn and track down the rest."

"You're right. We need to find them before it's too late," Rasha said. "You and Ebere did it. Thank you." Rasha reached out, surprising herself and Ladi, and gave the younger girl a fierce hug. "So, I suspect there's a story I'm going to want to hear eventually."

"Yes, you should know he's not innocent. He'll need to answer for his crimes, but he's also not the evil calculating muke we thought he was. I'll give you the details later. By the way, thanks for sending Zele. She was amazing and fast."

"I didn't send her."

Rasha and Ladi stared at each other for a moment, wondering how Zele knew. Then they both shrugged.

"There's too much to do. I better go," Ladi said, turning to head down the corridor.

Rasha was shocked and comforted to see Ladi being so mature. She was only fifteen but she was behaving so much like her older brother it was amazing.

"Be careful," Rasha called after her.

Rasha put her hand around her amulet and said a prayer of thanks for the lives of her friends.

## 31

THE PALACE OF ISHOLA WAS buzzing with activity by the time Ladi and Ebere left. There was still one more mission left. They had to reach the coast in order to find the shipment of beasts being transported and track it back to where their friends were being held prisoner.

Ladi was happy to see that their people were still in the trees. She'd dispatched the Wola to watch the coast for the next ship transporting beasts. They'd been on the perimeter, keeping watch for some time. When they arrived, the beach was a flurry of men carrying crates and preparing the ship for its departure. Tarrick listened to the report.

"Has there been any change?" he asked.

"No, sir, they've not had any communications out and after the second ship arrived, it was also loaded up. Both have been waiting for something."

Ladi and Ebere had been placed in the treetops near

Tarrick. It wasn't long before the ships were casting off, filled with more than a dozen kidnapped beasts each. They included at least three dragons, four bears and six wolves, according to the Wola who reported to Tarrick.

They watched the large ships cast off at last. Not one person was left on the beach. It took less than an hour for them to gain some distance in the water. Ladi felt her body tense as the ships were getting close to the edge of her field of vision. Ebere reached out a hand and touched her arm, keeping his eyes on Tarrick. He had excellent hearing, but his sight was less than her own. But he trusted Tarrick and he was indicating with a look that she should too. So, when she could barely see the ships, she looked to Tarrick.

"It's time, get ready to take to the sky," Tarrick said in a low voice. The message was carried to the rest by way of his signal. His long white wings extended away from his body. He didn't move from the tree top until the ships were almost out of sight on the edge of the horizon.

Tarrick and another lifted Ebere and Ladi from the tree tops and carried them across the water. With the ships just barely in view on the horizon, Tarrick led the way while the other Wola stayed well behind him. After a few hours, they had travelled so far over the crystal blue water that they needed to be passed off to other Wola in order to avoid flight fatigue. The air here had grown slightly cooler and the clouds above them thick. It was clear that it was harder to see the ships ahead and Tarrick increased his speed in order to keep the ships in sight.

The ships came back into Ladi's view and she knew they'd reached their destination. When the Wola caught up to them, they had to circle around in order to avoid being seen from the ground. Most collapsed in the trees on either side of the coast where the large ships were docked.

While the Wola were catching their breath, Ebere and Ladi made their way down the trees to the ground. On foot, they moved to where the sailors were unloading the drugged animals. The large crates on wheels were rolled off of the ship and onto a large dock that extended out to meet them. Each of the containers had a large metal hook on either side to link them. The first cages were the largest ones holding the dragons. They were linked, followed by the large bears, then the wolves and smaller animals came last.

The train of containers were pulled until the last motorized utility vehicle attached its front to the end. It pushed from the rear while the lead vehicle pulled, and they were soon disappearing into the woods while the ships remained empty.

"We need to follow them, now," Ladi said.

Ebere followed her as she dashed through the trees after them. Tarrick appeared out of nowhere and joined them in the pursuit. Ladi didn't look back. She could hear the distinct rustle of the leaves that she'd associated with the Wola coming out of the tops of the trees. Ladi could smell the encampment before she reached it. It was iden-

tical to the one she'd infiltrated near Adalu more than a
rotation ago now.

She held up an open hand to slow down the others.
Tarrick must have waved them out to spread out because
before long, several Wola were stretched along to the right
and left of where Ladi crept toward the encampment.
They watched her and when she stopped, they stopped.
Ladi followed her nose and the stench of the place told her
all she needed to know about the camp.

Ebere put a hand on her shoulder.

"There's an arena here," he said.

"What?" Ladi tilted her own head but couldn't make
out the sounds of cheering that she usually heard this close
to an arena.

"I can hear the beasts fighting." Ebere's head was tilted
slightly to the right.

"We need to stop the fighting and round up the
captors. There will be more there than there were guarding
the cages," Ladi said.

Tarrick nodded understanding. "I'll see to the arena
with my people. Can you handle the guards?"

Ladi looked at Ebere, who nodded, his lips set in a thin
determined line. Even after everything he'd done, she still
trusted him. He'd explained his reasons and they were sound,
though misguided. Looking back over the last few months,
hadn't she done the same thing? He'd asked her that exact
question back at his mother's home. She had to agree that, to a
point, she was also willing to save her friends ahead of herself.

He'd taken it a step further by allowing others to pay the ultimate price, however, that wasn't something she could ignore. It was like a weighted ball that rolled around in her stomach whenever she thought of it. Ladi pushed it down now and moved to the left where she could smell the stagnant cages.

Ladi led Ebere and a dozen Wola through the woods toward the larger enclosure that she knew existed. She found it but it was larger than she'd expected, and she noted more guards than there had been before. They were a mix of bird-men and bull-men. She watched more than a dozen guards just milling about in the area. Crouched behind a large boulder, she watched them walking around until a loud horn sounded and the guards started running toward the arena. She let them go and when it was clear, they ran from the trees to the enclosure. Inside, a couple of guards put up some resistance.

Ladi and Ebere moved in with swords swinging and dropped them with several strokes. The Wola charged the enclosure and, using their own weapons, they broke open every single cage they found. Ladi ran toward the back of the arena. She knew that was where they kept the feistier and high-spirited animals. She was shocked to see Browl in one of the cages.

"Get me out of here," he growled at the sight of her.

Ladi swung her sword hard and with one hit, the lock broke and Browl charged out.

"My cubs," he growled.

"Browl!"

It was his mate calling from another cage placed above him.

"I've got her, you get them," Ladi said as she climbed up to her enclosure.

She found swinging her sword with one hand while holding on to the side of a cage far more difficult.

"I got it," Ebere said, coming up from behind her. As she dropped to the ground, he leapt and swung, knocking the lock off.

Grella, now freed, ran after her mate.

"We should follow them," she said to Ebere.

"Go, I'm right behind you," he said.

"We're coming too," Merrick said, moving forward with Erima.

Ladi stopped mid-turn and threw her arms around them.

"I'm so glad you're okay," Ladi cried. She didn't realize how much guilt she was carrying until she saw them both standing in front of her. They were battered and bruised, but both standing. That's when she noticed their wings. Each of them had a broken wing.

"Your wings are damaged."

"They'll heal," Merrick said, putting a hand on her shoulder.

"We knew you'd come," Erima said, putting her hand on Ladi's other shoulder.

"Come, we should get to the young," Ebere said, pulling Ladi back.

Ladi didn't know she'd been crying until he ran a light

hand over her cheeks and she felt the wetness pass to his fingers. She pulled back her shoulders and nodded. Then the four of them ran out of the larger enclosure, looking for the smaller one.

"I don't know which way they went."

Ebere tilted his head to listen.

"They're not far." He started running and Ladi had to struggle to keep up.

They arrived in time to see Browl and Grella fighting off six bull-men guards while the smaller enclosure holding their young had roared to life. The cubs inside were growling, howling and making every perceivable sound of discomfort.

Without a word, Erima and Merrick turned and maneuvered themselves behind the guards, pushing them forward into Ladi and Ebere's waiting swords. They rushed inside the enclosure to free the young.

Ladi and Ebere stood back to back, fighting off the bull-men guards until they fell to the ground. Grella and Browl finished off their aggressors and soon there was no resistance. The children were still inside, crying, and Ladi and Ebere rushed inside ahead of the wolves and discovered why the young weren't free.

"One more step and I slice her throat." Erima was held from behind by a bird-man, and his long knife was tight against her throat. His colorful wings were pulled tight against his body as he stood his ground in front of the cages. Merrick was already standing with his palms out.

"I promised to let you go. Please, you don't have to do this."

Merrick's eyes had softened and he took an almost imperceivable step forward. Ladi wanted to give him a chance to get close.

"He's right. We won't hurt you if you let her and the young free." Ladi lifted her hands palms up.

Grella growled behind her and when the bird-man's eyes flew nervously to her, Ladi took a side step to block the angry mother's face.

"There's only one way out of here and I'm not letting anyone go as long as I see you crowding the door. Get back!" The bird-man's knife swung out in the direction of Browl who'd crept up on his left. When he did so, it gave Merrick the space to reach for Erima and get her out of harm's way.

"I said get back." The bird-man reached into the nearest cage and grabbed the ruff of a wolf cub, pulling his small face forward and placing the knife close to his snout. The others backed away, crying. The captured one growled and snapped.

"Not my baby!" Grella howled.

"Everybody back," the bird-man said, seeing he had the upper hand.

"Trust us, go outside, give him some space," Ladi said, looking at Browl.

"Please," Grella howled and her babies howled with her.

Browl used his teeth to tug on her ear as they both

685

walked slowly out of the small enclosure. It gave the bird-man some relief to see the parents backing up. He didn't understand that the entire enclosure was surrounded with parents. Ladi wouldn't be the one to enlighten him, but she did have an idea for how to get him away from the children. Ladi stepped forward.

"Let the young cub go, you'll never be able to get out of here with him. Take me," she said, walking confidently forward.

"Ladi, no," Ebere said reaching for her vest but she stepped into the range of the bird-man with her hands up.

He dropped the cub and turned her around, putting the knife to her throat.

"Let's go," she said, walking into the knife and pulling the bird-man forward.

Soon, the others were backing up and they were stepping into the light.

"Free the babies," Ladi said without looking at Ebere and the others.

She kept putting one foot in front of the other. When the bird-man's knife slipped she winced at the pain but kept him moving forward and away from the young.

It was then, stepping out of the enclosure and surrounded by angry parents, that he realized his mistake. He gripped the back of Ladi's vest hard scratching her back. But she had scars there and it didn't hurt as much as it would have before. He hadn't noticed that she'd pulled a short sword from her hip. She kept it loose on her belt and it came away with a slight click that the bird-man didn't hear.

Ladi pretended to stumble just enough to twirl her sword low. She used her body to throw the bird-man off balance. Then, with a practiced move, she swung the sword up between his arm holding the knife and her face. The short sword nicked his feathered arm and before he could recover, she pulled her long sword and it came down hard across his chest. He fell to the ground and was devoured by beasts before she could turn around.

The cubs now free and the parents reuniting with them, Ebere came out of the enclosure and to her side. He lifted her chin and winced at the sight of the small cuts she felt on her neck.

"That was a very risky and foolish thing you did back there," he said.

"I did what I had to do," Ladi said. "I wouldn't let that cub die when I knew I could save him."

Ladi looked up to the sky, wondering how things had gone in the arena. The sight of Wola circling the sky was a comfort. That meant they'd secured the area. They didn't have to wait long before Tarrick appeared.

"The arena is shut down. The animals are safe," he said.

Ladi's shoulders slumped with fatigue. "The cubs and young are also free and reunited with their families." She nodded in the direction of the smaller caged enclosure.

"I see," Tarrick said with a smile.

Grella approached, her head hung low and one cub on her back.

"Thank you," she said, bowing her head low to Ladi.

Ladi reached out and stroked the top of her head and the head of her cub. He'd been the one the bird-man grabbed that she replaced.

"I would do it again, no matter what," Ladi said.

Grella lifted her head and nodded as she returned to her family. Browl was already wrestling around with his other cubs.

"How do we get them home?" she asked out loud.

"The ships?" Ebere asked.

Ladi walked over to Browl, who tore his cubs away long enough to talk to her.

"We can prepare the ships but it will take some time before you all can return to the other side of the water. Will you be all right here until then?"

"We're not leaving," Browl said. "My family and many of the others have decided that we like this land and we'll stay here."

"Oh," Ladi said, not bothering to hide her surprise.

"It's more comfortable here and we'll have plenty to hunt and eat," a nod toward the remains of the feathers on the ground made his point.

"I see," Ladi nodded. "I'll miss you, old friend."

"I am with family and friends here too. You are welcome to return."

"Thank you," Ladi nodded to him and he dashed off with his family into the woods.

As it turned out, none of the beasts cared to return. The dragons were able to roam as they wished and the Wola were returned to their people. With their broken wings, they were carried across the blue expanse along with Ladi and Ebere.

When they reached the other side again, the Wola needed time to recover. Ladi and Ebere waited for the others.

"I appreciate all of your help in this. I can honestly say I couldn't have done it without you," Ladi said to Ebere, not quite meeting his eye.

"I was happy to give it and I'm glad you trusted me enough to allow me to try to redeem myself a little. I made a huge mistake and I'll have to live with it for the rest of my life."

"Yes, you will," Ladi reached for him and he threw his arms around her.

Ladi pressed her face to his chest, the ache in her stomach spreading to her chest and throat. She could barely speak. One look in his eyes and she knew she was in love with him.

Ebere didn't hesitate. She'd been expecting the passionate desperation like before. Instead, he leaned down and kissed her on the mouth, a soft and gentle exploration. Ladi was on the tip of her toes and letting him pull her so close until nothing could pass between them. His kiss warmed her aching belly and made her dizzy. When Ebere pulled back, she gripped him by the shoulders, unwilling and unable to let go.

"I'm sorry," she said.

Ebere looked down at her his eyebrows drawn together in confusion. When Ladi stepped back he saw two Wola had taken up position behind him. His shoulders fell and the look of betrayal on his face threatened to split her in two.

"You didn't trust me to turn myself in," he said.

Ladi shook her head. "I didn't trust myself. So, I made sure to have Tarrick take care of it for me. The timing and execution of it was his."

The Wola stepped forward, each taking an arm.

"Where will they take me?"

"The palace. The prince and the council will hear your side of the story and make their decision," Ladi said. Her voice felt stilted and artificial.

Ebere nodded and as they pulled him away, he called her name. That stopped them and her, giving him time to say one thing more.

"Wait, I want to be clear. I love you, more than anything, and I probably always will."

Ladi nodded once and before the tears threatened to choke her, she turned her back to him. She waited for the sound of their flapping wings to dissipate before she fell to her knees and cried.

## 32

THE PALACE BUZZED WITH ACTIVITY
the night of the ball. Servants covered the
entire building with imported flowers and showered the
guests with food and drink. Now the kingdom had come
out on the other side of the disease, it was time to get on
with things. The New Choosing would be announced after
the final ball. The royals, potentials, and their families
were invited back to the palace to celebrate. They'd lost
two of the potential ladies and one prince to the disease
that swept the eleven kingdoms, but even their families
were invited.

Prince Bashir wanted this ball to bring people's attention away from the disease and its mysterious cure. When
Rasha explained to him what would be involved in
accepting the cure, he'd agreed without contest. When he
learned about the origins of the mermaid necklace as a

boy, he always imagined he'd wear it as a man just like his father had. But he didn't hesitate to heal the breach between the kingdoms by returning the shell necklace to the Majiwa. The leather band that belonged to the first prince was also returned to Karmir. He insisted that the items remain in their respective kingdoms side by side, as had the couple themselves. The Majiwa leader was so pleased that he attended the ball. It was his first time on land for such an occasion.

Every royal in the kingdom joined in the festivities. The parents of the lost princesses were able to appreciate the tribute that Prince Bashir had done for them in the east wing. Many of the mothers gasped with grief and joy at seeing their precious daughters memorialized on the walls of the palace forever, many of the families still grieving their losses.

Prince Bashir and Princess Chiza maintained their facade of indifference during the festivities. The Choosing would be announced at the end. They didn't want to spoil it by giving away the surprise, although a blind man could have seen that the two of them were in love. They couldn't keep their eyes off of each other the entire night and whenever there was a moment he could touch her without being obvious, he did. Rasha caught the subtle way he brushed her neck with his fingertips to adjust her necklace or the way they stood near each other with the backs of their hands touching.

"Makes you sick watching them, doesn't it?" Jak said into her ear. He handed her a glass of fermented juice.

It was so good to have him at her side again. She'd missed his quick banter.

"Don't be jealous," she said, at the same time throwing a smile and nod to a young man who walked by and bowed in their direction.

"I'm not jealous. I just don't believe everyone in the room is fooled by the two of them. He's already chosen her, what's with the pretense?"

"You've clearly never been to one of these before." Rasha angled her body toward him, but she kept her eyes on the room. "Look around, don't you understand what this party's really about? It's an introduction to royal society. All of these young people are the future royals and the old royals are strutting around reminding each other of who's got the most jewels or power or both."

"I don't see anyone here except you," Jak whispered. He was so close to her ear, the hairs on her neck stood up.

"Blushing, I understand. He must have said something scandalous." Silae came up and put her arm through Rasha's.

"Not really, I was just complementing the princess on her amazing look this evening."

"You're welcome, if it had been up to her she'd be wearing her courier's rags."

"Well then, thank you very much, she looks stunning."

"I'm still here," Rasha said with as much annoyance as she could muster.

"Yes, and what are you doing here when you should

both be out there dancing?" Silae clucked her tongue and shook her head.

"She doesn't like dancing." Jak shrugged and then draped an arm around Rasha's shoulders. She shrugged him off and removed her arm from Silae.

"Pity, it's really fun," Silae moved to stand between Rasha and Jak and put her arm through his.

"I'm standing right here," Rasha said, then crossed her arms.

"Shall we?" Jak asked, pulling Silae out to the dance floor.

A second later, Rasha closed her shocked mouth. She shouldn't be surprised, they were both notorious flirts.

Chiza stood across the room and watched the two go out onto the dance floor before she crossed the room to talk to Rasha.

"I wouldn't let that gorgeous beauty dance with my boyfriend if I were you."

"He's not my boyfriend. Besides, what do you know? You and the prince have already made your claims on each other and yet here you stand, watching him dance with every other potential in the room."

"They're not really potentials when they don't have a chance," Chiza said as she smirked into her drink.

"You're a wicked thing now aren't you?" Rasha was happy to see Chiza up and around. She'd been confined to her room longer than any of the others and had only just started walking around on her own.

"I'm sorry, you're right. I shouldn't be. There was a moment there where—,"

"Don't finish that thought." Rasha turned to her friend and grabbed her shoulders. "You made it and he loves you and that's all that matters."

Chiza smiled and when Rasha let go of her, she leaned her head on Rasha's shoulder. "When did you become such a romantic?"

"Is it romantic to state the truth? I didn't know." Rasha spotted someone on the edge of the room who didn't belong, his pointy ears and large paws blending into the background. "Excuse me, I have to go take care of something. I'll be back."

"Dance with him, make sure you're the last and he'll forget every other girl he danced with tonight." Chiza gave Rasha a light push on her back.

The little cub was fighting with the curtain by the time she reached him. He growled at it and refused to let it out of his teeth until Rasha lifted him to her face.

"You don't belong here, little fellow. I promise we'll find you a good home too, but this party is a little too big for you." He stared at her in that way that made her think he understood, then his little pink tongue flew out of his mouth and licked her nose. "Uck!" She held him out at arms' length to the nearest servant.

"Sorry, your highness, he got away from me." The young maid was at her elbow, taking the little beastie into her hands. "It won't happen again."

"It's fine, they're mischievous at this age," Rasha said.

The young maid tucked him into her arm and dashed out of the room, away from the guests. He'd already caused a bit of a stir as the royals didn't like barn animals of any kind sharing the night with them.

---

$\mathcal{T}$HE NIGHT ENDED WITH A final celebration of love and romance. The royals were invited up to speak in front of the crowd about their most romantic notions and experiences. Soon, it was a competition to see who was the most romantic. Even her own parents were obnoxiously ready to share their true love story. The young all stood around looking embarrassed for themselves and their families.

By the end of the night, everyone was drinking to their success in marriage and romance. A large bouquet of white flowers was brought into the room. Attached to each flower was a name card and on the card was a potential. Each one of them pulled out their flowers in turn. The only person who didn't have a flower was Chiza. She turned around, looking surprised as Bashir crossed to the center of the room and bent down on one knee. He held up a necklace made in the image of The Eye of the Universal. The rainbow swirls of color surrounded by silver eyelids hung from a silver chain.

"I choose you and if you choose me, we'll love each other for eternity."

Chiza's tears of happiness spilled over onto her cheeks as she accepted his offered gift. He draped the chain around her thin brown neck. Then he turned her toward him and captured her mouth with his own in a deep and luxurious kiss. All the royals cheered. Although, Rasha noted a lackluster applause from Chiza's father. He'd be giving up more than his share of gems to make their marriage happen. Even though society in general hadn't forgiven him for trying to play two sides of the Choosing, he'd been welcomed to the palace for this special event.

Jak reached over from beside her and grabbed her hand, lifting it to his own lips. While everyone watched the happy royals, he pulled Rasha out onto a nearby balcony. They slipped through the sheer curtains and the cool air outside greeted them.

"It's so hot in there," Rasha said, waving a hand in front of her face.

"Yeah," Jak said as he turned to look out over the gardens. The summer air held the scent of the flowers that filled the room behind them. He still held her hand and even when she tugged, he didn't let go.

"We should congratulate them," Rasha said, speaking of Bashir and Chiza. Her own heart raced as she waited for Jak to speak.

He took in several long breaths but still didn't say anything. Rasha didn't know what he had in mind but couldn't shake the feeling he was about to ask her something.

"What are your plans after you leave here?"

This wasn't the question she was expecting. He'd said 'your plans' as if he didn't include himself in them. She imagined it then if she had to choose her next move what would she do. She'd been a courier for three rotations despite the fact that she hadn't been commissioned to deliver anything in the last rotation she retained her license. There were several options open to her, and she wanted to be honest with Jak about her ideas. Maybe he'd even want to go with her. What worried her was if he didn't want to go, would she still go through with it?

"I'm a courier. But I don't want to stay on Bolaji forever. I may extend my territory to off-worlds."

Jak didn't seem surprised as he nodded.

"There are so many places to see and I'd like to visit other planets in our system before I'm too old and too comfortable."

Jak didn't say anything for a long time, as if he were considering it.

"What about Zele? Will you bring her with you?"

"I hadn't considered it. I don't think a courier gets a space vessel big enough to carry a dragon."

"Something to consider, I guess." Jak spoke as if he had no feelings about it one way or the other. What was he getting at?

"I'm not leaving them until all those remotes are destroyed and the animals are protected."

"I've been considering that dilemma. If the beasts have their own hunting grounds in the North, then that will spare the rest of the kingdoms. It also gives them the freedom to settle without fear of humanoids trying to take control of them."

"Their own kingdom of Adalu, land of the beasts?" Rasha wondered what the council would say to that idea. "The council might take issue with it. There's still life outside of the palace, they might not take to sharing Adalu with the beasts."

"Whether they like it or not, Bolaji is their home. They deserve a piece of it." Jak's jaw was set in a firm line.

Good, they needed another champion. Ladi had done all she could, but it was time for others to step in and help the poor animals.

"What are your plans after all this?" Rasha pulled her hand away and gestured to the palace.

"I don't know yet," Jak said.

He hadn't mentioned her in his plans. She hadn't mentioned him either. Was that the point he was making? The music inside got louder and people were dancing all around the room. Her parents must have retired for the night as they were no longer drinking and eating. They were usually the last to leave a party, but perhaps with the anxieties of the day they were just tired. Rasha caught sight of Chiza and Bashir laughing and dancing in the center of the guests. Could she ever be that happy? She looked at Jak's outstretched hand, asking her to dance, and thought, perhaps, someday.

## 34

*I*T WAS EARLY MORNING BY the time the festivities died down. Rasha climbed the stairs to her room alone. She'd left Jak on the dance floor. There was nothing worse than a long goodbye. She'd make time to see him later. Ladi was notably absent, but after dealing with Ebere and the beasts, she didn't blame her for wanting to spend time with her own family. Ebere was tucked safely in a cell for the moment while the council met to decide his fate. He'd done some good but until they found Omi, he was their only guilty party. Ebere would have to answer for what they'd done.

Rasha was passing her parent's door on her way to her own room when she heard voices inside raised in anger. Rasha caught the tail end of their conversation.

"You can't do this. You've kept it from them long enough." Aunt Sochi was in her parents' room and arguing with her father.

Rasha heard him pick up something and throw it against the opposite wall where it shattered with a crash.

"You don't scare me," she said.

"Please, both of you stop. Don't push him," her mother said.

Whatever was going on, it didn't concern her, but it seemed urgent. She didn't need the sword at her back to propel her forward, but she didn't get the chance to say so.

"Why don't we all go in and see what the fuss is about?" Omi spoke from behind her. He held the sword up to her neck when she turned to see who'd snuck up on her.

The three adults stopped and turned when they entered. Her aunt and father were nose to nose with her mother holding one shoulder of each. Sochi was the first to move. She lifted her hands as her eyes flew from his hand to the knife he held at Rasha's back. Rasha shook her head when she saw her aunt's hand move to her waist.

"I wouldn't do that if I were you," Omi said as he pressed the knife deeper into Rasha's side.

Rasha let out an uncontrolled wince but kept her hands up.

"Son, what do you want?" Her father said, raising his own hands and stepping between the young man and his wife.

"Interesting choice of words, father."

Rasha watched her father's eyes widen in disbelief then squint to scrutinize Omi.

"Father?" Rasha asked as she watched her father's face deepen in color.

"That's right, sister, you and I are blood related."

"No," Rasha's mother said stepping from behind the king. "It can't be." Her eyes flew to Sochi's. "Is it him?"

Sochi shook her head. Rasha had difficulty following the conversation. She tried to piece together what Omi had said in the woods with what was happening now and it just didn't make sense.

"Don't move, Aunt Sochi. I'll strike her down right in front of you all, don't think I won't," Omi said between clenched teeth. His jabs were sharp as he became more agitated. "She's taken everything from me."

"Who told you?" Rasha's father asked.

"I discovered the truth a few rotations ago when I learned I wasn't the legitimate child of my parents. I was raised in Buku and played with the prince, but I never dreamed I was one. Then I learned the truth."

Rasha's mother shook her head.

"Sorry to disappoint you, mother, but I'm here to take what belongs to me."

"You poisoned half the world to get to this throne?" Rasha said angrily. "You'd jeopardize our relations with the beasts and every species off-world to satisfy your revenge?."

"Not revenge, birthright."

"You're wrong," the king said.

"You're sick," Rasha said at the same time.

"Tell him, tell him the truth," Rasha's mother said,

looking from Sochi to the king. "He deserves to know. They both do."

"If I tell him, then everything will come unraveled. I can't throw away all we've worked for."

Omi's grip on her faltered for the first time and she stepped to his left, pushing him forward while holding the hand with the knife. He struggled, but she took him down quickly, placing her foot on the back of his neck and stretching his arm back until he dropped the knife. Before he flinched to grab it again, Sochi had her sword out and pointed at his nose.

"Don't you dare move," Sochi said, "I'd hate to hurt my only son."

Rasha lifted her foot off of Omi's back and dropped his arm. She stared at her aunt then back at Omi.

"Your son?" Rasha asked. She thought she knew everything about her aunt.

It felt like a betrayal to find out she had a child. Then Rasha's gaze fell on her father. He paced back and forth, he mumbled something to himself before running a hand over his face.

"Let him up," he said to Sochi. She complied but kept the sword on him.

Rasha crossed to her left and out of reach, even though his knife remained safe in her hand. Still struggling with her own feelings, she tried to listen as the three adults in the room took a breath. Her mother sat down and fanned herself as if she'd lose consciousness. Her father stopped pacing. He put a hand on Omi's shoulder and one on Sochi's sword, lowering it to the floor.

"You've been mislead. I'm not your father. You think you've been robbed of the throne, well so do I." The king glanced at his wife before continuing. "We were unable to produce an heir. Left with few options, we did what we had to keep the royal family line intact. My sister's indiscretion gave us an opportunity that we wouldn't otherwise have been able to use."

Rasha looked at her aunt's face and saw she'd flushed a deeper purple.

"Xeku?" Rasha asked.

"No," Sochi shook her head. "There was another, he's long dead now. Our love was a passionate affair that our families wouldn't permit, each wanting to keep their royal lines as pure as possible," she scoffed. "Now look at the mess we made."

Rasha was shaking her head. "But technically he is royal."

"Of course he is, but his father's family refused to allow us to marry. I became pregnant and before I was able to tell him, his family sent him to fight in a battle between the Buku and the Vol. He died there, and I never saw him again. All that I had left were my babies." Sochi glared at the king and Rasha realized what she'd just heard.

"Babies?"

Sochi nodded. "Yes, twins. One girl and one boy. One Chilali purple and one white of the Buku." Her eyes filled as she looked between Rasha and Omi.

Then Rasha looked at Omi, shaking her head.

"No," she said. Her mother was fanning herself and the tears were flowing down her face. "You mean, you're my mother?" Rasha wanted to laugh and cry at the same time. Instead, a sound like choking escaped her throat.

Sochi nodded. "And Omi is your twin brother. Your father thought it best that I not raise either of you as my own. It ensured a pure purple child would inherit the throne and neither of you would ever learn the truth."

Rasha's rage was replaced with hurt as her aunt—no, her mother spoke. She'd never understood why she didn't take after either of her parents. It explained a lot. Sochi's undying devotion to her while her parents kept her at arms' length all while pushing the throne on her. Omi, hadn't blinked in a minute as he looked from Sochi to the king, shaking his head. All of that revenge and it got him nothing in the end.

"So you see, neither of you has a true claim on the throne for as long as I'm alive."

"Liar!" Omi crossed the room in two strides and stood nose to nose with the king. "If you die, the throne falls to the nearest male. I'm your sister's son. I have as much a right to the throne as her." He pointed at Rasha.

Rasha's shoulders fell. Now she understood.

"They didn't want you because you're not purple. You? Represent Chilali and not be the precious purple? No, that would be too much." Rasha let out an incredulous laugh. "Ironic, isn't it, your highness?" She spat out the title sour on her tongue. "I never wanted the throne, and he always did." Rasha threw Omi's knife down on the floor and it clanked until it hit the rug near a chair behind her.

"What's my brother's name?" she asked. Omi seemed surprised, as if he hadn't even thought to ask the question.

"You are and have always been Rasha. I insisted on it. Your brother's name is Karil."

Rasha repeated the name to herself and Karil did the same.

He'd tried to kill them all for the Chilali throne. Her brother had tried to kidnap Ladi and Zele. How could the two of them share blood, let alone a mother, and be so different?

Now they all stood in the room together, regarding each other as if for the first time. In a way, Rasha realized it was the first time they were meeting each other, knowing who each and every person really was to her.

Karil seemed to be doing the same. He looked down at his hands and then clenched them into fists.

"I'm nothing," Karil said, looking down at the floor.

Sochi moved to stand by him. She started to reach for him, but at his angry glare, she dropped her hand back to her side.

"That's not true. You're the child of two parents who loved each other and were separated by unfortunate circumstances. You have a mother who loves you despite what's transpired because not a day has passed when you weren't in my thoughts." Her eyes went to Rasha and she felt the power of that love behind her eyes. Hadn't it always been there?

Hadn't she always, in the back of her mind, in her heart of hearts, wished that Sochi had been her mother all along? Why did it break her to know that it was true? It might be the knowing that the king and queen never really did care for her as their own. They didn't really love her, they wouldn't love her. She was just the twin with the purple skin who inherited the throne. Rasha wanted nothing to do with any of it. She'd wanted a connection to them. The family that she'd always wanted was based on a lie. Her real father was dead and her brother was both a muke and a twyllo. How could she forgive Sochi, her mother, for the lie that brought them here? She didn't have an answer. She walked out of the room and didn't look back.

## 35

*J*AK FOUND RASHA STANDING OUTSIDE of the Ishola Palace by the pond. The grounds were dark and the only light came from the full moons above. He didn't touch her, but she must have sensed him staring at her because she shifted back and forth as if uncomfortable with being watched. He waited a minute, then stepped across the bridge and leaned over the rail beside her. Rasha was upset about something her parents had said to her. When did she ever leave their presence with her dignity still intact?

Jak didn't ask her why she was standing out on the pond by herself. He didn't ask her how her parents were doing. He didn't ask her anything. She'd tell him when she was ready and not a minute before.

"The Choosing went well, I think. Of course, no one was surprised but I think it will be a good match. The hardest thing about being with someone is trusting them.

If you don't trust them, there's no amount of attraction that will overcome it." Jak picked up a rock and threw it across the water, making waves. "Ever notice how no matter how small the pebble it makes the same number of waves as a large stone. The size of the ripples may change but no matter what, the little waves meet the shore."

Was her news a big stone or a small pebble? It felt like it might be a big stone. Jak picked up another rock, a larger one, and tossed it into the water just to prove his point. The waters rippled and raced to the edges of the pond. They were both quiet for a long time. Rasha lost track of how long they stood there before she broke the silence.

"Sochi is my mother and Omi is actually my twin brother, Karil," she blurted out.

Jak turned to stare at her to make sure she wasn't joking. She gave him a raised eyebrow in response. He let out a long whistle. But he didn't say anything right away. He needed to gather his own thoughts first.

This was a big stone kind of problem, he decided. He looked down and found a smooth rock and weighed it in his hands before tossing it out over the water.

"Your twin has a rightful claim to the throne, but your father isn't keen on an illegitimate heir," Jak stated things in summation. He'd understood what the obstacles were, but she wasn't done.

"He's also not purple. A true problem for a people too proud of their color. Not that it matters now that he's in prison."

Jak nodded but didn't say anything more. He had a million questions but probably not as many as she had.

"How's Omi—I mean, Karil handling his emprisonment?"

"I don't know. Since he hasn't tried to escape that might be a good sign." Rasha huffed out half a laugh. "But Sochi, she's trying with him. I've been told that he gets daily visits from her. If there's any good left in him, she'll find it."

Jak threw another stone across the water. It skipped four times before it disappeared into the black water.

"What do you want to do?" He asked.

"I can't do anything about him right now. But eventually he'll need to answer for his crimes. He killed people to get to my family. They may not be who I thought they were, but we're still family."

"Will you and Sochi mend?"

Rasha thought about it for a moment. Hadn't Sochi been her favorite aunt? Could Rasha forgive her for being pressured into making a choice that separated her from her own children?

"Yes, but not today," Rasha said.

That would complicate things, but he wasn't sure for how long. There was something he had been wondering about, only he wasn't sure if it would take her mind off of her problems or add to them.

"Yinka and the children? Have you heard anything? Did they make it?"

Rasha shook her head.

Jak felt his stomach revolt against the food he'd forced down earlier. He knew their survival had been doubtful from the start. Despite being one of the first villages affected, he'd been hoping they had survived. He looked at Rasha's face and saw the hard edge she used to hide the hurt. She'd hold on to the guilt for a while, just like she'd done with the fighters they'd lost the rotation before.

"Have you told anyone about your plans?" He asked.

Rasha shook her head.

Jak pushed himself up from the railing and moved to stand behind her. Maybe there was a way he could help her, if she let him. She probably wouldn't turn to him, but he could hold her. He stood behind her and wrapped his arms tight around her. He'd been prepared for her to push him away but she didn't. Instead, she turned around and buried her head in his chest. It broke him. No matter what happened he would never forget this moment, and he vowed within himself to make her smile for the rest of his life.

## 36

---

*I*N THE FRONT THREE ROWS of the
audience, Ladi sat with the other twenty-five
courier graduates while their friends and family looked on,
the sun above them high in the summer sky and the crowd
erupting as each new graduate received their orders. The
remainder fidgeted as they waited for their turn to receive
commissions and assignments. Ladi walked up to the plat-
form and received her official courier's license and number
with the entire class watching and her own family in the
audience.

"Moren, Ladi, courier number 72513." The audience
erupted in applause and Rasha tried hard not to cry.
They'd given her one number off of her older brother
Lu. Rasha called in a favor and requested the special
number.

Ladi looked like she was going to cry, her eyes filling
with emotion. She held it together, squaring her shoulders.

Afterwards, she crossed the stage before taking her seat in the second row again.

After the ceremony, they got a look at their first assignments at the same time. Ladi opened her communicator and read her first delivery and smiled. Unable to contain her excitement, she almost leapt over the rows of seats to get to her family. She would assist on a delivery from the seventh kingdom of Winaka to Ishola.

"That's wonderful, darling," her father said.

Her mother and father wouldn't let go of her, even after she showed them her first official assignment in Winaka. Rasha looked over at Jak, who grinned. They both had similar experiences. At her own graduation, her aunt—well, her mother Sochi was there for her and cried tears of joy and pride at that first commission.

"We're so happy for you," Rasha said and pulled Ladi into the biggest hug she had ever given. "Promise me you'll stay out of trouble."

"I can't promise that, but I'm sure I'll blow your records out of the water."

"We'll see," Jak said and pulled her in for a hug too.

Ladi let her parents into the circle. They wanted her to themselves tonight.

"We have something for you," her mother said as she swiped another tear from her cheek.

"Stop that, now, we're happy for you sweetheart," Ladi's father said, pulling them both into his arms. Then he pulled something out of his pocket.

"Your brother would be so proud. He knew this day

would come long before any of us did." Her father pulled out a small object no bigger than two fingers thick and half the length.

Ladi's eyes grew large. They all recognized it right away. A small recorder used for short personal messages.

"Thank you. I can't believe he did this." Her voice was almost a whisper.

"You shouldn't be so surprised. He was your biggest supporter." Her mother gave her shoulder a pat. "Let's go, supper is waiting and I want you to get a proper night's sleep before your big trip."

Ladi waved to the rest of them and Rasha felt something in her heart ease as she clutched her amulet, wishing Lu could see his little sister now. She'd surprised them all. She'd been despondent when she'd returned from rescuing the beasts. Turning in Ebere to the prince must have been the most difficult thing she'd ever had to do. It had taken a few months, but she was finally coming around and today, her smile was so genuine it reached her eyes.

Jak must have been reading her thoughts again, because he said, "She seems better today, right?"

"Yes, much more like her old self." Rasha wasn't sure she could forgive Ebere as easily as the others had. She and Jak had personally seen too much of the consequences of his actions to forget it for a long time.

"His sentence wasn't death, that's something," Jak said, speaking of Ebere and putting an arm around her shoulders. Again, his own thoughts lined up with hers.

Rasha didn't brush him off this time. She didn't mind him holding her anymore.

"Let's go," Jak said, suddenly lowering his arm and taking her hand to pull her along.

"Where are we going?"

"I'll show you. Come on."

"WHAT ARE WE DOING HERE?" Rasha asked as they sat down at a corner table of the inn where Silae worked.

"Saying goodbye to friends," Jak said.

The bar of the inn was filled. They'd grabbed one of the last tables. A new waitress came to their table and took their drink orders. She was young with a short spiky crop of blonde hair and permanent markings drawn from her collarbone to her neck.

"Have you decided what you're going to do about your little Temi and Zele?"

Rasha shook her head.

"I can't take them with me. As much as I want to, this off-world life, I don't know what to expect."

"Expect that you're going to need a domesticated beast for protection and a semi-domestic flying creature for stealth missions."

"Yeah, until the day I return and find that my dragon and my pet are done waiting for me to find them food and decide they'll eat each other." Rasha laughed, "No, I can't risk it. They'll have to stay here. I'm leaving little Temi with Chiza and Bashir. They'll take good care of him. Zele is a dragon, she'll be fine without me."

Rasha felt a tinge of pain at the loss of them both but tried not to let it show. Jak was staring at her hard in the face, waiting to catch any change in her expression. He was so annoying.

"You're really leaving?" Silae asked as she threw her arms around Rasha's shoulders.

She hadn't seen the dark-haired beauty sneak up behind her.

"I am."

"Will you two ever come back?"

"Yes, I still have family here."

Rasha's eyes dropped to the table when she said family. She still wasn't used to thinking of her parents as her aunt and uncle and her aunt as her mother.

"Did you hear about Poobari?"

"No, what happened to him?" Jak asked.

"Some off-worlder killed him. They're scrambling to fill his position. The couriers have been coming in all day talking about it. I guess one of them found him dead at his desk."

Silae took the drinks from the new waitress and ordered a large plate for them to share.

"It seems someone posing as an off-world courier did

it and then left. They couldn't find anything missing, but how would you know at that smelly dump?"

Rasha nodded, but her mind was already racing. Who would kill old Poobari? He had enemies, sure. When you dealt in shady business, it was likely that you'd eventually have some unsavory characters oppose you. But enough to kill? That was something else entirely. What did they want from him that he wasn't willing to give up? What did they take?

"I see your thoughts as if they were playing outside your mind and on this table." Jak leaned over and rested his chin on his fist, regarding her with interest. "What are you going to do?"

"Nothing, I'm not the authorities. I'm a courier."

"An off-world courier," Silae said, slipping into the chair next to her. "You could do a little investigating, maybe find out what happened to poor Poobari."

"You two are a couple of mukes. I'm not doing any such thing. I'm using my shiny new credentials to fetch and deliver. I can't hold any loyalty to one people over another, or one planet over another."

Jak and Silae gave each other knowing looks as if they didn't believe a word she was saying, which only irritated her more.

"No, I won't. But I will have a drink and remember our fallen—I don't even know what to call him," Rasha said as she held her glass half way to her mouth, trying to think of a word that described her relationship with Poobari.

"Friend?" Jak offered.

Rasha shook her head and lowered her glass to the table.

"Ally?" Silae asked.

Rasha tilted her head to one side and pondered it for a moment. No, that wasn't him either.

"Associate." Rasha picked up her glass and took a drink. The others did the same.

"I can't stay here chatting with you all night, I have other customers and besides I've got a date coming," Silae said and ran a hand over the front of her apron. It did little to cover her bosom and long bare legs.

"Who's the victim?" Rasha asked with her face in her cup.

"Very funny, princess. He's someone I met at the Ishola palace."

"Who?"

A commotion at the front door drew their attention. A tall muscular Wola with long black hair entered. His large white wings tucked behind his back as he entered carrying an array of wild flowers.

"Tarrik?" Jak asked as they both stared.

"Yeah, he brought us supplies when we needed them. I'll tell you all about it over drinks some time. See you two later. We've gotta fly." Silae giggled as she whipped off her apron and tossed it and the flowers to the new girl.

"I didn't see that coming," Rasha said as she finished her drink.

"You didn't see me coming, either." Jak laughed.

"No, I didn't."

Rasha could admit that when they'd met, she never imagined she could like him. Now, he was her closest friend and something more. He'd swept into her life like everything else the last rotation and a half and changed everything.

Jak stood up and held out his hand.

"We've gotta fly."

"Yes, early morning fetch on Musa."

They walked out of the inn and through the trees to a small clearing where their flyer sat.

"I'll drive." Jak placed a light hand on the small craft's door.

"No, I'll drive," Rasha said, squeezing between him and the door.

"I thought you hated mechanical vehicles?" Jak said, pinning her to the door with his body.

Rasha knew she was at a disadvantage. Jak was taller and built stronger than her, but that wasn't the reason she let him keep her there between him and the door. She understood something she didn't believe was possible before. When you really liked someone, it was okay to let them have the advantage sometimes.

"Motorized ground vehicles are clunky and unsophisticated." Rasha draped her arms around Jak's neck and felt the shift in advantage go to her. "I love flying."

Jak's eyes glazed over as he stared at her mouth. Rasha's lips parted, and he crushed his lips to hers in a hungry and passionate kiss. When he pulled back, she wasn't sure she had the advantage anymore as they were both out of breath. She managed to get inside the space craft and climbed into the pilot seat. She tapped in the start code and released the controls as she prepared to take off. Jak sat down in the seat beside her and tapped on the display monitor, initiating their map and plotting their course.

"Which do you like better, riding dragons or flying spaceships?" Jak asked.

"Why don't you strap in and find out?"

# EPILOGUE

*M*ost great love stories never end well, mine was no exception. However, before everything fell apart, it began the way most love stories do, with a lie.

It was an unusually warm summer in the kingdom of Chilali that year. Ball gowns and parties for my brother the king and his wife bored me. They invited royals from neighboring kingdoms but tensions were still high among the newer kingdoms. Many of them refused to attend. Not that it mattered since no one of interest ever came.

The scents and sounds of varied life outside the castle walls propelled me into the hills to escape my constricted family ties. I avoided the cliffs keeping to the inner woods where I could find the best game. Dressed in thin leather skins and boots, I ventured to the forest on the hunt for wild beasts. After an hour of tracking, I had one in the sights of my bow. The two-headed duali lifted one head to smell the air while the other continued to graze. It didn't have the olfactory abilities of a tuskin but with two heads it was still a prize to catch one. Their skins made fantastic coverings in the winter. Both heads looked up startled by something it caught on the wind. The duali bolted into the trees away from whatever had taken it by surprise, ruining my careful shot.

"Yatz!"

A moment later, a man came crashing through the trees and threw me to the ground. He clamped a rough hand over mouth as I struggled to get away from him. I couldn't breathe under the full weight of him bearing down on my chest. Panicked I kneed him in the groin and clamped my teeth down to remove his hand and take a full breath.

I'm not sure which made the most difference but in any case was free and I scrambled to crawl away from him. I overestimated his recovery time, and I fell face forward when he landed on my back. Then he whispered something in my ear that convinced me that lying underneath him was better than trying to get away.

"There are bounty hunters right behind me."

My blood froze, and I knew whatever this stranger's intentions he'd kept me from becoming the hunted. A princess would be ample bounty for someone looking to make money off of any kingdom. It was the main reason my brother didn't want me gallivanting across the countryside and why I dressed as a peasant.

There were many who might still recognize me. They

could extort coin from the king. Without a husband, I was his charge. If my brother's marriage did not produce a child to the throne, my first-born would ascend to rule the kingdom. This was the law in almost all eight kingdoms of Bolaji.

When he was sure they were out of danger, the stranger rolled off of me and held out a hand to help me to stand. I ignored it getting to my feet without his assistance.

"Sorry, Miss, I was just trying to help."

"If you hadn't knocked me down in the first place I wouldn't need it. I'll be fine without you. I lost my prey because of you. But I'll forgive you for ruining what would have been an otherwise good day."

"You're the princess of Chilali."

I felt my mouth drop open in surprise and clamped it closed. How could he know me?

"I should have recognized you, even in disguise," he said brushing off the front of his pants.

"I don't know what you're talking about. Not all of us look alike," I said hoping he didn't notice the hesitation in my response.

Instead, he laughed.

"I've seen a lot of purples in my life but you're the most beautiful. I wouldn't forget you."

"Go about your business and I won't call the royal guard on you," I said holding my head high.

"I'll forgive you for kicking me, but I'm hardly concerned you'll call the guard. You don't want them to catch you out here any more than me. A couple of royals playing peasantry isn't good for the families you know."

Then I recognized the green eyes and smirk.

"You're the prince of Buku."

We'd spent hours together in the first kingdom as children. His soft green eyes and dark brown hair had been almost feminine then. Now, he'd grown into the handsome features. It had been years, it was no wonder I'd forgotten him. Buku and Chilali weren't neighboring kingdoms and thus not the best of ties. Hadn't he just called me the most beautiful purple he'd ever seen?

I did my best to recover from the shock of recognition.

"Yes, I remember you and my brother coming to blows and rolling on the castle floor."

"He walked away with a bloody nose," he said.

"But he walked away."

I brushed the rest of the twigs and dirt from my own clothes and snickered at him.

The prince laughed and I couldn't resist smiling in return. He had an infectious laugh so full of mirth I couldn't help myself.

"Bracken." he held out his hand as if to clasp my arm like a man.

I gave him my hand, and he turned it over to kiss the back.

"Sochi," I said. I cleared my throat as my voice had dropped an octave and gone raspy. "What brings you to Chilali?"

"I'd meant to spend the day as a commoner among

your people but it seems the bounty hunters followed me. My parents are having a difficult time with a few of the neighboring kingdoms and there seems to be a price on my head."

"What a shame." I feigned a yawn. "Well, it's been lovely chatting with you, but I've got to get back. It's getting too dark to tell my brother, the king, I've been out alone."

I turned to leave, but he grabbed my hand again, stopping my abrupt exit. The look I gave him and his hand would have withered anyone else.

He didn't let it deter him from his next question.

"Can we meet again?"


BRACKEN'S EYES and question were still on my mind an hour later at dinner with my family. Before I could answer the question, two guards dispatched from the castle arrived to escort me back. They never saw Bracken.

"Is there something wrong with your meal, Sochi?"

My mother's keen eye even at her advanced age was quick to notice any change in me.

"No, mother, I'm just not that hungry. May I be excused?"

I ignored their looks of concern and retired to my rooms upstairs. Living in the castle was killing my soul a little every day, and I dreamed of living on my own. Since my father's death, a shadow had settled over the castle. No light or life filled the halls or rooms anymore. So it only took a moment after my door closed to notice the change in the room. I pulled out the small knife I carried strapped to my leg.

"I know you're here," I said looking into the shadows of the room.

"I didn't get your answer, so I took it upon myself to visit," Bracken said.

He stood up from the sitting room chair and stepped out into the light.

"How very forward of you," I said, returning the knife to its place.

We stood a breath apart in the middle of the room. He didn't touch me but I could feel the heat emanating from him. His lips broke out into a smile. I had to take a step back to catch my breath. But his arm reached around my back keeping me close and with his other hand he tilted my chin up forcing me to meet his eye.

"Your spirit is strong, but it's your face that's disarmed me. Please let me call you mine until the end of time."

Warmth crept into my cheeks and I felt the purple blush before I pulled away.

I wish I could say that I pretended not to like him before giving in.

I didn't.

Bracken of Buku and I were lovers from the first night. After months of sneaking around, we agreed to tell his parents and then mine. We loved each other, and we wanted to marry as soon as the news was public. Our marriage would forever join our two kingdoms. But we were a week too late.

The news came that the princess of the first and ruling kingdom of Adalu was ready to begin the Choosing. Bracken's parents were so excited they packed him up and sent him on his way. His mission, of course, was to win the hand of the princess. Determined to elevate their status and lives forever every kingdom with an eligible son did the same. They knew that whatever happened to him they'd done their duty securing a place among the favored of the first kingdom.

I received a letter from Bracken a day after his hasty departure.

> *My dearest love,*
> *Please understand that for the sake of my family I'm going to the first kingdom but not to marry or even curry favor with the princess. I will do everything in my power to make myself less than palatable to her. My heart belongs forever to you and life in the first won't poison it. Remember me in the cold evenings of the winter months. My warm thoughts are always with you. Take care my love and I will see you in the spring. We will announce our engagement and our wedding at the same time. Nothing can tear us apart, for we are of one soul and one body. Patience my darling, and we will be side by side once more. My undying love,*

*Bracken*

I wish he hadn't signed it that way. It would forever taunt me. Bracken never made it to the first kingdom. He was killed in a freak accident on the road to Adalu. Days after learning of his death I discovered I was pregnant with his child. I told my brother the truth about our romance. He promised to raise my child as his own. He and his wife were desperate for relief from ridicule. It would also relieve us of any embarrassment over my lack of a legitimate union and heir. In my grief, and sorrow over the loss of Bracken I agreed. I couldn't fathom raising a child alone without him. I believed being in the child's life as an aunt would be enough. However, as the days passed and my belly grew larger, I regretted the hasty decision to give up our child. I felt comforted knowing I still held a piece of him.

When I grew too large to walk the palace, the doctor restricted me to my bed. The baby was taking everything away from me, my energy, my blood, my food. Nothing seemed to be enough for the two of us.

At last, the time came for the baby to come and to everyone's surprise, there were two. A pale pinkish boy with eyes like his father and a purple girl with wisps of silver-white hair like her mother. They were gifts from the Universal.

My brother, however, had no desire to raise my son. A male who would never be purple could never rule.

"We can't keep him," he said, without a glance at the boy.

"What? But he's mine. I don't care if he's not Chilali purple."

"No. We can't raise him here."

"I'll care for him myself. There's a small cottage on the hill. We won't be a bother to anyone."

"It will be too much of a coincidence for you to bear an illegitimate child at the same time as my wife. Her shame is already known in over half the kingdom. Send the boy to live among his own people."

He raised a hand to silence my protests, and I bore down on the pain of my breaking heart as I stared down at my son wondering what to do. Hadn't I lost enough?

My brother snatched my daughter from my arms and took her to be with his wife. I looked down at my son and wept for what could have been. When I had the strength, I went to Bracken's parents. They were still grieving the loss of their son but I had hoped to bring them some consolation.

I showed them first the letter from Bracken then our son. Only a week old he was already the image of his father. Their reactions were nothing like I expected. The disgust on their faces was enough. But they condescended to tell me the letter to a lover proved nothing since my name wasn't on it. They threw me out with the declaration that my son and I would never be welcomed in the castle of Buku.

I clutched my twice rejected son to my breasts and

wept on the side of the road. The Buku royal gardener and his wife offered me solace. Tears streaming down my face they lead me to their humble home on the grounds behind the castle. Forcing a cup of tea down my throat I told them the story of my woes.

"We watched Bracken grow up and become a man. He was a good person and would have made an excellent king. We'll miss him," he said.

I let the tears fall down my face no longer bothering to wipe them away.

When my son became too upset to hold the gardener's wife reached over and picked him from my arms, cooing until he calmed. He seemed fascinated with her.

"My wife and I have always wanted a son," he said as he looked over at them.

I glanced from him to his wife. They had kind eyes. The gardner would give my son a loving home. My decision made, I kissed the forehead of my baby boy and returned home. My empty arms were heavier than when I'd left.

When I returned to the castle of Chilali, I packed my things and said goodbye to my daughter. I warned my brother that I'd keep our secret only if my daughter was allowed to visit me as often as she liked. Then I made the cozy cottage on the hill my home. My brother and his wife never asked me what became of my son.

## WANT MORE?

*Want to see how it all began? The First Kingdom is a free gift when you sign up to get author updates from T.S. Valmond.*

### A ROMEO AND JULIET STORY WITH A FANTASY TWIST

Sanee and Adera became friends long before they understood what it meant to hate those who were different. They fell in love in secret against the wishes of their families. Determined to be together when ripped apart, they each embark on a journey to find a land only rumored to exist where they could be accepted and live in peace.

The feuding tribes of Bolaji have never had peace but this epic war comes to a head when border battles intensify over the disappearance of the two young lovers, forcing Sanee and Adera to make unimaginable choices.

# APPENDIX 1

## BOLAJI GLOSSARY

BAKED BETI - a lasagna-like meal

DUALI - a two headed deer-like animal with a thick skin and no antlers

FANGLEDORT - an idiot

GUMP - a mushroom or small animal

MUKE - a crazy person

MULKIS - fool/foolish

NIRAMAYA TREE - the healing tree that resides underwater in the kingdom of Majiwa.

PIKO - a peacock-like bird

PUMSEED - a stupid or slow person

RANGLEFORT - rat

ROTATIONS - years

RUINS - messed up

SLITHERING STOLKEN - snake

SNORK - idiot

TUSKIN - a bull-like beast used for pulling and riding

TWYLLO - a small brained bird/idiot

YATZ - an exclamation

## BOLAJI KINGDOMS ABBREVIATED HISTORY (IN ORDER OF ALLIANCE)

**1. ADALU** - Also known as the first kingdom is the coldest and most northern kingdom. The people here are the most diverse representing all other kingdoms. Here is where royals and the purest royal lines are joined to provide a central ruling family. The ruling council is made up of royals from the remaining kingdoms that assist the Adalu royal family in caring for the needs of the kingdom. The heir of the king and queen has a royal ball during the age of ascension called the **Choosing.** At this time they pick a future bride or groom from among the allied kingdoms to rule alongside them once they take the throne.

**2. KARMIR** - This is the origin of the red people with jet black hair. Known for their legendary fighters and hunger for power. They worship the sun god **Thelion**. A Karmir prince was the first ruler of Adalu.

**3. CHILALI** - A purple people with white hair in their youth and small pointed ears. This is the birthplace of Rasha Indari Jenchat. Their primary belief is in the Universal god. It is generally believed that the **Universal** created all things and is one of the oldest of the known gods.

**4. TERO** - The green people with large ears. They are one-half of the twin lands and they specialize in advance hearing and listening technologies. Most have brown hair and brown or blue eyes. They are largely non-religious and scientific people. They are known for their advanced skills in espionage. Their alliance with Joro preceded their entrance into the kingdoms of Bolaji.

**5. JORO** - A kingdom of green people with large eyes. Close cousins of the Tero they are similar in stature and physical ability. They are the other half of the twin lands and they specialize in visual technology. Most have brown hair and brown or blue eyes. They worship the nature goddess **Mat`ka of Poda**. They have an affinity with all things natural in their lands including the animals.

**6. MAJIWA** - The kingdom of the mermen and mermaids. They come in an array of colors. Their portion of land was a gift of peace from the first five kingdoms. Their eyes are solid black and blink horizontally. A kingdom who only ever went to war with the Karmir. They use a combination of vocal singing and hand gestures to communicate underwater. Over time they have learned how to communicate with the land dwellers. Polytheistic in their beliefs there are just too many gods and goddess to name here. They are the only kingdom to have a ruling member in Adalu before their official alliance with the other Bolaji kingdoms.

**7. WINAKA** - These human settlers were once displaced from a distant planet and come in a variety of colors. Their history is fragmented and cloaked in mystery. Some believe that they and the Buku have a similar ancestry since their variety in color and appearance seem to match. They've had border disputes with their nearest neighbors the Vol and Buku.

**8. VOL** - The frost white people who originated in the North but moved south in search of warmer climates and more lush farming grounds. They are considered a godless tribe and also the purest. They are one of the kingdoms that still resist racial mixing. They've had border disputes with their nearest neighbors the Winaka.

**9. BUKU** - This is another set of human settlers were once displaced from a distant planet and come in a variety of colors. Little is known of their origins. There is no record of their religious beliefs or customs. They've had minor border disputes with their nearest neighbors the Winaka.

**10. SIDOA** - One of the newest kingdoms of Bolaji, they've never ruled from Adalu. Their kingdom is also one of the smallest. These humanoids are dark brown in color. Due to their small population, they've never battled with the other kingdoms. Their people have recently discovered precious stones inside caves on their land making them one of the richest kingdoms ever. This has also increased their need for miners. They are mostly farmers and the land is tropical and warm. The majority worship the Universal god.

**THE WILDS** - The untamed and lawless lands where outcasts go and thrive outside of the lands and rules of the kingdoms of Bolaji.

**11. ISHOLA** - The last kingdom to join Bolaji is made up of winged-men and women. They are from the far side of the Wilds where they live in the tallest trees in the world. During an agreement for more warriors, they attain kingdom recognition and legal rights for Ishola thus dissolving the lawless Wilds. Their religious beliefs and official history are not yet public knowledge.

# ACKNOWLEDGMENTS

This series started as a dream of ten kingdoms on the faraway world of Bolaji. The premise was that a princess might have other goals in life than ballroom gowns, dances, or being married off to a prince. The very next morning I drew the map of the kingdoms and started outlining the book.

It would never have seen the light of day if it wasn't for the support of my outstanding family and friends. I couldn't do this without their love and encouragement.

I also owe a special thanks to my husband for his encouragement and bringing my map to life in a way that only a true artist can.

Many thanks go to my editors Ellen Campbell, Emily Gibbons, and Jessica West that made these stories readable and polished.

Thanks to my cover artist FrostAlexis who did an

amazing job of showing the strength of my purple leading lady.

Last but not least, I want to thank my VIP readers who gave me valuable feedback improving the book in its final stages.

Like most stories, this one has no finite beginning or end. I hope you'll continue to enjoy more of my stories.

# ABOUT THE AUTHOR

Hi, I'm **T.S. Valmond** the science fiction and fantasy author currently residing in Canada with my husband and dog in an undisclosed location. One can never be too careful when exposing the secrets of powerful governments, worlds, and illegal aliens.

(Yes, they're watching.)

I was into science fiction and fantasy long before Browncoats, Trekkies, and a Jedi were cool. Like my readers, I long for the days when Reality TV didn't mean anything and entertainment was entertaining.

When I'm not writing I'm–

Nope. I'm always writing.

Printed in April 2019
by Rotomail Italia S.p.A., Vignate (MI) - Italy